Proud, untamed, passionate rulers of
desert kingdoms, used to wealth and
luxury, these two powerful sheikhs draw
their strength and conviction from the
barbaric, extreme beauty of their lands.
And they have decided to wed!!

THE DESERT

INNOCENT QUEEN

Two sensual, exotic novels by favourite
authors Jane Porter and Lucy Monroe

THE DESERT SHEIKHS
COLLECTION

THE DESERT

Sheikh's

INNOCENT QUEEN

JANE
PORTER

LUCY
MONROE

MILLS &
BOON

All the characters in this book have no existence outside the imagination
of the author, and have no relation whatsoever to anyone bearing the
same name or names. They are not even distantly inspired by any
individual known or unknown to the author, and all the incidents are
pure invention.

Mills & Boon, an imprint of Harlequin (UK) Limited,
Eton House, 18-24 Paradise Road, Richmond, Surrey TW9 1SR

THE DESERT SHEIKH'S INNOCENT QUEEN
© Harlequin Enterprises II B.V./S.à.r.l. 2011

King of the Desert, Captive Bride © Jane Porter 2008
Hired: The Sheikh's Secretary Mistress © Lucy Monroe 2008

ISBN: 978 0 263 88755 6

025-0411

Harlequin (UK) policy is to use papers that are natural, renewable
and recyclable products and made from wood grown in sustainable
forests. The logging and manufacturing processes conform to the
legal environmental regulations of the country of origin.

Printed and bound in Spain
by Blackprint CPI, Barcelona

King of the
Desert,
Captive Bride

JANE
PORTER

Jane Porter grew up on a diet of Mills & Boon® romances, reading late at night under the covers so her mother wouldn't see! She wrote her first book at age eight, and spent many of her school and college years living abroad, immersing herself in other cultures and continuing to read voraciously. Now Jane has settled down in rugged Seattle, Washington, with her gorgeous husband and two sons. Jane loves to hear from her readers. You can write to her at PO Box 524, Bellevue, WA 98009, USA. Or visit her website at www.janeporter.com

**Don't miss Jane Porter's exciting new novel,
A Dark Sicilian Secret, available in May 2011
from Mills & Boon® Modern™.**

PROLOGUE

SHEIKH Khalid Fehr read the message posted on the Internet bulletin board again.

American Woman Missing in the Middle East.
Help desperately needed. My sister disappeared two weeks ago without a trace.
Her name is Olivia Morse. She's twenty-three years old, five-four, 105 pounds, blond, blue eyes. She speaks with a Southern accent and is on the shy side. If anyone has seen her or knows her whereabouts, please call or e-mail me. Her family is frantic.

In his tent, sitting at his laptop computer, Khalid reread the last sentence—*her family is frantic*—and felt a heavy weight lodge in his gut.

He knew what it was like to be frantic about a family member. He knew how it felt to be an older brother panicked about a sister. He'd once had two younger sisters and then one day they were gone.

He scrolled back through the message on the Internet bulletin board and discovered an earlier message from the same Jake Morse.

Missing American woman! If you've seen this woman please call or e-mail immediately.

There was a photo attached and Khalid clicked on the attachment and waited for the photo to open.

It finally did, although slowly due to the connection being via satellite phone, and Khalid found himself looking at a black-and-white photo that had to be a passport photo. White-blond hair. Light, light eyes. Pale, translucent skin. She was definitely pretty. But what really held his attention was her expression, the tentative smile and the look in her eyes—shy, curious, hopeful.

Hopeful.

His chest tightened and he leaned back in his chair, away from his desk.

His sister Aman used to look at the world that way. She was so much shyer than Jamila, the more outgoing twin. Aman's tenderness and quiet sense of humor always brought out the best in him, brought out the best in everyone, and when she died a week after Jamila he'd felt his heart break. His heart had never been the same.

Frowning at the computer screen, he ran his palm slowly along his jaw, the short, rough bristles biting at his skin. And again he looked into this missing Olivia's eyes and tried to imagine where she was, tried to imagine her circumstances. Was she sick, hurt, dead?

Had she been kidnapped? Murdered? Raped?

Or had she disappeared by choice? Was there someone, something, she was running from?

It was none of his business, he told himself, rising from his computer. He'd left city life and civilization behind to live in the desert, far from violence, noise and crime. He'd chosen solitude because he hated how most people lived.

But what if this were his sister?

What if Aman or Jamila had gone missing?

They wouldn't, he brusquely reminded himself. They'd been princesses—royal—and security detail had followed them everywhere.

He didn't know this Jake, didn't know anything about the man, but he could still see the words he'd written, could still hear the plea for help echo in his head.

Turning at the edge of his tent, Khalid looked back at his computer, at the enlarged black-and-white photo. Olivia Morse, twenty-three years old, five foot four, and one hundred and five pounds—if that.

With a snap of his wrist he flung the tent flap back, exited his tent and called for one of his men.

He might live in the middle of the Great Sarq Desert and he might be a nomadic sheikh, but he was still a king, one of the royal Fehrs, blessed with power, wealth and infinite connections. If anyone could locate this American, he could.

CHAPTER ONE

HE'D found her.

It'd taken three weeks, a small fortune, two private investigators, the help of Sarq's secretary of state, a lot of secret handshakes, deals and promises—as well as some threats—but at last he was going to see her.

Sheikh Khalid Fehr ducked to enter through Ozr Prison's low threshold. He was escorted past the men's wing to the women's side of the prison, the foul smell of overflowing toilets and unwashed bodies so overpowering his stomach rose in protest.

At the entrance to the women's prison wing his male guard handed him over to a female guard who examined Khalid's paperwork.

The female guard, covered head to foot by her black robe, took her time reading through his paperwork, and Khalid stifled his impatience. Ozr had the reputation for being one of the worst prisons in the world—it was a place notorious for the lack of human rights—but finally the female guard looked up, nodded curtly. "Follow me," she said.

He followed her through one low arched corridor after another, deeper beneath the old fortress which had been turned into Ozr Prison a half century ago.

As they walked through the corridors, hands reached out, and voices in Arabic, Egyptian, Farsi and even English begged for help, for mercy, for a doctor, a lawyer, anyone, anything. Ozr was the last place on earth any man would want to be. God only knew how it was for a woman, as once you entered through the prison's gates, you discovered you'd earned a one-way ticket. Once you were in, you never came out again.

One of Khalid's friends from high school had gotten into trouble in Jabal and after being arrested was tossed into Ozr was never heard from again. Khalid's father, the King of Sarq, had made enquiries and then entreaties on his son's friend's behalf all to no avail.

Jabal, bordered by four countries including Egypt and Sarq, remained a dangerous dictator state, with international travel warnings in place, warnings that Olivia Morse had obviously ignored.

The guard stopped before a cell that was empty except for a woman sitting on a narrow cot, her knees drawn to her chest, wisps of blond hair escaping from her black veil.

Olivia.

Khalid's chest tightened, a visceral reaction to seeing her for the first time.

In her passport photo she'd been pretty, fresh-faced, a hopeful light in her blue eyes. But the young woman sitting inside the cell didn't look like the photo anymore. The woman inside the cell appeared vacant, even half-dead.

"Olivia Morse," he asked, stepping toward the bars.

Her head briefly lifted but she didn't look at him.

"You are Miss Olivia Morse, aren't you?" he persisted, his voice pitched low.

Liv sat on the cot, legs pulled up against her, her arms wrapped tightly around her knees, trying to make herself smaller.

Maybe she wasn't really here, and maybe there wasn't another bad man standing outside her cell demanding information, threatening another interrogation, interrogations that always ended with a beating.

Didn't they understand yet that she had no answers? Didn't they understand she was as confused as they were? She'd been had. Duped. Destroyed.

Liv closed her eyes, bent her head and pressed her forehead against the bony curve of her knees. Maybe if she just kept her eyes closed she'd disappear. Dissolve. Wake up in Alabama again.

God, she missed home. God, she missed Jake and Mom and everyone.

She should have never dreamed of pyramids and beautiful waves of sand, shouldn't have wanted to ride a camel or explore the ancient tombs.

She should have been happy staying home. She should have been happy just being a travel agent, booking other people's exotic vacations.

"Olivia."

The man spoke her name quietly, urgently, and fear rose up in her, fear that something bad was going to happen again.

Turning her head away, she choked in broken Arabic, Arabic she'd learned to protect herself from another blow during the endless interrogations, "I don't know. I don't know who she was—"

"We'll discuss the charges later," he interrupted, speaking flawless English, English without a hint of an accent. "There are a few things we need to settle first."

Liv shivered. The fact that he spoke English only made her more afraid, and fear and fatigue were the only things she understood anymore.

"If I knew who she was, I'd tell you, I would. Because I want to go home—" She broke off, took a quick, unsteady breath, exhausted from the interrogations. The guards came for her at all hours of the night and then they'd skip her meals, trying to break her, trying to get the information they wanted. "I want to help you. I'm trying to help you. Believe me."

"I do," he said almost gently, and his tone, so different from the others, was her undoing.

Scalding tears filled her eyes, tears so hot they stung and burned as if filled with salt and sand.

Reaching up, she swiftly wiped her eyes dry. "I want to go home," she whispered, her voice shaky.

"And I want to see you return home."

No one had said that to her since she arrived. No one had given her the slightest bit of hope that she'd ever leave this horrible place.

Liv slowly turned her head and looked at him. The corridor was dark, shadowy, but the shadows couldn't hide his height or size. He wasn't a small man, or a stout man, not like the ones who'd interrogated her before. He was considerably younger, too.

He was robed, but his robe was black and embroidered heavily with gold. His head covering was white, pristine-white, and while the cloth concealed much of his hair it only served to emphasize his hard, strong features.

"I'm here to get you out," he continued, "but we don't have much time."

Torn between hope and dread, Liv clutched her knees to her chest, her thin back robe rough against her skin. All of her clothes had been confiscated with the rest of her things at the time of her arrest. In place of her skirts and jeans and T-shirts she'd been given this robe, and the thin, stiff linen garment she wore beneath the robe, which was little more than a slip. "Who sent you?"

The man's expression was neither friendly nor encouraging. "Your brother."

"Jake?"

"He asked me to check on you."

She lurched to her feet and then grabbed the wall for support. "Jake knows I'm here?"

"Jake knows I'm looking for you."

Liv exhaled in a dizzy rush, her fingers pressed to the damp stone wall. "They said I'd never leave here. They said I'd never get out, not until I confessed, and gave up the names of the others."

"They didn't know you were connected to powerful people," he replied.

Liv blinked, her head swimming. "Am I?"

"You are now."

She moved to the front of the cell and grabbed the bars. "How? Why?"

"I am Sheikh Khalid Fehr, and I'm here representing the royal family of Sarq."

"Sarq borders Jabal," she said.

"And Egypt," he answered. "It will be a diplomatic feat to get you out of here today, and time is short. I need to have the paperwork finalized, but I will return—"

"No!" Liv didn't mean to shout, she hadn't intended her voice to be loud at all, but panic melted her bones, turning her blood to ice. "No," she said more softly. "Please. Don't leave me here."

"It's just for a few minutes, maybe a half hour at the most—"

"No," she begged, her voice breaking, her hand snaking through the bars of the prison cell to clasp the sleeve of his robe. "Don't leave me."

For a long moment he said nothing, just stared down at her hand, his thick black lashes fanning the hard thrust of cheekbone, his skin the color of burnished gold. "They won't free you without my completing the necessary paperwork."

Her fingers tightened in his robe. "Don't go."

"I'll be back, I promise."

"I'm afraid here," she whispered. "I'm afraid of the guards. I'm afraid of the dark. I'm afraid of what happens when prisoners disappear." Her gaze clung to his, desperate, pleading. "The prisoners don't come back sometimes. They don't and I hear screaming, terrible screaming."

"I'm only going down the hall," he said. "I will be back soon."

"But they won't let you back. They won't. I know how this

place works. The American ambassador came once and he never returned."

"There is no American ambassador in Jabal," he answered. "It was a trick they played on you, a trick to try to break you."

She gripped his robe tighter. "Are you a trick, too?"

Deep grooves bracketed his mouth. For a long moment he didn't speak and then when he did, his voice dropped, deepened. "It depends on your definition of a trick."

An icy shaft chilled her. She jerked her head up, stared at him, stared hard as if she could somehow see the truth. "I don't know what to believe anymore."

"Just know I will be back. As soon as I can."

"Don't forget me," she whispered.

"I won't, and I will be back sooner than you think."

She couldn't look away from his eyes, couldn't look away in case he was making promises he didn't intend to keep. She'd been duped once more. She was beginning to think she'd never leave Ozr, never see her family again. "What if they take me away first?"

"They won't."

"They have other entrances, and different rooms. They might take me—"

"They won't."

"How do you know?"

His gaze fell to rest again on her hand, where it clutched his sleeve. "They'd be fools to try that now, with me here. They know I've seen you, they know we've spoken."

She nodded stiffly, her insides cold. She heard his words but they did little to comfort. She'd been here too long, seen too much. The guards did what they wanted when they wanted without fear of retribution.

He pulled free and was gone, disappearing down the dark corridor and all she could think as he walked away was *Come back. Come back. Please.*

* * *

Although the wait seemed endless, the sheikh did return, and with him were two prison officials.

She didn't know what to think when one of the officials unlocked her cell door and called her forward. But once the door was open, she didn't hesitate, moving quickly towards Sheikh Fehr, blindly putting her trust in him. But what choice did she have? She couldn't stay here. Anything would be better than Ozr.

Liv walked close to Sheikh Fehr back through the narrow tunnels and out the door into the dazzling sunshine. It was astonishingly hot out, and bright, and the fierce light sent her reeling backward, her legs crumpling beneath her.

Sheikh Fehr was there as she stumbled, swooping to catch her before she fell to the stone steps.

Liv had instinctively thrown her arm out to break the fall and her hand ended up being crushed to Sheikh Fehr's chest, her palm flat against his hard body, his chest a thick, dense plane of muscle.

"Oh," she choked, her fingers lifting sharply, and yet she couldn't move her hand away, her arm trapped, locked, between his broad chest and her body.

"Did you twist your ankle?" he asked, his voice so deep and husky that it made her think of the sun-drenched pyramids with their elaborate hidden treasures.

She shook her head and struggled to free herself, needing to be on her own feet again and away from this dark, silent man who filled her with both awe and terror.

"It's just so sunny," she answered unsteadily.

He placed her on her feet even as he kept one hand on the small of her back. With his other hand he removed his sunglasses and put them on her face, carefully sliding the glasses onto her nose. "You haven't been outside in a while."

It was a statement, not a question, and Liv didn't know if it was the sudden and strange intimacy of being so close to this fiercely intimidating man or the intensity of the sun, but she felt weak all over again, her legs like jelly beneath her.

Dipping her head, the glasses, which had already been too big for her small face, slid to the tip of her nose. "You'd better take them," she said, reaching up to remove them. "They're too big for me."

But Sheikh Fehr didn't take the sunglasses. Instead he returned them to her face and firmly pushed the frame onto the bridge of her nose. "They might be big but they'll give your eyes a chance to adjust," he said flatly, his flinty tone discouraging argument, even as a series of dark cars appeared, heading toward them.

A group of robed men emerged from one of the cars and Liv shrank closer to Sheikh Fehr's side, moving so close she could feel his solid frame and the warmth emanating from his body.

He extended a protective arm, keeping her there at his side. "Do not fear. They are my men and they're here to make sure we get to the airport safely."

She nodded but her fear and worry didn't go away, and wouldn't until she was back home with Jake and her mom. There was too much here that felt foreign and unfamiliar. She'd wanted the unfamiliar, it's why she'd traveled to Middle East in the first place, but she hadn't expected problems, nor danger, not like this.

She'd chosen Egypt and Morocco because they looked unique and picturesque in the travel brochures. She'd poured over the travel brochures, too, lingering over photos of the pyramids in the late afternoon sun, camels setting across the desert at sunset, and treasures and artifacts on display at the Egyptian Museum in Cairo.

She'd read and reread the itineraries of the Nile cruises, imagining stopping at each of the different ports with a different temple and excursion for every day. She'd shop in the souks, purchase practical wool rugs, buy kebabs from the street vendors and have the adventure of a lifetime.

She'd never seriously considered the possibility of getting

into trouble. But then, she'd never been in trouble before. Liv had always been the good girl, the one that followed all the rules and did everything she was told.

One of Sheikh Fehr's guards opened the back door of the tinted-windowed sedan, and Liv turned to Sheikh Fehr, her gaze searching the hard, expressionless features. She was putting her life in his hands and she didn't even know him. "Can I trust you?" she asked, her voice all but inaudible.

His dark eyes bored into hers, his high cheekbones creating shadowed hollows above a firm, unsmiling mouth. "Perhaps I should be the one to ask that question. I've put my name, and my reputation, on the line for you. Can I trust you, Olivia Morse?"

Something in his dark, shuttered gaze sent shivers racing through her. She had the distinct feeling she was dealing with an altogether different sort of man than she'd ever dealt with before. The problem was, her experience with men was limited, and the one man she was close to—her brother, Jake—was as uncomplicated as a man could be.

Sheikh Fehr, on the other hand, struck her as quite complicated.

"Yes. Of course you can trust me," she answered huskily, trying to ignore the sudden rush of butterflies in her middle.

"Then we should go," he answered, gesturing to the open car door, "because you're not safe here, and you won't be safe until we reach my country."

In the close confines of the car, Liv dipped her head, tucking dirty blond hair back behind her ears. She was filthy, and was certain she smelled even worse. She craved a shower or bath, had never wanted to bathe as much as she did right now.

"I'm sorry," she said, realizing that the sheikh was watching her as the car sped along the road through the desolate countryside to the capital. "I know I'm in desperate need of a shower…." Her voice drifted off apologetically.

"I was thinking that your brother will be so glad when you call him later."

"Yes," Liv agreed, eyes suddenly stinging as intense emotion rushed through her. "I was beginning to lose hope that I'd ever get out of there."

"You're lucky," Khalid answered. "Most don't."

"Why don't they?"

"They don't have the power."

"I didn't have any power," she said, voice soft.

"No. But I did."

"You've done this before…helped people like me?"

"Yes."

Her lips parted to ask him more, to find out who he was, and why he'd risk his own safety to help others, but he'd turned his head away to stare out the tinted window and the hard set of his features discouraged further conversation.

Almost everything about him discouraged conversation. Dark, big and powerfully built, she found him incredibly intimidating.

Sheikh Fehr had towered over her when they stood side by side waiting for the car and she had to believe he was at least six feet tall, if not taller. He was also quite broad-shouldered, with an athletic build. His skin was deeply tanned, with strong, rugged features that spoke of sun and wind and hot, stinging sand.

"We're approaching Hafel, the capital city of Jabal," Sheikh Fehr said. "Did you see any of the city before your arrest?"

Liv shook her head and, glancing down at her lap, she glimpsed the inside of her wrist where yellow and blue bruises remained. She also had more bruises high on her arms, but her robe covered those. "I never got as far as Hafel."

"Where were you arrested?"

"On the main road between the border and Hafel." She made a faint sound, part misery, part disbelief. "One moment I was on the bus, and the next I was on my way to Ozr."

When the sheikh didn't answer Liv looked up at him. "Are we stopping in Hafel now?"

"No," Khalid answered as the capital city, a city thousands of years old, appeared before them. The city boasted relatively new modern office buildings that rose over and between crumbling Roman ruins. "Although it's a fascinating city, a city most of the Western world knows nothing about."

"Have you spent much time here?" she asked.

"Once upon a time."

"What changed?"

"Everything." He hesitated. "When I was a boy my father had a close friendship with the Jabal king, but the king was overthrown twenty years ago and the country is ruled by someone far different now." His lips twisted cynically. "This is the first time I've been here in four years and until last night, I wasn't even sure they'd allow me in."

"Why not?"

"I get people out of prison, whisking them off to safer places. The government here doesn't like it." He shrugged. "They don't like me."

Liv's stomach did a peculiar somersault. "So why did they let you in?"

He briefly glanced out the window, his shoulders shifting carelessly before glancing back at her. "I paid off several high-up officials."

Drawing a quick breath she felt her stomach fall again and wondered if she'd ever feel safe again. "You *bribed* them?"

"Didn't have much of a choice." He dark eyes rested on her face, his expression grim. "It was either that, or allow you to go before the Ozr Prison judge in two days' time, and believe me, you wouldn't have survived the sentence."

Liv bit her lip and looked away, out the window. They were approaching the city center, which was far more cramped than the modern neighborhoods. Smoke rose from food stands on the street corners. "It would have been harsh," she said.

"It would have been deadly," he agreed.

"And I just wanted to have an adventure," she said, her voice low. "I never imagined this nightmare."

The driver slowed, then braked to a complete stop. The sheikh's wireless phone suddenly rang and he answered it, his eyes on the line of police cars ahead.

"The nightmare," he said, echoing her words as he hung up the phone, "isn't over yet."

Liv leaned forward to get a look at the police officers ahead. "What's happening?"

"We're to be questioned," he answered shortly, his features hardening. Turning his head, he looked at her, a close, ruthless inspection that was as thorough as it was critical.

"Pull your headscarf forward," he directed. "Hide all your hair and wrap the fabric across your mouth and nose so that as much of your face is covered as possible." He retrieved the sunglasses from the seat and handed them to her. "And keep these on. Don't take them off unless I tell you to." Then he opened the car door and stepped out, slamming it shut behind him.

CHAPTER TWO

THE nightmare isn't over yet.

Sheikh Fehr's words rang in her ears as he walked from the car. The driver had locked the car doors the moment the sheikh left the vehicle and she watched Sheikh Fehr now, heart in her throat, as a group of uniformed officers approached him.

From inside the car she could hear their muffled voices outside. The officers practically surrounded the sheikh, but he appeared unruffled.

They were speaking Arabic and she understood nothing of what they were saying other than there seemed to be a problem, and from the way the officers kept gesturing to the car, their voices growing louder, she had a sick feeling that the conversation had something to do with her.

Several long minutes passed and then Sheikh Fehr turned to the car and opened the back door. Liv ducked her head as the officers crowded around to get a look inside. Terrified, she kept her head down, her eyes closed behind the oversized pair of sunglasses.

After what seemed like eternity the car door slammed shut and shortly after the sheikh climbed back in the car. The chauffeur immediately started the ignition and pulled away.

Liv nervously laced and unlaced her fingers. "Is everything okay?" she asked, as they left the narrower, old city streets behind for the wide boulevard that ran along the North Africa coast.

"Yes."

When it became clear he didn't intend to say more she added, "What did they want?"

"They wanted to know if I'd legally entered their country and if I'd done anything illegal while here."

"Have you?"

"No and yes, but that's not what I told them. I couldn't tell them that or you'd be in one of their cars heading straight back to Ozr."

"So what did you tell them instead?"

He hesitated a moment, then plucked the sunglasses from her face, calmly pocketing them inside his robe. "That I was escorting a female member of my family home."

But he wasn't, she thought, her uneasiness growing. "Did they believe you?"

His expression turned mocking. "They know who I am, and they saw I had the proper paperwork. There wasn't much they could do at that point."

He was setting her newly heightened inner alarm, the one that should have been working when she agreed to carry Elsie's bag in her backpack.

Her inner alarm hadn't been attuned to danger then, but it was now, and Liv knew from Sheikh Fehr's tone, as well as his evasive answers, that there was something he wasn't telling her. Something wasn't right. She didn't know what it was and she very much wanted to know. "The officers were upset about something," she persisted.

He shrugged. "It's a cultural thing."

She leaned forward. "Tell me."

"We're a man and woman traveling alone together."

"So?"

"We're not actually related, which is illegal in Jabal."

Liv sat back against the seat, her fingers curling into her palms. "So they could rearrest me," she whispered.

"Not if we get out of here first."

They reached the small business airport in less than thirty minutes, the airport built on the outskirts of the capital city. The chauffeur drove them through the airport gates and right out onto the deserted tarmac, pulling close to the jet's stairs.

The jet was long, sleek and narrow, the body a shiny silver with a discrete gold-and-black emblem on the tail. Sheikh Fehr walked Olivia to the jet's stairs. "Go ahead and board," he told her. "I need to speak with the pilot about our flight plan."

She nodded and, holding on to the handrail, climbed the steps. A flight attendant greeted Liv as she entered the plane.

"We'll be leaving soon," the flight attendant said, leading Liv to the grouping of four enormous club-style leather chairs that made up one of the plane's sitting areas. "Do you have any bags or luggage for me to stow?"

Liv shook her head as she sat down. "I don't have…anything," she said, reaching for the seat belt.

"So your luggage has been sent ahead?" the flight attendant asked.

"Unfortunately, I've lost everything," Liv answered, and suddenly, remembering how she'd been callously stripped and searched, she shivered. They'd confiscated everything that first night. Her backpack, her passport, her clothes, her makeup bag. All of it. The only thing she had was what she wore, and even that was a prison-issued robe and headscarf.

The flight attendant saw Liv shiver. "Cold?"

"A little," Liv admitted, still chilled from the weeks and weeks in the dark, dank cell. It'd been so awful, so unbelievable. She still couldn't understand how she'd ended up at Ozr. She'd never broken a law in her life—well, except for driving over the speed limit, and even then, it had been five miles over the limit, not twenty.

"Would you like a blanket?"

"Please." Liv smiled gratefully.

"Poor thing. Have you been sick?" the flight attendant asked sympathetically as she crossed to the wood-paneled cabinet and retrieved an ivory cashmere throw and small pillow, the ivory blanket the same color as the supple leather seats.

Returning, the flight attendant unfolded the blanket and draped it across Liv's legs. "And just between you and me, I think the air conditioner is a little too efficient. Now, how about something warm to drink? Coffee, tea?"

"Coffee, with milk and sugar. If that's not too much trouble."

"None at all."

The flight attendant disappeared into the jet's galley kitchen and Liv sank deeper into her seat. This was surreal, she thought, tugging the blanket up to her shoulders. An hour ago she was still locked up in Ozr and now here she was, on a private jet, being waited on hand and foot.

While Liv sipped her coffee on the plane, Khalid joined his pilot in the final preflight inspection.

"We've a change of plans," Khalid told the pilot.

The pilot looked up from his clipboard. "We're low on petrol. The airport refused our request to refuel."

"I'm not surprised. We had a little problem on the way here."

"Is that why we're not going straight to Sarq?"

Khalid nodded. "Can't risk involving my brother in this. There's enough tension between Sarq and Jabal already. I won't drag Sharif, or my people, into an international incident."

The pilot's attention was suddenly caught by a line of cars on the horizon. "Police," he said, nodding at the line of cars racing toward them. "Are they coming for you?"

"That, or my guest, or us both," Khalid replied, dispassionately watching the cars grow closer.

The pilot patted the side of the plane. "Then maybe it's time to go."

Liv looked up as Sheikh Fehr and the pilot boarded, the pilot drawing the folding stairs up and then securing the door. Sheikh Fehr stopped to speak to the flight attendant and then continued down the aisle to take a seat across from Liv.

"Are you not feeling well?" he asked Liv, seeing the blanket wrapped around her.

"I was cold," she answered, feeling the engine turn on, a low vibration that hummed through the entire plane.

Sheikh Fehr's eyes narrowed as he inspected her. "You are quite pale. I wonder if you're coming down sick."

"I'm not sick. Just chilly. But I'm getting warmer." She started to fold the blanket up, but the sheikh put out a hand to stop her.

"Don't," he said. "If the blanket is keeping you warm, there's no need to put it away."

As the jet began to taxi toward the runway, she resettled the blanket on her lap and glanced at him from beneath her lashes. Against his white head-covering, his skin was a tawny gold, while his eyebrows were inky slashes above long-lashed eyes the color of bittersweet chocolate.

His features were almost too angular, too strong. His forehead was high, his cheekbones were prominent, even his nose was a trifle too long. It should have made him unattractive. Instead it gave him a rugged, and very primitive, appeal.

As she looked at him, a window behind his shoulder, she caught sight of a flashing red-and-blue light.

Her eyes widened as she spotted the line of cars trailing the jet.

The sheikh glanced out the window. "Police," he said matter-of-factly.

She looked at him, her stomach tumbling, the fear returning. "What do they want now?"

"Us," he answered.

Us, she repeated silently, as the jet began racing down the runway, faster and faster until they were off the ground and soaring up, up, into the air.

Liv sat glued to the window.

Within ten minutes they had lifted high above the congested streets of the capital, and as they climbed higher, green fields came into view before the green faded to a khaki gold, and then even the gold hue faded, leaving just pale khaki.

"What happened in Ozr?" Sheikh Fehr asked abruptly. "What did they do to you?"

Liv jerked her attention away from the landscape below. "Nothing," she answered quickly, too quickly, and from the creasing of the sheikh's eyes, she knew he knew it, too.

"Ozr isn't a nice place," he said. "I can't imagine they were nice to you."

She suddenly pictured her life of the past four long weeks. The terrible food, the lack of sunlight, the lack of exercise, the taunts, the accusations and the endless middle-of-the-night interrogations. "I'm here now."

His jaw tightened. "Barely," he answered quietly, his gaze meeting hers.

She suppressed a shiver and turned away, unable to hold his intense gaze, or dwell on her weeks in Ozr. She was out now. That's what mattered. She was out and soon she'd be going home.

"The view is beautiful from here," she said, determinedly turning her attention to the landscape below.

He gestured toward the stretch of brown and beige beneath them. "That's the Great Sarq Desert. It begins in Southern Jabal and stretches through much of Sarq, my country, and is one of the largest deserts in Northern Africa, consisting of thousands of miles."

"I've read quite a bit about the Great Sarq Desert," she said shyly but eagerly. "I read that thousands of years ago the desert was once a lush tropical landscape, that there are elaborate rock paintings in the mountains depicting everyday life. Is that true?"

He nodded. "Yes, and scattered oases are all that's left of that ancient tropical landscape."

"Oases used by traders and their caravans," she added, her gaze glued to the empty plains below. "Before the trip I was reading a book on the area, and it said that in ancient civilization the desert here was the corridor that linked Africa with the coast, and the world beyond. Everyone utilized the desert corridor. The Romans, the Phoenicians, as well as the early Greek colonists—" She broke off, flushing. "But of course you know all that. It's just...new...to me."

The look her gave her was frankly appraising. "I didn't know American women cared about geography so far from their own homes."

Her eyebrows lifted. "You can't judge America, or Americans, by what you read in the news."

"No?" he mocked.

"No." She held her breath for a moment, battling her temper. "Just like it'd be unfair of me to judge all the countries in this area by what happened to me in Ozr."

The rest of the flight passed in silence. Liv tried to blank her mind, desperate to ignore the questions and worrying thoughts racing through her head. She leaned back in her chair and turned her attention to the landscape below and for a short while, it provided the much-needed distraction.

The vast desert, with its contrasting hues of tan and orange, burnt amber and rust, maroon and even a few shades of purple, held her captivated as flat expanses of sand gave way to gently rising sand dunes, which led to even higher hills. She'd never thought the desert could have so many contrasting colors. It was breathtakingly beautiful.

Before long the hills completely disappeared and desert sand gave way to the Red Sea, the deep turquoise colors a vivid contrast to the view they had left behind. Liv was again craning her head to see out the window as they flew over the coast of the African continent. Brilliant blue water sparkled below as it suddenly dawned on her that they weren't headed to Sarq but a different destination.

It had to be Dubai, she thought. It was one of the most cosmopolitan cities in the Middle East and a place very far removed from Jabal. "Are we headed to Dubai?" she asked, as the plane tilted slightly, giving her a wider view of the Arabian Peninsula looming on the horizon.

"No, we're going to Baraka. I have friends there and you'd be safe. But tell me, how is it that a girl from a small Southern town knows so much about the Middle East?"

"I pour over travel brochures all day," she said, but from his expression she could see he didn't understand. "I'm a travel agent," she added.

"So you're a world traveler."

She shook her head regretfully. "No. I don't usually travel. I just book trips for other people. This is my first real trip. Until now I'd never been out of the U.S."

Suddenly the nose of the plane tipped and they seemed to be changing direction again. Sheikh Fehr frowned and reached for his seat belt. The flight attendant moved toward them at the same time.

She knelt at his side and spoke quietly in Arabic. "The pilot said we've a problem. We're dangerously low on petrol. We need to land almost immediately. Fortunately we've been given permission to land in Cairo."

"Good. Thank you," Khalid answered, glancing at Olivia, knowing that things were beginning to get a little more complicated than he liked.

By being diverted at the last minute from Baraka to Egypt he wouldn't be able to process Olivia swiftly. He'd planned on having her checked out by a doctor then put on a private jet to New York tonight. Instead they were landing in Cairo, which meant they'd need to find a place to stay, and since he couldn't use his preferred pilot and jet, nor the doctor he normally used, he'd need to find another way to get her quickly and quietly attended to. Unfortunately, it wouldn't be today, or tonight.

Olivia turned just then to look at him, her blue eyes wide, almost pinched, in her pale oval face. She was still wearing her headscarf, but the fabric was loose around her neck, exposing her delicate features.

"What's wrong?" she asked, fear in her voice, the same fear that made her eyes turn to lapis.

"We've had a change of plans," he answered.

Her forehead creased. "*Another?* Why? What's happened?"

"Out of petrol, or as you Americans call it, gas. So we're landing in Egypt instead of Baraka."

He wasn't sure what he expected, but her sudden smile stunned her, her blue eyes widening with excitement. "Egypt?" she repeated. "I was on my way to Egypt when I was arrested. Will we have time to see the pyramids in Giza?"

"Unfortunately not. We'll be landing and hopefully taking off as soon as we refuel. We need to get to Baraka tonight."

Her gaze searched his as if trying to see what he wasn't telling her. "Why?"

"You want to go home, don't you?"

She nodded slowly, clearly puzzled. "But if we don't make it out tonight, we'll just go tomorrow, right?"

He wasn't ready to tell her that things were a lot more complicated than she knew.

For the past ten years he'd operated his version of an underground railroad. He specialized in rescuing innocent people and he'd enlisted some powerful friends to help him. People like Sheikh Kalen Nuri, the younger brother of Baraka's King Malik Nuri, and Sheikh Tair, leader of the independent state Ouaha.

In the past few years Kalen and Tair had helped him with dozens of impossible rescues, and they'd pledged to help with Olivia's, but first they had to get to Baraka.

"We want to reach Baraka tonight," he said tersely, unwilling to give up his initial goal. "I need to make a few calls," he added, rising from his seat. "Relax, try to get a little sleep. I will be able to tell you more once we're on the ground."

Twenty minutes later they touched down, the jet landing so smoothly that Liv didn't even realize they were on the ground until the pilot began to brake, slowing the jet's speed.

After taxiing to the terminal the jet sat on the tarmac, not far from the executive terminal. Khalid didn't appear and the pilot hadn't emerged from the cockpit.

Liv, seeing the flight attendant on the plane phone, flagged her down. "Are we refueling?" she asked.

But before the flight attendant could answer, Sheikh Fehr walked from the cockpit back to Liv's seat.

"We're staying in Cairo tonight," he said. "I've a car waiting. Let's go."

Liv shot him an uneasy glance. He was angry. She felt his tension wash over her in dark brooding waves. Something had happened. Something not good.

"What's wrong?" she asked, unbuckling her seat belt and rising to her feet. From her window she could see a black car outside, waiting not far from the plane.

"We can talk later," he answered, extending a hand, his black robe with the gold embroidery swirling. "Come. Traffic will be heavy. We need to go."

She put her fingers in his, shuddering at the sharp hot spark that passed between them. She wanted very much to take her hand back but was afraid of upsetting him.

Once seated in the car, their driver sped on and off highways and Liv marveled at the way Sheikh Fehr traveled.

She'd never met anyone who owned his own jet and employed his own pilot and flight crew. Even though she worked in the travel industry, she thought of flying as booking a ticket on a commercial airline, then going to a crowded airport for an endless wait in a long security line. Maybe it was just the U.S., but modern travel meant canceled flights, missed connections, lost luggage, no meal service and irritated flight attendants. In short, flying was far from luxurious, and definitely not glamorous. But Sheikh Fehr's jet was sumptuous, as was his fleet of cars.

The fact that he had access to a fleet of cars in different countries, never mind the security, made her wonder about him, and his power.

What kind of man could accomplish the things he did?

What kind of man risked life and limb for a stranger?

Unless he did it for money.

Hiding her worry, she shot another glance his way. Could he be a mercenary of sorts?

The thought made her skin crawl, nearly as much as her disgusting black prison-issued robe and lank headscarf did.

Self-consciously she reached up and touched the headscarf she still wore. The flight attendant hadn't worn one and Liv wondered now if it was still necessary. "Can I take this off?" she asked.

"Please. In Jabal we didn't have a choice, but here in Egypt, and my country of Sarq, it's optional."

"Some women want to wear the veil?"

"They view it as protection, shielding them from leering eyes and inappropriate advances." His gaze swept over her. "You will need something else to wear though. That's obviously a prison-issued robe."

Liv plucked at her robe's stiff, coarse fabric. "I can't stand this thing," she confessed, her voice dropping. "It's all I've worn since they arrested me and I hate it. I never want to put it on again."

"You won't have to. And once we're at the hotel, I'll make sure the robe's properly disposed of."

"Thank you." Tears inexplicably burned the backs of her eyes and she had to squeeze her eyes shut to hold the emotion in. She was just tired. Overwhelmed by the day. There was no reason to cry. She'd be home soon. If not tonight, then tomorrow. And everything would be all right. She just needed to call her mom, or Jake. Once she heard their voices she knew she'd be okay.

"So we are staying in Cairo overnight?" she asked.

"Yes."

"Why?"

He shifted, shoulders shrugging impatiently. "My pilot was concerned about the plane. He was afraid there was a fuel leak and wanted it checked out before we flew again."

"Sensible."

"Yes."

But from his tone, she knew the sheikh didn't agree and she was hit with another wave of homesickness. She was tired of strangers, tired of short-tempered men and women. She just wanted to go home. Back to the people who knew her and loved her, and back to people she loved.

"Can I call my brother now?" she asked, her voice wobbly with the threat of tears.

"Maybe we should wait a little longer, until you've seen the doctor."

His words were a one-two punch and Liv stiffened. "A doctor? Why?"

"It's routine. Standard practice whenever someone's been released—"

"How often *do* you do this?" she interrupted.

"Often enough to know that you need to be checked out and cleared for travel."

"But I'm fine," she insisted. She didn't want anyone touching her, didn't want anyone looking at her or poking at her or coming near her. She'd had enough of that at Ozr. "I'm fine."

His dark gaze pierced her. "It's not an option, Miss Morse." His tone hardened. "You have to. I can't take any chances.

You've been in Ozr for weeks. The place is a breeding ground for all sorts of diseases."

"I doubt I've caught anything and if I have, I'll deal with it at home." *With my doctor*, she silently, furiously added.

Sheikh Fehr might have rescued her from Ozr, but she couldn't completely trust him. She didn't trust anyone here anymore. These countries and cultures were far too different from hers.

Her longing for home had become an endless ache inside her. She missed her mom and brother. She wanted her mother's delicious Sunday pot roast, and her melt-in-your-mouth mashed potatoes and the best brown gravy in the world.

She wanted Pierceville with its sleepy Main Street and big oak trees and the old Fox theater where they still showed movies. She missed Main Street's angled parking and the drugstore on the corner and the two bakeries with their cake displays in the window.

"You won't be given permission to leave the country if you're not cleared for travel." He spoke slowly to make sure he was heard. "And if you're not cleared for travel, you don't go home."

Home.

That word she understood, that word cut through her fog of misery.

Turning away to hide the shimmer of tears, Liv stared out the car window, the stream of traffic outside a blur.

"Whose rule is that?" she asked thickly. "Yours, or the government's?"

"Both."

Biting her lip, it crossed her mind that maybe, just maybe, she'd jumped from the frying pan into the fire.

Khalid Fehr watched Olivia turn her face away from him. She was upset but that was her choice. He had to be careful. He took tremendous risks in helping people. At the end of the day, once someone was safe and en route to their home, he wanted to go home himself, back to his beloved desert.

The desert was where he belonged.

The desert was where he found peace.

"The doctor's a personal friend," he said quietly, only able to see the back of her head, and then when the sun struck the outside of the window, it turned the glass into a mirror, giving him an almost perfect reflection of her pale, set face.

She looked lost, he thought. Gone. Like a ghost of a woman.

Her fear ate at him all over again, stirring the fury in him, the fury that was only soothed, calmed, by acts of valor.

It was ridiculous, really, this need of his to save others, this need to unite families torn apart, to return missing loved ones to those who waited, grieved.

He wasn't a hero, didn't want to be a hero, and this wasn't the life he'd ever wanted for himself. He'd loved his studies, had enjoyed his career, but that all ended when his sisters died.

Thinking of his sisters reminded him of Olivia and her brother Jake and all her family had gone through in the past five or six weeks since she disappeared. "I'm trying to help you," he said quietly.

"Then send me home," she answered, her voice breaking.

His jaw jutted. She wasn't the only one who couldn't go home yet. He couldn't, either, and he wasn't much happier about it than she was.

Anytime he took these human rights cases on, he moved swiftly, moved a person in and out in a day. These rescues always took place within twenty-four hours and then he was home again, back in his quiet world of sky and sand. Back in anonymity.

Today was different. Everything about today's rescue was different. And that didn't bode well for any of them.

CHAPTER THREE

A HALF hour later they reached the famous Mena House Hotel, a historic hotel on the outskirts of Cairo.

Liv leaned forward to get a glimpse of the historic property but saw little of the hotel's entrance with the dozen black cars lining the drive and virtually blocking the front door.

"It looks like the President of the United States has arrived," she said, staring at all the cars and security detail. "I wonder who it's for?"

"Us," he answered cryptically, as security moved toward their car, flanking the front and back.

She jerked around to look at him. "Why?"

He shrugged as the door opened.

"Your Highness," one of the men said, bowing deeply. "Welcome. The hotel is secure."

Liv didn't move. She couldn't. Her body had gone nerveless. "Who *are* you?"

"I'm Sheikh Khalid Fehr. Prince of the Great Sarq Desert."

And then it came together, all the missing pieces, all the little things that hadn't added up. Sarq. Fehr. The family name, Fehr. "Your brother is King Fehr," she whispered.

"Yes."

"You're…royalty."

His broad shoulders shifted. "I didn't ask for the job. I inherited it." And then he climbed out of the car.

They were escorted through the opulent, gilded lobby to a private elevator that glided soundlessly up to the royal suite, which occupied the entire penthouse floor.

Their suite consisted of two enormous bedrooms and ensuite baths opening off a central living area. The suite was dark, the windows curtained, but then the butler drew the curtains back and the suite was flooded with late-afternoon sunlight, and the most astonishing view of the Great Pyramid.

"Incredible," Liv murmured, standing at the window, hands pressed to the glass.

"There's a balcony in each of the bedrooms," the butler offered. "Very nice for a morning coffee or evening nightcap."

She could only nod. She didn't want to move, or be distracted. She just wanted to stand here and feast on the most amazing thing she'd ever seen.

The golden stone pyramid soared...gigantic, mythic, spectacular.

This is why she'd traveled so far from home. This is what she'd wanted to see. Ancient wonders. Relics of a glorious past.

But then Khalid Fehr spoke. "The doctor is here, Olivia."

Her insides did a quick freeze and she slowly, reluctantly turned from the window. A woman in a dark slack suit and wearing a dark scarf around her shoulders stood next to Khalid.

"I'm Dr. Nenet Hassan," the woman said briskly. "I'm a friend of Sheikh Fehr's from university. The exam won't hurt, and it won't take long, either. We'll just step into your room and get it over, shall we?"

Liv wouldn't even look at Khalid as she headed for her bedroom with Dr. Hassan close behind. She didn't want the exam, didn't need a checkup, but no one seemed to be listening.

Fortunately, the exam was as quick as Dr. Hassan had said and in less than ten minutes the physician was putting her instruments away. "You're healthy," Dr. Hassan said. "And I know you're dying for a bath so go ahead, enjoy. I'll have a word with Sheikh Fehr and see myself out."

Khalid was waiting for Nenet as she emerged from Liv's room. "Well?" he demanded.

"She has some bruises but they're not specific to any injury."

"She hasn't been beaten?" Khalid asked bluntly.

"She does have marks and the odd bruise or cut, but that's to be expected. It's a well-known fact that the female guards are far harder on the female prisoners than the male guards are on the men. They're just more aggressive, although the abuse leans toward the mental instead of the physical."

"What about drug use?" he asked.

Nenet lifted her head, and her somber brown gaze searched his. "You suspect her of using?"

"No. But you never know."

The doctor's expression remained speculative. "I didn't see needle marks, or anything else indicative of drug abuse."

"Good," he answered, turning away to look out the same window that had so completely captured Liv's imagination earlier.

"Do you really intend to marry her?" Nenet asked, catching Khalid off guard. "Or is it just another baseless rumor?"

His forehead creased and he turned from the window to look at the doctor over his shoulder. "How did you hear?"

"How did I hear? Khalid, it's all over the news! A high-ranking Jabal official announced that you'd visited his country today to bring your betrothed home." Nenet swallowed hard. "And this…this…American…she's your *betrothed*?"

None of this was supposed to be happening, Khalid thought. He was supposed to have freed Olivia from prison, zipped to Baraka in his jet, had her cleared by a doctor and then hurried onto a waiting jet provided by Kalen Nuri, and then she'd fly home and he'd fly back to the Sarq desert in his jet and it'd be finished. No naming of names, no police chases, no publicity.

"I don't know that this is an appropriate conversation for us to be having," he said flatly.

He'd once dated Nenet Hassan during his second year of graduate school, but the pressures on both of them had been intense, and then when his sisters had died, he'd broken the relationship off. Nenet had written long letters to him, saying she'd wait for him, promising he could take all the time he needed to heal, but Khalid hadn't wanted time to heal. He hadn't wanted to heal. He just wanted out. Away. Gone from the life he'd lived and the people he'd known.

"Forgive me, Khalid. Please don't be angry. I know it's not my place," Nenet added quickly, trying to ease the tension and awkward silence, "but I can't ignore what you're doing. It wouldn't be right."

"And what am I doing?" he asked even more gruffly.

"You know what you're doing. I know what you're doing. But stop. Don't. Don't sacrifice yourself for her." Grief darkened her eyes. "You aren't merely a good man, Khalid, you are a great man, and a man that has suffered enough. You owe her nothing, especially not your future, or your freedom."

In the bathroom, Liv stood in the middle of the marble tiled floor for what seemed like forever.

The bathroom was beyond decadent. The decor was reminiscent of the Great Pyramid outside, with pale ivory and gold limestone pavers on the floor and more buttery-colored limestone surrounding the deep bathtub.

A series of three glass-covered jars rested on the tub surround. She lifted each of the lids and smelled the different scented bath salts—verbena, orange blossom and hyacinth—and suddenly a lump filled her throat, making it hard to breathe.

She'd been in hell for weeks and just when she thought there was no hope, she was plucked from her cell and rushed to the airport. Now she was in this palatial suite with a palatial bath furnished with thick, plush towels and exquisitely scented bath salts and fragrant designer shampoos.

It was strange. Impossible. Overwhelming.

The transition was too much.

Leaning over the marble surround, she turned on the water. While the tub filled she stripped off her hated robe and the black sheath she wore under the robe and balled the fabric up and smashed it into the rubbish bin beneath the vanity.

Naked, she examined herself in the mirror. Even to her eyes she looked too thin, gaunt, with yellow and purple-blue bruises on her arms and legs. Turning part way, she studied her back and spotted a big fading bruise on her hip and a newer bruise on her left shoulder.

But the bruises would go and she'd recover and she'd be home. Soon. Soon, she repeated, dumping in two scoops of the verbena-scented bath salt before sliding carefully into the hot water.

The bath felt like heaven and she soaked until the water cooled, forcing her to action by shampooing and conditioning her hair.

Later, clean and wrapped in the soft white cotton sateen robe found hanging on the back of the door, Liv left the bathroom for her bedroom and then realized she didn't know what to do next. She had no clothes. She didn't feel comfortable wandering around the suite in just a robe. The conservative climate of the Middle East made her aware that she shouldn't be sharing a suite with man she didn't know.

Fresh anxiety hit and out of an old nervous habit, she began chewing her thumbnail down, chewing it to bits.

She had to go home. She needed to go home, and even thought the hotel was gorgeous, and this was probably the only time in her life that she'd ever stay in a five-star property, she couldn't enjoy it. Couldn't appreciate the high ceilings, the tall windows and the exotic decor, not when her mother and her brother were waiting for her and worrying about her.

Crossing to the table near her bed, she picked up the phone

and asked the hotel operator to put through a call to the States. The operator answered that she couldn't make the call for her, but gave Liv the international codes so Liv could dial the call from her hotel room.

Liv was scribbling the codes down when a knock sounded on her bedroom door. Her heart skipped. "Just a minute," she called, swiftly trying to dial the string of numbers, then making a mistake in the middle and having to start all over again.

"We need to talk." It was Khalid's deep voice on the other side of the door.

Fingers trembling, she finished inputting the long sequence of numbers. "Okay," she called back. "I'll be out soon."

There was a pause. "We should really talk before you call home," he said. "There are things you should know, things that you might, or might not, want your family to know."

She could hear the ring of her mother's line. Liv gripped the phone more tightly. She suddenly wanted to hear her mother's voice more than anything in the whole world.

"Olivia," Khalid continued, his deep voice unnervingly clear despite the door between them, "you don't have a passport any longer, and it could be difficult to get another issued soon. Perhaps we should discuss a way to break the news to your family without frightening them?"

She could hear the ringing on the line. Could imagine her mother looking for the phone, wondering where she'd left it this time.

Eyes smarting, emotion thick in her chest, Liv hung up before her mother could answer.

She couldn't worry her mom. She loved her too much.

Beseiged by conflicted emotions, Liv walked to the bedroom door and opened it. Khalid stood on the other side, his robe discarded in favor of exquisitely tailored European-style clothes: dark slacks, supple black leather belt, crisp long-sleeved cotton shirt the color of espresso and black leather shoes. His dark hair was cut short and sleek, emphasizing the strong lines of his face.

He didn't even look like the same person and she didn't know why his transformation felt like one more blow.

Nothing was what she'd expected. Imagined.

Nothing made sense.

Pressing her hands into her robe's pockets, she took a quick breath for courage. "Sheikh Fehr, in the car, you said to wait to call my brother until after I'd seen the doctor, and I waited. Now you tell me not to call home because I don't have a passport and I shouldn't worry my family." Her eyes met his and held. "I don't know what to believe anymore."

"Maybe we should sit down."

"I don't want to sit. I just want the truth."

"As you, yourself know, the truth is complicated."

She blinked, puzzled. "What does that mean?"

"You were charged with smuggling drugs, and the drugs were found on your person—"

"In a bag I was holding for a friend!"

He shrugged. "But it was in your backpack, in your possession, making you responsible. Complicating the truth is the fact that this 'friend' disappeared and we have no proof she ever existed."

"That's not true! I had her bag. Her cosmetics. Her toiletries."

"Who is to say they aren't yours?"

She stared up at him, appalled. "You don't believe me? You think I did it—"

"I never said that. I was just pointing out that truth isn't always what it seems, just as my freeing you, isn't quite what it seems, either."

She suddenly felt very woozy, her head starting to spin. "I'm beginning to feel dizzy."

His brows pulled in a fierce line. "I knew you were better off sitting."

Ignoring her attempt to brush him off, he put one hand to

her elbow and the other to the small of her back—a touch that scorched her even through her thick robe—and escorted her to the plump upholstered chair in the living room.

"I'm not going to break," she said breathlessly, her heart hammering unsteadily as heat washed through her. She could feel his hand despite the plush robe, could feel the press of his fingers against the dip in her spine, and it made her head spin even faster.

"I know you're not going to break," he answered, making sure she was safely ensconced in the chair before stepping away, "but you've been through a traumatic ordeal, and unfortunately, it's not over yet."

Liv stared up at him, battling to get control over her pulse and her thoughts. "I'd think the American embassy would step in now, accelerate the process of getting me home."

"They'd like to, but they work with the local government, and Jabal is lobbying very hard to have you returned to them for sentencing."

She made a soft sound of disbelief. "Can the Jabal government extradite me from here?"

"No," he answered, standing above her, arms folded, his expression downright forbidding. "At least, hopefully not."

With a trembling hand Liv pushed a damp tendril of hair away from her face, trying to sort out everything he was saying, stress and exhaustion making the task even harder than it should be. "That doesn't sound very reassuring," she said hoarsely, blinking back the sting of tears.

"It's not meant to be. You should know the truth, and the truth is, things are…unpredictable…at the moment."

His response just added to her fears. "I won't go back to Jabal," she choked. "I can't. I *can't*—"

"I know, and I wouldn't let you go back."

She looked up at him, scared, so very scared, and bundled her arms more tightly across her chest. "Why are you doing all this? Why are you helping me?"

"Your brother posted a message for help on the Internet. His message came to my attention."

Her chest felt so hot, and her emotions felt ragged. She didn't know if she could—should—believe him. "You did all this just because you saw a message on the Internet?"

"Yes."

Who did things like this? Who broke into prisons and rescued people? *"Why?"*

His shuttered gaze rested on her face, his expression as blank as the tone of his voice. "Your brother said your family was frantic." He paused for a split second before adding, "It touched me."

Her brow wrinkled as she digested his words, thinking it was odd to hear him use the word *touched* when he struck her as emotional as one of the limestone statues she'd seen carved into the wall of the Ozr fortress turned prison. "And you acted alone?"

"Yes."

"But if you weren't working with an embassy or government, how did you get me released?"

He made a rough, mocking sound. "The old-fashioned way. Power. Blackmail. Intimidation."

"Isn't that illegal?" she asked, trying to keep the horror from her voice.

"Blackmail is never pretty," he answered. "But it was you or them, and it's not as if the guards were good to you. The doctor told me she found bruises on you, bruises I'm certain you didn't inflict on yourself."

She just looked away, towards the window with the spectacular view of the pyramid.

Khalid dropped to his haunches, crouching before her, and turned her face to him. "No diplomatic measure would have ever gotten you freed from Ozr. Jabal doesn't care about diplomacy. They don't recognize diplomacy. They only recognize power and money. I did what I had to do, and I don't apologize for it. At least you're here, safe and alive."

Liv felt his fingers on her chin, felt the fierce heat in his eyes and the coiled tension in his powerful frame. She was simultaneously fascinated and terrified by the fire in his dark eyes. He intrigued her and yet intimidated her. He was hard and fierce and remote, and yet he'd also come to rescue her when no one else had, or would. "But not free," she whispered.

"Are you free to go home, back to Pierceville, Alabama? No. Are you free of the prison cell?" He hesitated for a fraction of a second and then stood again. "For now."

For now. The words echoed loudly in her head. She was free only for now.

"But money alone didn't buy your freedom," he added. "It required honor. My honor."

She gave her head a slight shake. His honor. It was such an archaic-sounding word, so old-fashioned it didn't even make sense to her. "I don't understand."

"I vouched for you," he said bluntly. "I told them you were mine."

She blinked at the word *mine*, heat flooding through her, heat and shyness and shame. *Mine* was such a possessive word, a word implying ownership, control. It was a word two-year-olds loved, but not one she would have expected to come from a man. At least in the United States you'd never hear a man refer to a woman as his. "How could being… *yours*…free me?"

"By claiming you, I have personally vouched for you."

She was even more confused than before. "Claimed me… how?"

"I said you were my betrothed."

Betrothed? The archaic word didn't make sense for a moment and then it hit her. *"Engaged?"*

Appalled, she saw him nod.

"Because of our…relationship…you are protected for the time being."

Liv's mouth opened but she couldn't make a sound, couldn't think of a single thing to say. Instead shock washed over her in gigantic mind-numbing waves, and before she could think of anything to say, the butler materialized with a tray of small sandwiches, pastries and a large pot of tea. He placed the tray on the low table in the living room and served them both sandwiches, pastries and tea, before departing.

Liv stared at one of the small open-faced sandwiches on her plate. "We're not really engaged," she said at last, finally finding her voice.

"I gave them my word," he said bluntly.

"Yes, but that was to get me out. That was to free me—"

"And I did, but we had complications on the way out of Jabal. Remember that police stop earlier today? They'd come for you. They'd learned that you'd been released from Ozr and they'd been given instructions to seize you. The only way I could protect you was by claiming you. And once I claimed you, they couldn't touch you."

"But you will still send me home, right? You are going to put me on a plane first thing in the morning…." Her voice trailed off as she stared at his face, his expression hard and unyielding.

She tried again. "If you were going to send me home earlier, what has changed?"

"Everything. It has been announced by the Jabal government that we are engaged. They cannot be faulted. It is what I told them, and my honor is based on my word. My word is central to who I am, and to who my family is. I…we Fehrs…do not break our word."

"We're not really going to get married."

"Today at Ozr you said you wanted out, you begged me to get you out, and I did what you asked me to do."

It was just beginning to hit her that she'd celebrated her release from the Ozr prison far too soon.

Her panicked gaze searched the fierce lines of his face, the high brow, the long aquiline nose, the generous but unsmiling mouth, as tremors of fear coursed through her. "There must be another way. There must be some other way…."

He didn't answer and his silence terrified her. "Sheikh Fehr," she pleaded. "Don't tell me we have no other options. I can't believe there aren't any other options."

"There is another option," he said flatly. "And you're right. It's not a done deal yet. You can choose to return to Ozr—"

"To Ozr?" she interrupted, stunned. It'd been hell, sheer hell, locked up there. No sunlight, no bathroom facilities, no running water to speak of. "People die there all the time!"

"It isn't a good place," he agreed.

She bolted up from her chair, nearly upending her plate. "So why would you think I'd want to go back there?"

"Because as of now, those are your only two options. Marriage to me or a return to Jabal."

She sank back down, her legs suddenly impossibly weak. Her gaze clung to his, trying to see, trying to understand if he was absolutely serious. "But you don't want to marry me. There can't be any possible benefit for you!"

His upper lip curled. "None that come to mind."

"So why?"

His features hardened, his dark eyes almost glittering with silent anger. "What would you have me do? Let you rot in prison for the rest of your life? Tell your brother to be glad you're in prison because you're at least not dead?"

She dropped her gaze, her cheeks flaming. Jake would have been desperate, too. He'd always been so protective of her, the quintessential big brother. "You don't have to do this. You didn't ask for any of this—"

"Did you smuggle the drugs?" he demanded harshly, abruptly.

Her head jerked up. *"No."*

His shoulders twisted. "Then I have to do it. If you are innocent, how do I stand by and do nothing? How do I explain to your brother that your life has no value? That his love for you means nothing here? How do I live with myself knowing that all your lives have been laid to waste over someone else's mistake?"

"You're one of those men with a hero complex," she said, feeling desperation hit. "I've read about people like you. Heroes are ordinary people who do extraordinary things—"

"I'm not a hero," he interrupted roughly. "But I did go to Jabal and you are here now, and we've got to get through this."

"But marry…" Her voice faded and she stared at him with disbelief. "It seems so extreme, so…impossible."

His dark head, with his crisp, short black hair inclined. "It's not what you'd choose, or what I'd choose, but it was the only way. Is the only way."

"For *now*," she said.

He said nothing, just stared at her.

She raised her chin, silently defiant. *For now*, she repeated, making a vow to herself that she'd never be forced into marriage, nor marry a man she didn't love.

There was another way out of this. There had to be.

Turning her head away, Liv looked out the window again. The sun was beginning to drop in the sky and long gold rays of light haloed the Great Pyramid.

"Finish your tea," Khalid said, his voice flat, authoritative. "Then we'll go shop. We're entertaining tonight and you'll need proper clothes to impress our distinguished guests."

She reluctantly tore her gaze from the window and glanced back at Khalid. "Who are we entertaining?"

"Friends from Jabal and Egypt who come to celebrate our engagement tonight."

Liv's blood froze, her insides turning to ice. "Jabal officials will be here tonight?"

"You don't need to be afraid," he answered. "They will see you, but they won't speak to you, not without permission from me, and I won't give them permission."

She nodded once.

"But you will have to look happier than that tonight. Tonight's a party, so finish your tea, and then we'll go shopping."

She stared at him in horror. A party tonight to celebrate their engagement? Jabal officials coming here, to their hotel? "I have to pretend we're engaged?"

"Don't worry. I'll see you properly clothed, and I realize you can't shop in your prison-issued robe. Dr. Hassan was kind enough to pick up something from an Egyptian designer we both know. She brought it with her, and it's hanging in the hall closet now. I don't know how well it'll fit, but there's a dress, coat, some undergarments and even a pair of shoes."

"The point isn't the clothes—"

"But it is," he interrupted. "We're having a small party here tonight and you have to be properly attired, so finish your tea and then get dressed as I've arranged to have a stylist meet us in an hour and traffic is going to be ugly."

CHAPTER FOUR

HAVING finished her tea, Liv studied herself in her bedroom mirror. The wheat-colored linen dress and matching coat hung on her slim frame, but the fabric was gorgeous, as was the warm color that reminded her of the pyramid outside.

She'd lost a lot of weight in the past month, her body more angular than attractive. She frowned and combed the brush through her hair, leaving the unruly white-gold strands tumbling loose past her shoulders.

Downstairs in front of the hotel, one of Sheikh Fehr's black Mercedes sedans waited for them. Soon they were driving across Cairo to the First Residence Complex, which is where the luxury shopping mall was also located.

Khalid told her that the First Residence Complex, which included the First Residence Shopping Mall and the Four Seasons Hotel, was the most coveted real estate in Cairo and the place all the stars and sheikhs and heads of state hit when they visit the city.

"But you don't stay there?" she asked, catching glimpses of handsome palm trees lining the broad cornice as the last glints of dying sunlight warmed the creamy paint on the building facades.

"I usually do when I'm here, but on the plane you mentioned your love of history and geography and I thought the Mena House would appeal to you."

"You chose it for me?"

"Yes."

Liv felt that painful tightness in her chest again, and, flustered, she dipped her head, surprised, flattered, but also confused. "Thank you."

The car slowed before an elegant domed building. "We're here," Khalid said, as his driver came around to open the back door. "And I believe your personal shopper is here waiting for us, too."

Indeed, a smart-looking woman in a dark suit stepped toward the car as the driver opened the door. She'd obviously been waiting for them and she bowed deeply to Sheikh Fehr, and gave a smaller bow to Olivia. "I'm Val Bakr," she said, her long dark hair braided and pinned up. "I'm a personal shopper and I'm here to make wardrobing you as quick and efficient as possible."

She led Liv through the shopping center to a selection of designer shops where she'd already selected dozens of outfits for Liv to try on. Khalid accompanied her in each shop, but he sat off to one side and silently observed the fittings.

By the end of the hour Liv had tried on a staggering array of dresses, skirts, slacks, jackets, blouses, gowns, shoes and coats. Raffia totes were added to the pile of clothes, along with small clutches, swimsuits, belts, hats, scarves, and even robes and nightgowns.

The clothes were stunning. Cotton and silk white trousers, off-white patent pumps, a jade-green crocodile belt, a cotton cardigan with real pearl buttons. The rainbow-hued Louis Vuitton bag got its color from pretty leather buttons adhered with a tiny gold ball. The green Valentino heels had a rhinestone bow. The sea-foam green silk chiffon dress had sweet ruffles at the neck and then a high-waisted belt covered in semiprecious stones.

Khalid didn't even hand a credit card. He just nodded at the pile and asked for everything to be sent to him at the Mena Hotel and then he took Olivia's arm and walked her back to his car.

"You can't possibly really buy all that," she said in protest as they exited the elegant shopping mall.

Khalid didn't answer. He just gestured to the car's open door, but Liv hesitated. She could still remember how Val had stood elbow-high in tissue and boxes and garment bags. "Sheikh Fehr, I saw the price on the bag—which alone was seventy-five hundred dollars. I don't even own a *car* worth seventy-five hundred dollars."

Khalid sighed and glanced at his watch. "Miss Bakr has impeccable taste and everything she selected is perfect for our needs."

"But all those clothes! They must cost thousands and thousands of dollars."

"You need a proper wardrobe."

"But this is too much. A couple skirts, a few blouses, a pair of sandals. But certainly not all the designer labels, and those extravagant accessories...and you must admit a seven-thousand-dollar purse—"

"Please get in the car," he interrupted quietly, but in such a no-nonsense tone that Liv gulped a breath and complied.

Inside the car he added, "We do not argue with our women on the city streets, and our women do not disagree with us in front of family, friends or strangers."

Flushing with embarrassment, Liv went hot and then cold and hot again. She was just trying to save him money. She'd only been trying to make things easier. "I'm sorry. I wasn't trying to be disrespectful. I just didn't want you spending so much on me. There was no need."

"But there is," he corrected. "It's what people will expect of you. You now represent me. You are my fiancée, and here in the Arab world, I am very well-known."

"But you must understand I can't pay you back for these things," she protested huskily. "My mom certainly can't. She's nearing retirement, and Jake can't, either. He's a carpenter. He builds houses for a living."

Khalid sighed. "I don't expect to be paid back. But I do expect your respect, and cooperation. I have put my name and reputation on the line for you. I am risking my personal and family honor, and honor is everything here. Honor is the difference between life and death."

It was dark now and the streetlights and building lights illuminated the city blocks.

"My job is to protect you, but you must allow me to protect you. You must trust me when I say we are in a difficult, and dangerous, situation."

Khalid's warning sent a shiver through her. How many times had Jake virtually said the same thing? How many times had he told her the world wasn't a nice place, the world wasn't a safe place, especially for a girl from a small Southern town?

But she hadn't believed him. She'd thought Jake was a pessimist. Now she knew differently.

"Are you listening?" Khalid asked.

"Yes," she answered hoarsely. The things Khalid was telling her terrified her. It wasn't the life she knew. It wasn't how she'd been raised.

"I do not mean to frighten you," he added after a moment, "but I need to impress upon you the importance of appearances. We must be discrete. Everything we do will be observed by others. Everything we do—individually, or together—will be documented, analyzed and discussed. The only time you are truly free, or truly safe, is when you are alone with me."

She gave a short nod to show him she understood.

Khalid fell silent, his forehead creasing, his expression turning brooding. "One more thing. I phoned your brother earlier, while you were finishing your tea. I told him you were safe. I told him you were with me. And I told him you would personally phone later tonight and he said he'd look forward to speaking with you, but in the meantime, he sends love and extends to us his heartiest congratulations."

Liv's blood froze. "Congratulations?" she whispered, through impossibly cold, stiff lips.

"On our engagement."

"You *told* him?"

"I had to. He's going to read it in the paper soon. I thought he'd rather hear the news from us."

"But we're not really going to get married," Liv choked, fingers balling into fists in her lap. "It's just a ruse, a facade to buy us time."

When Khalid didn't answer she felt downright hysterical. He couldn't be serious about marriage. There was just no way. No way. And how was it possible that she'd left prison only to be forced into marriage? Apparently it was just one jail in exchange for another. "I can't do it," she said fiercely, "and I won't."

"Then tell that to the Jabal officials who are coming to see us in an hour or two," he said, doing little to hide his annoyance. "Tell them you're not really my fiancée, tell them it was all a mistake and you'll see what will happen when you get me out of the way. Olivia, I am the only one keeping you from that prison. I am the only one who can, and the only way I can is by offering you my name, my life and my family's reputation."

She hung her head, closed her eyes and dragged in a breath, and then another. "Why does it have to be jail or marriage? Why?"

"Because this isn't Europe, or America, and you were charged with a very serious crime. A crime which can carry the death penalty."

"But why did you have to tell Jake that I was getting married? He didn't have to know. It hasn't happened, and it might not happen—"

"He was going to read it in the papers tomorrow or the next day. I thought he'd want to know first. I thought he'd want to be prepared."

Jake wasn't going to understand, though. Jake knew her. He knew she'd only dated a little and had never had a proper boyfriend. When it came to men she was still ridiculously sheltered and the last thing she'd do, ever, was jump into a relationship with a man she didn't know, much less a man from a culture so very different from hers.

"Jake's just going to be more worried," she said. "It's only going to make things worse."

"It can't be much worse for him that it already is," Khalid answered shortly. "He's had his hands full these past few weeks and the truth is, you are safer with me than you were in Ozr."

"What do you mean, things can't be much worse for him than they already are? What's happened back home?"

Khalid abruptly turned the interior light on, flooding the car with yellow light. "Your mother took the news of your disappearance badly—"

"What do you mean 'badly'? How badly?" she interrupted.

"She had a heart attack—"

"No!" Liv pressed a hand to her mouth. "No," she repeated, voice muffled. "It can't be."

"I understand she's better. She's stable, and resting, but she's still not strong and your brother has been caring for her. Otherwise he'd be here now."

Liv shook her head, her thoughts wild and chaotic. Her entire world had been upended and she couldn't get her bearings. "When did she have the heart attack?"

"A week ago."

With an unsteady finger she reached up to dash away tears before they could fall. "Are you sure she's okay?"

"She's back home. She's sleeping a lot right now."

"That's why you didn't want me to call home earlier."

"Yes."

Exhaling slowly, she drew another painful breath. "I'm not ready to lose my mom. I just lost my dad a couple years ago."

"You must be strong now. You must believe that everything will work out. Everything will be fine."

"Do you really think everything really be fine?"

He gazed down at her for a long, level moment. There was a fierce intelligence in his eyes that reminded her of a hawk or falcon circling before making its kill. "Yes." His long black lashes dropped, concealing his fierce, dark eyes. "It may take time, but things always do work out. One way, or another."

Returning to the hotel, Liv discovered their suite had been transformed. Fresh flower arrangements covered the living room tables while the dining room table had been turned into an elaborate dinner buffet with another huge white-and-purple floral arrangement at the centerpiece.

Soft music played from hidden speakers and a uniformed waiter finished prepping the beverage table, while another moved around the room, fluffing pillows, dimming table lamps and lighting floating candles.

Liv stood in the hall, awed and more than a little bit intimidated by the transformation. In the shimmering candlelight, the faded tapestries on the wall, the dark wood furniture and the rich exotic fabrics covering the couch and chairs seemed almost otherworldly, and Liv realized all over again how far from home she was. How far from anything she knew or understood.

The butler appeared and bowed. "Your attendants are here," he said to Olivia. "They are waiting to help you dress."

Liv shot Khalid a perplexed glance. "My attendants?"

"Miss Bakr thought you might feel more confident tonight if you had help preparing for the party. She sent her favorite stylists. One to do your hair, and the other to…to…" His voice faded and for a moment he looked nearly as perplexed as Liv. "I actually don't know what she's for, but Miss Bakr insisted you have her."

Not entirely reassured, Liv slowly entered her bedroom, not sure what she'd find. Two Egyptian women waited for her. They'd been deep in conversation when Liv arrived but they broke off abruptly to greet her.

"We don't have much time," the hairdresser said briskly, steering Liv straight into the bathroom, where she'd already laid out hair appliances on the marble counter. The curling iron, flat iron and hot rollers were all plugged in, heating, while the blow dryer lay close by, along with a half-dozen bottles of lotion, pomade and hair spray.

"Simple," the other woman said, taking one of Liv's hands in her own to examine her nails. "Tonight it is all about you. Simple. Beautiful. Elegant."

"A goddess," the hairdresser added. "Tonight, you shall be a goddess."

The hairdresser urged Liv to sit down on the chair they'd pulled into the bathroom and while she turned her attention to Liv's clean but tousled blond hair, the other one started in on a pampering manicure.

While they worked she snacked on fruit and cheese and crackers Khalid had sent to her. A glass of champagne also arrived but she didn't dare touch it. She hadn't eaten much in days and feared the alcohol would go straight to her head. However, the assorted cheeses, sweet apricots, grapes and savory flatbreads were delicious and Liv ate virtually everything on her plate.

By the time her hair and nails were finished, Liv felt unusually relaxed and ridiculously spoiled. To have not one, but two, women fuss over her while she snacked on cheese and crackers struck her as incredibly decadent, but she wasn't in a position to argue. Tonight was important. Khalid had made that very clear and she was going to do everything in her power to make a good impression on the visiting officials.

"And your clothes have now arrived," the manicurist said. "We'll just get you into your dress, make sure everything fits exactly so and then leave you to your party."

Her party.

The suggestion was laughable but Liv didn't laugh. She shivered, suffering from a sudden fit of nerves.

She was scared. Nothing could go wrong tonight. She couldn't—wouldn't—go back to Ozr.

Fortunately her attention was drawn to getting dressed. She was to wear a beautiful ivory-pleated gown, the ivory shimmering with threads of gold. A gold collar encircled her throat, the collar the width of her hand and heavy with gold and jewels. The dress was long, touching the tips of her champagne-colored high heels.

The hairstylist had curled her hair in loose waves, and then pinned strategic pieces up so that her hair looked like a golden waterfall with loose tendrils around her face. The manicurist wasn't to be outdone. She swiftly applied a deft application of makeup, including sooty eyeliner, a swirl of black mascara and a soft golden blush on Liv's cheeks, and a touch of golden gloss on her lips.

"You look perfect," the manicurist said, stepping back to examine her handiwork. "So fresh and young and charming, just the way a princess should."

Liv smiled gratefully even as she heard the door open and close. From the sound of voices she knew that the guests had arrived and her smile disappeared as her stomach flipped…a maddening somersault that had her clutching the sink.

"It's going to be fine," the hairstylist said, patting Liv on the back even as Liv leaned over the sink, trying to catch her breath and calm her queasy stomach. "Everything is fine, and you are going to make His Highness very proud. Now go. Enjoy your party."

Her party. A party where she had to pretend she was engaged to Prince Khalid Fehr, Sheikh of the Great Sarq Desert. How could she do it? She was just a girl from Pierceville, a girl who'd never had more than twelve dates in her entire life.

Her stomach rose up again in protest. She couldn't do it, couldn't go out there, not if the Jabal secretary of security was here….

But then she thought of her mother, and Jake, and the sheikh himself. They were all counting on her, depending on her to be strong.

And she could be strong. She would be.

Khalid watched Olivia enter the room, the long, loose pleated ivory and gold gown emphasizing her slender frame and delicate beauty. With her head up, her shimmery blond hair slid along her bare shoulders, the curls long and loose like the pleats in her dress.

She'd been pretty in her passport photo and troubling in prison, but entering the room she was simply stunning and Khalid watched her, by turns surprised, proud, hungry, possessive.

The gold arm rings on her slim biceps hid the bruises on her upper arms. Her fair hair, curled and twisted back from her face, revealed her elegant features, her pale, flawless complexion and her astonishing goddesslike composure.

He knew she didn't want to be here tonight, knew she'd been terrified to face the secretary of security from Jabal, but one wouldn't know it looking at her. Her expression was serene, her blue gaze focused, intelligent, poised.

Beautiful, he thought, she was beautiful and so small and fragile and not of this world.

And she was his.

His.

Khalid's body grew hot, tight, his chest constricting with emotions he didn't know he could feel.

He wanted her, and he'd protect her. Forever.

"She doesn't wear a head-covering or robe," the Jabal official said under his breath, turning an accusing eye to Khalid.

"She doesn't have to," Khalid answered evenly. "She's here with me."

"But you parade her like a—"

"Careful," Khalid interrupted. "She is my future bride, and

I have vowed to protect her with my life. I will not allow anyone to insult her."

The secretary of security clamped his jaw together, his nostrils flaring, and for a moment he couldn't speak and then he choked, "If she really is your betrothed, when is this wedding going to take place? Because it is unlawful for an unmarried man and woman to be together like this, unchaperoned—"

"But she is chaperoned. Her attendants are in her room now." The corner of Khalid's mouth lifted sardonically. "Perhaps you'd like to meet her attendants personally, Mr. Al-Awar?"

One of the Egyptian dignitaries interjected. "That is not necessary, Your Highness, your word is good enough for us, and may I extend our warmest congratulations on your coming nuptials?"

"Thank you," Khalid answered, keeping an eye on Olivia as she stood at the far end of the living room. She looked very small and vulnerable standing on her own and he found himself wishing his brother Sharif was here tonight with his American wife, Jesslyn. Although Jesslyn was now the Queen of Sarq, she was a former schoolteacher and one of the kindest, most genuine women Khalid had ever met. Jesslyn was just the sort of woman Olivia needed in her corner right now.

"When are these nuptials?" the Jabal official pressed. "I haven't heard a date mentioned, which troubles me, and my government. If your engagement is just a hoax—"

"If you've come to insult me, then perhaps it's best if you go now before I take personal offense." Khalid fixed his attention completely on the secretary of security.

"The paperwork stated she was a family member."

"And she is." Khalid's upper lip curled.

"So there will be a wedding."

"Royal weddings take time and my family is scattered at the moment. Once we can bring us all together on a mutually agreeable date, the ceremony will take place."

The Jabal official was silent a long moment before awkwardly nodding his head. "Very good. And congratulations again."

"Thank you." Khalid smiled, showing a hint of his teeth. "And now I shall join my fiancée, but I do hope you'll stay and enjoy our hospitality. The hotel chef has outdone himself and there is much to sample." With a nod he left the men and headed to Olivia.

Olivia watched Khalid walk toward her. While she'd dressed, he'd also changed, donning the traditional Arab robeing.

"Enjoying the party?" he asked on reaching her side.

She nearly smiled at his ironic tone. "It's not much of a party."

His warm gaze slowly swept over her, resting indulgently on her upturned face, lingering even longer on her lips. "I promise that one day we'll throw you a proper party, one with lots of interesting people."

"As long as there's no one from the Jabal government there, I'll be happy."

He glanced toward the dignitaries now crowding around the buffet, piling their plates with food. "I'd tend to agree with you there."

Before she could respond he turned back to look at her. "You look beautiful tonight. Like a goddess." His dark gaze met hers and held. "And I don't give compliments often. I also never say what I don't mean."

Liv's insides felt funny, and her chest grew tight as though she'd swallowed an air bubble, but she knew it was nerves, and this odd emotion he stirred in her. This morning she'd thought it was fear. Now she wasn't so sure. "Thank you. I'm glad you approve."

By the time Liv went to bed an hour and a half later, she was so exhausted she was asleep the moment her head touched the pillow.

In his room, Khalid didn't find it so easy to fall asleep. Usually when he closed his eyes he found absolute silence, and darkness, a stillness that wrapped him completely, blanketing thought, emotions, need. But tonight when he closed his eyes he saw eyes, blue eyes, eyes with long sooty lashes, eyes that were too big in a face that was too small and pale.

But he didn't want to be thinking of Olivia, didn't want to become emotionally involved—or attached—in any way.

He hadn't left his desert and isolation to become entangled in a relationship. He liked being a bachelor, enjoyed his life as a loner, and yet suddenly marriage seemed like a very real, and very constraining, possibility.

And he was the one who'd vowed to never marry.

Khalid passed a hand over his face, trying to erase the picture of Olivia from his mind, trying to create the desert's stillness, but he couldn't shake Olivia's blue eyes, couldn't erase her shock and fear from his mind's eye.

He was still lying awake hours later when he heard her scream. It was a piercing scream and Khalid was on his feet immediately, bursting through the door separating the two bedrooms in the royal suite to flick on the light.

But once in Olivia's room he discovered she was still asleep.

Standing motionless in her doorway, he watched her sleep, wondering what it was that had made her cry out, and hesitating in case she called out again. But minutes passed and she didn't cry again. Instead she slept on, her long blond hair spilling across the pillow, her left hand curled beneath her cheek and chin.

Sleeping, all the worry and pain disappeared from her face. Sleeping, she reminded him of a young girl with all her hopes and dreams still before her.

He'd just turned out the light and was closing the door, turning to leave, when Olivia's voice reached him.

"'Night, Jake," she said sleepily, her voice soft in the darkness.

Jake. The big brother.

His jaw suddenly flexed, tension and pain rippling through him. He'd once been the big brother, too, to younger sisters, too.

But they'd died over ten years ago. They'd died and there was absolutely nothing he could do for them.

Maybe that's why he was here, risking life and limb for Olivia. She was someone's little sister.

"Good night, Olivia," he said quietly, closing the door behind him, and as the door shut, he realized why he couldn't sleep earlier.

Olivia was waking him up. Making him feel again. And feeling emotions *hurt*.

Feeling was the last thing he wanted to do.

CHAPTER FIVE

KHALID was woken by the sound of his phone ringing. Groaning as it continued to ring, he reached out and grabbed the small wireless phone from the table beside his bed.

He recognized the number immediately. His eldest brother, Sharif.

Answering, he rolled over onto his back. "You're a king and a newlywed," Khalid said, his deep voice husky with sleep. "What are you doing calling so early?"

"You promised me you wouldn't break any laws."

Khalid rolled his eyes. "I didn't."

"The president of Jabal wants her back."

"He's not the president, he's a dictator, and the Red Cross and United Nations are both extremely concerned by his regime's disregard for human life."

"Khalid, this is serious."

"I know it is," Khalid answered mildly, but both of them knew that Khalid was the Fehr brother least likely to compromise. "And Olivia's not going back. Not now, not ever."

Sharif sighed heavily. "You freed her by illegal means."

"I rescued her from Ozr, which is synonymous with hell and you know it."

"You claimed her. You claimed her as your fiancée."

"Yes, I did."

"That's a lie—"

"Not if I marry her." Khalid nearly smiled at Sharif's sharp intake.

"That's ridiculous," Sharif protested tersely. "You've spent the past ten years making it clear that you're not interested in people, or relationships or emotions. You've pushed everyone close to you away. You don't even return phone calls—"

"She's in trouble."

"The world's in trouble, Khalid. That doesn't mean you can save everyone."

"I'm not trying to save everyone."

"No?"

"No."

Sharif muttered something unintelligible before adding, "They believe your Miss Morse is part of a huge drug ring."

"She's not," Khalid answered flatly.

"But what if she is?"

Khalid fell silent. He'd considered the very same point. What if Olivia wasn't innocent? What if she was part of this drug smuggling ring? What if the others were just better at the game and she was the one who got caught?

What if there weren't any others involved?

What if she'd lied to everyone about everything?

"I've run a background check on her," he answered after a moment. "There is nothing in her past that indicates she has the experience, or worldliness, to pull something like this off. She lives in the middle of nowhere—a small town in the south—and it's a genuine small town, population thirteen thousand."

"Just the kind of girl to crave fame and fortune."

"Her mom's a homemaker, her older brother is a carpenter and builds houses."

"Khalid," Sharif said, a caution in his voice. "You can't mean to marry her—"

"Why not? You married a schoolteacher. I can marry a travel agent."

"Not funny. I knew Jesslyn for years. She was best friends with our sisters. Furthermore, she wasn't a criminal."

Khalid, uncomfortable with the mention of Aman and Jamila, rolled into a sitting position, naked save for the sheet partially covering his lap. "I won't marry a criminal."

"Not even to save her. Because I know you. You have this thing about rescuing broken creatures, but marriage is different. You can't damage your name—our name—for someone like that. It's not fair to my children, or our brother—"

"I know," Khalid interrupted, smothering his irritation. Sharif had always played the heavy. It was a role he seemed to relish. "I've a week to uncover the truth, and I promise you, I intend to do everything I can to uncover the truth."

"What if a week isn't enough, brother?"

Khalid ran his hand through his short hair, trying to comb it flat. "Then we're all in trouble."

Hanging up, Khalid stepped into a loose pair of cotton pajamas and walked to the balcony, where he drew the curtains open, revealing the pyramid bathed in pink morning light.

One week, he thought. One week wasn't long. He had a lot to do in seven days, a lot to learn, and the best way to learn was to observe.

He needed to get Olivia alone, away from the crowds and noise and distractions of Cairo. He needed to find out just what happened that day she was arrested. He also wanted to find the group she'd been traveling with, including the elusive Elsie, who'd allegedly given the drugs to Liv to carry.

So the first order of the day's business was to ensure Liv had phoned home last night as she'd promised she would before she went to bed.

The second was to make their engagement official—which included putting a ring on Liv's finger.

And the last was to learn more about this fiancée of his, and the best way to do it was to leave urban Cairo behind for the old Egypt, the one of pharaohs, temples and archaeological digs.

Liv was already awake and dressed in a pretty blue-and-white seersucker sundress when Khalid appeared. She'd been sitting in the living room having coffee and flipping through one of the many newspapers the butler had presented her earlier.

"It's everywhere," she said, looking up when Khalid entered the room. "It's in every paper, on the front page, and again inside other sections. Your engagement is front page news."

"Our engagement," he corrected evenly, reaching for one of the papers off the table. He was dressed very casually in a European wardrobe of dark slacks and a long-sleeved white shirt with the cuffs folded back.

"When does this end?" she choked, sitting up taller. "How does it end?"

"It doesn't. We're in this together. For better or worse," Khalid said, shooting her a hard, narrowed look. He'd just showered and his hair was still damp, his jaw freshly shaven. "It could be worse, too. You could still be in Ozr."

She just looked at him, her stomach a bundle of nerves. Perhaps he didn't find the idea of a marriage of convenience intolerable, but she did. She wanted to love the man she married. She wanted to be wooed and won, swept off her feet, and fall head over heels in love.

She wanted a proper wedding, too, but then, didn't every girl? Over the years Liv had imagined her wedding in detail, from the white silk dress to the pale pink floral swags in the white steepled church.

"I'm not marrying a man I don't love," she said almost fiercely, her cheeks burning. "And when I do meet him, Sheikh Fehr, I'm not getting married without my mother attending."

"I appreciate your romantic sentiments," he answered,

dropping one paper and reaching for another. "I do. And as a man who had two younger sisters, I understand how important romance is for you women. But romance isn't practical. And romance isn't going to save you so I suggest letting go of the fairy tale to focus on reality. By the way," he continued, "how did you sleep last night?"

"Well enough, I suppose," she answered hesitantly. "Why?"

"No bad dreams?" he persisted.

She frowned at him, trying to remember if anything had disturbed her sleep. "I don't think so."

"All right. Good. And you do look better today. You still have those shadows under your eyes, but at least you've got some pink in your cheeks. Yesterday you were very pale."

"I was exhausted," she admitted.

"Were you able to call your family before you went to bed?"

She nodded, recalling the brief five-minute conversation. Her mom and brother were on the phone at the same time and her mother still found it difficult to speak for too long without getting winded, so Liv and Jake did most of the talking, but even then, they were both quite careful to say nothing that would upset their mother.

"It was fine," she said. "I was tired and not as talkative as I could be. But at least they know I'm safe, and, well…and they don't have to worry anymore." She hesitated. "I was surprised, though, that Jake didn't mention your call to him, but maybe he didn't feel right talking about it with Mom on the phone."

"I imagine he's doing his best to protect your mom." The edge of his mouth curved. "It's what men want to do for their women, whether it's their wife or their mother."

Intrigued by this revelation, she probed for more information. "Are you close with your mother?"

"No," he answered, and instead of elaborating glanced at his watch. "Feel like shopping?"

Liv wrinkled her nose. "Not particularly."

"You don't enjoy shopping?"

"We shopped yesterday."

He looked at her strangely, deep grooves forming on either side of his full mouth, his upper lip slightly bowed, but not quite as full as his sensual lower lip. For the first time she noticed he had a hint of a cleft in his chin. Definitely handsome, if not completely overwhelming.

"Women love to shop," he said.

"I don't, unless I'm buying travel books or history books or something that I can read." She watched his face, trying to gauge his reaction, but his expression was perfectly blank. "I was actually hoping we could go sightseeing." She hesitated. "See the pyramids or visit the Sphinx."

Before Khalid could answer, the suite's doorbell chimed and the butler emerged from a back room to go to the door. Liv could hear the door open, and then listened as he greeted someone and then the door closed again. The butler entered the living room with an older Egyptian in a dark suit following close at his heels, a large leather briefcase in one hand.

"Your Highness," the older Egyptian said, greeting Khalid with a deep bow. "I hope I didn't keep you waiting."

"Not at all," Khalid answered. "We were just discussing the day."

The man bowed again. "Is there someplace in mind you'd like to do this? Shall I join you there in the sitting area, or would you prefer to move to the dining room?"

Khalid glanced at Liv where she sat, and then into the dark dining room. "I think the light is better here," he answered, "and Olivia is already comfortable. Let's just do this where we are."

"Excellent." The man carried his briefcase to the low coffee table between the upholstered pieces of furniture and set his briefcase down. It wasn't until he placed the briefcase on the table that she noticed it was handcuffed to his wrist.

Shocked, she watched him take a tiny key from another

pocket and undo the clasp on the handcuff, before turning his attention to the locked briefcase.

Glancing at Khalid, she realized he wasn't at all surprised by the elaborate security measures. Then when the man opened the briefcase, she understood why.

It was filled with diamond rings. Rows and rows of diamond rings in the velvet-covered, foam-lined briefcase. There had to be at least twenty rings, maybe thirty, and the diamonds were enormous. They started in the three- or four-carat range and went all the way to three or four times that size.

But not all the diamonds were the traditional clear stone. Parts of the rows glittered with pastel light, and a dozen rings featured the incredibly rare and costly pink and yellow diamonds.

Each diamond was cut differently, too, and the shapes and styles dazzled her—marquise cut, emerald cut, oval, pear. The settings were all unique, too, with prongs inset with diamonds, the bezels paved, every setting glittering with fire and light.

"I know you said you don't enjoy shopping, but I do think you should pick the ring you'll wear," Khalid said.

"It's not just a ring," the Egyptian jeweler said soberly, "it's a symbol of your commitment, and you'll want a ring that will always remind you of your love and vows—"

"Khalid," Liv murmured, rising to her feet. "May I please have a word with you?"

"Of course," he answered, "but we can speak freely here. Mr. Murai is an old friend of my family's and has been in the jewelry business a long time. You are not the first jittery bride-to-be he has helped."

Liv's frustration grew. Khalid was deliberately misunder-standing her. "I'm just overwhelmed," she said. "I don't think I can make this decision today. Perhaps at the end of the week...?"

"I want my ring on your finger," Khalid answered bluntly. "It's important to me. It's important to my people, and it's im-portant to my family."

"But I don't know anything about diamonds or jewels—"

"Which is why Mr. Murai is here. He's not just the best in Cairo, he's one of the best jewelers in the world. Most of the royal families use him."

But she didn't want to wear a ring, especially not a ring like this. None of these was just a simple band, but a statement of wealth, a statement of style and lifestyle—all things Liv wasn't comfortable with.

"I understand you want me to wear a ring," she said, swallowing with difficulty, "but these rings are too much. They're so elaborate, and large and more than I need."

"Miss Morse, I understand this can be overwhelming," Mr. Murai said kindly. "Selecting one's ring is often a very emotional decision and it requires time and thought. Please, won't you sit down again and tell me a little about what you'd like? There's no hurry, no pressure. We shall take as much time as you need, we will try every ring, and if nothing pleases you, I shall go, search out more beautiful choices and bring them back to you."

Liv looked up at Khalid as the jeweler spoke and she stared at him hard, wanting to tell him that she still wasn't happy even as she knew that Khalid would have his way.

She couldn't fight with Khalid in front of the jeweler. Khalid had said appearances mattered. He said everything they did would be scrutinized, including her wardrobe, her jewelry, and what she wore—or didn't wear—on her ring finger.

Slowly she sat back down on the couch. "I don't know very much about diamonds," she said, her voice pitched low.

"That's fine, I can teach you what I know."

She nodded, aware of Khalid standing behind the jeweler, aware that he'd hardly glanced at the case of jewels. Instead his entire focus seemed to rest on her.

"Do you have any favorite pieces at home?" the jeweler persisted.

She blushed shyly. "I don't own very much jewelry, just an opal ring my brother's former girlfriend brought me back from Australia, and a pearl necklace my father gave me when I turned eighteen."

"No diamonds?" the jeweler asked.

"No diamonds."

"Well, then, we will make sure your first is exactly right for you." Mr. Murai gestured to the front row of diamonds. "I don't know if diamonds are truly a girl's best friend, but I do know diamonds are timeless. The popularity of the cut might come and go, but the stone itself remains the most popular of all gemstones.

"There are three very popular cuts at the moment," he continued. "The marquise, rose and cushion. All the rings in this front row are one of those cuts. As you can see," he said, lifting one of the rings and tilting it to catch the light, "the marquise cut is boat-shaped, pointed at both ends and one of the most popular cuts today although it dates back to the 1700s."

She watched him tip the ring this way and that, amazed at how the ring glowed all the way through, glinting with bits of fire and light. "It's very pretty."

He glanced up at her. "But not right for you?"

"It's very dramatic," she answered.

Smiling, Mr. Murai replaced the large marquise cut diamond ring and picked up another. "This is a rose cut, and the rose cut was developed in the sixteenth century. As you can see, it's a very glamorous, very elegant look. Some people think it's classic Hollywood, others see it and think of the crown jewels. You'll notice there's a flat base and all the facets radiate from the center."

It was beautiful, but not her. The setting was beautiful, too, but it just felt too…old, too much like what a grandmother might wear. Not that her grandmother had ever owned a diamond bigger than a half carat.

"Not for you," the jeweler guessed, slipping the ring back

and reaching for another. "This one dates to the 1600s and it's known as the cushion cut. Note the square or rectangular shape and the rounded corners. Many people think a diamond's brilliance is particularly enhanced by this cut."

"That's gorgeous, too," she said, but there was no way she'd ever wear a ring that big, or a stone that large. "How big a carat is that?" she asked, just out of curiosity.

"Just under twelve carats."

"Heavens," she choked, recoiling. "Twelve carats? Who could afford that?"

"Your fiancé," Mr. Murai answered evenly, putting the ring back. "His brothers. Their friends."

"I'm sorry, but I find it almost offensive—" She broke off apologetically. "I just couldn't in good conscience ever wear something like that when I know half the world is starving. It doesn't seem right."

Khalid abruptly moved forward, leaned over the open briefcase and searched the trays of rings. "That one," he said, pointing to a two-and-a-half-carat yellow pear-shaped diamond in a platinum band. Smaller diamonds sparkled at the prongs.

Mr. Murai took the ring out of the case. "One of my favorite rings," the jeweler said, twisting it to capture the light. "Very classic, and very, very elegant."

It was beyond beautiful, and it wasn't something she would have ever chosen to try, but there was something in the shape and the design that captured her imagination.

"Try it on," the jeweler encouraged.

Uncertainly Liv slid the ring onto her left hand and gazed down at the flawless diamond, the palest yellow. The ring made her skin look creamy, while the stone itself reminded her of sun and sweet, ripe fruit and lemon meringue.

She turned her hand to the light, then dropped her hand low and finally brought the ring up near her face to inspect the exquisite setting more closely.

"It suits you," Khalid said quietly.

She looked up at him, her cheeks flushed. "It's the most beautiful ring I've ever seen."

"Is there anything else you'd like better?" he asked.

"No," she answered breathlessly, curling her fingers, feeling the weight of the stone against the back of her finger and the smooth warm fit of the platinum band on her skin. "But it's too much, far too much—"

"That is the ring," Khalid said, turning to Mr. Murai. "Can we have it sized this morning and returned to us before our noon flight?"

Mr. Murai nodded. "Not a problem."

"We'll leave for the airport at eleven-thirty," Khalid added.

Liv looked at him, and then back at the ring, which was still enormous at two and a half carats, and yet it was also beautiful, beyond beautiful, and she couldn't believe it was going to be hers.

It shouldn't be hers. She wasn't really going to marry Khalid. She was going to go home and get back to her job and become just Liv Morse again, but until then, would it be so awful to actually wear something this lovely? God knows, she'd never have anything like this again.

Girls like her didn't own jewels. Girls like her just admired them in magazines.

"I'll have the ring sized immediately," the jeweler answered, "and will personally bring it back to you."

After Mr. Murai left with his briefcase of rings, Liv stood at the window with the view of the Great Pyramid, feeling increasingly pensive.

She shouldn't have said yes to the ring. It wasn't proper. Nice girls—*good girls*—didn't accept expensive gifts from men, much less from men like sheikhs and desert princes.

Her mother would have another heart attack if she knew Liv was even wearing a ring like that.

"It's just a ring," Khalid said flatly, standing not far behind her. "You haven't damned your soul yet."

She glanced at him over her shoulder. *"Yet."*

His generous mouth with that slightly bowed upper lip curved in amusement. "Most women love trinkets."

"Sheikh Fehr, yellow diamonds aren't trinkets."

"I don't think you can continue with the Sheikh Fehr title now that we're engaged."

"But we're not really engaged."

His faint smile disappeared, and his chiseled features grew harder, fiercer. "On the contrary, we really are, and in just a few hours you'll have the ring to prove it."

CHAPTER SIX

MR. MURAI returned to the hotel by eleven with the sized ring and by eleven-thirty she and Khalid were in the car, heading for the airport.

At Cairo's executive airport they boarded the royal jet for Aswan, the southernmost outpost of ancient Egypt, a city five hundred and fifty miles south of Cairo.

During the first half hour of the flight, Khalid stared out the window, reflecting on the early morning phone call from his brother.

Sharif had been wrong about several things, but he had been right when he said that Khalid had pushed people away and severed relationships. Khalid didn't want anyone dependent on him, much less emotionally dependent. He needed space—freedom—and he wasn't ready to give it up.

He'd do what he had to do to get Olivia home, but this wasn't about love. It wasn't about emotion. It was duty. Pure and simple.

The flight attendant appeared to tell them she would soon be serving lunch, and proceeded to set up a table that locked into the floor in between their club chairs, turning the sitting area into a cozy dining room.

Liv glanced at Khalid as the flight attendant spread a pale gold linen cloth over the table. She didn't want to be intimidated by him but there was something overwhelming about him. She didn't know if it was his silence, or the stillness in his powerful frame, but he reminded her of the desert he lived in. Remote, detached, aloof. A desert—and a man—she wanted nothing to do with.

Horrifying tears suddenly started to her eyes. She reached up and knocked them away with a knuckle. She hadn't cried in Ozr. She certainly wasn't going to cry now, but she'd gotten her hopes up. She'd thought—imagined—she was free. She'd thought that once she left Jabal with Khalid she was just one step away from home. But instead of home, they were setting off on a different journey. A new journey. A journey she wasn't ready, or willing, to take.

The flight attendant served their first course, sizzling prawns, on the Fehr royal china, with its distinctive geometric gold-and-black pattern that struck Liv as exceptionally Egyptian.

Baked red snapper in a lightly spiced tomato sauce followed the sizzling prawns, with a minted pomegranate yogurt on sliced grapefruit presented for dessert.

They ate with almost no conversation or discussion, which did little to ease Liv's nerves. "We don't eat like this on commercial air flights," she said awkwardly as the last of the dishes were cleared away. "Especially not in economy." She took a quick breath, adding in a rush, "Not that you'd ever fly economy."

His brow lowered. "I'm sure I have once."

She waited a good minute, and Khalid was still thinking. "You haven't," she answered for him, "or you'd remember. It's horrendous, especially on international flights when you have to sleep sitting up and you can't because you've been cramped for so long.

"There's no room for your tray table," she added, "no room to lean back, no place for your legs or feet, and the people sitting on either side of your seat hog the armrests, which squishes you even more."

He grimaced. "I'd never fly if I had to fly like that."

"I actually didn't think it was going to be so bad. I sell coach tickets all the time but it was miserable. I just kept thinking once I arrived in Morocco the trip would get better…." Her voice faded and she stared out the window at the impossibly blue sky.

After a moment she drew a deep breath and looked back at Khalid. "I honestly don't know how everything went so wrong. I thought I was being careful. Cautious. I avoided going out on my own, didn't dress provocatively, never allowed myself to be alone with men…" Her voice drifted off as she shook her head. "I'm just so disappointed. Not just with the world, but with me."

"Why are you disappointed with yourself?"

"I thought I was smarter. Better prepared. I thought I could take care of myself and instead I end up arrested and in prison." She clasped her hands in her lap. "But it's my fault I ended up there. I have no one else to blame but me."

"And how is it your fault?"

Liv struggled to explain it, but the words didn't come. How could she make him understand exactly what had happened that day? It was already such a blur. Just remembering the day she was arrested filled her with cold, icy despair. She bit into her lower lip as she searched for the right words.

"I offered to hold Elsie's bag," she said at last, her voice unsteady. "I had a backpack and she had that awkward purse. I told her to slip her purse in my backpack so she wouldn't lose it."

Khalid listened intently. "Did you know Elsie well?"

Liv shook her head. "No, we'd only met a couple days earlier. She was part of this big group of people in their twenties from Europe, the U.S. and Australia. There were guys, girls, a very friendly international crowd. A lot of them had met while traveling through Spain, and then they crossed from the tip of Spain into Morocco, and that's where I met them. We traveled around Morocco for a week before deciding we'd go to Jabal."

"Why Jabal?"

"We missed the bus to Cairo and it seemed like an adventure. No one really goes to Jabal anymore, and yet everyone heard it was cheap and we could catch a bus to Cairo from Jabal's capital."

"That was the destination—Egypt?"

"We all wanted to see the pyramids and the tombs. That's why I ended up joining them in the first place. I was trying to be smart, proactive. I thought I'd be safer traveling with a group of people than being on my own—" She broke off, realizing all over again how wrong she'd been, and the shock of it, and the anger over it, surged through her, wild, fierce, uncontrollable.

"If you hadn't come…" she said, her voice muffled. "If you hadn't come I would have never gotten out."

"But I did come, and I've promised you my continued protection."

She lifted her head to look at him and her eyes met his and held. His eyes were so dark, so commanding, that she couldn't look away, and Liv didn't know if it was the heat there in his eyes, or his slightly rough rumble of a voice, but shivers raced through her, shivers of hope and fear, anticipation and curiosity.

He was so very much a man—confident, controlled, a little ironic, a little intimate. The combination was incredibly dangerous, especially for someone like her who had such limited experience with men.

With the table now collapsed and once again stowed, she found she'd missed the protection it offered.

The table had created a sense of distance and space, and with it gone, Khalid seemed even more imposing than before. He was sitting close, very close, not even an arm's length away, and even though they weren't touching she could feel him, feel his warmth and energy, and it was an electric awareness. Hot, sharp, dizzying.

Liv needed that table back, needed a barrier between them, because right now she felt very exposed, and vulnerable.

Maybe this is why women in the Middle East and Northern Africa hide beneath robes. Maybe they're not hiding their bodies from men, but from themselves.

Interesting how a man could change so much so fast. Liv had never felt delicate before, nor all that feminine, but Khalid made her aware of the differences between them, made her aware that he was bigger, taller, stronger.

He was tall and broad-shouldered and powerfully built. She was smaller, not even reaching his shoulder, and slender. But it was more than height. It was the way they were shaped. The way *she* was shaped. Her narrower shoulders. The swell of her breasts. The curve of her hip. The line of her thigh.

Her wardrobe only accented the differences between them, too. Everything he'd bought for her yesterday was feminine, each piece fresh, charming, stylish and of course perfectly made. Even her blue-and-white seersucker sundress, topped by a small white cardigan edged in lace, emphasized her delicate frame. The 1950s retro-style dress was innocent and yet flirtatious. The bodice molded to her breasts, nipped at her waist and then flared at her hips in a swingy skirt that hit just above her knees.

She shifted, increasingly fidgety, trying not to be aware of the bare skin of her legs, or the rub of the cotton fabric against her breasts. She didn't want to dwell on the parts of her that were covered, and the parts that weren't. Didn't want to think of how warm she was or how strange her body was feeling— tingly, antsy, unsettled.

Khalid had scooped her from Ozr, plucking her from a prison hell only to transform her into a virtual princess overnight. Frankly, it was a bit too Cinderella for her tastes and she didn't trust it. *Any* of it.

"Tell me about where we're going and what we're going to see," she said, trying to distract herself.

"We've left urban Cairo for old Egypt," he said, rising to pull a thick atlas out of one of the cabinets inlaid with exotic wood. "The Egypt of pharaohs and temples and archaeological digs."

"Now you're just torturing me," she answered, thinking he knew all the right things to fire her imagination. "Cairo wasn't on my must-see list of places to go. I wanted the old Egypt with its history and romance. Alexandria, Luxor, Aswan…"

"We'll be visiting Aswan today. Visiting two of those places. We're starting with Aswan and will end up in Luxor. Here, let me show you our stops on the map."

With the atlas opened to an enormous map of Northern Africa, Khalid showed her the border his country shared with Egypt. "You can see we're not far from southern Egypt, and Aswan is the southernmost city in Egypt. You can see why at one point Aswan was viewed as the Siberia of the Roman Empire. No one wanted to go through. It was a long way from Memphis, but Aswan's role in Egyptian history is significant. Those that ruled Aswan were responsible for patrolling the river, for keeping the border of Egypt safe."

Liv was listening, she really was, but as Khalid talked he found it hard to focus on anything except the fact that he was sitting near her, very near, the large atlas open between them. As he talked he drew a line along the Nile River and she found it fascinating to watch the way he used his hands.

He had beautiful hands.

A rather odd realization, she thought, wrinkling her nose, especially as she'd never even noticed men's hands before, but suddenly everything about Khalid was interesting. He was interesting.

She liked the color of his skin, the shape of his fingers, the creases in his knuckles and that tapered index finger as he lightly traced the river and the river valley.

Why was she even looking at his hand? Why was she feeling so edgy? They were just studying a map. He was talking about history. Temples. Monuments, for God's sake.

"Does that sound right?" he asked for a second time and Liv, realizing he was talking to her, jerked her head up and looked into his face, her eyes meeting his.

They were dark eyes, dark brown, so dark she couldn't see anything at all but his eyes. And long black lashes and a faint line between his strong black eyebrows.

"Yes," she said, sounding rather breathless.

The corner of his mouth lifted ever so slightly, and his gaze grew warmer, faint lines at the edge of those mysterious eyes. "Really?"

"Yes," she repeated, wondering why her skin just kept growing hotter and hotter. Her head felt light and her body felt strange.

"You weren't even listening," he flashed, challenging her.

She blushed. He was right. She wasn't listening to a single word he said, too intent on things she'd never noticed before, and emotions she'd never felt. Like a giddy excitement.

And a painful curiosity that burned for something she didn't quite understand yet.

"Okay. I wasn't listening," she confessed, crunching her fingers against her thigh, feeling the sharp press of the diamond, which seemed like nothing compared to the turbulent emotions inside her.

"I thought you were interested in the history."

"I am. I really am."

"But…?"

She could feel heat creep up her neck toward her face. "I don't know. I'm sorry. My mind's just racing. It's really hard for me to focus right now. I think I'm too excited."

His expression eased. "What part overwhelms you the most?"

"Uh, you."

Khalid suddenly grinned, a rare grin of flashing white teeth. The smile was so easy, so wide it reshaped his entire face and for a split second Liv saw a different man, one that had maybe once laughed a great deal, one that had relaxed more, lived more, enjoyed more.

"You're beautiful when you smile," she said, blurting the compliment before she had time to think it through.

His easy smile slowly disappeared, his expression turning speculative again even as they made a sharp turn and dipped, nose tipping for the quick descent. "We're on our way down."

On the ground a convoy of new Range Rovers waited. "More security?" Liv said as they climbed into the four-wheel-drive Range Rover designated for them. Other vehicles were in front, others were behind.

"Always," he answered as the door closed behind him.

"Is everything so dangerous here?"

He glanced at her and his hard features suddenly gentled. "I'm not going to take any risks when it comes to you."

And just like that, he stole her breath, sent her heart racing, her pulse thundering.

Khalid had been imposing in his *dishdashah*, but in his exquisitely tailored Italian suits, he looked so ruggedly handsome that she'd look at him and then moments later, want to look again. No man in Pierceville wore khaki linen suits, and certainly no one managed to look so casual and yet confident at the same time. The lapels of Khalid's jacket hit just so on his broad chest and the cocoa linen shirt was conservatively buttoned with only the top button undone near the collar.

As the car moved forward, she looked at him again, and didn't look away this time. She couldn't. He was just so…

So…

Sexy, she thought, gulping for air.

"There," Khalid said, leaning close to Liv in her window seat to get a better view, "that's Lake Nasser."

She turned to the window. They'd flown over the lake in their final approach, and the dark blue water of the lake had been intensified by the contrast of the desert everywhere else.

"It's enormous," she said, aware of Khalid's shoulder, and knee and thigh.

"It's man-made," he answered. "If we've time we'll visit Aswan Dam, but it's not my favorite place to go."

As he gestured, his broad shoulder brushed against her arm not far from her breast, and a lightning-hot shiver whipped through her. His body had felt warm against hers and hard, too, and just like his hands, she found herself obsessed with his close proximity.

Breathing in, she could smell the heady scent of skin and soap and spice, and it tantalized her, nearly as much as that brush of his shoulder so close to her chest. "You don't sound as though you approve of the dam," she said unsteadily.

Khalid's eyes narrowed. "I have a love-hate relationship with the new lake."

"It's new?"

"The dam was completed in 1971, but the architects of the plan knew a decade earlier that once the dam was complete, some of the world's greatest treasures would be doomed—completely submerged—beneath the huge lake being created behind the new dam."

"Are you serious?"

He nodded grimly. "There was an international outcry, and thankfully my father was one of the first to become involved in the conservation efforts to save these valuable Nubian monuments. From the 1960s until the 1980s he used his own personal resources to help finance the rescue efforts of the Nubian Rescue Campaign. He even participated on one dig where they dismantled the temple stone by stone to have the same temple rebuilt later at Abu Simbel."

Liv didn't know what to say. She suddenly felt very provincial. Her father had never done anything so grand in his entire life. Her father had been a good man, a kind man, but ultimately, he'd been rather simple. "You must be proud of him."

Khalid shifted his shoulders. "I'm proud of every country that participated in the conservation efforts. Archaeologists from Egypt, Sweden, Italy, Germany and France raced to move the massive structures, while other countries also helped underwrite the undertaking. In the end, fourteen monuments were saved—"

"But not all?" she interrupted.

"No. Some disappeared beneath the lake, and I suppose fourteen is better than nothing. Ten of those temples are at Abu Simel—which we'll visit tomorrow—and the other four are in different parts of the world, including one of my favorites, the Temple of Dendur, which has been reconstructed in New York City's Metropolitan Museum of Art."

"Why did four of the temples leave Egypt?"

"The Egyptian government wanted to thank the countries for their significant financial contributions."

"Did Sarq get one?"

"My father wouldn't even consider it. In his mind, the Egyptian monuments belonged in Egypt."

They drove to Shellal where a private boat ferried them to the Isis Temple complex built on Agilika Island. Liv had always been fascinated by stories of Isis, aware that by Roman times, Isis had become one of the greatest Egyptian gods, worshipped everywhere in the Roman Empire, even in distant Britian.

During the ride Liv listened, enthralled, as Khalid told her about old photographs his father had in his library, photographs taken at the turn of the century when Philae was one of Egypt's legendary tourist attractions. "In the early 1900s Philae was a wonder of the Nile. And I can't remember her words exactly, but Amelia Edwards, an Egyptologist, wrote about Philae in her 1877 book, that the island with its palms and colonnades seemed to rise out of the river like a mirage."

"Is Philae one of the places damaged by the dam?"

"Yes. The original Philae Island is now completely submerged, and the temples and artifacts were also submerged for a number of years. People would come out in little rowboats and peer through the water to try to get a glimpse of the sanctuaries lost below."

"I can't imagine all this underwater," she answered, tipping her head back to take in the enormous temple as the boat neared the bank of the island.

"It was a disaster. Horrible. People would row boats out here and try to peer through the water to see the ruins. Thankfully, in 1972 conservationists began to salvage the submerged temple and buildings by constructing a cofferdam around the island and draining the waters. The exposed temple was then disassembled stone by stone, before being transported across the Nile to this place, Agilika Island."

Their boat glided to the base of the Hall of Nectanebo, which Khalid told her was the oldest part of the complex. After stepping out, he assisted her out and together they walked north, through the outer temple court with its long line of colonnades to the entrance of the Temple of Isis itself.

As they explored the island with the various temples and gates and pavilions, Liv felt some of the darkness inside her ease, the sense of doom receding. If she didn't think about the engagement ring on her finger, or the prospect of marriage, she actually felt…happy. Happier than she had in weeks and weeks.

She was seeing ancient Egypt after all. She'd be taking the Nile River cruise she hadn't been able to afford. She'd visit the spectacular monuments on private tours with Sheikh Khalid Fehr, a real desert prince.

She glanced down at the sparkling diamond ring she wore and then bit her lower lip. The engagement, though, still didn't make sense. She loved Egypt. She liked Khalid. But she wasn't marrying him. She couldn't. She didn't even know him. It didn't make sense.

It was late in the afternoon by the time they returned from Philae to their convoy of vehicles. Climbing back in their Range Rover, Khalid told her they were heading to his family's Egyptian sailboat, a boat built for the Nile River, and their home for the next five days.

As they drove Khalid told her that the boat had been built by his father for his family's use but hadn't been completed until a month after his death.

"I think you'll like the boat," he added, "and our captain. He's worked the Nile for nearly forty years and he knows stories about the river that will fascinate you."

The sun was just starting to set when they arrived at the place where the royal sailboat, a magnificent flat-bottomed *dahabieh*, was moored.

For a private sailboat it was large, very large, but not nearly the size of the Greek yachts that sailed the Mediterranean. The *dahabieh* utilized the smart nineteenth-century design but improved on it by ensuring every room and suite was exquisitely furnished and completely comfortable, as well as luxurious.

On the upper deck, an awning covered much of the deck, with striped cotton curtains that could be untied later to shade the deck from the worst of the afternoon sun.

Beneath the top deck, but still above water, were the guest rooms, the living room and the kitchen, as well as the staff quarters.

Khalid's room, the master bedroom, was the largest room, outside the serenely and simply furnished living room. His room, located at the far end of the sailboat, had its own beautiful covered deck, the covered area supported by four hand-painted columns in cream, white and the palest gold.

While sunset painted the sky lavender and red, deckhands went around lighting the large antique lanterns on the upper deck and in the living room.

Liv loved the antique lanterns and the soft flickering light they created, but then everything about the royal *dahabieh* was romantic. Mysterious.

Khalid gave her a brief tour of the boat and then escorted her to her room, the second largest suite.

"We normally eat quite a bit later than you Americans do," he said, glancing around her room to make sure she had her luggage and everything was indeed in order, "but I know it's been a long day and we could eat sooner if you're hungry."

"I am hungry," she admitted. "But if you prefer to wait, I can wait. The last thing I want is to be a demanding guest—"

"You're not a guest anymore. This is your home, too, now. If you're hungry, we eat, and when you're tired, you sleep."

She swallowed hard. "Thank you."

His dark head inclined. "I'll meet you on the upper deck when you're ready. Dinner is usually served there. There's no need to wear anything formal, as we sit at a low table with cushions, but it is a chance to wear something comfortable, that is still a little more special."

"I understand," she answered. But once she'd closed the door she panicked. Not formal. Comfortable. But still special? What was that?

One of the crew had already unpacked her clothes, hanging all the beautiful new skirts and dresses, blouses, slacks and coats in the small closet with her shoes lining the closet floor. The drawers in the painted cabinet on the opposite side of the room were filled with the silk undergarments, stockings, purses and accessories Khalid had insisted on buying.

She flicked through her hanging wardrobe once and then again, finally settling on a chalk-colored cotton cardigan with patent-leather buttons and a nautical, ropelike detail on the sleeves. She'd pair the sweater with white cotton and silk slacks, and a pair of high raffia wedge sandals.

Hair combed and pulled into a low ponytail, face washed and refreshed with lotion and just a little makeup, she climbed the staircase to the upper deck where the lantern flames flickered and danced in the evening breeze.

Less than thirty minutes later they were sitting at a low table at the front of the deck, their table surrounded with pillows and covered in the most gorgeous silk cloth.

They were eating by candlelight, too, their table illuminated by a dozen jeweled candles, the candlelight a perfect complement to the steaming savory pilaf, delicately seasoned lamb, grilled seafood and sautéed vegetables.

It was so peaceful dining on the upper deck. She and Khalid chatted about their afternoon at Philae and compared notes on what each of them had liked best.

Khalid said he appreciated how the new island had been landscaped to resemble the old island as much as possible.

Liv said she loved the stories of Isis, and how devoted she'd been to her husband.

"He was also her brother," Khalid said, tearing a hunk off the bread to mop up the rest of the savory juice on his plate.

"I try not to think about that part," she answered, "because if I do, the story gets a little weird."

Khalid's dark eyes flashed with amusement. "What about the conception of their son, Horus?"

"The part where she reassembles her husband's dismembered body, brings him back from the dead, and um…conceives the baby…and then lets Osiris go back to the underworld? That's weird, too." She leaned back against one of the large pillows. "But it's also kind of cool. She was so devoted to Osiris. She loved him so much. Love like that is rare."

"You're a romantic."

She shrugged and smiled. "I'm a woman."

"And until now, single."

She looked at him, eyebrows half-rising. "Is that a question or a statement?"

"A statement." He shrugged. "Nothing in your background

report indicated you'd ever married, so I assumed you'd remained single." He paused. "You are single?"

Liv sat forward abruptly, no longer as calm or relaxed as she'd been a moment ago. "You had me investigated."

"I have to investigate everyone," he answered unapologetically.

"A hard way to live."

"It's the way I've always lived. The way my family lives." His deep brown gaze met hers and held. "Everyone we meet, everyone we invite here, everyone we spend time with is eventually investigated."

Her skin crawled at the idea of people's lives being examined, researched, investigated and yet he was so casual about it. "Did you discover any dirty, dark secrets in my past?" she demanded hotly. "Anything that shocked you?"

He shook his head, his expression shuttered. "No. You're just as sheltered as I imagined. A babe in the woods."

"You sound disappointed."

"Why would I be disappointed if you aren't experienced?"

Her heart beat faster. Even her palms felt damp. "Were you interested in my life experience, Khalid, or my sexual experience?"

"Are you a virgin, then?"

"I'm sorry. Did the background report leave something out?"

He leaned against his cushions. "Why are you angry?"

"I don't know. Maybe because you had a background check done on me and you know all my juicy little tidbits, but I know nothing about you. You're this big mystery and I'm supposed to be engaged to you."

"You *are* engaged."

She glanced down at the diamond glittering on her ring finger on her left hand. "I *don't* feel like we're engaged. To be honest, I don't feel anything at all."

"Then we have to change that, don't we?"

"How?"

He didn't answer with words. Instead he reached for her, drawing her into his arms and sliding one hand into her hair to cup the back of her neck.

It all happened so fast, so unexpectedly, that she didn't even realize what was happening until his head descended, blotting out the light.

Panicked, Liv stiffened, her mouth opening to protest even as his lips covered hers. His lips slowly moved across hers, coaxing, testing, teasing. She'd never been kissed like this, never kissed with so much control, so much expertise. He made her melt on the inside, made her belly ache and tighten and her lower back tingle over and over again.

Her hands rose to his chest, uncertain if she should push him away or bring him closer, but once her hands settled there, she felt the last of her resistance melt.

He felt good. He felt unlike anything she'd ever felt. His chest was hard, firm, thick with muscle that curved in smooth taut planes, and beneath her palm she could feel the beat of his heart, steady, sure, and somehow that reassured her more than anything else.

She'd never been with a man before, not a man like this. She'd only dated boys and young men, men who hadn't found themselves or their strength, but Khalid was strong, and brave, full of courage and conviction and he wasn't afraid to do what he thought was right....

Wasn't afraid to risk everything to save a woman...

His tongue traced her inner lip the same way his finger had traced the river on the map and she felt like liquid gold in his hands. Kissing Khalid was like kissing the sun; she could feel the desert in his veins, feel his great silent world of endless sand.

He deepened the kiss and she dug her fingers into his shirt. He was making her feel so much and the emotion burned in her, tightening her chest, making her feel hot, hungry, fiery.

When his tongue slipped all the way into her mouth she

trembled from head to toe, her knees clamping together so hard she felt a shock of intense feeling rush through her, a rush that left her dazed by its ferocity.

She wanted something new, something almost wild.

Passion, she thought, as his teeth nipped at her lip, eliciting yet another fierce, hungry response.

She wanted this, him, whatever it was.

His head lifted and his narrowed gaze swept her flushed face. "Tell me, little one," he drawled, his deep voice so husky it sounded hoarse, "do you feel anything yet?"

CHAPTER SEVEN

IN HER bed with moonlight peeking through the slats of the wood shutters, Liv replayed the kiss over and over in her mind.

No one had ever kissed her like that and, putting her fingers to her mouth, she marveled at how sensitive her lips felt now. How sensitive she felt, her body suddenly humming with a brand-new energy. A brand-new awareness.

She'd felt things she didn't even know existed and now the possibilities tantalized her. More energy and more excitement and more of that giddy, dizzying sensation and pleasure.

Lightly she rubbed her fingertips across her mouth, feeling the softness, the swollen lower lip, the curved upper lip, the inside of her bottom lip so much more sensitive than the upper.

Just touching her mouth made her insides tighten and turn over. Nerves and adrenaline and a hot, aching sensation low in her belly that made her want relief.

Relief, she repeated, even as it crossed her mind there would be no relief until she left Khalid and Egypt far behind.

It was the second night in a row that Khalid was woken by Olivia's scream. Tonight's cry pierced him and, racing to her room, he once again turned on the light, and once again found her fast asleep.

Troubled, he stood for a long moment in her doorway, the

moonlight spilling across her bed, illuminating her profile and the pale silk of her hair.

What was giving her the nightmares? Was it something from Ozr? Or had something else happened that she hadn't told him, something she wouldn't talk about in daylight?

He was still disturbed the next morning when he woke and dressed and joined Liv on the upper deck, where she was leaning on the rail, enjoying the morning sun. The soft breeze was playing with her pretty sea-foam dress, catching at the delicate pleats and making the hem swirl. The breeze was also playing havoc with her hair, blowing the silvery blond strands with carefree abandon.

She was as pretty as a picture, he thought, taking her in. Fresh, sweet and, after last night's kiss, extremely desirable, but he wasn't sure he liked this attraction. Didn't trust attraction, and definitely didn't trust emotion.

"Good morning," she said, turning her head to watch him approach.

"Good morning."

Liv gestured to a large boat passing. "I once booked a couple for their fiftieth anniversary on a Nile River cruise, but I had no idea there was so much traffic on the river. It's *busy*."

"It is busy, but apparently modern-day traffic is nothing compared to what it used to be. Until decent roads were built in the late nineteenth century, sailing the Nile was the main method of transportation. It's been estimated that in the Middle Ages there were thirty-six thousand ships plying the Nile."

"Thirty-six thousand?" she repeated, dumbfounded.

"The Nile is the heart of Egyptian civilization. Thousands of years ago Egyptians believed the earth looked like a pancake and in the center flowed the Nile River, while around the outside flowed the ocean. They also thought the sky was flat as well, and four poles held this flat sky up so that air and life could soar between earth and sky."

She glanced at a *felluca*, a small Egyptian sailboat, now passing their ship. "This is more beautiful than I imagined. It's so peaceful, and I love this area. It's very pastoral, very green."

"This entire part of the river valley is agricultural-based. You'll notice when we reach Kom Ombo—"

"Kom Ombo!" she interrupted excitedly, turning to face him, eyes growing round. "Isn't that where they have a monument to the crocodile god…oh…what is his name?" Reaching up, she tucked hair behind her ear, her white teeth biting her lower lip. "Sobek?"

He didn't want to like her, didn't want to respond to her, and yet her enthusiasm was appealing. She was appealing. "I'm always amazed at what you know about this part of the world," he said.

"Blame Jake," she answered, making a face. "He had a fascination with Egypt when he was a kid, probably from watching too many Indiana Jones movies, and acquired a huge collection of books on Egypt. In high school when his interests turned to girls, I laid claim to his Egypt collection."

"Smart girl."

She laughed, her blue eyes dancing with mischief and then slowly her smile faded. "Not that smart. I wanted to be an archaeologist but I didn't have the grades to get in to a top-notch public university, and didn't have the money to go to a really good private one. So instead of studying bones and digs I book travel packages to the Bahamas and Cancún."

"So go back to school, study what you want to study. You're still young. You've got time to pursue your dreams."

"You don't think I'm too old to go back to school?"

"For your information, you're still younger than I was when I started graduate school."

"What did you study?"

"Boring science stuff. Bones, dirt, digs, et cetera."

Her jaw dropped and her eyes widened, the sun painting her cheeks a soft rose. "Archaeology?"

"Mmm."

"You're Indiana Jones."

"Not quite," he answered, trying very hard to ignore her smile, her quick warm laugh, the way her eyes danced when she was happy. He'd never met a woman who made him hunger for more, who made him crave intimacy. He was the man who needed nothing but desert, sand and sun. He was the man who lived alone, a nomad dedicated to unearthing buried treasures, and understanding lost civilizations. He was a scientist, a scholar and a loner.

But Olivia was turning him inside out and he didn't want to be alone, he wanted her, to be with her.

She captivated his imagination, teased his mind, stirred his senses. Everything about her tempted him—her soft mouth, winged eyebrows, her golden silky tresses.

He shoved his hands in his pockets to keep from touching her. "Although I will say you're very entertaining."

"I used to make up stories to entertain Jake. He loved them, he'd laugh, but Mom didn't. She said one day my imagination would get me into trouble." She paused, her eyes suddenly darkening with shadows. "Isn't it funny how mothers are always right?"

Khalid frowned slightly, his eyebrows pulling. She was telling him something, he thought, telling him something important, too. He was a man who'd built a formidable career on bits and pieces. He knew how important one little fragment could be, knew every part was representative of the whole.

"Can I try to call home again later?" Liv asked abruptly, looking up at him. Some of the shadows were gone from her eyes. Some but not all. The shadows in her eyes added to his unease.

There were things she wasn't telling him, things that he needed to know.

What? he wondered, trying not to fear for her even as his loyalties were becoming increasingly divided. He'd always been loyal to his brother and family, but something in Liv called to him, something in her made him want to draw a line in the sand and protect her to the end.

"I didn't have a proper conversation with Jake," she added, "and I want to know how my mom is doing."

"Of course," he agreed, thinking it was a good idea because a call would occupy her while he did some research himself. "When we get back from sightseeing it'll be late afternoon here and morning there."

"Good. I'll call then."

He hadn't planned on kissing her again, not so soon, and certainly not in broad daylight, but with the sunshine playing across her face, warming her lips and turning her eyes to the same dazzling hue of the blue lotus, he couldn't resist her.

Clasping her face in his hands, he dipped his head, covered her lips, claiming them. Claiming her. As yesterday, she briefly stiffened, resisting, and then like yesterday, she gave in, melting into him.

Her surrender fired his hunger. Last night's kiss had been gentle and he wanted to be gentle now, but she tasted so sweet, and she tasted warm and she made him think of apricots and strawberries and he groaned against her mouth, deepening the kiss, plundering her mouth.

His body hardened and hardened again. Drawing her closer, he molded her body to his so that he could feel her slender curves, the pillow of her breasts, the narrow apex of her thighs.

He wanted her.

He wanted beneath her floaty, filmy skirts, between her pale slender thighs, inside her warm soft body.

Khalid felt fierce, carnal, *starving*. He hadn't wanted anyone, or anything, in years and now his desire consumed him. It was too raw, too explosive.

He needed her too much.

With a guttural groan he broke away, stepping swiftly back

to ensure he didn't reach for her again. "We'll go on shore soon. Make sure you have comfortable walking shoes," he said roughly, gazing off toward the shore, unable to even look at her.

Shaken, Liv pressed one hand to her mouth, feeling absolutely blindsided. What had just happened? Why was everything spinning so crazily?

The kiss just now was nothing like last night's kiss, either. This kiss had been hot, so hot, she felt singed, burned, her skin blisteringly sensitive, her legs too weak beneath her.

Last night's kiss had been so tender, so seductive she'd melted with desire. But this kiss punished. This kiss told her she wasn't in control. Not by a long shot.

Maybe that was what frightened her most. She had no control here. She didn't even know who she was here. Was she a prisoner, or a princess?

And standing there alone, she looked off toward the shore and spotted an amazing temple just there on the riverbank. "Kom Ombo," she whispered. They'd arrived.

The *dahabieh* anchored not far from the temple and Liv and Khalid walked the short distance from the port to the temple where they were met by their guide, an eminent Egyptologist Khalid knew and had asked to join them for the day.

"It is my great pleasure," the guide answered after introductions were completed. "Sheikh Fehr has helped me more than once. I am honored to show you one of my favorite temples because it is so unusual. Everything you will see at the Kom Ombo Temple has a twin. It is a perfectly symmetrical temple. Here, let me show you."

The guide couldn't have been more interesting as he pointed out how the Greco-Roman temple had been built with twin entrances, twin courts, twin colonnades and twin sanctuaries, but Liv kept glancing at Khalid, who was standing as far away from her as he could.

Why was he upset with her? she wondered. He'd kissed her.

Perhaps she wasn't supposed to kiss him back....

Perhaps he thought her too forward. After all, he was foreign. A sheikh. God knows what they wanted in women.

Frustrated, she forced her attention back to the guide and his description of the temple's twin sanctuaries. "The left, or western side, was dedicated to Horus, the falcon-headed sun god," he said, "and the right, or eastern side, to Sobek, the local crocodile god."

She glared at Khalid's back. Why wouldn't he even look at her? How childish was that?

Her temper suddenly got the best of her, so she marched over to Khalid and tugged on his linen shirt.

He turned his head to look down at her, his expression flinty, his rugged features set in uncompromising lines.

She lifted her chin, refusing to be intimidated by his fierceness. "You don't scare me," she hissed.

"Good," he growled, turning back to listen to his friend.

Liv stared at Khalid's broad shoulders and strong back before tugging on his shirt a second time. "You can't be mad at me."

He barely turned his head, giving her just a glimpse of his aquiline profile. "I'm not mad."

Not mad? He'd ignored her for the last hour. Hadn't spoken to her except for the introduction to his friend the eminent Egyptologist and acted like he was the only one of the tour, always walking a couple paces ahead of her, standing arms crossed as though he were some kind of impenetrable fortress.

She stepped closer to him. "I did nothing wrong. *You* kissed me. You can't be mad at me."

Khalid turned around so fast that Liv had to take a swift step backward. Khalid reached out, clasped her wrist and tugged her back toward him. "I'm not mad," he said in the quietest imaginable voice. "You did nothing wrong. We're supposed to be enjoying Kom Ombo."

"Then why won't you even look at me?" she asked, trying

to keep her hurt from showing. "You're acting like I've got the plague."

Khalid's dark gaze burned hot and he studied her for an endless moment before bending low to whisper in her ear. "I am trying to ensure you remain a virgin until we marry, *habiba*, but am finding it very difficult to keep my hands off you."

Liv colored, blood surging hotly to her cheeks. "Oh."

"Oh," he mocked, reaching up to caress her flushed cheek. "Now you see."

"Sorry."

"Of course you're sorry."

He stroked her cheek again, sending hot rivulets of feeling throughout her body. "Don't say you haven't been warned."

Blushing hotter, she dipped her head and moved away from Khalid, putting distance between them again.

He wanted her.

She swallowed hard as her insides did a crazy flip. Egypt was getting more dangerous by the day.

Their guide resumed his tour, leading them through the temple's damaged entrance, where he pointed out a small shrine to Hathor. The shrine, he explained, was now used to house a collection of mummified crocodiles. "Note the clay coffins," he added, pointing out the coffins. "They were dug up and moved here from a nearby sacred animal cemetery."

"Amazing," she whispered, overwhelmed. She was in Egypt, touring the very temples she'd read about fifteen years ago. She was sailing the Nile, exploring the old tombs, sleeping on a royal *dahabieh*. "Mummified crocodiles. Who would have thought?"

Khalid had heard her. He smiled faintly. "You'll like this next spot then," he said. "It's the small pool where the crocodiles were raised."

An hour later they were in a private car, leaving the riverside temple behind. Khalid had arranged for them to go to Daraw to see the famous camel market. Camels were being sold when they arrived, but it was a slow day, Khalid told her. Sundays were the busiest day with upward of two thousand camels exchanging hands.

"Who buys all the camels?" Liv asked, watching the haggling between buyer and seller with great interest.

"Most go on to Birqash, which is north of Cairo, and they're put on the market again. Buyers in Birqash will often send them to other Arab countries."

They stopped for a tangy frozen ice and found a toppled sandstone wall partially shaded by a towering palm tree where they could sit and eat.

"This is perfect. I was getting really hot," Liv confessed, savoring the cold, slightly creamy, slightly sour treat when she noticed that Khalid hadn't even tried his frozen ice yet. "You don't like yours?"

He looked at her sideways. "You have nightmares," he said gruffly. "Last night you had another one. You cried out, and it's not a small cry, but piercing. Disturbing—"

"I'm sorry."

He shook his head impatiently. "I want to know what's bothering you. What do you dream about?"

She searched his face, trying to see past his shuttered gaze. He had such a remarkable face, his low eyebrows straight above hooded eyes. His nose was long and yet it only emphasized the fullness of his mouth and that faint cleft in his chin. There were times, like now, when he was more rugged than handsome, but there were other times when he smiled and he became someone else.

She liked that someone else very much.

"I don't remember my dreams," she said, her heart suddenly aching. She wished she knew Khalid better, wished she understood him better. Maybe if he smiled more she'd feel easier around him. But she didn't feel easy. She was scared, scared of all the things she couldn't control. Like him. The engagement. Her future.

"How do you feel when you wake up?" he asked.

She thought for a moment. "Worried."

His brows lowered. The lines deepened around his mouth. "Worried about what?"

Looking into his face with his dark, serious eyes she felt a tug in her chest, another pull on her emotions. "Everything," she said, trying to smile but failing.

His frown deepened, a strong line appearing between his black eyebrows. "Tell me so I can help you."

Liv didn't understand the pressure in her chest or the tightness at her throat. She didn't understand the strong urge to reach up and smooth the frown line from between his eyebrows, either. It crossed her mind that Khalid frowned too much. He needed to smile more. "I'm okay," she said. "I am. Don't worry about me. You've worried enough. You've done more than enough. Now eat your ice before it all melts."

By the time they returned to the *dahabieh* it was late in the afternoon and Khalid gave Liv his wireless phone to use to call home.

But before she called, she took a shower in her en suite bath, rinsing off the day's dust and grime, and then slipped into a long, loose cotton shirt that reached midthigh. Curling up on her bed, she phoned Jake's cellular number and the call went through straight away. Unfortunately he was once again with their mom and unable to say much, but apparently their mother was doing much better and Jake was going back to work full-time now that he'd found a nurse to stay with their mom during the day.

"That's great," Liv answered, trying to be enthusiastic when in truth, she couldn't imagine her mom needing nursing care. How bad was the heart attack? And had the heart attack been followed by a stroke? But Jake wasn't telling and her mom didn't talk a lot, content to let Jake and Liv catch up.

After about ten minutes of chitchat Jake said he had to go to finish getting ready for work.

"I'll see you soon," Liv told them, blowing kisses into the phone and hanging up before she broke down in tears.

Things weren't right at home. Things weren't right here, either. She'd never felt so helpless in her life. What was she supposed to do? What could she do? The answers eluded her.

Exhausted, Liv stretched out on her bed, pulled the light cotton quilt up over her legs and fell asleep.

She was still napping when a knock on her door woke her up.

Sleepily Liv tumbled from bed to open her door. One of the ship's crew stood on the other side. "His Highness invites you to join him for dinner," he said with a small bow.

Liv assured the crew member that she would be right up, shut the door and glanced at her watch.

Eight o'clock.

She'd been sleeping for hours.

Liv dove into a celdon silk caftan, which was heavily embroidered and beaded at the collar. She wore narrow white trousers beneath the caftan and flat Egyptian-style sandals on her feet.

Worried about the time, she left her hair loose but did scoop up a pair of gold jeweled earrings out of the jewelry box to complement the exotic caftan.

She was upstairs in record time, taking the stairs two at a time, and when she reached the top she turned the corner so fast she ran straight into Khalid, colliding so hard she went reeling backward.

Khalid reached out and grabbed her, putting his hands on her shoulders to steady her. "What's wrong? What's happened?"

Bewildered, she looked up at him. "I'm late. I've made you wait."

Khalid's dark eyes fixed on her with intimidating intensity. "You're running like a madwoman because you were late to meet me for dinner?"

"Yes."

His gaze searched hers for a long, penetrating moment and then he tipped his head back and laughed, a huge deep laugh which made his white teeth and his eyes shine with a hint of tears. "*Habiba*, you make me feel like a king."

And realizing he was enjoying that she'd run at top speed to meet him, she shook her head.

"You're not fair," she said primly. "You don't play by the rules."

"The rules? And which ones would those be?"

"The ones that say desert sheikhs are barbarians that expect to be waited on hand and foot."

Khalid's lips twitched. "I think, little one, you need a new set of rules. Yours are outdated. Desert sheikhs today do not expect to be waited on hand and foot. They're far more interested in giving pleasure and making love." And, checking his smile, he gestured to the table covered in a rich violet silk cloth, and decorated with a low arrangement of dark purple lilies, completed by tall, thick cobalt-blue stemware. "Dinner?"

Dinner was entertaining. They were served endless courses of mouthwatering seafood and grilled lamb and seasoned vegetables followed by live entertainment. Musicians and dancers performed for them on deck and Liv sat on her pillow, an arm around her knee as she watched the swirling dervish of dancers. It was great fun to have authentic musicians and dancers on board and when they were finished Liv clapped until her hands stung.

"The trip just gets better and better," she said to Khalid after the musicians and dancers made their final bow and disappeared from the deck. "I'll never forget this trip, never in a thousand years."

He gave her a peculiar look. "We'll have more river cruises in our future."

Liv bit her lip. Did Khalid really think they were going to end up together? Did he really believe they'd ever marry?

Glancing down at her left hand, she studied the yellow diamond engagement ring. She was living the most amazing, fantastic and yet bizarre dream. She felt like Alice in Wonderland. She'd fallen down the rabbit hole and was having great adventures and lots of fantastic experiences, but she knew she'd soon wake and Khalid and Egypt and this beautiful river would be gone.

"What are you thinking?" he asked, tugging her toward him.

"Nothing."

"That's not true. You suddenly looked...sad."

"I don't know what's real anymore," she whispered. "I don't know what to believe."

Khalid dropped his head, kissing her lightly, fleetingly, and even as heat flared within her, his lips brushed her cheek, traveling with tantalizing slowness across to her ear.

Lightly he bit her lobe, his warm breath sending shivers through her. She squirmed at the pleasure, overwhelmed by her body's sensitivity. She had no idea her ear, or her neck, could feel this way and as his lips grazed the hollow below her ear, his tongue tasting her skin, she arched against him, arching so that her breast pressed into his hand, and his knee rubbed close to her thighs.

He rubbed her nipple, massaging it between his fingers until she felt absolutely wild. She wanted more, but she didn't know how to ask for it, didn't know if she could even ask for it.

Instead she turned her head blindly, trying to find his lips, craving his lips on hers.

His head lifted briefly, his gaze locking with hers and holding. His expression was so somber, so penetrating, that she shivered all over again.

As she shivered, Khalid dipped his head to cover her mouth with his. He kissed her as though he and only he knew the secrets of her heart, and he and only he could bring her out of the darkness. Reaching up, she clasped his face, savoring his warmth, the flutter of his breath, and the spice and musk of his skin.

She liked the feel of his mouth against hers, liked the way his arm pulled her close, liked the pressure of his knee between her legs and the crush of his chest against her tender breasts.

"We can't do this here," Khalid said against her mouth before lifting his head. "I don't know what I'm thinking."

"Then come to my room."

"No." He barked a rough laugh, his dark eyes lit with a possessive fire. "I'll walk you there, but only to lock you inside."

CHAPTER EIGHT

KHALID knew he'd lost his mind the moment he met Olivia, but now he was getting dangerously close to losing control.

Body burning, he followed Liv down the narrow stairs to her suite of rooms, his gaze riveted to the very feminine sway of her hips and the round, firm curve of her derriere. Watching her though was sweet torture, his groin growing harder by the second, his shaft already so erect it hurt to walk.

He wanted her more than he'd ever wanted a woman, and yet he wasn't going to take her. He'd never made a business out of deflowering virgins—especially since that seemed to be Zayad, his middle brother's, specialty—and with Liv's freedom at stake, Khalid was determined to do everything right.

At her bedroom door, he gave her a gentle push inside. "You'd better lock it fast," he said, his voice husky.

Instead she reached for him, catching his sleeve in her hand and tugging him toward her.

Liv knew she was playing with fire, knew she just might get more than she'd bargained for, but right now she welcomed the heat, especially if it would answer whatever it was burning her up on the inside.

"Five minutes," she whispered, feeling like the devil, feeling bad, wicked, but also knowing that once the truth came out, once everything became known, she'd never have this chance again. She'd never have him again.

"I won't make love to you," he said, even as she pulled him into her room.

"Fine. Just kiss me some more," she answered, locking the door behind them.

"You're only going to drive us crazy."

"We're already on the way to crazy," she answered un-steadily, her legs shaking as she approached Khalid one nervous step at a time.

"You are going to marry me," he said, arms folded over his chest, his expression enigmatic. "It's not a choice. It's some-thing we must do now."

"Can we forget marriage—"

"No."

She felt nearly feverish as she looked up at him from beneath her lashes. "Let's just forget wedding talk for five minutes."

"No."

"Come on."

"No."

She took the final step toward him, closing the distance between them, her thighs against his thighs, her breasts to his chest, her hands on his waist to hold her steady. "You want to kiss me," she whispered, her voice low and husky.

"I want to kiss you so badly that my body hurts," he answered, his jaw flexing.

"So do it."

He sat down on the bed and pulled her between his knees so that she stood before him. Watching her face, he slowly lifted her caftan and then kissed her flat stomach and leisurely took his time, kissing his way higher.

She gasped at the warmth of his mouth on her bare skin, and the tingling sensation of his mouth on her rib cage, and then at the sensitive spot just beneath her bra.

She gasped again when he kissed her through the delicate silk bra, and then closed his mouth on her taut, aching nipple. His mouth felt hot, wet, and as he sucked her lower belly clenched, and clenched again. She gritted her teeth, burying her hands in his hair as he sucked and caressed her nipple until she felt as though she were as wet and hot between her thighs.

His hands slid from her waist down to her hips, his thumbs stroking her hipbones through the thin fabric of her trousers.

She was making little whimpering noises now. She knew it but she couldn't stop. She craved his touch, craved release, craved satisfaction.

But then his mouth lifted and, holding her firmly by the hips, he pushed her back a little and then a little more until there was distance between them.

"Khalid," she protested, reaching for him.

"No," he answered roughly, as he stood and moved away. "You're beautiful," he added, his jaw set, his cheekbones flushed with deep color, "but I won't take anything that isn't mine."

Liv tossed and turned all night. Her body felt hot, wanton, desperate. She felt desperate. She'd never wanted anyone, or anything, the way she wanted Khalid, and yet she was never going to have him.

He wouldn't make love to her until they were married and she wasn't going to marry him. She wouldn't—couldn't—do that to either of them.

Waking early, Liv stripped her nightgown off and took a stinging shower, deliberately turning the water to a chilly temperature to try to cool her hot blood down. It sort of worked, too, she thought, shivering as she turned the shower off and grabbed a towel.

At least it worked until she thought of Khalid and his dark brooding gaze, and his full soulful mouth, and that hint of a cleft in his chin.

She loved looking at his face, loved that his nose was a little too long and his forehead a little too broad and his cheekbones a little too severe. She loved that he looked like a man and he kissed like a man. She loved that here in Egypt he'd woken something inside her, something she didn't quite understand yet, but felt powerful and fierce. All she knew was that it felt stronger than lust and deeper than desire.

Growing warmer by the second, Liv searched her wardrobe, looking for the coolest, calmest pastel shades she could find, eventually selecting tailored, sand-colored linen trousers, which she paired with a slate-blue jersey-organza petal top that came with matching shell necklace.

Dressed, she gave her image a once-over in the floor-length mirror attached to the back of her bathroom door and nodded approval. With her hair drawn into a low knot at the back of her neck, her bare shoulders now lightly sun-kissed, she looked composed, controlled, even disciplined, which was exactly what she needed to be today.

There could be no more kisses, caresses, stolen moments of lovemaking.

She was going to leave. She didn't know exactly when or how, didn't know where she'd go, but there had to be another way out of Ozr without further implicating Khalid. He didn't deserve to be dragged into her mess. He was a good man. He deserved better, and one day when he married, he deserved to marry a great woman.

Before leaving her cabin, Liv grabbed an ivory pashmina and then headed to the upper deck to watch the sunrise. One of the crew brought her a pot of coffee and some apricot-and-almond-filled pastries.

The sunrise stained the horizon the most tender shades of pink and lilac, making the ancient Nile Valley look young and new.

Liv took a quick breath, bewitched by the sunrise and the way it changed the sky, the water and the land. The Nile was magical.

But it wasn't just the history of the river that held her spell-bound, it was the luxurious and yet authentic *dahabieh* itself.

The sailboat was in perfect harmony with the wind and sun, and there were moments where Liv was convinced she'd traveled on a time machine and had gone back one hundred, two hundred years, to a time when traveling was elegant, even sumptuous, with long lingering sunsets and cool pink sunrises and the wind blowing through the palms lining the river's great banks.

Khalid appeared at her side even as the captain steered the *dahabieh* toward the riverbank and dropped the anchor at Edfu, where they were to spend the day.

The port seemed exceptionally busy and noisy for a sleepy agricultural town and Liv wondered about the large crowd gathered on the riverbank.

"Are they waiting for a boat?" she asked Khalid as they prepared to disembark.

"No," he answered, studying the crowd, too. "My security tells me they've come to see you."

"Me?"

His eyebrows rose. "You're the new princess of Sarq, and they're curious to see my bride-to-be."

With the sun rising higher, the day was already considerably warmer and Liv took off her shawl and slowly folded it while studying the noisy crowd. "I'm not princess material."

"You don't know that."

"But I do," she said, dropping the scarf on one of the deck chairs. "I'm from a small town of thirteen thousand, and until you rescued me from Ozr, the most important man I'd ever met before was the mayor of my hometown, a man with some very mild celebrity status as he owns a car dealership and stars in his own television commercials."

He laughed softly, appreciatively. "But now you've eclipsed your mayor. You're a star, a celebrity in your own right."

Liv shot a skeptical look at the throng. "I'm going to disappoint them."

"How?"

She shrugged helplessly. "Look at me!"

He did, his gaze slowly sweeping over her from head to toe. "You're beautiful."

She just shook her head. She didn't feel beautiful. She felt like a failure, a walking disaster. "My mom raised us to have good manners, and of course she instilled in me good old-fashioned Southern hospitality, but royalty?"

Liv laughed weakly, thinking of the lessons she and Jake had been taught as kids. She and Jake were to be practical and pragmatic, honest and hardworking. They were supposed to do well in school, always be respectful, and never boastful. No lofty dreams in their family. No shooting for the stars. Just safe, steady jobs and safe, steady lives. "I know who I am, Khalid, and I'm a very simple person. I'd be ashamed of myself if I put on airs, acting like someone I'm not."

"Then don't try to act like a princess. Just be yourself, and you'll be perfect."

She looked up into his face, her eyes meeting and holding his. "Perfect for what?"

His gaze warmed. "Perfect for me."

The crowds didn't fully disperse after they disembarked, but they gave Khalid and Olivia space as they toured the Temple of Horus, the most completely preserved Egyptian temple.

Having already visited Isis's Temple, Liv was up-to-date on her Egyptian mythology and knew that Horus was the son Isis had conceived with Osiris, her dead, dismembered husband, and that Isis raised Horus in secret, so that he could later avenge his father's death.

Liv was most fascinated by the scenes painted on the Passage of Victory's narrow walls. The scenes depicted the fierce battles between Seth and Horus, and Khalid stood close by to explain to Liv the symbolism of some of the battle scenes.

"In this one, Seth has been turned into a hippo," Khalid explained.

"He's a tiny hippo, too," she answered, grinning at the artist's fanciful rendition.

"Seth's small size symbolizes his loss of power. Being reduced in size and shape, he has become less dangerous."

They walked farther down and Khalid pointed to the final scene, where Seth the tiny hippo was now a hippo-shaped cake and being eaten by the priests. "The priests eating the hippo cake is the ultimate statement. They've destroyed Seth completely."

She knew Seth was the evil uncle who'd killed his brother, Horus's father, but it was still a rather horrible depiction. "It's a sad end," she said, turning to face Khalid. "Hippo cake for priests?"

Khalid laughed quietly, and put his arm around Liv. "Let's head back. We can stop in the bazaar on the way and pick up some souvenirs if you'd like."

They hadn't done any shopping so far and Liv, not a big shopper, wasn't sure she wanted the hassle of the crowded shopping bazaar, but Khalid promised no one would push too close. "Everyone knows who we are, and they know I've security everywhere. They'll give us our space."

She'd seen how foreigners were treated in other touristy shopping bazaars, but was willing to give it a go if Khalid would deal with the aggressive sellers.

Shopping actually ended up being more fun that Liv expected. Khalid was confident, and comfortable haggling with the different shopkeepers. One vendor in particular caught her eye, his booth displaying absolutely gorgeous scarves. Liv stopped just to look, but Khalid, noting her interest, glanced at the shopkeeper, who quoted a price that made Khalid's eyes roll.

The shopkeeper tried again, cutting the price by twenty percent.

Khalid just stared at him.

The shopkeeper knocked another ten percent off.

Khalid took Liv's arm and they walked away.

A minute later the shopkeeper chased them down, four different scarves over his arm. "Please, please, Your Highness, I give one of these to you for your beautiful bride. My gift. Free. Please."

Khalid smiled faintly. "One is free. How much are the others?"

The vendor bowed his head, offered a price. "They're now half off the price he originally quoted me," Khalid said to Liv. "They should still be cheaper."

But Liv felt badly for the shopkeeper. He was trying so hard to make a sale. "But fifty percent off is good, and he's trying awfully hard."

"That's his job," Khalid answered.

"Yes, but he's offered a free gift."

"It's not free if we buy the others."

Liv glanced at the old man with his wrinkled little face and his bright dark eyes. "But we've helped him, right?" she whispered.

Khalid sighed and shook his head. "You are too soft," he chided, "but if you want—"

"Yes."

"Fine." Khalid spoke rapidly to the shopkeeper, who bobbed his head and hurried back to his stall to wrap up the scarves for them.

By the time they returned to the boat they were both starving and ready for lunch.

They were served beneath the canvas shade on the upper deck, and over grilled lamb and beef kebabs they laughed about their shopping experience.

"I have never bought any of that stuff before," Khalid said, with another wry shake of his head. "Most of it is junk."

"I know, but I couldn't resist the little brass statue of Horus."

"It'll look great next to your brass pyramid paperweight," he mocked.

She wrinkled her nose. "Okay, maybe I didn't need both, but how do you buy from one guy, and not the next?"

"Easily," Khalid answered. "You just say no."

They were still sitting at the table talking when one of the crew members approached and bowed. "You've a phone call, Your Highness. It is His Excellency, King Fehr."

Khalid glanced at Liv. "If you'll excuse me?" he said.

"Of course. I'm perfectly happy here," she answered with a smile.

And she was happy, she thought, leaning back against the cushions. She felt comfortable, relaxed, as though this boat— and this life—was really hers.

She was still waiting for Khalid to rejoin her, when she heard his voice and she turned around to welcome him back, but he wasn't on the upper deck. It took her a moment to realize he was actually one deck below, still speaking on the phone.

"We've just a few days left," she heard Khalid say. "The government has stepped up their pressure. I'm getting daily e-mails and phone calls now."

Liv frowned and leaned forward, trying to listen more closely. She knew she shouldn't eavesdrop, but she couldn't help herself.

Was Khalid really being pressured? He'd never told her. He'd never mentioned the calls or e-mails, either.

Chewing on her lip, she waited for whatever he'd say next.

"I know what I promised you, Sharif," Khalid was speaking again, "but she's not a criminal. I would never marry a criminal. You know how I feel about marriage—" He broke off, listened to something his brother was saying before continuing. "No, you're right. I never intended to marry. I never wanted a wife, but it's a little late for that. I've made a commitment and I intend to honor it."

Khalid's voice grew more distant. He must have been walking in a different direction and soon his voice faded away altogether.

Liv stared at the ruins they were passing, but the magic was gone. She couldn't see anything, think of anything, except for what she'd overheard.

Khalid and his brother, the King of Sarq, were fighting over her. King Sharif Fehr didn't want Khalid to marry her. Worse, Khalid didn't want to marry her, but would out of duty.

Biting into her lower lip, she tried to suppress the ache inside her chest.

She didn't want to marry someone who didn't want her. She couldn't imagine marrying a man who dreaded a life with her.

But what were their options? If Khalid was really being pressured, what could they do?

She could try to run away, but she wasn't sure how far she'd get, especially with no money, no ID and no passport.

She could try to convince Khalid to put her on a plane anyway, but then there was his honor and reputation.

The whole thing overwhelmed her. The problems kept piling up.

A few minutes later Khalid appeared at her side, taking a seat among the cushions on the shaded deck. For a long moment she just looked at him, trying to understand this man who'd risked everything for her.

For several minutes he said nothing and Liv clasped and unclasped her hands, suddenly nervous with him all over again.

Khalid fixed his brooding gaze on her. "Tell me what really happened that day you tried to cross the border."

Her shoulders slumped beneath the weight of her secret. There were times she thought he didn't believe her. Times she suspected he thought she was lying. "But I've told you at least a dozen times—"

"Tell me again. Maybe there's a piece you left out, maybe there's something more you can tell me. I have men working on your situation around the clock. My brother Sharif has had Sarq's top investigators looking for this Elsie, too, but so far we've come up with nothing. No clues. No direction. No progress."

Guilt weighed on her. "I'm sorry. I'm so sorry I got you involved in any of this. You thought you'd rush in, rescue me and be done with me. Instead, you're stuck."

His brow creased. "You make it sound like I'm some kind of victim, but I'm not. I'm not stuck or trapped. I'm a man. I chose to go to Jabal to help you, and I've chosen to continue helping you."

"But you don't want to get married."

He sighed, revealing a hint of frustration. "It wasn't on my personal agenda, but things happen. Such is life."

She studied him, seeing the creases at his eyes, and the lines bracketing his mouth. He looked tired, more tired than she'd realized, and her chest squeezed tight. "Why didn't you ever want to get married?"

He shot her a swift glance from beneath his lashes. "Who said I never wanted to marry?"

She'd tipped her hand, inadvertently revealing that she'd overheard him on the phone. Now she shrugged evasively. "You've made it clear that you live a solitary life in the desert, and I'd be lonely living so isolated in the desert, but you seem to like it."

"I've avoided emotional entanglements, yes—"

"Emotional entanglements? Is that how you view relationships?"

His shoulders shifted. "They are."

"You don't like people?" she persisted.

"I like the desert. It's peaceful."

"People aren't peaceful?"

Drawing back, Khalid stared at her hard. "You ask a lot of questions for someone who doesn't have a lot of answers. I think it's time we turned the focus back on you, and the hunt for the elusive Elsie."

Liv winced at his tone. She heard his frustration all over again. "She is elusive, isn't she?"

"Yes, and I don't understand it. No one has ever seen this person you've described. No border authority, no passport agency, no embassy official. And yet to get into Egypt you have to have a valid visa. You can't just enter without the proper paperwork but there is no one in Egypt—or any other Middle Eastern country—by that name or description. Are you sure Elsie intended to visit Egypt?"

"It's what she'd told me."

"But when you were all on the bus and you were stopped at the border, where did she go? Did she get off the bus? Did she get through to Jabal? What happened? How did she vanish?"

"I don't know. I was pulled aside and I never saw the others again."

He rubbed the back of his neck. "We need to find her," he said finally, bluntly. "The clock is ticking and your future—my future—depends on us locating her, getting her proper identity and verifying your story."

"And if we don't? Can't?" she asked, her voice soft, hiding her desperation because she didn't know how to fix this, or solve this, and she was scared now that no matter what happened, it was all going to end badly.

But Khalid wasn't answering her question and the fact that he didn't sent shivers up and down her spine.

"Do you think she has another name, or identity?" Liv asked quietly. "Is it possible to have two passports?"

"Possible, but not always legal. It depends on her citizenship."

"What can I do?" Liv looked up at Khalid, hating her sense of helplessness, and wanting to help, wanting to make things better but not knowing how.

He shook his head. "There's nothing at this point. But I'll let you know."

The rest of the afternoon was spent in separate pursuits with

Khalid attempting to work in his suite but ridiculously distracted by his conversation with Liv earlier and her impression that he didn't like people.

Was that the impression he gave? Or was she just attempting to draw conclusions?

Either way, her question and assumption troubled him. He wasn't an uncaring man. If anything, he cared too much, which was why he'd exiled himself to the Sarq Desert.

Losing his sisters had broken his heart. He'd loved them, adored them, enjoyed them more than anyone else in his family. More than nearly all his friends put together. Jamila and Aman were so smart and yet wickedly funny, full of laughter and imagination, love and mischief. The fact that they were beautiful didn't even come into it. It was their spirit he cherished, their love of life.

That subsequent loss of life was a wound he couldn't seem to heal. Not after one year, not after ten. He missed them and finally he accepted he'd always miss them.

But the love and loss had taught him a lesson he'd never forget. Loving others, caring for others, hurt. Thus if one was going to care, it was preferable to keep those that one loved at a distance.

While Khalid worked in his room, Liv curled up in the sitting room downstairs with a book. Fortunately it was a good book, and Liv read for an hour before thoughts of home intruded.

Lifting her head, Liv stared across the room, seeing but not seeing the ornate side chairs and leather ottoman. Her mother had warned against this trip. Her brother had warned her, too, but Liv had wanted something other than safe and predictable. She'd wanted change and had been thrilled by the prospect of going somewhere new and exotic, somewhere filled with tales of adventure.

She'd had exotic, and adventure, too, but now she couldn't go home—not easily—and it was devastating, especially with her mom so ill now.

If only she'd stayed home. If only she'd been happy with safe and predictable.

A lump filled her throat. Her heart felt unbearably heavy. She hated that her dreams now hurt others.

Hating her train of thought, Liv forced her attention back to her book and the rest of the afternoon passed relatively quickly, although Liv was glad when it was dinner hour and she could join Khalid on the upper deck.

Dinner tonight was unusually subdued. Khalid seemed completely preoccupied and once they'd finished eating, he excused himself, saying he needed to return to his desk. Liv forced a smile, trying not to let him know she was hurt or nervous.

She watched him start to walk away but suddenly couldn't let him leave. Jumping to her feet, she called his name. "Khalid!"

He turned around to face her. "Yes?"

Her heart raced. She gripped her hands together. She didn't know what to say. She just knew she didn't want him to leave. "I'm worried about my mom," she said, blurting the first thing that came to mind.

"Have you talked to her lately?"

"Not really. Every time I call Jake stays on the line and directs the conversation. I think he's afraid I'm going to upset her."

"Her health is fragile. Your brother is just trying to protect her."

"I know, and my mom only lost my dad a couple years ago, and now this heart attack. But I'm worried. I'm worried that something worse will happen if I don't come home soon, and I don't know if I can live with the guilt if anything did happen because of me. She didn't want me to come on this trip. She was adamant that I not go."

He looked at her a long moment before speaking. "So why did you make the trip?"

"I wanted to see the world." Her voice dropped. "I wanted to see what life was like."

Khalid stared off into the distance for several minutes before slowly turning his head to look at her. "Now you've seen it," he answered, his voice strangely hard, "and now you know the sacrifices we make to protect those we love."

CHAPTER NINE

Khalid disappeared down the stairs, and the staff immediately began to clear the table and cushions away, before dimming a half dozen of the antique lanterns. Once the deck was virtually empty, the staff gradually headed to the lower decks to tackle other tasks.

Standing alone on the semidark, deserted deck, Liv thought the night seemed endless. Mysterious.

The moon was only half-full and, closing her eyes, she took a deep breath, trying to calm herself, trying to relax. With her eyes closed, she focused on the sounds around her, listening to the water lap the side of the boat, hearing the breeze rustle palm fronds on the shore.

This is how it must have been to travel the Nile River in the old days, and right now she felt as though she'd stepped from the pages of a history book, or an E. M. Forster novel.

Drawing another breath, Liv opened her eyes and looked up. It was late and the stars glittered above, the sky so deep it looked glossy black, a sweep of onyx overhead. The warm breeze continued to blow, rustling the canvas awning, and whispered through another grouping of palms on the riverbank.

Tipping her head back, she savored the way the moonlight cascaded over the landscape, illuminating the swathe of river in brilliant white and silver light.

It was so bright that the fragments of towering temples lining the riverbank looked like they'd been hit with huge Hollywood spotlights, each of the sculptural shapes glowing in 3-D and taking on life of their own.

She could almost imagine Cleopatra climbing the crumbling stone steps and appearing between ancient limestone pillars and columns decorated with intricate shapes and designs, and Liv knew she'd never forget this trip.

Egypt might seem beautiful and magical with all its glorious history and Khalid might be a handsome desert prince, but what he wanted her to do, what he believed they should do, was as impossible as her becoming an Egyptian queen.

She wasn't from here, she couldn't stay here, she needed to go home. To her world, her family, her people.

She needed to go soon. She had to stop waiting for the right moment to present itself. Instead she needed to make the right moment happen. She needed to start looking for opportunities to make her escape. It wouldn't be easy, but staying here, marrying Khalid, would be worse.

He didn't want to marry her. He was marrying her out of duty. And she didn't want to marry anyone who didn't love her, who didn't passionately want her.

But then she pictured Khalid, and the way he looked at her, and that expression he would get in his eyes, and she felt a frisson of feeling.

No one had ever looked at her the way he looked at her. No one had ever treated her the way he treated her.

Maybe he didn't love her, but he did care for her in his own way.

Could that be enough for marriage?

Could caring and duty be sufficient glue?

Perplexed and ambivalent, Liv stayed on the upper deck to read, curled up in a chair, a soft blanket thrown over her legs. She read for hours even after the crew blew out some more of the lanterns at the far end of the deck, leaving just those near her lit.

Hearing footsteps behind her, Liv turned to look over her shoulder. Khalid, still wearing the white shirt he'd worn for dinner, walked toward her, but now his shirt was half unbuttoned, revealing the high, hard planes of his chest and the burnished gold of his skin.

He wasn't smiling and his dark gaze raked her from head to foot. "You shouldn't be up here by yourself. It's not safe."

His rebuke felt like a slap. "It's your boat," she challenged, hurt. "Your home. I thought I was safe with you."

"You are safe with me. But I wasn't here. And until we're married, you must be careful."

The wind was blowing and as she tipped her head back to see his face she had to catch her hair and hold it away from her eyes. "What if we don't marry?"

He stood taller, his shoulders thrown back. Making a rough inarticulate sound in the back of his throat, he turned his head sharply to fasten his burning gaze on her. "I won't do this now. I'm tired—"

"But, Khalid, we have to face the truth."

He threw his head back, lifting his face to the moon, and for an endless moment he didn't speak. Finally he said, "I gave them my word."

She swallowed hard. There was no compromise in his voice. No compromise anywhere in his stony features. "What if it's not right…what if we'd both be miserable—"

"I gave them my word. I have staked my honor and reputation on you."

Her insides hurt, her stomach cramping violently. Those weren't the words she wanted, needed, to hear. She didn't want to hear honor or duty, responsibility or reputation. She wanted more.

She wanted love.

Khalid took a seat next to her. "It will not be all bad with me," he said more gently. "I promise I will treat you with kindness and respect. I promise no one in my household, no one connected with me, no one who works for me shall ever treat you with anything but courtesy. You are mine. You are in my safekeeping, and I have made a solemn vow to protect you." His gaze met hers, held. "Forever."

She pressed a trembling hand to her middle. "And my family?"

"It is my hope they will come for the wedding."

"And after that?"

"You will live with me."

"In your...desert?"

"Yes."

"But would I ever get to leave? Ever be allowed to return home?" she asked, her voice faint.

His brow creased and his lips compressed. For a moment he stared off into the distance before turning his head to fix his piercing gaze on her. "Yes, you could. Eventually. After you give me my first child. But if you left me, meaning you chose to move back to America, the child would have to stay with me."

"What?"

He shrugged. "Our child would be heir to the Sarq throne. All Fehr children are raised in our country, in our culture. It is custom and law." Then he stood, and extended a hand to her. "Come, let me see you back to your room. It is late. I will not rest easy until you are safe in your room."

The soft swish of the wind in the palm fronds was the only sound as she followed him across the deck. As she slowly climbed down the stairs the wind whispered in the palms the same thing over and over. *You are doomed.*

You are doomed, doomed, dead.

Later that night Liv's terrified scream woke Khalid up, and this time when he went to her room, he turned on the light and woke her up as well. He'd had enough of the night terrors. He wanted to know what it was that upset her night after night. Wanted and needed to know what she was hiding from him because she was hiding something and he was beginning to fear the worst.

"What is it?" he demanded. "Tell me your dream."

Liv sat up in bed, her hair a mess, her eyes a bruised blue. "It's nothing," she said, but her lips were pinched and she was pale, too pale.

"I'm not accepting that answer," he said, walking around the bed and taking her wrist in his hands, where he checked her pulse. "Your heart's racing. You're terrified."

She just stared at him, her eyes far too big again for her face. It was the same look he'd seen when he'd appeared outside her cell in Ozr. A vacant, half-dead expression. The expression of one without hope.

"Olivia, I want to help you."

"I know."

"Then let me help you."

Tears filled her eyes. "You can't."

The despair in her eyes, the grief in her voice, hurt him. He couldn't bear for her to feel this way.

"Olivia," he said firmly, "I know you've been through a great deal in the past month, but the worst of it is over, I promise. We will find her. And when we find her, all this fear, all this worry will be behind us."

But that was the problem, she thought, searching his dark eyes. She didn't want Elsie caught, not if she was going to be dragged off to Ozr. Ozr was horrible, hideous and Liv couldn't send anyone there, much less another girl, and certainly not Elsie.

Maybe Elsie had committed a crime, but she also had a good side, and a big heart. From the very first day they'd met, Elsie had taken Liv under her wing, making sure Liv always had a safe spot in the hostel, a seat at the table. Elsie, fluent in four languages, translated everything for Liv.

"Let's talk about the wedding," Khalid said, changing the subject. "We haven't discussed our plans but we should, especially since we want your family here. I can send my jet over for them, and if a doctor clears your mom for travel—"

"She's not going to be cleared, not after a heart attack."

"Then it'll just have to be your brother. But at least you will have some family—"

"Stop. I can't do this. There's no point talking about weddings. I can't marry you. I can't, Khalid. It's just not right, and you can't make it right by forcing me into marriage."

"But I'm not forcing you. It's your choice, entirely your choice. The last thing I want or need is an unhappy bride. I've lived with an unhappy mother. I don't need a miserable wife."

She blinked, so surprised by the revelation that she didn't even know how to answer.

"And you're right, I might not be some Disneyland prince sweeping you to his castle on a white stallion," he added, "but I am offering you my protection. Perhaps it doesn't sound romantic, but safety, companionship and shelter are also important."

"I agree that safety and companionship are important, especially after what I've been through, but a marriage without love?" Liv drew a deep, shuddering breath. "A marriage that's based on a paper contract instead of emotions? How will that make anything better?"

"It'll save you from returning to Ozr, which could just possibly save your life."

She took another breath and this time held it, trying to slow her thoughts, as well as manage her emotions better because Liv knew when she was emotional she couldn't think properly and she needed to be able to think now.

"In theory," she said carefully, "we're exchanging one prison for another."

"I am not a barbarian—"

"I didn't say you were. But your culture treats women very

differently than my culture and it frightens me. I can't imagine living in Sarq and you've said that's where you live, and you've also said I'd live with you."

His jaw jutted with anger. "In my culture, mothers, wives and daughters are respected."

"Is that why you cover them with robes and veils?"

"Women are robed to protect them. We understand that a woman's honor and virtue is her most valuable possession so we guard it zealously."

"It's not just the robe and veil, it's the other loss of freedoms. I've noticed that in the Middle East women rarely go anywhere on their own. Instead they run errands and shop in groups, and many, if not most, of your marriages are still arranged, aren't they?"

"Yes, many, if not the majority, of our marriages are arranged, but we view it as a positive thing, and these arranged marriages are just as warm and real as the marriages in the West."

He sounded so reasonable, every bit the scholar and philosopher, but she didn't trust his argument. She couldn't accept that an arranged marriage brought the same joy—the same emotion and passion—of a love match. "Was your parents' marriage arranged?"

"Had to be. My father was a prince, soon to inherit his father's throne. His family spent five years looking for the right woman."

"And that was your mother?"

"No. It was another woman," Khalid answered wryly, "but she died unexpectedly just two months before the wedding and my mother was found as a replacement."

"No wonder she was unhappy," Liv muttered.

His lips compressed. He was trying not to smile. "My mother was thrilled—initially—to be married to my father and my father was very happy with her."

"So what changed?"

He looked down at her, his expression suddenly grim. "She never felt like my father's equal. He was royal, she was a commoner and it ate at her, little by little until she was obsessed with the fact that he had blue blood, royal blood, and she did not."

"Why would it matter so much to her? Did people treat her differently?"

"Some," he admitted.

"Your father?"

"No."

His swift, decisive answer made her brows pull together. "He respected her?"

"He loved her."

Liv felt a strange prickle of feeling. "How do you know?"

"He told me." Khalid's gaze locked with hers. "When he was dying he asked us, his sons, to always take care of our mother as he loved her and worried about her and dreaded leaving her."

For some reason his simple words nearly undid her. Emotion rushed through her and her throat ached, and her chest hurt, and she bit down hard to keep the intensity of her feelings from showing.

It was ironic, despite the distance between countries, and cultures, how similar people were, how similar love could be. When her dad knew he was dying, he had the same fear for their mom. He'd begged her and Jake to remember their mom, to take care of Mom, make sure she wasn't alone too much, make sure she went out with friends, and even dated again someday.

She blinked away the sting of tears. "That sounds like my father. He was worried about my mom, too." She paused. "But they married for love and despite what you say, it worked. They were happy, very happy, and that's what I want, too. I want to fall in love and feel like I'm the most important thing in the world to someone. I want to be special…cherished, and I want it to last. Not just for five months or five years, but forever, and relationships like that aren't from being forced together. They're from choice."

"So make the choice," he said quietly. "Stop fighting against fate—"

"It's not fate!"

"And get on with life."

"Right. Just marry you and move to Sarq and live wherever it is you live," Liv said hotly, sitting up in bed.

"That sounds good."

"No, it doesn't. I know nothing about you. My God, Khalid, I don't even know five things about you."

"Yes, you do. You know five. Try," he insisted, folding his arms across his chest and looking every bit the imperial warlord.

Furious with him, furious with herself, furious that she'd gotten them both in this ridiculous and yet tragic situation, she began to tick off what she knew. "Your name is Khalid Fehr and you are a member of the royal Fehr family."

"That's one and two," he said encouragingly.

She rolled her eyes. "You've an older brother and I think, but am not sure, that you live somewhere in Sarq."

"Very good."

She shot him a frustrated glance as she wrenched a hand through her messy hair. "That's not very good, Khalid, it's terrible. We've spent four days together now and you're still virtually a stranger."

"You know more than that, little one. For the past four and a half days we've had dinners and dates, and excursions."

"Dates," she said, rising up higher on her knees. "Did you just call our…sightseeing…dates?"

"Isn't that what you call it in the States? When a man courts a woman—"

"We're not courting."

"We should be since we're engaged."

Liv covered her eyes and collapsed onto her bottom on the bed. "You're courting me."

"Do you prefer wooing? It is an old-fashioned word, but perhaps it has the element of romance that you seem to crave?"

She peeked at him from between her fingers. "Can we not discuss this anymore? It's not going to help me sleep better."

He allowed himself a very small smile. "You fight this, you fight us, and yet it's natural between us. We are right together whether you're willing to admit it or not."

"How can I admit something I don't understand or trust? You are a mystery to me. Yes, I can see that you are a powerful man with a luxurious lifestyle, but that doesn't tell me who you are, or what you care about, or what you believe in."

Khalid didn't answer. He looked at her so long, his expression so intense and penetrating, that she felt as though he could see her terrifying secret.

"You know the real me. You just don't want to admit it because that would change everything, including your false sense of control." His lips twisted, his expression hardening, glints shining in his eyes. "Easier to ignore the obvious and play dumb."

Liv's jaw dropped. "That's not true."

His eyebrows rose. "Then tell me what you know, what you really know and I'll then tell you what you don't know. Fair?"

"You're an archaeologist," she said in a small voice, "and you come from what I think is a big family. Your eldest brother is the king in Sarq and he sounds as though he is a good leader and a good brother." She glanced up at him from beneath her lashes. "And you respect his opinion but you don't always agree."

She noticed Khalid's eyebrows rise. She'd surprised him with that one but he didn't contradict her. "I don't get the feeling that you spend a great deal of time on digs, anymore, but I could be wrong," she continued, trying to shuffle through all her memories and impressions. "You're compassionate and dislike injustice, and that's what I know," she concluded quietly.

He looked at her, eyes narrowing, jaw firm, and then he nodded. "Good enough." And then he left.

Morning came far too early for Liv and instead of bounding out of bed as she had on other mornings, she rolled over and groaned into her pillow.

She'd slept badly. Her head ached. And her stomach felt like it was a bundle of nerves.

And she hadn't even seen Khalid yet.

Burying her face deeper into her pillow she let out a muffled scream. She couldn't do this much longer. She couldn't. The stress was becoming too much.

By the time she dragged herself in and out of the shower and into a white eyelet sundress her mood had sunk even lower.

In the white girlish dress with her hair in a ponytail and red coral beads around her neck she looked sweet, pure, and it felt like one more nail in her coffin.

Glancing at her hand, she caught sight of her elegant yellow diamond engagement ring and yanked it off, unable to continue with the charade.

Tucking the ring into her jewelry box she left her room for the stairs. But as she climbed the stairs to the upper deck, her chest felt tight and her throat squeezed closed.

She couldn't continue here, like this. She had to go. First chance she got today, she'd leave.

Khalid was already at a table having breakfast and reading when she arrived on the upper deck. The table was a traditional table, too, one with four legs and regular chairs. There were glasses of juice on the table, a large pot of coffee, a basket of flaky pastries and more fruit. It was such a normal-looking breakfast table, such a normal-looking morning, that she felt the backs of her eyes burn.

This is what she wanted, she told herself. Normal. She just wanted to get back to normal.

Sitting down at the table, she glanced at the papers stacked in front of Khalid. Mountains of reading, she thought, glancing at the computer printout. "E-mails or research?" she asked, reaching for her juice glass.

"Both," he answered, looking up at her with a faint smile. "I have good news."

"You do?"

He leaned forward, elbows resting on the table. "They've found Elsie."

Liv felt like she'd been hit with a bucket of ice water. *"What?"*

"They're taking her into custody this morning and once they have her in custody, they'd like you to come identify her."

Liv just looked at him, her brain unable to process anything that he was saying.

"Amazing news," he added, with a shake of his head. "I was close to giving up hope."

He was talking and she was listening but she couldn't believe it. Couldn't. How was it possible? "Did they say where they found her?" she asked, her voice shaking.

"No," he answered, his head dropping to scan the e-mail in front of him.

"Or who she's traveling with?"

"No. Only that she's been located and they'll need your help to prosecute her properly."

She balled her hands in her lap, her heart thudding so hard it made her queasy. "Who told you?" she asked, her voice shaking.

He glanced up at her, a black eyebrow cocking. "You don't look well. Are you okay?"

"Yes." *No.* Biting into her lip, she felt anything but okay.

Khalid slid the top sheet of paper toward her so she could

read it herself. "It's from one of my detectives. He's been working in conjunction with the Egyptian police and since it's an Egyptian detective making the arrest, I imagine that Elsie's here in Egypt just as you said—" He broke off, his attention caught by her bare hand. "Where's your ring?"

She covered her left hand with her right. "In my jewelry box."

His forehead furrowed. "Why aren't you wearing it?"

She sidestepped his question. "I'll get it before we go ashore."

Her breakfast arrived and she focused on her fruit and yogurt, struggling to get a half-dozen bites down before she stopped eating altogether. "What do you think they'll do to her?" she asked, an unbearable weight on her chest.

Khalid looked over at her. "Send her to Ozr."

Oh, God. Not to Ozr. Not there.

Liv pressed her fingertips to her eyebrows, pushing at the terrible pain throbbing there. Her headache from this morning was just getting worse and worse while her stomach heaved.

There was no way she could do this…no way she could get through this….

Khalid pushed his paperwork aside. "Are you worrying about her?"

Eyes closing, she nodded, trying hard to hold back the sting of tears. She felt sick, so sick, so very, very sick.

"Liv, you can't blame yourself. You're not responsible for Elsie—"

"Ozr's a terrible place," she choked, cutting him short. "It's hell. *Hell.*"

"She didn't care about you," he reminded bluntly.

She could only shake her head. Things were bad, very bad, and they were just going to get worse. "I don't feel good," she whispered. "My head hurts."

"Do you get migraines?"

"I haven't had one before, but my head feels like it's going to explode now."

"Why don't you go downstairs, back to your cabin where it's cooler and darker?" Khalid suggested, standing. "Try to sleep. See if that helps."

"But aren't we supposed to go ashore?"

"We can skip Esna. Just spend the day on board, a proper cruise."

She lifted her head and looked at him, tears in her eyes. "Can we do that?"

"Of course." He frowned, concerned. "Liv, this is good news. Elsie's arrest changes everything."

She couldn't listen to any more, and she pushed to her feet. If she didn't get downstairs soon she'd begin crying here. "I'll be in my room."

"Good. Rest, catch up on your sleep. Tomorrow we'll explore Luxor."

Liv spent the rest of the morning in her room resting but when Khalid stopped by her cabin at noon to see if she felt like lunch, she agreed to join him on the upper deck under the awning for a light meal.

"You've been crying," Khalid said as Liv joined him on the deck.

Self-consciously she moved farther away from him, going to stand on the opposite side of the shaded deck. "I washed my face."

"I can tell by your eyes," he answered, dropping onto the low couch with the thick ivory and sand pillows. "How are you feeling?"

"Better," she fibbed, wishing she had a pair of sunglasses, something to hide her eyes from him.

"Come, sit here by me. We're having an informal meal. We'll just eat our lunch here on the couch."

"Aren't you hot?" she asked, leaning against the railing and lifting her ponytail to get her hair off her neck.

"You'll be cooler here on the couch with the fan."

But she didn't want to sit on the couch, and she didn't want to be close to Khalid. She was wound too tight. Wound to the breaking point.

"Olivia, what's wrong?" he asked quietly, not at all fooled by her attempt to avoid him.

"I think I'm just exhausted. I think it's good that we're just cruising today," she said, arms bundled across her chest. "I didn't realize how tired I was. Maybe we don't need to stop in Luxor tomorrow. Maybe we should just keep sailing."

"Not stop in Luxor?" He gave her an odd look. "But Luxor is the highlight of a Nile cruise."

"I know, but it's going to be hot and crowded, isn't it?"

"We'll have our own guide, our own private tour just as we have every other day." He rose from the low sofa and crossed the deck to stand before her. "I can't even believe you'd want to pass on Luxor."

"I've just had enough," she choked, her voice rising to a nearly hysterical pitch. "I've seen lots of ruins and monuments and it's enough—"

"Wait. Stop," he interrupted, cutting her short, before taking her chin and tipping her face up to his. "This is all about Elsie, isn't it? You're afraid to face her."

"Yes, I am afraid. I'm terrified."

"Don't be. I'm here, and I'll be with you every step of the way."

My God, he didn't get it. He didn't have a clue. "Khalid, I can't do it. I won't—"

"Won't?" he thundered. "What do you mean, won't? This isn't an option. You can't save Elsie and yourself."

"Well, I won't send her to Ozr. I can't send her to that place. I couldn't send anyone to that place."

"You might want to think on that decision, because it's you or her, Olivia. That's the choice."

CHAPTER TEN

SHE jerked her chin free and spun away from him. "I won't do it, I won't make the choice—"

"Then I will," he interrupted, his deep voice rough. "We are together in this, and I will not allow you to throw away your future, your freedom or your happiness."

"This isn't your decision to make," she answered hoarsely, bitter tears burning her eyes. "We're not together and we might be together now, but we're not a family. Your family is in Sarq. My family is in Pierceville. And those are the people we must be loyal to."

His dark eyes glittered. "I vouched for you."

"Then you made a mistake," she flashed, her emotions running so hot she knew she'd lost control. "And you made a mistake about me."

There, she thought. She'd said it. She'd told him. He'd made a mistake.

He took a step back, ran a slow hand through his hair. "We're running out of time, Liv." Khalid still sounded angry, but she heard something else in his voice now, a different emotion, one far colder, and darker and hollow. "The clock's ticking."

She'd begun to know his face so well and yet it looked different now. He seemed different. Remote. Detached.

"Let's forget Luxor," he said. "Let's just fly straight to Cairo in the morning and you can identify Elsie and then you and I can get on with our lives, and put this behind us before it spirals any more out of control than it already has."

"And if I don't identify her?" she asked faintly, perspiration beading her temple, her nape and brow.

"You mean if you *refuse* to identify her?"

She nodded stiffly, her heart thudding so hard it hurt.

"I'd return you to Jabal," he said without hesitation.

She couldn't look away from his eyes. "You would do that?"

"The Jabal government is threatening military action against Sarq. They want to escalate this into something deadly. I won't do that to my brother or my country."

Heartsick, she didn't answer, she couldn't.

"Something has to be done," he added wearily.

And still she just looked at him, too sad, too frightened for words.

But her lack of answer seemed to break something in him.

His features grew harder, colder, like granite sheathed in ice. "Knowing how I feel about my family and my country, how can you refuse to do this?" he demanded, his voice cutting and low. "Knowing that I have sacrificed so much for you, how can you not do this one thing for me? It would take five minutes of your time."

"Khalid," she choked, her hands clenching and unclenching. "It's not that I won't, but I can't—"

"Five minutes!" he repeated, his tone scathing. "Five minutes to identify her and we'd be done, gone from there. Five minutes and we'd be finished with this chaos and fear."

She was long past heartsick. She felt half-dead. He was looking at her with such disgust that her heart seemed to shrivel up.

"They hurt me in there," she said after an endless painful silence, "and they'll hurt her, too." But as she finished speaking, Liv could tell that Khalid wasn't even listening anymore. He'd turned his back on her to face the riverbank with the high narrow limestone walls. They were passing through a narrow gorge and the rocks rose high on either side, the rugged cliffs chiseled by thousands of years of sun and wind and rain.

"I thought I knew you," he said lowly, bitterness etching each word hard and sharp. "I thought I understood you—"

"She was my friend," she blurted, balling her hands at her sides in fists of sheer terror. "Even if she betrayed me, even if she did, I couldn't hurt her. Couldn't betray her. You must know me by now. You must realize I'm not that kind of person." Her eyes itched, burned. "I'm not vengeful. I'm not cruel. I wasn't raised that way and I can't change. I can't change who I am. Not even to save myself."

He didn't respond. He just stared at the wall of ivory and gold stone surrounding them even as her heart pounded wildly out of control.

Finally he slowly turned to face her. "You knew she had drugs, didn't you?"

"No, of course not—"

"So why would you protect her?"

"Because that's the kind of person I am."

"Foolish!"

"No more foolish than you," she railed furiously. "You come rescue me and you're a hero. But I try to help someone else and I'm a fool."

His upper lip curled derisively. "She had nearly a kilo of cocaine hidden in her cosmetics."

Her stomach rose in protest. "And how do we know for sure it's hers?"

"Because it was her bag. You know it was her bag. And surely you must have gotten suspicious when she never used the cosmetics—"

"But she did! When Elsie washed her face, or brushed her teeth, she used that little bag. She carried it everywhere...." Her voice drifted off as she understood what she'd said.

Khalid made a rough, mocking sound and Liv's eyes smarted. "Maybe if I'd traveled more," she added quietly, "maybe if I had more experience with different cultures I would have realized something was odd, but I found Elsie's eccentricities charming. I thought she was charming. I thought she was my friend. I liked her. I really did."

"And look what she did to you."

"Yes, look. It's bad. What she did was bad, but I can't condemn her, not to Ozr, not to a life sentence."

He looked at her without a hint of sympathy. "They're not going to just drop the charges, Olivia. Two governments have spent endless hours of manpower investigating this Elsie. My brother Sharif has been up night after night trying to find a peaceful solution, one that would free you while releasing Egypt from responsibility even as he ensured Sarq's safety." Khalid shot her a forbidding look. "Not an easy task."

She trembled inwardly. "Is there any way to get her freed?"

"For the love of God, woman!" he roared.

"I'm sorry, Khalid," she whispered, lifting her head. But when she looked up, she realized her apology had gone unheard. Khalid was gone.

Liv sank onto the low couch, shell-shocked. Although the canvas awning protected her from the harshest rays of the dying sun, she could still feel the shimmering heat and see the sun bronze the cliffs a darker gold.

She couldn't stop thinking about Elsie, couldn't forget the terrible darkness of Ozr, couldn't forget her own hopelessness before Khalid rescued her.

And maybe she was too naive, and maybe she was too trusting, but what if Elsie hadn't smuggled drugs? What if Elsie was set up? Blamed for something she didn't do? What if, and yes, this was a big what-if, but what if there never were drugs? What if the Jabal border officials made up the charges?

Liv's chest squeezed tight with grief and sorrow.

She couldn't accuse Elsie, or condemn her. She'd been taught to forgive, to forgive and forget.

But what about Khalid...and his brother? They'd all done so much to help her....

Drawing her knees up, Liv wrapped her arms around her legs and pressed her forehead to her knees.

Khalid had said something had to be done, and he was right. It was also her responsibility to do something. So what could she do? How could she fix this? How could she fix it with the least amount of damage? How could she minimize the impact for Sharif and the various government officials?

Accept responsibility.

Touching the tip of her tongue to her upper lip, she realized she needed to turn the lies into truth.

It would be hard, very hard, but at least she'd finally have a clear conscience. At least she'd feel like herself again. Good. Honest. Caring.

It'd be hard for her family, especially her mother, if she didn't return to the States, but Mom had Jake, and Jake would always take good care of her. Sons did love their mothers.

With a quick, deep breath she lifted her head, fixed her gaze on the rough rocks rising up on either side of the river and, drawing another breath, slower, deeper, she accepted responsibility. The sandstone cliffs blurred as her eyes filled with tears.

Maybe Ozr wouldn't be so bad the second time.

Rising, she went downstairs to sit at the writing table in the rarely used living room, opened the top drawer and drew out stationery and a pen. It took her several efforts to find the right words and the right tone but finally she was satisfied.

Sitting back in the chair she read:

To Whom It May Concern,
I, Olivia Morse, of Pierceville, Alabama, confess to carrying drugs illegally into Jabal from Morocco. I admit

sole responsibility. No one aided or abetted me and I am
guilty of the crime for which I'm charged.
I write this of my own free will.
Olivia Anne Morse

Carefully Liv signed her name beneath the brief confession
and, folding the sheet of stationery in thirds, slipped it into the
envelope, sealed the envelope and then walked to Khalid's
room where she slid the letter beneath his closed door.

The rest of the day crept by with agonizing slowness. For a
long time Liv remained on deck hoping Khalid would return
for lunch. He didn't. And then she remained, hoping eventually he'd come up for air. He didn't.

It was growing hotter on deck, too, and by three o'clock Liv
couldn't handle the heat or her lack of activity and retreated to her
room, where she lay on her bed and just stared at the empty space.

What was going to happen now?

What was Khalid going to do?

Frightened, she curled onto her side, her throat aching.

Lying still wasn't helping though. Her inner turmoil and
tension just continued to grow, her cabin's four walls emphasizing the fact she was trapped.

There was nothing she could do right now. Nowhere to go
at this moment in time. No one who could help.

Later that evening a dinner tray was brought to her room and
after the crew member had gone Liv glanced at the tray sitting
on the foot of the bed and felt an eerie flashback to Ozr. There
her dinner was brought to her cell on trays, too, although dinner
in Ozr was watery soup or lumpy rice and this meal smelled of
mouthwatering seasonings and spices.

But still, she knew what a tray to her room meant.

Khalid didn't want to see her. He wanted nothing to do with
her. Not that she blamed him. She didn't like herself very
much, either.

She hadn't touched her tray when a half hour later a knock sounded on her door. Opening her door, she discovered Khalid standing on the threshold. The letter was in his hand.

"What the hell is this?" he demanded, shaking the letter in her face.

It wasn't the reaction Liv expected and she took an involuntary step backward. "I won't send Elsie to Ozr, and I don't want your country on the brink of war. You said something had to be done. I'm doing it." The words tumbled from her, one after the other. "This way everyone is okay. You, your brother, your country—"

"What about you?" he roared, dropping the letter and marching toward her to seize her by the shoulders. "What about you?" he repeated, shaking her fiercely.

He made her feel boneless, her teeth chattering together, but her pain was nothing compared to the anguish she heard in his voice.

"I'm doing my best," she choked. "I'm doing my best to fix this—"

"And break everyone's heart?" he interrupted, his dark eyes black.

"But I have to do this, I have to make things right."

His fingers tightened on her shoulders. "You've no idea of your value, do you? You have no concept of the depth of your family's love. Two weeks ago when I first contacted your brother and told him I'd located you in Jabal at Ozr, he offered to switch places with you. He told me he'd go there in your place. He insisted I negotiate with the Jabal government and allow him to be sentenced instead of you."

Khalid's eyes were no longer dry. He shook his head, his hold on her fierce. "He meant it, too. And I knew what he meant, and I suddenly knew who he was. Who *you* were. I knew what kind of family you were and I vowed to get you home to him, no matter the price, no matter the cost. It was the least I could do."

Liv's eyes felt hot and gritty and she had to blink to keep tears from welling up.

"I will honor my promise to your brother, because it is what I would want one to do for me."

"But why?" she asked, torn between fury and heartbreak. "Why do you care so much?"

"Because I know how Jake feels. I know how a man feels when he can't protect his family. I had two younger sisters and I loved them. I would have done anything for them, and I'd like to think that if they were ever in trouble, someone would have helped them. Someone would have reached out to them just as I have reached out to you."

"Where are your sisters now?"

"Dead." He said the word so harshly, it reverberated in the room.

"How? When?"

"Does it matter?"

"Yes. To me, yes, and obviously to you, too."

His eyes burned down into hers. "They died in Greece, on holiday. They went on vacation and they never came back."

"That's why you help people." She looked at him wonderingly. "You don't want them to suffer the way you've suffered."

"We have not come this far to lose you now," he answered instead before releasing her.

Khalid turned and stooped to retrieve her confession, which he promptly tore into a dozen strips. "The captain has the authority to marry us," he added tersely, "and has agreed to perform the ceremony tonight. The ceremony will be performed on the upper deck at ten o'clock."

Liv's mouth tasted dry as sand and she couldn't speak even if she wanted to.

Khalid walked to the door of her cabin but paused in the doorway. "I know marrying me isn't the answer to your romantic dreams but if it reunites you sooner with your family, then it is the right thing to do." He left the room then, shutting the door firmly behind him.

Alone in her cabin, Liv leaned against the bedroom door.

He'd had sisters, and they'd died and as though to atone for the sin of not being able to save them, he spent his life trying to save others.

It was mixed-up, messed up, wrong.

And it wrenched her heart in two.

The tears she'd been fighting to hold back, fell, and once the tears started, they didn't stop.

Sliding down the door, she sat on the ground and buried her face in her hands and cried as though her heart had cracked. And maybe in a way it had. Khalid, a prince, was giving up everything for her. What was she doing for him? Fighting his every move to try and save her?

She thought of Khalid as he had looked just before he walked out the door. So proud and fierce, so regal, so…beautiful. The past few months in Ozr had been a nightmare and then suddenly there he'd appeared, a desert prince determined to save her. He left her breathless every time he got too close. But he also made her feel safe. Protected. He'd believed in her when no one else here in this foreign land would.

Liv took a shuddering breath and slowly wiped away her tears.

She couldn't undo her mistakes. She couldn't change who Elsie was, or what she had or hadn't done. But she could make things easier for Khalid. If he thought the best course of action was to get married, she'd do it. She'd go along with his plans as long as it lasted.

Pulling herself together, Liv went to her en suite bath to bathe and wash her face and prepare for tonight.

The only white dress she had was the white eyelet sundress she'd worn earlier and Liv couldn't imagine putting that back on. Instead she looked through the extravagant wardrobe Khalid had purchased for her in Cairo. She did have several long gowns which would work. There was the pleated ivory-and-gold goddess dress she'd worn that first night in Cairo when the Jabal and Egyptian authorities came to their suite at the Mena House, but that dress didn't seem right, either, not with the memories she had of that evening.

No, she wanted to wear something new, something she'd never worn, things that couldn't be tainted with memories of anything else. Because this might be a marriage of convenience, but it was still a wedding, and even if it wasn't the wedding her mother had imagined putting on for her, it counted.

She was marrying Prince Khalid Fehr, Sheikh of the Great Sarq Desert, and she wanted to be beautiful for him.

Knowing she only had a half hour left until the ceremony's appointed time, Liv selected a creamy draped gown in the softest, lightest jersey fabric imaginable. The fabric stretched over her right shoulder, leaving her left bare. The fit was smooth, elegant, and molded to her breasts. A band of silky jersey wrapped her narrow waist and the gorgeous fabric, the color of French vanilla ice cream.

The dress wasn't white, and it wasn't stiff with petticoats and lace and all the things a Southern bride wore, but it was somehow better, more appropriate for Egypt and a wedding on the Nile.

Liv combed her hair into two braids and then twisted the plaits together low at the nape of her neck, securing them with little jeweled pins Khalid had given her. She'd thought the pins were exquisite, and yet also beyond ridiculous when she discovered the jewels were real—tiny diamonds and citrines studding the hairpins—but now, sliding them into her coiled hair, it was perfect.

She applied mascara with a very light hand, a touch of sooty gray eyeliner, a bit of rose-gold blush and a shimmer of rose-gold gloss on her lips.

Inspecting herself in the mirror she felt beautiful, calm, regal. She wore no veil. She had no jewelry other than her ring, which reminded her to get the engagement ring out from her drawer and put it back on her finger. She had no flowers to carry. All she had to give Khalid was herself.

With a glance at the clock in her room she saw it was time to go upstairs. Her stomach did a little flip, alive with nervous butterflies.

It's okay, she told herself, taking a breath and sucking her stomach in. It's just Khalid. Your desert prince.

Upstairs Liv discovered the deck had been lined with white candles. Pillars of white candles were everywhere, and the abundance of pure white light made up for the lack of any other ornamentation.

The wedding ceremony was short. The captain, a forty-year veteran of the Nile River, performed the brief ceremony. Their vows weren't just witnessed by one or two people, but all twelve crew members, who stood grouped behind them at a respectful distance.

The captain spoke the words in both English and Arabic and Liv answered when required.

Khalid wore a white *dishdashah* and a white *shumagg* with a black *ogal* to hold the head cover in place.

He looked fiercely beautiful, and extremely male, his broad shoulders dwarfing her, making her feel incredibly small and fragile.

She looked up into his face as he said his vows, lost in his dark eyes and the sensual fullness of his mouth. Then, vows completed, the captain declared them husband and wife, and legally wed.

With the ceremony over, Khalid accepted the congratulations of his captain and crew before escorting Liv from the upper deck, downstairs to his room.

Liv's calm disintegrated and suddenly she felt like a child dressed up as a bride. She'd never thought it through this far, but of course she should have. He was a man and she was a woman and obviously attracted to him. Obviously married, they'd take the next step...consummate the relationship, something he'd refused to do before, when she was a virgin and in his protection.

But everything had changed. She might still be a virgin, but in the course of fifteen minutes she had become legally his.

CHAPTER ELEVEN

PULSE racing, Liv followed Khalid down the narrow hall and when they reached his room at the far end, he opened the door and allowed her to enter first.

The lights were dimmed and the walls—painted a cream color and delicately stenciled in gold, apricot and teal, glowed in the flicker and shine of candlelight. Great brass candelabras covered the late nineteenth-century side table and there were more on the big mahogany bureau.

The suite felt like something from another world, the fabrics rich, sumptuous, and the furniture a unique combination of Egyptian and British antiques. Beaded pillows were stacked near the headboard, while a rich teal and crimson and gold spread covered the rest of the enormous bed.

Liv glanced at the big bed with the jewel-tone silk coverlet and quickly glanced away, growing warmer by the second, her gaze falling to the only place that seemed safe—the hardwood floor darkly stained and buffed to a glossy shine.

Khalid moved around the room, lifting off his head cover, opening the glass doors, turning on the ornate ceiling fan to create a stronger breeze.

Liv watched him, feeling very much like the amateur.

When he finally turned to face her, she was gripping her hands tightly, insecurity and apprehension getting the best of her. "I don't know how to do this," she confessed. "I'm sorry."

"Do what?" Khalid asked, moonlight spilling across him and onto the bedroom floor.

"This," she whispered, gesturing to his bed, the candles, his room. "I've never…you know."

Khalid saw the fear in her eyes and he felt a pang of remorse. He hadn't handled any of this well today, hadn't been the most diplomatic, either.

Leaving the door, he walked to her. Reaching her side he discovered she was shaking, and her fingers were folded together in front of her as if in prayer.

He nearly smiled, but again seeing fear in the hard set of her jaw, the firm press of her lips, the desire to smile faded. Tilting her chin up, he gazed down into those huge blue eyes, eyes the color of lapis.

"You don't have to know how to do anything," he said, his hand sliding along her jaw and down her throat, where he could feel the wild beat of her pulse. Her heart raced, drumming through his fingertips. He left his fingers there, covering that wild staccato. "I know what to do. That's my job."

In her long cream-colored gown, the soft fabric draped to highlight and reveal the elegant line of shoulder, the full curve of breast, the small waist and feminine hip. He was reminded of the glorious Egyptian god Isis.

Dipping his head, he kissed the side of her neck and the pale expanse of her jaw and then the corner of her lips. Her lower lip quivered and he kissed the quiver.

Liv shivered as Khalid's mouth brushed the corner of her lips. He was kissing her lightly, fleetingly, and she closed her eyes, and tried to relax by concentrating on what was happening now instead of what would happen *then*.

Then would be sex, but now was sensual, seductive, sweet. With her eyes still closed, she felt his cheek graze her lips and she took a deep breath, drinking in the smell of him and that warm musk-and-spice-and-soap smell that was so uniquely his. He'd shaven before the ceremony and his cheeks and jaw were incredibly smooth.

As he caressed her, she lifted her hand to explore his throat and jaw, wanting to discover the very texture of his skin. Touching him like this awed her. He was so big, so powerful, and his face had the same strength in its very shape.

Lightly she traced the lines in his cheekbone and chin, along his jaw and across each eyebrow and finally the forehead. Touching him, she breathed him in again, her senses flooded by heat and spice and skin. It was like being in the bazaar again—the warmth, the seductive scent—and it was all the exotic beauty of him.

Khalid caressed the length of her, waking her entire body, making her ache and crave, her body tightening, her breasts peaking, nipples growing taut beneath the silky fabric of her gown.

"I love this dress on you," he whispered, stroking the flare of her hip, and from the small of her back to her bottom.

The hum of his voice in her ear was almost as much of a tease as the stroke of his hand over her skin. She felt hot and the elegant ceiling fan didn't seem to do much to cool her or the room down.

She gasped when Khalid lifted her long skirt to slide his hand along her bare thigh. His skin on hers felt even better than skin through clothes and she was impatient to feel more of his body against hers.

She moved her hands across the front of his robe, trying to figure out how to get it off. "Can we remove this?" she asked.

"Later," he said, his teeth lightly nipping at her neck. "First I want to know you."

He unzipped the zipper hidden in the seam of the gown; her dress suddenly came tumbling down and Khalid lifted her—naked except for silk panties, bustier and jeweled shoes—onto the bed.

Kissing her shoulder, he unhooked the lace-and-silk bustier and peeled it down, covering one suddenly exposed nipple with his mouth. Liv arched against the feel of his hot, damp mouth on her even hotter skin and reached up to dig her fingers into his hair, needing contact as his tongue flicked and licked her taut aching flesh. She wanted more, much more. He didn't seem to feel her urgency though, and took his time kissing and caressing both breasts, and then her rib cage and down her flat belly to the silk barrier of her panties.

As he kissed her hipbones he slid his hands beneath her bottom, lifting her slightly and making her insides feel so hot and wet she was afraid she'd melt in his hands. "Khalid," she choked as he stroked her mound through the now damp white silk.

He ignored the plea in her voice, concentrating instead on the incredibly tender skin on her inner thighs, his tongue exploring that small hollow between her inner thigh and the elastic of her silk underwear.

Liv didn't know if she wanted to push him away or trap him between her thighs when he put his mouth on her, kissing her through the silk, his lips covering, wrapping her tight, hard nub. She'd never felt anything like this in her life and she grabbed at his shoulders, her hands pressing against the thick muscle. When his tongue stroked down the silk to trace the lines of her inner lips she bucked, finding the sensation and friction overwhelming.

"No more," she begged. "No more, not like this. This isn't fair. I want it fair. You have to take your clothes off now, too."

He was slipping her silk panties off, and parting her knees, parting them to kiss her without the silk interference.

Liv cried out as his tongue touched between her, a light caress that became bolder, alternately licking and sucking until she felt drenched with her own desire.

"Please, please," she pleaded, her voice so hoarse she didn't even recognize it as she tugged on his robe. "Take this off, please."

The robe finally came off, as did the rest of his clothes. Heart in her throat, she watched him climb back onto the bed and straddle her. His body was a map of muscles and planes. She couldn't resist touching his abdomen, with the hollows and cuts in the muscle, and below his lean torso was a very big, very intimidating erection.

Nervously she touched the end of his shaft, the head surprisingly hot and silky in her palm. Curious, she wrapped her other hand around the thick shaft, sliding her hand from tip to pubic bone and then back again. His hissed breath caught her attention and, looking up at him, she saw the dark color in his cheekbones and the primal hunger in his eyes. He liked it, she thought, feeling surprisingly powerful. She could do something he liked and she wanted to do it again.

Gripping tighter, she stroked the length of his shaft, a little faster, a little harder, and she felt him tense, saw his thick black eyelashes drop, his lips parting in a silent groan of pleasure.

Abruptly he seized her hand, lifting it from his body. "You'd better stop," he growled, "or I won't be able to make love to you the way I want to."

Feeling very provocative, she linked her hands behind his neck and drew his face down to her. "How do you want to?"

He kissed her hard, deeply, passionately, kissing her until she shivered and danced beneath him. Lifting his head much later he answered, "Thoroughly."

And then he was kissing her again, stealing her breath and her body and her will. He moved her legs, his thighs inside hers, and as he stretched over her she felt the tip of his erection nudge her.

"I don't want to hurt you," he whispered, kissing the side of her neck, and then her throat and back to her lips.

"It won't always hurt, will it?" she asked, barely able to concentrate on what he was asking when his hands were on her breasts and his palms rubbed slowly across her sensitized nipples.

"No," he answered, dropping his head to suck one peaked nipple even as he positioned his shaft at the entrance to her body.

She tensed as his fingers brushed her damp curls and he soothed her by kissing her again. His kiss deepened as he entered her slowly. Fortunately her body was wet and welcoming and only once did the pressure become too much. She pressed at his chest, holding her breath, feeling panicky.

"Hurts?" he murmured in her ear.

She nodded, afraid to exhale.

"Look at me," he said, smoothing her hair back from her brow.

She did, and what she saw in his face—in his eyes—made her clasp his face and kiss him, kiss him to tell him how much it mattered, how much she appreciated everything he was and everything he'd done.

And, kissing him, her heart exploded wide open and her body accepted him and he was with her, completely with her making her feel more than she'd ever felt in her life.

Khalid, she whispered as his powerful body surged into hers, *my husband*.

The first time they made love she didn't have an orgasm. The second time they made love she had two, and after shattering against his hard, sinewy body a second time, Liv felt as though she, and her life, had been turned inside out and upside down.

Khalid had changed her. Khalid hadn't taken her virginity, he'd made her feel cherished and beautiful. He'd made her feel like a woman.

In the morning breakfast was brought to her in bed and Liv dragged herself into a sitting position only to discover she was ridiculously sore. Khalid, hearing her whimper, appeared from the en suite bath where he'd just finished showering and dressing.

"What's wrong, little one?" he asked, buttoning his linen shirt.

She grimaced as she adjusted the tray on her lap. "I'm a trifle sore, thanks to your not-so-little one."

He grinned, obviously pleased, and Liv shook her head, amazed at the male ego. "So what are our plans?" she asked. "I wasn't sure what was going to happen today. Do we have to go somewhere, do something to formalize the wedding?"

"No, we'll finish the cruise as planned, here in Luxor," he answered. "I love Luxor. It's my favorite Egyptian city, and my Egyptian friends know it's my favorite city and they expect us here today. But dress in something cool," he said, leaning over the bed to kiss her. "The Valley of the Kings can get hot."

Liv had read that Luxor was the world's greatest open-air museum and she immediately understood the significance when presented with the Theban necropolis to view the royal tombs.

Luxor, with its wealth of monuments, ranging from the Valleys of the Kings and Queens to the Colossi of Memncon, was old Egypt, deep Egypt like the one she'd read about in Jake's books.

Their guide was another good friend of Khalid's and he'd gotten them access to the Tomb of Nefertari, which strictly limited the number of visitors to protect the fragility of the ancient tomb.

It was a hot day already, even hotter inside the tomb, and Liv began to wilt. Their guide was exceptional, but very detail-oriented and as the temperature in the tomb continued to climb her discomfort increased.

Once Khalid looked at her, a questioning light in his eyes, but she forced a quick smile, not wanting to worry him, especially when she knew how much he enjoyed this particular tomb.

But his gaze held hers longer than necessary and she felt her chest squeeze tight, her heart filled with the most bittersweet emotion imaginable.

If only she'd met Khalid in different circumstances.

If only they'd met on an airplane or on a street corner in passing. If only, she thought wistfully…

From the Valley of the Queens they traveled on to the Valley of the Kings and it was even hotter by the time they faced the first set of stairs, due to the sun rising high in the sky.

"Why were the royal tombs built here?" Liv asked the guide, fanning herself, as they paused part way on the flight of steps. The Valley of the Kings was all desert, barren limestone rock and sizzling heat.

"Some believe the tombs were carved out of the mountains to help with the journey to the afterworld," the guide answered, "and others think that once the first tomb was built here, it just became the popular thing to do."

"Either way," Khalid suddenly added, arms crossed, "the Egyptians' mummy specialists definitely knew the desert was an ideal place to store a corpse."

She shuddered. "Yuck."

"But that's what these are, little one. There are sixty-two tombs opened. They expect there are still that many to discover."

"That's a lot of dead bodies."

He laughed softly and they continued hiking, climbing eighty steps up one of the mountains before creeping down through a huge cave that smelled musty and dank.

Liv wrinkled her nose as they squeezed through uncomfortably narrow passages. She didn't like the close confines, particularly coupled with the mind-boggling temperatures. Liv told herself that it would soon pass, but as the guide led them deeper into the tomb Liv felt like she was suffocating. She couldn't catch her breath and her head was beginning to spin again.

"Too hot?" Khalid's voice murmured close to her ear and she nodded, feeling yet another spike in temperature, aware all over again of Khalid's large, hard frame so close to her own.

"A little," she admitted.

"Let's go out," he said, touching her low on her back. "We've seen enough."

His light touch flooded her veins with fire, her body remembering him, her body already craving him. "No. No, this is incredible. I've never seen anything like it and if I leave now, I might never have the chance to see it again."

"All right," he agreed reluctantly, and they reached the bottom of the cave without further incident.

On reaching the bottom, Liv understood why this tomb was such a favorite of tourists. Oval-shaped, the tomb was exquisitely painted with astonishing hieroglyphics on every wall, while the ceiling was a gorgeous azure blue.

Liv stared up in awe. "It's beautiful."

"It is," Khalid agreed.

Liv lingered behind Khalid and the guide to have a closer look at the hieroglyphics. Other tourists were in the tomb, too, and there was some gentle jostling as everyone jockeyed to see the decorations that illustrated the ancient Egyptians' thoughts and ideas and expectations for the afterworld.

Bumped twice by a particularly aggressive tourist, Liv was just about to return to Khalid's side when a uniformed Egyptian took her arm. "Ma'am, please step away from your group and come with me."

"I'm sorry," Liv said, trying to tug her arm free. "I don't understand. What's wrong?"

"Just come with me, ma'am."

Absolutely stunned, Liv's stomach fell even as she experienced the most painful déjà vu. She'd been through this before, she'd been hauled off the bus in Jabal and it'd gone from confusing to terrifying in less than twelve hours. Now she feared the worst. Why had she been singled out? What was happening?

Khalid suddenly appeared at her side. "Take your hand off her now."

The uniformed officer bowed. "Your Highness, forgive me, it's for your protection."

Khalid's eyes narrowed. "You dare to suggest that I need to be protected from my own woman?"

"Your Highness, we have observed suspicious activity in the

tomb today and believe Miss Morse is involved in illegal activity here."

Khalid's features hardened, his dark eyes glittered. "Do you have proof?"

"If we could check her bag."

"If you were in my country, I'd have you hanged for your insolence."

The official sweated even more profusely. "We respectfully request permission to go through her belongings."

"No."

"Your Highness."

"You've insulted my wife, you've insulted my family and you've insulted me. I suggest you call your chief of police because there is going to be hell to pay."

The guards stepped back to confer and Khalid reached out to take Olivia's hand in his. "No one will touch you," he murmured. "No one will take you from me. I promise."

She clung to his hand. "Khalid, you must believe me. I wouldn't take anything. I'm not a thief. I'm not a drug smuggler."

"I know."

"Do you?" Her gaze searched his. "Do you really? Because there's no way I could do what they say—" She broke off as the officers returned.

"Your Highness, if you and Miss Morse—"

"*Princess* Fehr," Khalid corrected.

"If you and Princess Fehr would follow us, a helicopter is coming to take us to the police station."

The helicopter transported them from the sweltering Valley of the Kings to Luxor's police station, where the chief of police awaited along with a half dozen other officials. Khalid greeted three of them by name and as it turned out, two of the officials were from Sarq, the third an Egyptian lawyer who was close friends with the Fehr family.

Liv was seated in a small room just around the corner from the conference room. She couldn't see everyone, but she could hear the voices and she knew from Khalid's tone that he was very, very angry.

The meeting in the conference room lasted less than an hour and when it was finished, Khalid took her hand and walked out of the police station without looking back.

They climbed into another helicopter, this one sent by King Sharif Fehr for their use. "What happened in there?" she asked, catching sight of Khalid's grim expression. "What's going to happen now?"

"Nothing."

She leaned forward. "What do you mean, nothing?"

"It's over."

"What about Elsie? What's happening to her?"

"They've dropped the charges and she's being sent home tonight."

She looked at him, her brow deeply furrowed. "So there were no drugs? She was falsely accused?"

"I don't know, and I don't know if we'll ever know. But the fact that someone from Jabal would attempt to plant drugs on you here raised so many red flags that the entire case has been dismissed."

She said nothing for a moment. "The case wouldn't have been dismissed, though, if it weren't for you. You didn't just save me once, you saved me twice."

He shrugged uncomfortably. "I promised to protect you."

"You helped Elsie, too."

He shot her a sideways glance. "You wanted me to, didn't you?"

"Yes."

They flew to Cairo, where they boarded the Fehr royal jet. As the jet taxiied down the runway and then lifted off, Liv was briefly blinded by the setting sun's brilliance, the long, late afternoon rays turning the desert orange and red as though the sand itself was on fire.

Egypt had been riveting from start to finish, she thought, biting into her lower lip as the plane's wings tipped, blocking the view below.

They were served a meal, and Liv could only pick at her salad. Khalid was silent and he didn't eat, either. The flight attendant didn't comment as she cleared their virtually untouched plates.

"Are we going to Sarq?" Liv asked Khalid after their table had been removed.

He'd been staring out the window since takeoff, his gaze shuttered, his expression strangely remote. "Not yet." He hesitated. "I have some things to take care of first."

Liv watched him covertly, worried. He hadn't been the same since the accusation in the tomb and she wished she knew what he was thinking. Was he mad at her? Embarrassed? Disappointed?

"Are you mad at me?" she asked uncertainly.

"No."

"But at the Valley of the Kings—"

"It's over."

His short, terse answers did little to relieve her anxiety. Something was bothering him. But what?

She longed to press for a real answer, but at the same time didn't feel entitled to push him. He'd done so much for her, helped so much she felt she needed to respect his need for space…privacy. If he wanted to talk to her, he could. He would. He'd never had a problem talking to her in the past.

And yet as the flight passed with no interaction between them her sense of isolation grew.

For the first time she realized she could handle him being mad at her. She could even handle him not talking to her. But she couldn't handle not knowing what he was thinking.

She didn't like being shut out. It hurt.

It was dark by the time they arrived in Paris and raining. It wasn't a freezing rain, but Liv still felt chilled as they crossed the airport tarmac to enter the stylish executive terminal.

As always a chauffeured car waited, this time a beautiful dark gray Bentley that swiftly transported them to the historic and sumptuous Hotel Ritz.

They dined in their room, the presidential suite, served by their own personal waiter. Khalid was even more remote during dinner and Liv felt increasingly alarmed.

In the past eight hours he'd built a wall around himself and from what she saw, he wasn't going to let her over, or through. At least not yet.

At bedtime Liv didn't know what to do. They'd only been married one day and one night, and last night had been her first night sharing a man's bed. She didn't know what to expect tonight and, after changing into her white nightdress edged with pink lace, she stood uncertainly in the middle of the bedroom.

Khalid appeared in the doorway, his brow furrowing as he looked at her.

"You are angry with me," she said huskily, her fingers twisting together, a nervous habit she'd never been able to break. "Tell me what I did so I won't do it again."

"It's not you."

"Khalid—"

"I think it's better if we don't talk tonight," he interrupted emotionlessly. "I'll sleep on the couch in the living room. It folds out into a bed. The butler has already put sheets on it for me."

Liv fought to hang on to her composure. "But why are you sleeping there? Why aren't you sleeping with me?"

"A lot has happened this week."

"Yes."

"I think we could both use some alone time."

"I don't."

He shrugged. "I disagree. You've been through a lot, little

one. Your head is spinning so fast you don't even know if you're coming or going."

She stared at the rose-and-gold patterned carpet with the bits of royal blue. "You're sorry you married me."

"It shouldn't have been under those conditions, no."

"But it was under those conditions," she answered, lifting her head, meeting his gaze.

"Something I regret."

"Why?"

"No woman should be forced into marriage. Last night I forced you—"

"You didn't!"

"I'm deeply sorry. I wanted to protect you—"

"And you did." She crossed to him, reached out with both hands to his arm. He was warm and solid and yet he felt even more distant than before. He was disappearing before her eyes, becoming a stranger all over again. "Khalid, all you've done is help me."

"Good." And, bending his head, he kissed her on the cheek near her mouth, the feel of his lips sending electric sparks throughout her body. "Sleep well. And no more bad dreams tonight."

She watched him turn and leave. "I don't have them anymore," she said, calling after him.

He hesitated in the doorway. "Why not?"

"You made them go away."

CHAPTER TWELVE

AFTER a fitful night's sleep, Liv didn't want to get out of bed but Khalid pushed open the curtains, waking her. "Feel like seeing Paris?" he asked.

She pushed up onto her elbow, looked out the window and saw the rain. "It's raining."

"It always rains in Paris. Come, get up, get dressed. We'll go have breakfast and explore the city. You'll enjoy it. You can't come to Paris without seeing something."

He seemed so much like his old self that Liv couldn't help smiling back. He'd apparently resolved whatever was bothering him yesterday. "Give me a half hour to shower and dress."

"I'll order you some coffee."

He disappeared and Liv jumped from bed, excited to discover Paris with Khalid. He'd made Egypt magical. Imagine what he could do for the most romantic city in the world.

The morning passed quickly. After a breakfast in a charming café, they were then off to see some of Khalid's favorite historic sites including the nearby Place de la Concorde—site of the infamous guillotine—and then down the Champs-Élysées, the seventeenth-century garden promenade that had become an avenue connecting the Concorde and the Arc de Triomphe.

The rain let up as they wandered around Montparnasse, with

its artist studios, music halls and café life, but by the time they reached the Eiffel Tower, it'd started again, the skies a steely gray.

"I'm too wet," Liv protested with a laugh, getting drenched despite the umbrella Khalid had carried over their heads.

He stopped on the pavement and pushed a wet tendril of hair from her cheek. "Yes, you are." He looked at her so long, his expression intense. "Time to go."

Stepping into the street, he hailed a taxi cab, one of the many that flooded the streets of Paris. The taxi pulled alongside the curb and Khalid opened the back door.

"Go," he said, gesturing for her to get in.

She just stood there, beneath his umbrella in the pouring rain. "Go?" she asked dumbly, hearing the *ping ping* of the rain on the umbrella. "What do you mean, go? Go where? Go do what?"

"Go home. Go back to where you belong."

She reached up to wipe a wet splash from her cheek. "But we're married—"

"It can be annulled. You were coerced into marrying me. It wouldn't stand up in court."

But what about me? she wanted to ask. What about us? Instead she grasped for straws. "What about Jabal? Won't their government go after you? Won't they try to ruin you—"

"It's been dismissed. It's all over. But even if it wasn't, they can't ruin me." His lips curved, twisting. "I'm too powerful for them to ruin."

"But your name…and that whole issue of honor. If I leave you, won't that hurt you and your reputation?"

He shrugged. "You left me. You ran away. What am I to do?"

The taxi driver stuck his head out the window. "Come on, come on, I don't have all day."

Khalid's dark eyebrows lifted and, looking down at Olivia, he smiled that wry, heart-wrenching smile of his. "He's in a hurry, little one. You'd better go."

Olivia couldn't believe this was happening. It's what she'd

wanted, it's what she'd fought so hard for, and yet now that she had it, now that it was happening, she didn't understand it. Wasn't ready for it at all, wasn't even sure it was right. Khalid had never been her jailer. He was her rescuer, her hero.

She gave her head a slight shake. "I don't know—"

"Go to the U.S. embassy. They're expecting you. They know the story. You've just managed to escape from me and you've nothing on you—no wallet, no passport, just the clothes on your back—and you must get home. They'll see you home."

"But surely my ticket—"

"Paid for."

"My passport."

"Taken care of."

Her eyes burned. He'd been planning this for a while then. He'd known all along he was going to release her. And yet he'd never let on. He'd played his part, played it all the way out.

"Why?" she whispered, wanting to touch him, wanting to wrap her arms around him and feel his warmth and strength and courage.

His courage. Perhaps the thing she loved best about him.

He shrugged. "It's what I'd want someone to do for my sisters." And then he gave her a gentle push into the cab. "Be careful out there, princess. Remember that there are many wolves in sheep's clothing."

Before she even knew how, she was seated in the backseat, the umbrella folded and put away. Rain slashed down in long wet streaks. Liv leaned out the open door, pushing a wet sticky strand of hair from her face. "Will I ever see you again?"

Khalid's dark gaze met hers and held. "Maybe."

"Only maybe?"

"If you need me." And then he bent, cupped her cheek and kissed her lips, slowly, tenderly, before stepping back and slamming the taxi door closed.

The taxi sped off and Olivia turned and stared out the back

window through the slashing rain. She caught Khalid's profile before he turned away and then another car was behind them and he disappeared from sight altogether.

The flight from Paris to New York was endless. Khalid had bought her a first-class ticket on Air France, which meant her seat became a real bed with real sheets and blankets and not just one, but two very soft down pillows.

She practically had a flight attendant to herself. The flight attendant served her a five-course dinner and glasses of wine and champagne, but even with all the amenities and attentive service Liv couldn't stop thinking.

Or feeling.

She'd only just gotten married—a bride of only two days—and now it was already over.

Pulling the blanket to her nose, she pressed the soft fleece to her mouth and tried to think of something else. Tried to think of anything but the man she'd married and the man who'd sent her home.

But it's what you wanted, she reminded herself. *You made it clear that your family was in Pierceville and that's where you belonged.*

Had she been wrong?

In New York Liv caught yet another flight, this one bound for Arkansas, where her brother would meet her plane and drive her the three hours home.

During the flight to Arkansas she once again tried not to think, tried not to remember, not the fiery sands of Egypt or the towering pyramids or the mirage-like Nile winding through the fertile river valley.

She wouldn't remember the man who appeared outside her cell like an avenging angel sent from heaven to bring her home.

She wouldn't remember how he faced down an entire country to secure her release.

She wouldn't remember his dark eyes and the expression in them when he looked at her.

And most of all she wouldn't remember how it felt to be in his arms when he held her close. She wouldn't remember the thick, smooth muscles of his chest or the hard thighs or the flat abdomen or the warmth of his golden skin as he covered her, moved over her, filling her.

She wouldn't remember that she'd come so close to losing her heart completely, wouldn't remember that she'd been just one kiss away from being lost to his desert and his power forever.

Her plane touched down in Arkansas without a bump, the landing so smooth that it wasn't until they were drawing up to the gate that she'd registered that they'd landed. She was home.

With all the security headaches in American airports, she knew Jake would have to wait until she exited to baggage claim, It was as she was walking toward the baggage carousel that she heard him say, "If you aren't a sight for sore eyes."

Jake, she thought. She turned around and looked up into the bluest eyes in the world. Tall, handsome and kind, he was the best brother, and she threw herself in his arms, hugging him hard, hugging him to make up for all the things she could never tell him. He'd never understand what had happened to her these past six weeks, and she didn't want him to understand. It'd just upset him more and they'd all been through enough.

It was time to move on. Time to get their lives back to normal.

"Mom's dying to see you," he said gruffly when he finally let her go. "She wanted to come but I didn't think she needed a six-hour drive."

"But she's doing better?" she asked as Jake took her carry-on bag off her shoulder and slipped it over his.

"Much better."

"Good."

He looked her up and down, taking in her slim navy sleeve-less dress, which she was wearing with knee-high black suede boots with a small kitten heel. "You're all grown-up," he said, stepping back, "and with a new wardrobe."

"Khalid," she said. "He chose the wardrobe."

"Khalid?" Jake frowned, and then his brow cleared. "You mean, Sheikh Fehr."

She nodded.

"He has good taste," he said.

She nodded again and Jake studied her for an uncomfortable moment. "Were you two really engaged?" he asked.

Liv opened her mouth to say yes, to tell him they'd actually married, but then something in his expression held her back. Jake was afraid for her, afraid of what had happened when she was halfway around the world. "Briefly," she answered, thinking her answer was at least true.

"Is that why you're wearing that enormous ring?"

She'd forgotten all about the yellow diamond and she covered it with her hand, the sharp edges and large stone now so familiar.

"I'm assuming it isn't costume jewelry," Jake added.

Her heart ached all over again. "It's real."

"Your sheikh had a lot of money."

"I couldn't have gotten out of Ozr or Jabal if it weren't for him."

"I'm not criticizing him. I'm grateful."

Her eyes burned and she blinked hard. "Me, too."

Her brother studied her for another long, silent moment. "I'm glad you're back, Liv. We've missed you." He wrapped an arm around her, dropped a kiss on her head. "Now let's get you home. Mom's made dinner and baked you her famous banana buttermilk cake."

Reaching Pierceville, Liv was struck by how green everything was, particularly after her weeks in the desert. It was also humid, which was typical of the south. Fortunately her mom's house was cool and dinner was waiting, along with her mother's homemade cake, which had been a family favorite since Liv was born.

Liv slipped her ring off before dinner and put it in her jewelry box in her room before joining everyone at the table. Even though her mom had lost weight and appeared more frail, she was in great spirits and beamed at Liv throughout dinner.

"My Olivia is home again," she repeated for the fifth time as Jake carried in the cake.

"And not going away anytime soon, I hope," Jake said, placing the cake on the dining room table.

Liv thought of Khalid and his dark eyes and hard features and yet that full sensual mouth that kissed her so tenderly. She pressed her hands together beneath the table. "Nope," she answered, hating the lump that filled her throat. It was what it was, she told herself, and it was over.

But in her room that night Liv couldn't sleep. She didn't know if it was the jet lag or all her pent-up emotions, but sleep eluded her. After an hour of tossing and turning, she gave up. There was no way she was going to sleep, not with her mind racing and that huge, empty feeling inside her and, leaving bed, she headed for the kitchen.

Turning on the kitchen light, Liv opened the refrigerator to pour herself a glass of milk and cut another sliver of her mom's cake. But once she'd cut the cake and had the milk she realized the empty feeling inside her wasn't about food. It was about Khalid.

She missed him. She missed talking to him. She missed his voice. She missed seeing him and having meals with him and most of all missed that hot, electric feeling she got when he looked at her.

If she had his number she'd call him right now. But she didn't have his number and she didn't know how to reach him. She didn't even know where he lived.

The palace in Sarq?

The desert?

Some archaeological dig?

Stabbing her fork into the cake, she tried to ignore how hurt she felt.

He was her husband. He wasn't supposed to send her back. He was supposed to want her with him.

The next month passed exquisitely slowly. Liv dragged herself to work at the travel agency every day and yet, with each passing day, she liked the work less. Most of her customers didn't want to go anywhere. Most of her customers wanted her to book them a room on the Gulf Coast, or a package for four to Disney World. Her customers wanted round-trip air tickets to Chicago for a trade show or, the highlight of her month, an eco-tourism honeymoon to Costa Rica.

But other than that honeymoon trip to Costa Rica, there were no requests for exotic vacations, no interest in ancient ruins, scorching deserts or immense sand dunes shaped by the wind.

As the days passed, she found herself missing the deserts and sand dunes more and more.

She missed Khalid more and more.

When they were in Egypt, she'd been desperate to return to the States, but now that she was back, she didn't know why she'd been so anxious to return. Pierceville was boring. Her job as a travel agent was uninspiring. Her personal life was as empty as could be.

She wanted the colors of Egypt again, the golds and creams and khaki and sand.

She wanted the heat of the desert.

But most of all, she wanted her prince of the desert.

That brief wedding ceremony and the night in his bed had changed something in her heart, had changed the way she thought, felt, breathed. That ceremony had tied them together, united them together, an even though they were now thousands of miles apart she still felt like his, just as he felt like hers.

Her husband. Her hope. Her heart.

Without him, nothing was the same.

The weeks passed and summer was swiftly approaching. Liv's routine was to wake up, go to work, come home and make dinner, do laundry, do errands, go to bed and then wake up the next morning and start over again.

She didn't even mind the work. At least busy—hands typing, cooking, washing, folding—she found she didn't think as much, didn't feel as much. As long as she stayed busy.

Nights…they were another story and Liv had come to dread the night. They were endless. They were dark. They were quiet. And they reminded her of Khalid.

She needed him. She needed to see him. She needed to hear his voice.

She needed him back.

The next morning was Saturday. She had too much time on her hands, and after cleaning the house Liv decided to strip the beds and tackle more laundry. Hauling the sheets downstairs, she turned on the washing machine and started the first load.

"You're getting too thin." It was Jake. He stood in the laundry room doorway watching her.

"I'm fine," she answered briskly, adding the detergent to the wash.

"You're a stick and you don't sleep and you don't eat and you don't smile," he said flatly. "You've been like this ever since you returned from the Middle East."

Looking at her brother, she wondered what he'd say if she told him she'd hoped she'd be pregnant. She wondered how he'd react if she told him she was devastated she wasn't. She wanted Khalid's baby. She wanted him still in her life. She wanted…

"What's going on, Liv?"

"Nothing." She wiped her hands on the back of her shorts and tried to smile.

It was so ridiculous that she wanted to be pregnant. It was so impractical. But she needed Khalid. Not for a baby. But for her.

She loved him. Crazy loved him. Couldn't live, think,

breathe without him and yet, oh God, how was she to find him, and just go to him, and confess she loved him, and needed him, when he'd been the one to put her in a taxi and send her away?

"You've chewed all your fingernails off and you're wearing a hole in your bedroom carpet with all the pacing you do." Jake's deep voice was quiet, his tone patient. "This isn't the Liv I know."

It wasn't. She wasn't the Liv she knew, either.

Turning to face him, she had tears in her eyes. "Oh, Jake, what am I going to do?"

He leaned against the old door frame. "Do about what?"

"I thought I was pregnant—"

"Hell."

"No. I'm not."

"Praise God."

"No, it's not a miracle, either." She shoved her hands in the pockets of her shorts. "I wanted to be pregnant. I wanted to have his baby."

Understanding dawned in Jake's hazel eyes. "You love your sheikh."

She nodded slowly, tears filling her eyes. "A lot."

"You wanted to be his wife."

"I was." She swallowed hard. "Am. At least I haven't gotten the annulment papers yet."

"Olivia Morse."

She swallowed a second time. "It's actually Princess Olivia Fehr."

"Does Mom know?"

"No!"

"Good. Don't tell her. If she thought you got married without her being there…she'd have a stroke."

Liv sat at her desk, staring at the computer screen. She was supposed to be booking an airline ticket for one of her mother's friends to go see her daughter's new baby. Her mother's friend had just become a grandmother and was excited. Even Liv's mother was excited.

Liv just wanted to go away, far away, but had used all her vacation time for the year. And the following year.

That's when she looked up. And he was there.

In her travel agency. In a gorgeous suit with a white shirt and silk tie looking like a million bucks.

"What…" she said, before breaking off, aware that the agency had gone strangely quiet as all the other travel agents were staring. But of course they'd stare. Khalid Fehr was about the most exotic thing Pierceville had ever seen.

She rolled her chair closer to her desk, leaning forward to demand, "What are you doing here?"

"I need some help planning a trip."

Her lips parted and then she pressed them closed again. Glancing around at the other agents, she forced a small tight smile before gesturing to the chair in front of her desk. "Would you like to sit down?"

"Thank you. That's very kind of you."

She watched him sit down but it wasn't until he was seated across from her that she looked at him properly, really looked at him, and realized his gaze rested on her and only her.

"You've come a long way to get travel advice," she said, nervously straightening the travel brochures and folders littering her desk.

"But you told me you were good."

She stared in fascination at his mouth, and the way the one side curved up in that mocking, rueful way he had and she felt a shiver race through her. God, he was gorgeous, so gorgeous and he'd once been hers, for two days—

Or had he ever been hers?

She frowned, hopelessly confused.

"Where did you want to go?" she asked, striving to be as businesslike as possible.

"I'd like to see the world," he answered.

She tried to hide her bewilderment. "But you've seen a great deal of it already, haven't you?"

"Yes, but this time I'd like to see it all. I was thinking of devoting the next year to traveling around the world."

"That's a lot of traveling," she said, trying to hide her shock.

"There's a lot of world."

She picked up her pen to take notes. "When would you want to leave?"

"Soon."

His matter-of-fact answer made her stomach hurt. "And where would you like to end up?"

"Sarq."

A place she'd never seen, she thought, writing *soon* and *Sarq* on her pad of paper. "And how would you like to travel?"

"By my private jet."

"Right. A nice way to fly. Although I will say flying first class was quite comfortable...." She paused, looked at him. "Thank you for that ticket home."

"My pleasure."

She stared at him for a moment, her temper beginning to rise. "Were you glad to send me home?"

"It's what you wanted."

She opened her mouth to protest but realized he was right. It was what she'd thought she'd wanted. In the beginning. Before she fell in love with him. "What if I hadn't wanted to go home?"

He leaned across the desk. "Then you would have told me."

She couldn't look away from his beautiful face with his dark eyes, eyes that had caught her, captivated her from the first day she met him. "Why are you here?"

"I told you if you ever needed me I'd find you."

Her heart beat a little faster. "Yes."

"And apparently you do need me."

Her heart beat faster still. "Says who?"

"Your brother." The edge of Khalid's mouth lifted ever so slightly. "He wrote me and begged me to get you out of Pierceville. He said it was life and death."

A wash of emotion swept through her. She had to try very hard not to laugh. "Life and death?"

"Apparently so," he answered gravely. "Jake said you're in a terrible place. He said if I don't intervene immediately something bad will happen." Khalid's dark gaze searched hers. "Is that true?"

It was so good, so amazing to see his gorgeous face, to look into those dark soulful eyes, to watch that sexy mouth curve into a smile. "Yes," she whispered, her heart drumming a mile a minute. "It's all true."

"So I have to take action?"

"Yes."

His lashes dropped and his gaze rested on her mouth. "And just what am I saving you from, Princess Fehr?"

Her chest squeezed tight and her throat threatened to close. "A broken heart."

His face was utterly expressionless for a moment and then he smiled, that rare great smile of his, the one that transformed him from rugged into heart-stoppingly beautiful. "You love me."

Tears filled her eyes. "I do, I do, I do."

Suddenly he was around her desk and lifting her to her feet. He clasped her to him, his lips covering hers in a fierce, demanding kiss.

He kissed her until her head spun and her legs buckled and that horrible yawning emptiness inside her started to fill with warmth.

"I love you, my Liv," he said against her mouth. "I love you with all my heart."

"Are you sure?"

"Yes."

"Will you please marry me then?"

He lifted his head, pushed silver-gold strands of hair from her face. "But we are married."

"I know, but my mom doesn't know and she's desperate to have a wedding in the family and then a baby. Her friend Joanne's daughter just had a baby, making her a grandmother—"

Khalid cut her babbling off with another kiss, this one even hotter than the last.

"I think a wedding is a wonderful idea," he said having kissed her senseless. "It's time you met my family."

Aware that every single person in the travel agency was watching them, Liv turned around and, blushing, stammered out an introduction. "Everyone, this is my fiancé, Sheikh Khalid Fehr, and we're getting married."

The travel agents and customers cheered and, cheeks flaming, Liv turned back to Khalid. "So you don't really need travel advice."

He dipped his head, kissed her cheek and then the hollow below her ear. "But I do," he murmured. "I need to know where you want to go for our honeymoon."

"I don't care where we go," she answered, standing on tiptoe to give him another kiss, "as long as we're together."

"Jabal?"

She frowned. "Um, we might be safer in Sarq."

"I think so, too." And, scooping her into his arms, he carried her out of the travel agency. "Tell me you've got a decent hotel in this town," he said as he carried her into the summer sunshine.

She wrapped her arms around his neck. "Nothing special. Sorry."

"Do they have beds?"

Laughing, Liv kissed him. "Yes. But don't you think we should wait for our wedding?" she asked archly.

He growled in her ear, his arms tightening around her. "*No*. Sorry, little one, I've missed you too much. I'm desperate to make you mine again."

EPILOGUE

Later that night...

LIV sat with Khalid and her mom in her mother's living room. "It's going to be a big wedding, Mom," Liv said carefully, not wanting to frighten her mom. "I hope that's okay."

"How big?" her mother asked, still recovering from the shock of learning that Olivia was engaged and getting married to a sheikh quite soon.

"Um, a couple hundred people. Maybe." Liv cringed. "Maybe a few more."

Her mother reached for her glasses and put them on. "And who are all these people we're inviting?"

Liv shot Khalid a please-help-me-now look but he sat back, content to let her battle her way through this one. "Royalty," she said timidly.

Mrs. Morse turned toward her future son-in-law. "Your family."

"Yes," he answered gravely. "My family, along with our friends. Many of whom are royal in their own countries, too."

"I see." Mrs. Morse slid her glasses off and reached for her notebook. "I think we're going to need to increase our budget then."

Liv shot Khalid another desperate glance. "Mom, the Fehr

family would like to help with the wedding. They don't have any daughters and they hoped to put on the wedding…there."

Her mother's eyebrows rose. "*There?* In the desert?"

"Not all of Sarq is desert, Mom. There are cities, beautiful cities—"

"Have you been *there*?" she interrupted.

Liv flushed. Why was her mother doing this now? "No, not to Sarq, not yet, but I've seen pictures, and Khalid's told me."

"Well, that's very nice," Mrs. Morse answered in her best mother voice. "But you are my daughter and we'll do the wedding here."

"Here?"

"In Pierceville."

"Mom, there's no venue big enough!" *Or nice enough*, Liv mentally added.

"But of course there is if we plan an outdoor wedding. We can do something festive. Put up a tent and tables and that sort of thing." Her mother sat tall. "I've seen it done in magazines. There's no reason we can't have a tent and tables and chairs here."

Khalid reached for Liv's hand and kissed it. "I think that's a wonderful idea, Mrs. Morse. We'd love to be married here. And my family, and our friends, will be delighted to come."

"Excellent!" Mrs. Morse rose, beaming. "I'm going to call Joanne. Let her know the good news."

Liv turned on Khalid the moment her mother left the room. "Your family is coming to Pierceville?"

"Why not?"

"Khalid, your brother is a king. Your other brother is a billionaire and international playboy. They'll hate Pierceville."

"They'll love it," he answered, trying hard to check his smile and failing miserably. "Besides, if you get married here, you'll be Pierceville's biggest celebrity for life."

"That's not funny, Khalid!"

He pulled her into his arms, onto his lap and kissed her. "I think it is." He kissed her again, before his expression grew sober. "If it makes your mother happy to have you married here, why not? Where we marry, or where we live, doesn't matter. The only thing I care about is being together."

"That's a great answer."

"It's true."

She clasped his face in her hands, incredibly, hopelessly mad about this man. "I love you, Khalid Fehr, sheikh of the Great Sarq Desert and prince of my heart."

His dark eyes glinted. "Say it again."

"Sheikh of the desert?"

"No, that's a given. The other one."

She touched her lips to his. "You mean, prince of my heart?"

"That's it."

"You are."

"I know." He flashed, grinning wickedly. "I just like hearing it."

* * * * *

The Sheikh's
Secretary
Mistress

LUCY
MONROE

Lucy Monroe started reading at age four. After she'd gone through the children's books at home, her mother caught her reading adult novels pilfered from the higher shelves on the book case…alas, it was nine years before she got her hands on a Mills & Boon® romance her older sister had brought home. She loves to create the strong alpha males and independent women that people Mills & Boon® books. When she's not immersed in a romance novel (whether reading or writing it) she enjoys travel with her family, having tea with the neighbours, gardening and visits from her numerous nieces and nephews. Lucy loves to hear from readers: e-mail Lucymonroe@Lucymonroe. com or visit www.LucyMonroe.com.

Don't miss Lucy Monroe's exciting new novel, *For Duty's Sake*, **out in June from Mills & Boon® Modern™.**

For my homegirls on my blog
(http: //lucymonroeblog.blogspot.com/)—I love
our discussions, your enthusiasm for romance
and my books, and just having the chance to chat
with you every day. Thank you for taking the
time to be a part of my life. You all rock!

PROLOGUE

"Please, Your Highness, let me alert the sheikh to your presence." Agitation laced Grace's usual even tones as the doors to Amir's inner sanctum opened.

But then his family tended to have that effect on people—though rarely his always efficient and coolly composed personal assistant. Five years of exposure had almost made her immune, but an unexpected visit from a family member they'd both thought in Zorha was enough to unnerve even her.

Amir stood up behind his sleek, glass-topped desk. "I see you are still harrowing the help," he said to the tall man who'd opened not one, but both of the double doors leading into Amir's office.

Grace made an offended sound at his use of the word *help* while his brother simply strode into Amir's office with a somber air that belied the possibility of a simple family visit.

"To what do I owe the honor of your arrival?" Amir asked.

He had a feeling he already knew the answer, but admitting knowledge was as good as admitting culpability and he was not willing to do that...yet. But he should never have gotten involved with Tisa. The sex kitten had a love affair with the paparazzi that few could rival. However, at the time, Amir had needed a diversion badly and he had seen Tisa as the answer. For a while it had even worked.

Zahir did not answer, but simply stared at Amir for several tense, silent seconds. Being the youngest of three brothers had taught Amir many things, one of which was when it was politic not to talk. Now happened to be one of those times. He would not make the mistake of breaking the silence first.

He traded oblique look for oblique look with the man that could have been his twin but for the seven years that separated their ages.

They shared the same dark hair worn neither too short nor too long. While Zahir's was styled in a way that reeked businessman, Amir wore his in an artful tousle. They also shared the same square jawline, angular cheekbones and aquiline nose. All three brothers were tall, but he topped their brother Khalil by an inch, and at six and a half feet tall, Zahir exceeded them both in height. Taking after their father, they all had whipcord-lean bodies. Amir's muscles bulged slightly more from his time in the gym while Zahir showed the development of a man who spent time several hours a week riding. They were both dressed expensively, but while Amir favored designers like Hugo Boss, his eldest brother wore cool Armani.

Their matching brown-eyed stares did not waver until Grace cleared her throat and their attention swung to Amir's willowy assistant.

Below her red hair that was pulled back into a severe bun, her perfectly formed nose was wrinkled with displeasure. Full pink lips adorned with nothing but clear balm tilted in a downward curve. Behind the narrow dark frames of her glasses, her hazel eyes shimmered with disapproval at the brothers' stare down.

"Is this a meeting you need me for?" she asked Amir pointedly.

Bless her. Unquestionably loyal, she was letting his brother know that while Zahir might be in line to their father's throne, it was Amir who called the shots here in his New York office. She was also subtly encouraging his brother to answer Amir's initial inquiry without him having to repeat it.

Zahir might ignore him, but he would not show bad manners by dismissing Grace's question with his silence.

Zahir stepped forward and dropped a tabloid on the desk. It was quickly followed by one after another, each folded open to the page of interest—if the story wasn't on the cover, which it was with most of them. Every headline screamed some lewd innuendo about *The Playboy Prince* and his latest conquest.

Amir grimaced.

Grace made another noise of disapproval. And Amir had no way of knowing whether that disapproval was directed at him or his brother for bringing the scandal sheets into his office. Grace didn't think much of the revolving door in his bedroom, and she'd let him know it on more than one occasion.

Zahir looked at Grace. "You have something you wish to say, Miss Brown?"

Grace might be shy in most circumstances outside her role as his personal assistant, but here, she was in her element. No doubt, he was her employer. However, there was also no question that she reigned supreme in his office. At least in her own mind. They'd had a few *discussions* about that fact as well over the years.

She gave them both a look of displeasure. "I don't know which one of you gets the wooden spoon for having the poorest taste—Amir for getting involved with a media hound or you for bringing that trash here into the office, Your Highness." She straightened her inexpensive and incredibly ordinary suit jacket. "Regardless, I can see this is *not* a meeting I need to be included in, so I will take my leave."

With that she left, closing the doors with a definitive double-snick behind her.

Zahir actually smiled. "I thought Mother was a tough audience."

"Grace keeps me in line," Amir said with some humor, while he willed his libido back into check.

These moments of attraction for his indispensable assistant were coming too frequently for his comfort. But the spark in her eyes when she chastised his brother and him had lit a fire somewhere else entirely in Amir.

Zahir shook his head. "I only wish that were true." And just like that, the air of gravity was back.

"Tisa was a mistake," Amir admitted.

"Yes."

Amir refused to allow his pride to elicit offense at his brother's honesty. Tisa *had* been a mistake. In more ways than one. "Are you here on your own, or did Father send you?"

"Father sent me."

A cold fist tightened around Amir's heart. Some might think that King Faruq sending his eldest son in his place was an indication that he did not place as high of an importance on the message as he would one he delivered personally. However, Amir knew that was not true. Sending Zahir said more than Amir wanted to hear about how disappointed in him his father truly was. It implied the king was so angry, he did not even want to see his youngest son.

"You know, I realize that Tisa courts the limelight a bit too much and maybe I showed up in more than one story with her, but damn it…I never moved in with one of my flings like Khalil did with his mistress. He lived with Jade for almost two years before he decided to marry her."

And in any other universe that would have made Jade untouchable in the marriage stakes for a man in his family, but she had friends in high places. Their uncle had taken an interest in Jade and Khalil's romance and seen to it that Jade had a place in the royal family of Zorha.

Zahir's frown said how little he appreciated the reminder that his sister-in-law had been his brother's live-in lover. "Misdirection will not undo the results of your actions."

"You can assure the king that his youngest son will be more circumspect in choosing companions in future." Amir's jaw tightened against words he wanted to add, but would regret saying later.

"Unfortunately, such an assurance will not be enough. Our father has grown weary of you dragging the family name through camel dung. It is time for you to tame your wild ways permanently."

Once again, Amir had to bite back words it would be impolite to speak. But his father's and brother's attitudes grated.

He was loyal to his family and to his people. He had put the needs of each ahead of his own on more occasions than he could count. He lived away from his desert home to oversee the royal family's business interests. His position left him little time to himself and if he chose to spend that time with beautiful women in uncomplicated liaisons, how did that make him a bad person?

"I don't date innocents or married women. My companions are aware of the transitory nature of our association before I ever take them on the first date."

"So is the rest of the world."

Amir winced, but he said, "So what?"

"Your lifestyle reflects negatively on our family and our people."

"There is nothing wrong with my lifestyle."

"Our father does not agree."

"What does he want me to do, remain celibate?"

"No."

"Then what?"

A brief flash of pity flared in his eldest brother's dark eyes. "The king has decreed that you shall be married."

The king? So this was coming as a royal command. Camel dung was right. "And has he chosen my future wife?" Amir asked in disbelief.

Zahir had the grace to look at least a little uncomfortable. "Yes."

"That's positively medieval."

Again that short flicker of pity, but then Zahir's expression hardened. "Are you refusing the king's command?"

Foreboding skated up Amir's spine. He knew that to deny his father would come with a very heavy cost, maybe even his position within their family. His father almost never pulled royal rank, so when he did so, his family knew he would not be moved. If Amir refused to marry the woman his father had chosen, he might as well start looking for a new job. One that didn't have "prince" in its title.

He had been raised to do his duty and could not imagine refusing his father, unless the dictate were so untenable he could not possibly live with it. This one was not.

"I will marry the princess.... I assume the woman he's chosen is a princess."

"Actually, yes." If Zahir was surprised by his youngest brother's acquiescence, he did not show it.

"Who is it?"

"Princess Lina bin Fahd al Marwan." Zahir dropped another sheet of paper on the desk.

This one was a single-page dossier on the princess, including a picture of the beautiful woman. Maybe it wouldn't be so bad. The last thing he wanted was to marry for love and, if he was honest, he would admit that the transitory nature of the women in his life was starting to get old.

He wouldn't have chosen to marry for some time yet on his own, but he wasn't completely against the idea.

Besides, he had his own reasons for wanting a more permanent distraction than Tisa and the others like her. "When's the wedding?" he asked.

CHAPTER ONE

"WHAT DID YOU SAY?" Grace felt like Amir had just punched her right in the solar plexus, but all he'd really done was ask her a question.

"I want you to find me a wife."

She closed her eyes and opened them again, but he was still there, her gorgeous, totally sexy, only-man-in-the-world-for-her boss. The expression of expectation on his too handsome face said he had actually made the request that she was desperately hoping had been a figment of her imagination.

Hadn't it been awful enough when he'd announced to her a mere six weeks ago that his father had decreed Amir was to marry some princess from a neighboring sheikhdom? Grace's heart had shriveled and come close to dying at how easily her usually independent and stubborn boss had so easily submitted to his father's demand.

Then a reprieve had come for Grace's bleeding emotions when Princess Lina had ended up eloping with an old flame and nullifying the contract the two powerful sheikhs had signed. That had happened almost two weeks ago and Grace was just overcoming the jagged edges of pain left by the king's edict and his youngest son's acceptance of it.

Now Amir wanted *her* to find him a wife? Just kill her now because life couldn't get much worse.

Okay, maybe it could, but even plain PAs had the right to their moments of drama.

"What? Why?" He was happy in his serial liaisons, or at least he'd always acted like he was.

Definitely, he'd never fallen in love with any of them. As far as she knew—and she knew him better than anyone else in his life, including his family—Amir had not been in love since he was eighteen years old. Not that he admitted *now* that it had been love *then*.

But she knew the signs of a true and abiding love. Didn't she live with them on a personal basis every day?

Amir had loved his Yasmine enough to ask her to marry him. They were only engaged for three months, the wedding less than a month away—which in Grace's mind showed just how much he had loved the other woman to press for such a speedy wedding—when Yasmine was killed in a freak accident. It was Grace's personal belief that the loss of his first love had impacted Amir more strongly than he ever wanted to admit to himself or his family.

But even so, this was unbelievable.

"My father wants me to settle down," Amir said with a shrug.

How could he be so blasé about this? Didn't he care that he was breaking her heart into tiny, bitty, never-to-be-put-together-again pieces? All right, so he didn't know, *but did that excuse him?* The jury was still out on that one, just like it was out on the issue of the pain he caused her regularly with his little liaisons.

"But he hasn't said anything about selecting another wife for you, has he?" she asked with desperate logic.

"No."

"So…"

"I see no reason to wait on him to do so. If you find me a wife, at least I'll have control over the final choice and will get married on my own terms, not his."

Grace had to stifle a groan and the urge to smack her own forehead. She should have expected this. Amir was far too princely to let another man choose his wife. Now that he'd been given a reprieve, rather than wait for his father to exert control again, he would preempt the king by acting on his own. She understood the reasoning, respected it even, but no way in the world was she going to help him.

That was simply asking too much.

"No."

His dark chocolate eyes widened almost comically. "What do you mean no?" His shock at her refusal was so blatant, she could feel it like a physical presence between them.

"I mean that if you want to find a wife," she said very slowly and very firmly, "you'll have to do it *on your own*."

The shock melted under his obvious discontent. "Don't be ridiculous. I can't make this kind of choice without your input."

Her body jerked as if the words were knives directed at her heart rather than the backhanded compliment Amir intended them to be. "I'm not being anything of the sort. I'm your personal assistant, not a matchmaker. Finding wives is not even remotely in my job description."

"That's exactly right. Your title is *personal* assistant, not *administrative* assistant, because you help me with more than just business."

"The selection of a wife is way too personal."

"No, it isn't. You've picked out gifts for my companions, how is this any different?"

"How can you ask me that?" She loved this man more than her own life, but sometimes he was so dense she was tempted to question the obscenely high IQ level he was purported to have.

Amir leaned his hip against her desk and crossed his arms, a sure sign he was settling in for the siege. "We're just arguing in circles here, Grace. I need your help."

"No. I won't do it." She would never survive it.

It hurt enough to love him like she did and know there was no chance between the two of them, but to be forced to find a woman to hold the place she wanted more than anything? That was too much. Much, much too much.

"Come on, Grace. Don't let me down now. I'll make it worth your while."

That was all she needed, the promise of a bonus for doing the one thing she never, ever, ever—not in a million years—wanted to do.

"No."

Before he could continue the argument, the phone rang and Grace leapt for it like a drowning victim going for a lifeline. When she managed to drag the call out past a minute, Amir's natural impatience got the better of him and he pushed away from her desk.

The look he gave her over his shoulder said he wasn't finished with their discussion.

Amir paced his office. What was the matter with Grace? She'd been acting strangely ever since his father had insisted he marry. At first he'd thought it was because she was worried she'd lose her job when he took a wife, but he'd assured her the opposite was true. He couldn't imagine trying to function without his insightful and efficient PA.

She'd continued to act oddly and had only settled down in the last couple of weeks—since the marriage plans with Princess Lina had fallen through.

Try as he might though, he didn't understand why Grace was balking at finding him a wife. She didn't approve of his lifestyle any more than his father did. She'd made that clear enough, though she'd never gone as far as the king and suggested Amir resort to marriage.

He would think she'd *want* input into choosing the woman that would play a key role in her life. As his PA, Grace would no doubt find herself conferring with the woman Amir married in order to arrange schedules and the like. In fact, he would expect her to help select his spouse's personal assistant so the two would work together seamlessly.

Grace had to know this wasn't something he wanted, or even felt qualified, to do alone. She understood what he needed, often before he did. She would be able to find the best candidates to fill the role to complement his life.

He wasn't looking for love, but he didn't want a wife who didn't fit in with the lifestyle he was most comfortable living. Grace understood the sheikh under the Western clothing. She understood how important his family and home were to him, even if he lived in Manhattan and reveled in his New York existence.

He thought of how she had looked when he first asked her. Stunned. Totally shocked, which actually surprised him. He would have thought she would have foreseen this move on his part. She was usually much better at anticipating his actions.

She knew he didn't want his father controlling his life, even if the older man was King of Zorha. If not now, then sometime in the future, his father would come back with another parentally approved bride. Amir's only choice was to get there first. And he would have sworn Grace would realize that.

He had half expected her to have a list of suitable candidates already compiled. This intransigent refusal to help was completely out of character for her. Not to mention unacceptable.

It didn't help that Grace was kind of cute when she was startled like that. It wasn't a look he saw often and, frankly, that was probably for the best. He couldn't afford to ruin the most important relationship with a female that he had in his life for sex.

His mother might be hurt to know he placed Grace above her—and everyone else—in importance, but there was no contest. His PA impacted his reality in both big and small ways on a daily basis. No one had more influence on his day-by-day existence than she did.

Unfortunately, she was not the type of woman he could have a fling with and then go back to his normal life. Or he would have scratched this particular itch a long time ago. And he wouldn't have ended up with Tisa, either, thus preventing the subsequent edict by his father. Regardless, he recognized that working together afterward would be impossible.

He refused to risk something as important as his relationship with his perfect-for-him personal assistant for something as ephemeral as sex.

The fact that his desire to experience that side of his dowdy assistant was getting stronger all the time only enhanced his certainty that finding a convenient wife was the best course of action for him. Which meant he had to convince Grace to help him.

They both needed the protection. Because he knew that Grace would be far too easy to persuade into his bed. She watched him with an innocent hunger that had caused him to hide more than one hard-on behind his desk. He'd long since stopped questioning why a woman so unaware of—and poor at—showcasing her feminine attributes would affect him this way. He simply accepted that he craved pulling her long, curly mop from its tight bun and running his fingers through the red silk.

He also wanted to expose and taste the expanse of her alluring skin…the light dusting of freckles looked like sweet spice on the untouched creaminess. Did those delectable little dots cover her whole body? Were her delicious-looking apple-shaped breasts adorned with the cinnamon-looking specks?

Damn it. He had to stop thinking like this or he was

going to have to start taking midafternoon showers…of the cold variety.

He must convince Grace to help him find a convenient wife…the only kind he wanted.

Memories of the one emotional entanglement of his life and its aftermath sent chills through his heart. No love. No intense emotional connections. He was never going there again. Not in his mind, not in his heart and definitely not in his life.

Grace settled into her seat beside Amir at Fenway Park. They'd flown to Boston on business and he had surprised her with front-row tickets to see her favorite baseball team. She loved the Boston Red Sox and any other time would be absolutely ecstatic over his generosity. Only she had a bad feeling they were by way of a bribe.

He hadn't said another word about her finding him a wife in almost a week, but she was too smart to think he'd forgotten about it. That wasn't Amir's way. She'd worked with him for five years and couldn't think of a single instance when he had ever given up something he wanted after only one argument. He was much too confident and strong-willed to be easily dissuaded from a path he'd chosen.

And he'd made it clear he wanted her on that path, choosing with him.

This wasn't right. Or even remotely fair. She should be enjoying the game. Instead, her mind was whirling with ways to convince Amir she meant business and fears that she wouldn't be able to hold the line against him.

It was hard saying no to the man you loved, even if he saw you as a piece of handy office furniture.

Amir looked sideways at her. "Everything all right?"

"Yes. I'm really happy to be here. Thank you."

The smile he flashed her was both sincere and incredibly sexy. "I am glad. And you are welcome. You deserve much more."

Okay, so not a piece of office furniture. Guilt suffused her. She sighed. She'd be willing to bet that if asked, Amir would not only describe her as a top-notch personal assistant, but he would also claim they were friends, too. And they were. The truth was, Sheikh Amir bin Faruq al Zorha was her best friend. She was pretty sure he considered her the same or close to it.

The problem for her was that she longed to be more than his friend and knew that could never happen. He was so far out of her league, she might as well be considered a player in peewees, while he was definitely a top player in the major leagues.

None of which was anything new to her, so why was she allowing the situation to ruin her current experience? The answer was, she wasn't going to. This was a wonderful treat for an obsessive baseball fan like her and she wasn't going to diminish it with depressing, but old and familiar thoughts.

Grace forced her attention back to the men on the field. And if her senses were more in tune with the man beside her, no one had to know.

Amir had been biding his time before approaching Grace again about the issue of finding him a wife.

Whatever had caused her to be less than receptive the first time around would no doubt get better with time.

This strategy had worked before. He would put an idea to Grace and give her time to think about it. If her first reaction was negative, more often than not she would talk herself into it more effectively than he could. *Usually.* He was hoping this was one of those times. But if it wasn't, he'd taken care to soften her up with a trip to Fenway Park and was in the process of buying her a team jersey after a rousing win by her favorite team.

She'd chosen one that was made for men and obviously at least a couple of sizes too big. When he'd pointed out one that would have been more formfitting, she'd shaken her head.

He couldn't complain about her propensity to wear either shapeless or oversized clothing—or both—because it was one of her habits that helped him control the frustrating desire that plagued him around her. Though even that habit was rather endearing.

He had never known a woman so clueless regarding her feminine appeal, or how to showcase it.

For this small mercy, he could only be grateful.

He waited until they were in the limo before broaching the subject on his mind and in the end, she made it easy for him.

She settled back against the leather seat facing him. "Okay, what gives? As if I didn't know."

He poured her a glass of lime Perrier and himself a finger of vodka. Too bad she did not drink. Enhancing her malleability right now could only improve his cause. "If you already know, there's no point in me saying it."

She took the sparkling water. "Thank you."

He inclined his head.

She took a sip, regarding him over the rim of her crystal tumbler.

"Thank you also for not denying that tonight has all been about buttering me up."

Now that stung. "Do you really think so?"

She just shrugged, her hair for once not pulled up in a tight bun, but barely confined in a wild ponytail that made her look younger than her twenty-five years. She was dressed in a Red Sox T-shirt he'd bought her the year before and a pair of jeans that made her legs look a mile long. Thank goodness they were in her typical baggy style.

He gave her a chiding look. "You're not being fair, Gracey. And that's not like you."

She pouted, her lip protruding adorably, and he had to slam down on the urge to kiss her.

"Oh, all right…it's not all about buttering me up. Even if you didn't have something you wanted, you probably would have arranged tickets for the game." She rolled her eyes. "And bought me the jersey, which I'm sleeping in for the foreseeable future…so, thank you."

The image of Grace in bed was not one he could afford, so he thrust it from his mind with ruthless precision.

"I might have gotten regular box seats." Though he wasn't stingy with her and she knew it.

Grace had few passions and baseball was one of them. He indulged her as much as possible. An excellent PA like her deserved a few perks.

"Maybe…but regardless, I know you aren't above

using my good mood and sense of gratitude toward you for your own ends right now."

"If I were above it as you say, I wouldn't be a very good negotiator, would I?"

"I suppose not." She bit her bottom lip and looked out the window for several seconds of silence.

"What is holding your interest? It is simply the clogged traffic we encounter after every one of these events I've taken you to."

She sighed and turned her attention back to him, her hazel eyes troubled. "You want me to find you a wife."

"Yes." He had her, he knew it. And no, he didn't feel the least guilty for getting her in a moment of weakness.

She glared at him. "You think you've won, but you haven't."

"I will."

Her frown grew more fierce, but she didn't deny it.

"If you really wanted my cooperation, you should have arranged for me to meet Big Papi." Her eyes glowed with something that disturbed him on many levels.

"I have no desire to introduce you to your hero. Sports stars like him could benefit from having a good personal assistant, too. I will not lose you so easily." He said the words as a joke, but felt them deeply.

"You think so? I'll have to keep that in mind."

"I am not amused." The idea of her leaving him to work for the Red Sox's lauded designated hitter filled him with annoyance, even though he knew it was in no way possible.

She laughed, but then sobered almost instantly.

"I'm not saying I'm going to do it, but if I did, what are you looking for in a wife?"

The question caught him unaware, though it shouldn't have. He opened his mouth and closed it again immediately. Nothing came instantly to his normally agile brain.

She stared at him, the knowledge in her eyes growing. "You've got no idea, do you?"

"That's why I asked you."

"But Amir, this is *your* wife we're talking about. I can't just make a list of candidates and ask you to choose."

"Why not?"

"Because you have to tell me what you want first!" For some reason, her agitation made him feel better.

"You know what I want." Probably better than he did.

"You were happy with your father's choice."

"All but the fact that it was his choice, that is true." Was that pain that chased so quickly across her features? She had no reason to be hurt. It must be the subdued lighting in the limo playing tricks on him. "I prefer to pick out my own wife," he said when she did not respond.

"Then why are you demanding I do it?"

"It's different, and you know it. Now stop being difficult."

"I'm not the difficult one. How can you possibly expect me to do what you ask without giving me some guidelines in which to work?"

"Fine. She needs to be physically attractive."

"Is that all?" Grace asked with a sarcasm few could match.

"No. She has to be cultured and diplomatic."

"I see." Her formerly animated attitude had become subdued.

Was his lack of helpfulness bothering her that much? "I want to marry a woman who will complement me and my position, both in the business world and within the political realm when I am operating within my role as sheikh-slash-prince."

"I got that."

"Oh."

She sighed.

"I'm not sure what you mean by attractive."

"Are you being deliberately obtuse?" He would not put it past her. His PA could be very stubborn and going passive-aggressive was not outside of her repertoire.

"You think so? You once said you did not see what made Jade so special for Khalil. Obviously, you two have differing tastes. Most people do."

"But you know the type of woman that attracts me. You've seen and spoken with—hell, you've shopped for—the women I've dated."

"But one must assume these women lack something, or you would have married one of them by now."

"I am ready to marry. Perhaps if I had been before, I would be married to one of my former companions."

"But you never loved any of them."

"I don't plan to love my wife, either. This is a marriage of convenience."

"So, then what difference does it make if your future wife is attractive, or not?"

"Now you are being naive. A beautiful wife can only benefit me."

"You mean like a trophy wife."

"I mean like a feminine companion that will add to my *éclat*, not detract from it."

"That is so shallow."

"It is realistic."

"Whatever."

He had disappointed her…again. She was very good at her job, but still very innocent to the ways of the world. He decided to explain in a way that might embarrass her, but would not offend her sense of fairness.

"I do not wish the need to remain faithful to become a purgatory for me, either."

"So, you plan to be?"

"Faithful? Yes, of course. The men in my family are not philanderers."

"Everything you have listed up to now is superficial…what about you and she having interests, likes and dislikes in common?"

"Not necessary. It's not even preferred. As long as we are compatible in bed, we can lead totally separate lives."

She looked at him as if she questioned his sanity, which was frankly a marginal improvement over her doubting his integrity.

"That's not the best environment to raise children in, or didn't you plan to be a father?"

"I do not have to be a besotted fool to be a good father."

"Your parents love each other."

"So?"

"Are you saying you don't want that for yourself and your family? Not even a little?"

Thoughts of the only time he had ever known anything close bombarded his brain, leading to memories of Yasmine.

During the time right after Yasmine died, his mind shied away from those images, and the pain and weakness they represented. "Not everyone craves that kind of relationship. I definitely do not."

Her frown was back full force. "With an attitude like that, it would serve you right if I did it."

"That's exactly what I'm hoping."

But she wasn't listening, or at least she wasn't looking at him. She was too busy glaring out the window again. What was her problem?

Was it possible his ultra-efficient secretary who dressed dowdily and never dated had a severely hidden but equally deep romantic streak? It would certainly explain her negative reaction to his proposed marriage of convenience...both the one his father had decreed and the one Amir himself was trying to facilitate with her help.

It would also explain why she never dated. Because no matter how dowdily she dressed, he knew other men had to have noticed the latent sensuality in his Grace. But apparently she was waiting for Mr. Right...the knight in shining armor to come along and sweep her off her feet. In a way, he was glad she had this hidden streak of romanticism. It kept her working by his side rather than off dating and/or married to another man.

"Will you just think about it, Grace?" He played the card she'd never been able to ignore in the past. "Please."

Her gaze slid to him, another expression he could not read settled in her hazel eyes. "Okay, I'll think about it."

Victory was his, if he just waited.

Something of his certainty must have shown on his face because she pursed her lips with affront. "Don't look so smug. I may yet say no."

It was so unlikely as to be an impossibility, but he was savvy enough to her ways not to say so.

CHAPTER TWO

GRACE CURLED UP on the sofa in the living area of the two-bedroom suite she and Amir shared, pretending to watch an old Hepburn-Tracy movie on low volume. But all she was really doing was thinking about Amir.

He'd once told her that if his family knew of their traveling arrangements, it would upset his mother. In the next breath, he had laughed as if the idea of anything inappropriate happening between them was too funny for words.

And wasn't it?

She'd asked him what constituted attractive to him and he had pointed her to his former playmates after agreeing he had been perfectly happy with his father's choice for his future wife. Every one of those women fell in the realm of near physical perfection. He dated models, but usually stuck to women within his social set, women who dressed like they should be on the cover of a fashion magazine even if they weren't. And Princess Lina. She was a pocket Venus if there ever was one. Grace's hands went to her own small breasts and she frowned.

If she had to be as tall as a lot of men, couldn't she

have gotten the voluptuous curves to go with her height? Instead she was stick-skinny with what could charitably be called understated curves. Hugging the throw pillow from the sofa, she frowned. Amir had said not one word about personality or compatibility, unless she wanted to count sex. Was he really that shallow?

She knew he wasn't. So why was he willing to settle for a marriage of convenience with a woman who had little more to offer than her beauty and ability to be charming in social situations? He deserved so much more. His passionate soul *needed* more, even if he refused to see it.

This had to be the result of losing Yasmine at such a young age. He'd once told her the grief had led him places he never wanted to go back to. The men of the Zorhan royal family hated any semblance of weakness. Perhaps Amir even more than the others, because he was the youngest and felt he had something to prove.

It must have been difficult growing up an alpha male with two brothers of equally dominant natures. She often saw him chafing against that reality even now. But to resort to this? It wasn't right.

The *second to the last* thing Grace ever wanted to see was Amir in love with another woman. The *last* was him married to a woman he could never love. As annoyed as his current attitude made her, she couldn't help wanting him to be happy.

He wasn't going to end up that way married to some empty-headed beauty, who shared nothing in common with him but her ability to traverse the two worlds he inhabited and her prowess in bed.

Grace hugged the pillow more tightly, feeling lonelier than she had since first meeting Amir. From the moment she'd walked into his office at the age of twenty to interview for the position of personal assistant, he had changed her world. He'd filled it with light, warmth and sound.

The social awkwardness that usually plagued her did not touch her when she was with him. It was as if, standing in his shadow in her role as PA, she was part of him. He had nothing to be shy and awkward about and therefore neither did she on his behalf. She had felt at home in his office from the very beginning.

She'd also loved him practically from the first, not that she'd realized it. Sure, it had started as a typical crush on the gorgeous, wealthy prince—and even when she'd had a crush on him, she'd been singularly naive to what that meant. But Amir had quickly shown her that he was more than a rich and pretty face.

He cared about his family. He cared about the people of Zorha. He cared about the people of his adopted home, giving more to charities than most businessmen ever dreamed of doing. He was also kind to children and old people. It was such a cliché, but true. Not to mention, he was patient and generous toward his nondescript PA. Not patient and generous enough to consider her for the position of his convenient wife though.

For a mad moment, right at first, she had let herself imagine it was possible.

After all, hadn't he made a point of saying he didn't expect or even want to love his future wife? Even the idea that his wife must be able to move in his different worlds had fit Grace. She might have spent her entire life until she came to work for him being socially backward and tongue-tied in any situation that included more than two people, but she'd found her niche with him and learned to function as his personal assistant no matter where they were or who they were with.

Couldn't she have done the same as his wife?

Oh, sure, she mocked herself. Grace Brown, future princess. She could just see it. Not.

Ignoring the hot wetness tracking down her cheeks, she replayed the moment in the limo when she'd realized she could never put herself forward as a candidate for him to consider. Right up to that second, she'd still been harboring secret, crazy fantasies. Only when he had said he wanted to be attracted to his bride—so his vows of faithfulness did not create a purgatory for him to live in—had she known. One thing Grace was absolutely certain of, Amir did not want her sexually.

It was as that reality came home to her that her ill-conceived dreams shattered around her, leaving her already battered heart hemorrhaging.

Now, she sat, unable to sleep, considering what the future held for her. Pain. Yes. She saw no way around it. The man she loved with every fiber of her being was going to marry another woman. If she loved him enough and was strong enough, she was going to help him find that woman.

Why?

Because it was the one chance she had to ensure as much of Amir's future personal happiness as she could. If she continued to refuse to help him, he would end up marrying some beautiful icicle and think that was exactly what he wanted because it did not put his heart at risk.

Grace was not a fool, at least not a complete one. She knew he was avoiding any chance of being weak like he had been when he was eighteen. He did not want to hurt and she understood that. What *he* didn't understand was that loneliness within his marriage would chip away at his warm heart until it was as cold as he thought he wanted it to be.

She could not stand the prospect of such a thing happening to him. The only way she could help him avoid it was to find him a convenient wife that had the potential to be so much more.

If her own heart lost the final fight in the process, she would survive…somehow.

Amir sat down to the breakfast Grace had ordered them. Dark circles painted the skin below her eyes and her skin was even more pale than normal.

He frowned, concern making his voice edgy. "You look tired. Didn't you sleep well last night? Are you coming down with something?"

"I'm not sick, but I didn't sleep much, either." She smiled, a muted facsimile of her usual expression.

"Because of what I asked you to do?"

"Yes."

"If it causes you such concern, I withdraw my request." He did not want her losing sleep over this project. She worked too hard as it was. She had no more of a life outside his business than he did.

"That won't be necessary."

"What do you mean?"

"I decided to take on the assignment."

"But if it makes you like this…" His words trailed off, but he swept his hand toward her, leaving no doubt what he was talking about. "You look terrible."

She grimaced. "Thank you so much, Amir."

"This is no time for false modesty. Are you sure you are not ill?"

"I am positive. I am also certain that I am willing to help you find a wife."

Something inside him jolted, but he ignored it. "That is a relief."

She smiled, this one more genuine. "I'm glad."

"Thank you, but I do not want you making yourself sick. Tell me if it is too much."

She laughed. "Right. Like you won't be demanding the list in twenty-four hours."

"I am not that impatient."

"Yes, you are." But humor, not irritation, laced her voice.

Gratitude for her surged through him and he found himself standing up and walking around the table to pull her into a rare hug.

At first, she stood in rigid shock in his embrace, but then she relaxed, clinging to him. Her warm feminine body pressed tightly to his and inescapable arousal surged through him.

He did not let go.

She did not step away.

His head tipped down of its own volition as he instinctively sought to take in more of her scent. "You smell like cinnamon," he said against her yet-to-be-put-up mass of red curls. "And jasmine." The fragrance reminded him of home.

"Your mother sends me handmade soaps and hair products from her herbalist." Grace's face was buried in his neck and her voice came out a husky whisper.

He lifted his head and then tilted her chin up with his finger until their eyes met. "My mother sends you things?"

"Yes. Since after our first trip to Zorha when I remarked that I loved the soaps and shampoos I found in the palace baths."

"She likes you." He wondered why he had never noticed that before. Perhaps because he assumed others would like her. There was nothing unlikable about Grace. She could be shy and stubborn even, but she was not annoying.

"I like her, too."

"It pleases me that you do." She worked too close with him for it to be comfortable for anyone involved if she did not. Why hadn't he let Grace go yet? This hug was becoming something more, something he could not afford for it to become. He willed himself to step back, but his arms remained stubbornly around her. Now that she was looking up at him, her lips were an enticing few inches from his. They parted, her delicious-looking pink tongue just barely visible.

Her breathing increased and if he looked down and drew her suit jacket away, he knew he would see hardened nipples. Her response to his presence was one reason it had become so difficult to fight his own desires. He didn't do it. He had that much sanity left.

She was strangely silent, very unlike his Grace.

Even in her sensible inch-and-a-half heels, she was taller than most of the women he dated. Tall enough to be just the right height for him to tilt his head slightly and be kissing her. The temptation was growing by the second and her hazel eyes going dark and unfocused with desire were not helping.

She wanted him, but it was the desire of the innocent. She did not know how it would end. She was not one of his women. Grace was a far more permanent fixture in his life and he intended to keep it that way.

But right now, the temptation to taste that innocence was overwhelming.

His PDA's alarm went off, reminding him of an upcoming meeting at the same time that Grace's started beeping from the other room.

The interruption of the discordant beeping was what he needed to find the wherewithal to let her go and step back. "Potential candidates should probably be taller than the princess. You fit well in my arms."

He couldn't believe he'd said anything so easily misconstrued, but Grace didn't look triumphant.

Rather, her expression became carefully neutral as she turned away. "I'll make a note of it."

As she left to retrieve her electronic diary and briefcase, Amir castigated himself for coming so close to disaster. What was he thinking? Why had he hugged her when he was on such a sexual edge? Others might look at his no-nonsense assistant and think she was anything but seductive. Amir knew better. He knew just how dangerous the sweet innocent was.

And for that reason alone, he deserved the painful erection in his trousers and the sexual frustration he would be feeling long after it subsided. He knew better than to do something so stupid as to hug her.

If he had kissed Grace, it would have led inevitably to bedding her.

And then losing her.

She was too valuable a PA and friend to do something that idiotic.

This whole marriage thing needed to happen quickly.

Grace tried not to stare at Amir as he spoke to the software developer about investing in the man's company. It was harder than it usually was. For one thing, she'd done her research. This was a good deal only a fool would pass up and her boss was anything but a fool. But for another, she kept getting sidetracked by the way his designer sport-coat fit his muscular body. Which, for whatever weird associative reason, kept taking her mind back to what had happened earlier in the hotel room.

The problem was, she still wasn't sure what *had* happened.

Had he almost kissed her? It had certainly seemed like it. He'd definitely held her longer than your average hug between employer and employee. Did other employers hug their personal assistants? Certainly, Amir did not do so often. The last time had been her birthday two years ago. Why had he hugged her? At first she'd thought he was saying thank-you for agreeing to help him, but did a thank-you hug last that long? Did the hug fall under their "friendship?"

And if so, why do it now? Why not before he'd asked her to find another woman for him to marry?

But what she really wanted to know, thought she might die if she didn't figure out was: *had he almost kissed her?*

Was the hardness against her stomach a figment of her imagination or irrefutable proof that as impossible as it might seem, *she turned him on?* Or was she sliding into mad dreams again that were going to leave her crushed in their wake as any other she had woven around her too captivating employer? He'd pushed her away with further requirements about his future wife. Perhaps he had only held Grace that long to test the theory that he would prefer a tall woman. Most of the women he dated were at least two inches shorter than Grace's five foot nine.

How incredibly demoralizing if that was indeed the case. Then, what could be more lowering than to be asked by the man you were crazy in love with to help him find his future bride?

"Grace?"

Her head snapped up at the impatient tone in Amir's voice. Both men were looking at her.

"Did you get that?"

Heat climbing into her cheeks, she had to admit she hadn't and asked the other man to repeat himself. That was so unlike her efficient self, she knew she'd hear about it later from the sheikh. Jerry, the software developer, was awfully nice about it, smiling at her and asking very politely if she'd gotten it all the second time around. She found herself relaxing under his kindness and responded a bit more warmly than was her usual wont. She had a feeling they were going to end up being friends. She was sure she would have lots of opportunities to interact with him as she would be the liaison to Amir.

"It's too bad you are headquartered here," she said without thought.

"Or that the sheikh's office *isn't* here," Jerry said without missing a beat.

"I do not see either as a tragedy." Amir's tone was frosty and Grace had to stifle a sigh.

She smiled apologetically at Jerry. "He's still angry I wasn't paying attention just now."

"*He* does not appreciate being spoken about as if *he* were not sitting right beside you."

"My apologies." Jerry looked worried, so Grace did not say what was on the tip of her tongue.

In fact, she didn't say anything.

A few minutes later, when Jerry and Amir were making plans to share dinner and a drink to celebrate the deal, he asked if Grace would be joining them. Before she could get a word in edgewise, Amir said she had things to work on and wouldn't be able to.

She couldn't believe his effrontery and was ready to blast him the minute they got to the privacy of their suite, but Jerry had already dealt with enough of her boss's crankiness.

As soon as the door shut, she whirled on him. "What exactly is so pressing that I'm supposed to be skipping dinner to work on it?"

He glared at her. "You have agreed to find me a wife. Have you forgotten already?"

"I'm not headed toward dementia yet, though goodness knows working with you will send me there early."

"What is that supposed to mean?"

"It means that I find it beyond rude that you turned down a dinner invitation on my behalf simply because you think I should spend my off-hours working on your pet project."

"You've never minded putting in overtime before."

"You've never dictated when it should happen, and for your information, I had no intention of starting the great wife hunt tonight."

"Are you saying you want to have dinner with Jerry?"

"I thought that was obvious."

"Maybe I should just stay here and let the two of you make a night out on the town of it."

Had he lost his mind? "What in the world are you talking about?"

"You and Jerry. You appear to have gotten quite chummy."

"You're basing this on the fact I wanted to eat dinner with you?"

"You were flirting with him."

"I *never* flirt." She had no idea how.

"You *smiled*."

"And that is a crime now? You were smiling, too."

"I most assuredly was *not* flirting."

She took a deep breath and tried another tack. "Name the last business dinner I did not accompany you to."

"Last month, when I had dinner with Sandor Christofides regarding using his ships for importation of certain goods to Zorha."

This was getting beyond ridiculous. "I was in Seattle setting up for your arrival at the business conference!"

"You made no stipulation of where you were at the time…you simply told me to name the last dinner you had missed. So I did. Now, I expect you to work on my project."

"I'll work on it when I decide to work on it, and that is not going to be tonight when I could be having a pleasant dinner with a business associate."

"He is *my* business associate."

"What is the matter with you? You've never acted this way about me sharing dinner with you and an associate before."

Wasn't it bad enough he was planning to marry another woman, was he trying to ease Grace out of other areas of his life as well?

"I did not like the way Jerry looked at you."

"*What?* Like he pitied me for having such a churlish boss?"

Amir drew himself up and positively glowered. "I am not churlish."

"Dismissing me from your dinner plans without a by-your-leave certainly doesn't constitute polite behavior."

"So, we are back to that."

"We never left it," she said with exasperation.

"We are leaving it now."

"And that leaves *me* where?"

He had enough sense to look chagrined. "Would you like me to call and cancel so you will not be forced to eat alone?"

She was not a charity case. She might have been shy

and backward when she first came to work for Amir, but she'd grown a lot in five years. "Of course not, then Jerry would consider you inconsistent and that is hardly the impression you want to give a business associate."

"So, you will stay here and work on my personal project."

"No. I will find my own dinner out there." She pointed out the window. "I will no doubt return far too late to work on anything. Now if you will excuse me, I need to change into something besides business attire."

It was her turn not to give him a chance to answer as she marched into her bedroom, making mental plans for the evening as she went.

Amir stood in dumb transfixion as he listened to the silence left behind after Grace's door slammed shut. "I would prefer a wife who does not slam doors," he said loudly into the empty room.

The sound of another door, this one Grace's bathroom, shutting with noisy force was his only answer.

Damn it. What had happened? One minute he had been closing a lucrative deal and the next he was verbally fencing with a termagant. Had she been serious about going out on her own? Perhaps not as active as New York, Boston nevertheless had a distinct nightlife. And Grace planned to participate in it?

Never!

It was time for a trip home where the only nightlife was listening to the nocturnal sounds in the desert. Yes, definitely…he and Grace needed to go to Zorha. He could meet with his father and brothers and discuss their new business ventures while she cajoled his mother into sending her more fragrant soaps.

What to do about tonight? Clearly he had two options. He could include her in the dinner with Jerry, who had spent the latter part of their meeting all but drooling over Amir's dowdy assistant. Had the man no taste...or was he more discerning than most? Amir feared the latter. He feared even more that Jerry saw Grace as an easy mark and that she would prove to be one. She was ripe to be plucked from the tree of her virginity.

His other option was to allow her to go out for an evening on her own. In her current frame of mind, she was likely to do something she would regret later. As her friend, he was conscience-bound not to allow that. At least if she came with him to dinner, he could keep an eye on her.

And if Jerry thought he would be taking Grace home for a nightcap, he had a rude awakening ahead of him.

CHAPTER THREE

GRACE ADJUSTED her seat belt and looked out the window of the private jet at the wet tarmac. It was raining. Nothing new about that in New York in the spring. At least that was one good thing about heading to the desert. No dreary, gray days ahead. But other than the improvement in weather, she did not understand *why* they were headed to Zorha.

"Tell me again why we are going home?"

Amir said nothing about her slip of the tongue, though technically, they were headed to *his* home, not hers. Grace's home was a four-bedroom farmhouse in upstate New York. She still marveled at the fact that the former farmgirl, who had taken a two-year course in office management at a college near the city, had ended up a prince's personal assistant.

"Amir?"

He turned to face her, his dark brown eyes reflecting a question. "Yes?"

"What are you thinking about so hard that you didn't hear me?"

"I am always like this before going home. I am thinking of all that I miss and all that I will be happy to see."

She smiled. "Is that why we're traveling to see your family two full months ahead of our scheduled trip? You're homesick?"

Something odd passed over his gorgeous face, but it was quickly gone. "It is part of it."

"What is the other part, if you don't mind telling me?"

"I do."

"What? You mind?" The knot that had formed in her stomach the day she'd learned his father wanted him to marry a princess got tighter. Just as she'd feared in Boston, Amir was pushing her out of his life in small, but significant ways. "I see. Well, never mind then. Um…I'll just work on my report for your father."

"Your report for my father?"

"Yes. He wanted more information on the shipping deal. I mentioned that to you….you said it was fine if I wrote the report. Have you changed your mind?"

"No, of course not. I had forgotten, that is all."

"That's not like you."

"I have had some things on my mind."

Probably more things he did not want to talk about, so she didn't make the mistake this time of asking.

"Perhaps we could go over the candidates you have found for my project."

It felt funny talking about his future wife as a project, but Amir had taken an extremely businesslike view of the whole thing since the beginning, and that attitude had not wavered a single iota.

"I am not finished and I don't want to discuss it until I am."

"You said you knew I would ask for the list in twenty-four hours. It has been almost a week."

"I didn't say I would have it ready." She wasn't avoiding giving it to him for personal reasons. She *wasn't*. It just had to be right and finding women she thought would suit him and were worthy of him was no easy task.

"Perhaps if you spent more time on it than showing Jerry around New York."

She hadn't been surprised when Amir had arranged for her to have dinner with the two men that night in Boston, but she had only agreed to go because Jerry was expecting her. She had still been very angry with her boss. She *had* been surprised when Jerry turned up in New York two days later.

He had an unexpected, but necessary, meeting with his graphic designer for the software packaging.

"You were with us most of the time."

"I did not have other things I needed to be doing."

"We *always* have stuff on our to-do list. The only way to manage it is to know when to take a break."

"So, you chose to take a break with Jerry."

"As did you."

Amir's mouth snapped shut on whatever he was going to say next.

"If you are that worried about the project, I'll work on it instead of the report for your father. I'm sure he'll understand and even applaud the decision."

"That will not be necessary and we will not be bringing this particular project up to him."

"Fine."

He scowled at her victorious grin. "You are ruthless."

"I learned from the best!"

Amir watched Grace doze in her seat. She had been yawning long before she finished the report for his father and closed her laptop. Learned from the best indeed. He could let his smile at her cleverness show now. Grace was one of the few people in his life who could win an argument with him.

She shifted her head and the pale bruising under her eyes became more noticeable.

She was not getting enough sleep lately. *Was* his personal project taking too much of her time? Perhaps he should ask his mother to help her, but wouldn't that be like inviting his father's advice as well? Amir wanted as much of this decision as possible to be under *his* strict control. However, if it meant Grace getting sick from lack of sleep, he would compromise.

Perhaps his mother would be willing to keep the project a secret until his choice had been made.

He was surprised Grace had not asked what things had been on his mind. It was very unlike him to have forgotten she was writing that report for his father. Possibly that was further evidence of her worn state. In a way, he was glad she had not asked though. He and Grace had spoken on most subjects in the past five years, but he wasn't willing to discuss his libido with her. Especially when it was causing him so much stress in relation to her. He needed a woman, that was all. However, between arranging the last-minute trip home and his usual business duties, he did not have time to find one.

Even a sure thing.

Besides, when he'd made noises about going clubbing on the only night they had free before flying out, Grace had made her displeasure known. She had the ridiculous opinion that since he had asked her to find him a convenient wife, he shouldn't be seen with other women right now. Her romanticism showing again.

He didn't agree, of course. However, it wasn't worth arguing about in light of her cooperation regarding the trip. His decision to go home had been precipitous and despite the fact he was her boss, she could have put up any number of roadblocks to prevent it. The most worrisome obstacle being a refusal to accompany him.

She'd never done so before, but she'd been edgy lately and he wasn't about to risk it. Besides, if he gave her a completely free night, chances were she would go out on her own. Or she would make plans to see Jerry, who had conveniently followed them up from Boston.

Knowing the man was in the city had been the final impetus Amir had needed to invite Grace out to dinner to discuss their upcoming trip, rather than going clubbing.

She was in a vulnerable place, even if she didn't realize it. She was twenty-five years old and if he didn't miss his guess—and he almost never did when it concerned his ever efficient PA—she was still completely innocent. She wouldn't realize Jerry was only looking for a night or two of entertainment before returning to Boston. She wasn't like the women Amir dated. Grace was too giving for her own good and was apt to get her heart broken, especially with that heretofore unknown streak of romanticism coloring her views.

It was Amir's job to protect her. After all, he was her boss. She was his responsibility.

She made an adorable snuffly sound and turned in her seat. Why hadn't he noticed before how cute his assistant was? He was surprised more men like Jerry hadn't come out of the woodwork in the past. Amir had known for a while he found her sexually stimulating, but she was sweet...and...and cuddly.

How very odd. Or perhaps not so odd. After all "cuddly" was not a prerequisite for an effective personal assistant. It therefore made sense he had not noticed this trait before.

The question was, why was he noticing it now?

It all went back to the fact he hadn't dated since the fiasco with Tisa. He'd broken up with her a week before his brother had come to see him, which made it eight weeks since he had sought female companionship. Crass as it sounded, even in his own brain, his libido attested to that fact.

And there was no relief in sight. The lack of night-life in Zorha would not only keep his PA on a short leash, but it would also him as well.

There was no way he would risk conducting a discreet affair under the extremely watchful eyes of his father and his brothers. He chafed at the restraints returning to his family would bring, yet anticipated seeing them at the same time.

It had always been thus.

Being the youngest in a family of throwback dominant males—or at least that was the terminology his mother and Grace had used on his last visit—grated against his need to control his own life and at least influence the lives of those around him. There was something to be said for the way some desert kings split their rule into sheikhdoms overseen by their offspring, who ultimately submitted only to the king himself.

He supposed being sent to live in New York had been his father's way of doing the same thing. His father had sent his other brother, Khalil, off to operate as a diplomat, living in Greece. And King Faruq trained Zahir to take his place when he was gone.

Without realizing he was doing it, the whole time he'd been thinking about his father and brothers, Amir's fingertips had rested on Grace's smooth cheek. He traced the faint line of freckles and then the curve of her jaw, all the while knowing he had to stop touching.

She sighed, a soft, extremely sexy sound. Then she whispered his name and he had to fight the urge to kiss her sleep-softened lips. What was she thinking about to say his name?

CHAPTER FOUR

HE WITHDREW HIS HAND slowly, not wanting to wake her and wishing the contact was not having such a direct impact on the rapidly swelling hardness in his trousers.

"Would you like anything to drink, sir?"

Amir looked up to find the politely inquiring face of the plane steward. "A glass of Absolut."

"Yes, Your Highness."

"Sir is fine."

The younger man actually blushed. "I'm sorry, Your Highness, I should not have been so lax."

Oh, dear, his father's butler had been training the staff again.

"It does not bother me."

"I would like to keep my job all the same, Your Highness."

Amir nodded. He understood. Like too many things in his life, this, too, was dictated by his born role. Was he happy or frustrated that he had not been born to rule? He had never been able to answer that question. The only conclusion he had come to that was even halfway satisfying, was that he did not begrudge his brother the position. Zahir would make a fine king one day.

The steward returned with a rock glass of Absolut and a tall glass of Perrier water. "She instructed I bring it if you asked for alcohol, Prince Amir," he said, indicating the sleeping Grace.

The little tyrant. But Amir did not instruct the steward to remove the water. Grace firmly believed that alcoholic consumption should always be followed by that of water or healthy juices. Who was he to argue the point? He had never had so much as a dry mouth, much less a hangover since she came to work for him.

Memories of both from the time after Yasmine died left a bitter taste in his mouth even the vodka could not dispel.

He would never risk losing himself so completely again. The partying and drinking hadn't lasted very long. Three to four months at the most, but he still remembered the morning he had woken on the stone balustrade of the balcony outside his bedroom. He had slept there—maybe passed out—for several hours.

His room was on the second floor of the palace, so it was not certain that if he had fallen, he would have died. But he definitely would have broken something, and for what? So he could join the woman he loved in the afterlife? He was not that melodramatic—or weak.

Love. It was not an emotion he needed. A convenient wife would in every way be better than risking such emotional weakness again.

Amir finished both the Absolut and the water before leaning his seat back and closing his eyes. The lights dimmed around him, proving that the steward was not only obedient to his training, but attentive.

Grace woke up to the sound of a steady *thump-thump-thump* and a warm, firm pillow under her cheek. The subtle scent of Amir's cologne mixed with his natural essence told her subconscious who she was snuggled up against before her waking mind caught up. The lights were still low and all of the window shades had been pulled down so the cabin was only lit with a very dim glow from emergency lights.

She allowed herself to revel in the sensation of being cuddled by her boss, knowing that soon enough she would have to pull away. She did not want him to wake with his arms around her. She had no doubts that she was leaning against him because *she* had moved in the night, not because he had pulled her into his embrace. She almost laughed at the ludicrousness of the thought.

But she held her humor in even as she managed to control her need to nuzzle his chest and take in more of his masculine aroma. She would probably never be this close again.

At least not unencumbered by his conscious perusal as she was now.

She remembered the first time she realized what the sensations she experienced around him meant. She'd never wanted a man before. She'd never dated. Not once. Not even a pity date with her cousin's boyfriend's best friend, or anything like that. So, when her heart rate had increased in Amir's presence, she'd first chalked it up to her usual nerves.

When her breathing had become more erratic, she'd wondered if she was developing asthma. When her womb clenched and that place between her thighs that had never been touched by anyone but a doctor's clinical hand pulsed with some nameless need, she'd thought she was having muscle spasms.

She'd been mortified when she took her symptoms to the doctor only to be told by the kindly, but elderly GP that she was in lust.

She hadn't believed him, thinking he just didn't have a believable diagnosis for the things she'd been experiencing. But then, the next day, Amir had touched her…something very innocent, but it had sent all of her senses careening at once. Nerve endings she'd had no idea even existed within her had started buzzing and she'd been forced to stifle the insane urge to touch him back. Not so innocently.

Feeling like an idiot, she'd tried to read *The Joy of Sex* to figure out what was happening to her, but the book was clearly targeted toward sexually active people and she wasn't one. When she'd gotten to the chapter on light bondage, she'd about had a heart attack and slammed it shut, hidden it deep in a cabinet and never taken it out again.

Then she'd heard something another woman said and thought she ought to try reading romances. They were much better because at least they explained the whole connection between her physical symptoms and the psychological ones she'd been having as well. In some ways, she wished she'd never picked up her first book though, because the novels also peeled away the barrier between what she was feeling and the name for it.

She was in love.

Hopelessly. Head over heels. Probably never to be repeated. Drowning in it. Love.

Amir moved in his sleep and, trying to stay boneless, Grace shifted with him. It felt so good, this closeness. She closed her eyes and memorized the sensation for the years of loneliness ahead. She knew they were coming…he was already pulling away. How long before she was no longer his friend, and maybe even no longer his PA?

Banishing the painful thoughts of her future, she breathed in the scent of her beloved, her brain imprinting the sensation of her head on his chest, her ear to his heart, her breasts pressed to his side. If only this moment could last forever.

He moved again, his hand grazing down her back and settling against her hip. It felt so good. So *right*. Didn't he know she belonged here, in his arms? But of course he didn't because it was only in her heart, her fantasies, that this was the way things were supposed to be. And if she didn't move soon, things could get very embarrassing for her.

Very carefully, she pulled back, returning to her seat completely. She leaned in the opposite direction, against the cold bulkhead…the loneliness that was her life and her life to come settling around her like a funeral shroud.

Amir woke, fully alert as always. Grace was still sleeping beside him, her head against the wall of the plane. It didn't look like a comfortable position so he gently adjusted her until she was leaning back in her seat, with one of the small pillows they'd been given earlier resting under her cheek.

He shook his head at the steward, who was asking with hand motions if Amir wanted the lights raised. They had forty-five minutes before they would land, so he saw no reason to waken Grace before absolutely necessary. She needed her rest.

Fifteen minutes later, he allowed the lights to be turned on and asked quietly that tea be prepared for Grace while coffee was prepared for him.

The smell of the fragrant brew made Grace's nose wrinkle…then her eyelids fluttered…then opened. She smiled, not quite awake, her hazel gaze filled with an emotion he did not recognize and had no desire to name. "Hello, Amir."

"Hello to you, too."

She sat up, seeming to wake up more completely as she did so, and the open warmth on her face faded as the pillow he had placed under her cheek fell away. "Did I sleep long?"

"Several hours actually, but I slept for part of them as well."

"I know."

"You must have woken during the night. You usually do on these flights."

"Yes." Then, unaccountably, she blushed.

He frowned. "Is something the matter?"

"Nothing that a cup of hot tea won't cure," she said with what looked like a forced smile.

"I have asked the steward to prepare it."

"Thank you."

"I must take care of you, you belong to me."

She laughed, though her eyes reflected a sadness he did not understand. "This is not the Dark Ages, Amir. A sheikh's employee is not his personal responsibility or property. I don't belong to you."

He did not agree, but forbore arguing. After all, her words were rational; his feelings were not, but as she said, he had centuries of attitude to overcome.

Grace followed Amir into the private dining room of the Royal Palace in Zorha. While the room was used for meals for the royal family and only their closest friends, it was far from modest. It might not be even a quarter the size of the corresponding formal room, but it was every bit as luxuriously appointed. The teak floors were done in an intricate design that created a natural placement for the large circular marble table in the center.

King Faruq said that when the family dined together, no issue needed to be made of whose place was at the head of the table.

His opinion was deceptively egalitarian, but Grace knew better. The fact was, the king expected his sons not to have to be reminded of his position as top dog because they were unshakably aware of it. Nevertheless, she'd always found the oldest member of the royal family surprisingly likable.

In some ways, he even reminded her of her own father, a man who ruled *his* family with the same sense of entitlement, if not royal right. Both men cared deeply for their families, too.

Her father had seen how unhappy Grace was in her life in the small town she'd been raised in. He'd pretty much forced her to go to the city to take the business course. She hadn't wanted to, her shyness rearing its ugly head again. But her dad had simply put his foot down and Grace was no more capable of defying him outright than any of her other siblings. She'd thanked him later, though.

More than once.

He'd simply said it was good to see her happy and being the woman he had always known she could be. Her mom was a lot more emotional about it. The first time they'd seen Grace after she started working for Amir, the older woman had cried. With happiness. She'd said that it was the only time in her life, she'd seen Grace confident in herself.

Grace didn't know why she'd been such a shy kid, or why even now when she went home, she tended to shrink back into her shell at first. It was only at first though, which showed she'd grown as much as her father had thought she would…and should. Whatever.

Maybe her introverted nature had been the result of standing out in ways that made her feel self-conscious rather than unique. She'd always been taller than the other kids, even the boys until her last couple of years in high school. And her bright red hair that curled too much to be tamed made her easy to pick out in a crowd, no matter how big it was. Maybe it was simply being the second to the youngest in a family of eight children.

She'd not been the baby and she'd never seen herself as anything special.

Her sisters and brothers were all talented in different ways, but until Grace met Amir she hadn't known she could be someone special, too. Coordinating both his business and a big chunk of the prince's personal life was nothing to be dismissed as trivial though. It was anything but. If Grace made a mistake, millions of dollars could be lost or a country's government offended. She didn't make mistakes though. And that felt good.

Grace's thoughts had taken her through entering the dining room and sitting beside Amir's mother.

Queen Adara smiled. "It is a pleasure to see you again, Grace."

"Thank you, Your Highness. It's good to be back in Zorha."

"I am glad you think so. Amir loves his home."

Grace allowed a servant to place a linen napkin in her lap. "It is too bad he cannot live here full-time."

Adara nodded. "But it is the way of things. My husband wisely realizes that his sons would not thrive as they must if all three spent their lives permanently in our homeland."

"And because Amir was born last rather than first, he must be exiled to another country for most of the time?" Grace wasn't sure where the question had come from.

She certainly had no desire to offend the queen. It was just that she knew Amir would rather live in the desert, among his people, than New York, no matter how much he enjoyed the busy pace of life there.

Far from looking offended, Queen Adara's expression was one of warm approval. "He is lucky to have an assistant so loyal to him."

"I'm the lucky one. I love my job." Although she hated her newest assignment.

"And you are good at it. Good for my son. This pleases me." The queen reached out and squeezed Grace's hand where it rested on the table.

Amir looked up from his discussion with his father, his brows drawn together in a questioning frown. "What are you two plotting?"

Assuming he was concerned she was telling his mother about his search for a wife, Grace was quick to put his worries to rest. "We were merely discussing how much you love being here."

"Grace is saddened by the fact you cannot live here full-time," the queen added.

Amir looked startled. "You should not be saddened by it. You know I do well in New York."

"Yes, of course, but you would prefer to live here."

"I could not handle my family's foreign business concerns so easily from here."

Grace did not agree, but she was unsure how to voice her argument in the current company.

Before she could find the right words, the king spoke.

"It is the way life must be," he said with a finality that spoke volumes about his youngest son's future.

And for no reason she could fathom, Grace felt pain on Amir's behalf. After all, he *was* happy in New York, but his birthright dictated so much about his life. It was no wonder he wanted some say over the woman he ended up married to. Yet, the truth was even that was being dictated by the life he had been born into. Despite her own father's authority within their family, none of her brothers could or would be forced to marry before they were ready. For that matter, neither would she nor her sisters.

But Amir knew he was living on borrowed time in terms of choosing his own wife. The knowledge that he was as trapped in his course as Grace felt by it sent a wave of desolation, followed by pain-filled compassion, over her. She would do everything she could to make sure his life was as happy as it could be within circumstances that could not be changed.

"This begs the question what you were worried Grace was telling me," Queen Adara said, proving she knew her youngest son only too well.

"Was the report Grace compiled for you on the shipping agreement sufficient, Father?" Amir simply shrugged and changed the subject. He might be a youngest son, but he was by no means an easily cowed man. Even when it came to his royal mother.

"Yes." The king gave Grace one of his rare smiles in approval. "You understand both our business and our country well, Miss Brown."

"I would think that after five years, you could call her Grace," Amir said, mocking humor lacing his voice. He definitely wasn't totally willing to have his life and responses dictated by his role in life.

Shocking Grace, his father inclined his head in acknowledgment. "Grace."

"Thank you, Your Majesty."

"You may call me King."

Grace almost laughed out loud, but managed to stifle the urge in time. She knew King Faruq was perfectly serious and that he believed he was bestowing a special privilege on her. Which he was. After all, the only people allowed to shorten the title were his close friends and advisors and even most of them called him My King.

"It would be an honor, King."

Grace was not surprised when the queen made no similar gesture. Early in their acquaintance, she had invited her son's assistant to use her first name when they were in private. Grace had always considered the older woman more a friend than simply the royal parent of her boss.

Grace spent that night poring over the information she had compiled on possible candidates for Amir's wife hunt. Her dedication to the project had been renewed, if without improvement to her enjoyment of it. And, in her mind, that would take a miracle of the parting-of-the-sea variety. Still, she was determined to use their time in Zorha to finish compiling the list so he could begin his campaign when they returned to New York.

She was listening to the ballads on her iPod and totally focused on the Internet research she was doing when a hand fell on her shoulder.

She jumped and screamed, falling off of her chair and yanking the bud speakers out of her ears.

She looked up from her perch on the floor, a sharp pain in her hip telling her tomorrow there would be a bruise. "Amir! What are you doing here?"

Her heart was still beating madly and identifying her surprise visitor had not improved the matter at all.

He dropped to squat beside her, his hands roving over her body, no doubt to check for damage. "Are you all right, Grace? I did not mean to scare you like that."

"I didn't hear you come in" was all she could get past a throat constricted with instantaneous desire. Having him so close was bad enough, but her body was interpreting his impersonal touches as something much more.

"That is obvious." His probing had reached the rapidly forming bruise.

She winced and let out a slight gasp of pain.

"You *are* hurt," he said accusingly.

"It's nothing major, just a bruise." She needed to move away from him, but her body had stopped listening to her mind's dictates—where he was concerned—a long time ago.

"Let me see."

Bare her lower body to him? She didn't think so. "No."

"This is no time for your stubbornness, Grace."

"I'm not taking off my clothes so you can inspect the damage and fulfill some centuries-old responsibility factor your family has toward employees."

"It is nothing I have not seen before. You can keep your panties on."

"You are not my doctor and he is the only one who sees me like that."

"I wondered," Amir said, apropos of nothing. Then he stood, lifting her to her feet as well. "If you insist on a doctor, then you shall see a doctor."

"You can't be serious! I fell off my chair, not a second-floor balcony. I'll be fine."

Something passed over his face at her mention of the

balcony, but was quickly gone. "Nevertheless, we shall have you tended to."

"No." She put her hands on her hips and gave him her fiercest *I mean business* frown. "Absolutely not."

Patently unaffected, he said, "Yes. I must insist."

"Are you planning to carry me resisting all the way, because that is the only way I'm going to see a doctor for something so minor."

Amir didn't say a word, he just lifted her in his arms and started toward the door.

She screeched and pounded on his shoulder. "All right, you win!"

"You will go to the doctor under your own power?"

"No. You can inspect the bruise for yourself."

"And if I think it needs a doctor's attention?"

"I will bean you," she said unrepentantly.

"Resorting to threats of violence is no way to win a negotiation."

CHAPTER FIVE

"I AM NOT THE BULLY HERE."

"I am no bully!" He looked so totally offended and *hurt* that she had to sigh.

"No, you're not a bully, but you are irritating."

"Thank you so much," he said sarcastically.

"You can put me down now."

He did so, her brain trying to convince her it was with reluctance.

She stepped away, needing physical distance, but it did not help. Her body positively hummed with sexual energy from their close contact.

"So, let me see."

Knowing it was a bad idea, she complied, slipping her sleep shirt up high enough to reveal the purpling bruise on her hip. He reached out and brushed it oh so lightly. She shuddered and had to bite back a moan of wholly inappropriate pleasure.

"Is it that sensitive?"

"I'm just not used to being touched there." The honesty might be awkward but it was better than having him decide she needed to see a doctor after all.

Now *that* would be mortifying.

"It does not look as if any serious damage was done."

She dropped her oversized Red Sox jersey back into place. "I told you."

His thumb brushed over the spot one more time before he pulled his hand away.

It was all she could do not to demand he put it back and touch her far more intimately.

Doing her best to collect herself, she turned to face him. "You never told me why you are here."

"I saw that your light was still on."

"So? You decided to drop in and visit? Even when I didn't answer the door?"

"It is past midnight, Grace. I was concerned you had fallen asleep with the light on. I did not wish it to disturb your rest."

"So, instead, you scared me into falling off my chair."

"That was unintentional."

"No doubt. Well, now that you've seen I *did not* fall asleep with the light on, you can continue on to whatever you were doing."

"Not just yet."

"Was there something you needed to discuss?"

"Why are you still up? You have not been getting enough sleep as it is."

"You know I never sleep well the first night after a transatlantic flight."

"That was only true when we used to make the flights during the day. Once I adjusted the schedule so we could fly at night and you could sleep on the plane, it improved. Or so you said." His expression said he now doubted the veracity of her claims.

"It did. Does. I got to working…I wasn't tired." But an inescapable yawn belied her words.

Amir frowned. "You most certainly are tired. Why are you up?"

"What about you?" Changing the subject had worked in the past, but not always. "What are *you* doing up and about that you saw my light?"

"I could not sleep. I decided to go for a walk."

Her gaze flicked to her open balcony doors, through which she could see a star-filled night. "It's beautiful out there. I don't blame you."

"Would you like to accompany me?"

She wanted to, more than almost anything. But she couldn't. "Actually, I'm working," she admitted.

"On what?"

She couldn't believe he didn't guess, that he was going to make her say it. "My new project."

Recognition dawned, quickly followed by a glare of disapproval. "I told you that if it was too much, you were not to do it."

Yeah, right. "It isn't too much."

"Then why are you working at midnight when you so clearly should be sleeping?"

"Because I *want* to." She couldn't say she was in the mood to do the project, because that would never be the case. But she did want to finish it successfully for him.

"This is not acceptable. You need your rest. You will shut down your computer. I insist."

"If I go to bed right now, I won't sleep. My mind is

filled with information it is sorting through." She knew he understood this.

It was a trait they shared and had often led to midnight snacks together and chats because of it. The fact that they were in the office together so late often enough to make a trip to the all-night diner nearby commonplace indicated that perhaps they were both a little too involved with their work. Only for her, it was also the desire to spend time with him, no matter what guise that time came under.

"Then you will come for a walk with me. No more working."

"You said you wanted the list today."

"Correction, I asked if you had finished it. I did not give you a deadline for completion."

"But we both know that I need to do so soon or there is a risk your father will step in again with another choice of his own."

"I will take that risk, but your health will not be compromised."

He reached toward her computer. "Is there anything you need to save?"

"No."

He nodded and then clicked on the standby key before pushing her laptop closed. "Let's go."

She looked down at her pajamas. "I need to put something on, or I will shock your guards."

"More like instigate their lust."

She laughed as she was sure his comment was meant as a joke. Though the tease hurt, she wouldn't let him see that. As she'd promised him, she was wearing her new Red Sox jersey as a nightgown. It reached her midthigh, and she sincerely doubted a glimpse at her pale, gangly legs below the hem would inspire so much as passing notice, much less lust. Certainly not in the men who guarded the palace night and day, on top of the ultra high-tech security system his father had installed three years ago. She wasn't exactly centerfold material and they were trained to keep their focus wholly on their work.

She grabbed a pair of leggings and took them into the bathroom to don them. She came out a minute later and grabbed a pair of socks from the dresser a servant had unpacked her clothing into earlier.

Amir made a choking noise. "You think that is an improvement?"

She looked up from pulling on her socks and met his dark gaze. "What is the matter? Do you think my clothes will offend?"

"I think that if you plan to leave this room, you will put something far less revealing on."

"I'm not going to get completely dressed in a business suit, hose and dress shoes, Amir."

"I do not expect you to."

"Then what is your problem?"

"Those pants might as well be painted on."

"They're leggings. I wear them to work out."

"You wear them in public back in New York?"

"If you mean, do I wear them at the gym? Then, yes. Why is this a problem for you?"

"Because they are too damn revealing."

"What difference does it make? All they reveal is how skinny my legs are."

He shook his head. "You are serious, aren't you?"

"Amir…this is getting tedious. Am I going on the walk with you, or not?"

He didn't answer. Instead, he went over to her dresser and started opening drawers. He made a noise of approval and pulled out a pair of loose, wide-legged sweatpants and a matching jacket. "These will do."

"You expect me to change?"

"Yes."

"You know I think you are being ridiculous about this, don't you?"

He simply held the clothes out to her. Considering how intransigent he had been about the doctor, she should not be surprised. Sometimes, Amir got in these stubborn moods and her only choice was to give in or table the discussion for a later time when hopefully, he would be more reasonable. Right now, it was give in, or not go.

As often happened, her need to be with him took precedence, besides maybe the leggings *would* be considered inappropriate attire for a prince's companion here in Zorha.

She rolled her eyes to show she still thought he was being silly and went to grab a T-shirt to go with the sweats. Her nightshirt would look totally dumb hanging so far below the jacket.

Once she was dressed in what Amir apparently considered appropriate attire, they left her room. He led her down to the first level and out through the door near the kitchens, which opened onto the desert surrounding the palace rather than the courtyard in the center of the compound.

Grace did not worry about getting lost. Amir knew the desert as well as she knew her own tiny apartment's layout back in New York. He led her in the direction of a nearby oasis. Or at least, she thought he did. She was going on memories from other walks and horseback rides with him on previous trips, all of which had occurred during the day.

Amir took a deep breath. "I love the smell of the desert."

All she could discern was the dry fragrance of sand. She was sure he was noticing a lot more.

"I'm sorry you miss this so much when you are in New York."

"So you said at dinner."

"You *were* listening."

"No, I asked my mother later for a more complete account of the conversation."

"Why? Didn't you trust me not to tell her about your wife hunt?" She'd thought that was his worry at dinner, but the fact he had not believed her subtle assurance to the contrary rankled. More than that, it hurt. She would trust *him* with her life.

But not knowledge of your love, a small voice said inside her brain and it sounded suspiciously like her father's tone when he chided her for her shyness.

It would only cause stress between us. He doesn't want my love, she argued back.

Are you sure about that? the voice asked.

Yes! She wished she wasn't.

"Of course," Amir said, interrupting her argument with herself. "Grace, you would never betray my confidence."

"I'm glad you realize that."

"I wanted to know what had prompted your comments."

"Did you figure it out?"

"Not really, no."

"You are my friend, Amir. I want you to be happy." For her, it was that simple. Even if she had not loved him.

"I *am* happy, Grace."

"You would be happier living here."

"No, I would not."

When she would have argued, he laid his hand on her shoulder to silence her and then left it there as they walked and he explained. "I do miss the desert when I am away from it. I miss my people, my family…all of it. But, Grace, when we are here, I also miss New York. I prefer the faster pace of life in the city on a regular basis, though I admit it is a relief to retreat here occasionally."

"You couldn't dally with your women here," she said in sudden, unpleasant understanding.

Amir laughed. "What an old-fashioned term."

"Perhaps I'm an old-fashioned girl."

"You are a treasure, dear friend."

Warmth spread through her, dispelling the coldness of her realization. "Thank you."

"According to you, I am no longer allowed to dally anyway."

She chuckled at that. "I am not your father, I cannot order you to comply with my wishes."

Amir stopped, the full moon lighting the night sky almost as bright as day and casting his face in its cool glow. "You have more daily influence on me than any other person, Grace."

"I wouldn't put it that way."

"Perhaps I should not, either," he said with an amused smile. "You will begin to think you can boss me around."

That made her laugh. "Don't worry, Amir...I will never make the mistake of believing *anyone* could boss you around."

"My father?"

"Even him. You acquiesce to his commands because you choose to do so. If he ever demanded something you could not accept, you are strong enough to walk away from your family rather than to comply."

"Like Princess Lina did."

"Do you think her family disowned her? They certainly haven't publicly and the press release about her wedding had a picture with her aunt and uncle with her and her new husband the day after they were married."

For a moment, Amir looked sad. "Her father is more dictatorial than my own. I think it is a distinct possibility."

Grace had met the princess's older brother at a function at the palace once, though not the younger sister. "I don't see her brother turning his back on her."

"Perhaps, but I guarantee my brothers would follow my father."

"I think you are wrong." The princes were fiercely loyal to one another. Even if Zahir had brought the news of their father's edict to Amir.

"It is a moot point as I have no intention of being placed in a position where I have to defy my king."

"I know. I don't know if I said, but I think you are

smart to preempt his next move as you are doing." No matter how much it hurt her.

"I take your good opinion for granted," he said rather arrogantly. "It is not as if you do not tell me when you think I am doing something stupid."

This was true. She smiled. "You're right."

He shook his head again, a pained expression on his face. "You have no idea what you are doing, do you?"

"I'm standing in the moonlight with my best friend."

"Am I your best friend, Grace?"

"How can you doubt it? I have almost no time for other friendships."

Now guilt painted his features. "Perhaps we should adjust your working hours when we return to New York."

She shrugged, though pain lanced through her again. Just like on the plane, she saw this as further proof that he was pulling away from her, from their friendship. He didn't *want* to be her best friend.

"Are we going to the oasis?" she asked.

Looking around them with longing in his dark eyes, he sighed. "Actually, I think we should get back to the palace and into our beds."

"I'm sorry."

"For what?"

"I know you planned a longer walk than this, but you are insisting on returning because you are taking care of me." And once again, she knew it would do no good to argue.

"We can both use some sleep."

But he still would not have returned so soon without her. And while that did make her feel genuinely bad, she also stored away the sensation of being cared for so kindly. If she was right and her future with him would be markedly different than her past, she would need as many warming memories as she could accumulate to take her through the colder times to come.

Amir walked into Grace's room without invitation for the second time in less than eight hours. Though he had knocked just as he had the night before. Just as then, there had been no answer. Last night she'd been listening to her music and had not heard him. He discovered that this morning, she was still sleeping. Deeply enough that she had not woken to his firm knock.

He stopped beside her bed and shook his head. She looked so peaceful, which only brought home how stressed she had been lately. She'd hidden it well, but even in her sleep on the plane she had not relaxed enough for him to see the difference. Being in Zorha was good for *her* as well.

It was almost seven and he was sure her alarm was set to go off then. He picked up the travel clock, incongruous to the décor that would have done an ancient harem proud. He didn't know what his mother had been thinking when she had assigned Grace to this bedroom. However, she was never given a different one, no matter when they came to visit or how many guests the palace was holding. He had never requested his mother change the arrangements because Grace had been overtly charmed by her accommodations and Amir liked to see his invaluable assistant happy.

Shrugging off his mother's idiosyncrasies and Grace's

unexpected reaction, he flicked through the options on the small digital clock until he had turned off the alarm.

He quietly put it back on the side table. Clearly, Grace needed more sleep. If she would not listen to him, he would take matters into his own hands. The very fact that she had not woken to his knock or his presence testified to that truth. The bruises of exhaustion under her eyes actually looked better than they had yesterday and he was determined they would disappear entirely. He walked across the room and pulled the heavy drapes over the exit to the balcony, shrouding the room in a false dusk.

A day of rest would not go amiss, either. With that thought in mind, he unplugged her laptop and carried it from the room, closing the door silently behind him.

He found his mother and asked her to convey his plans for the day to Grace when she woke. He also told the queen that he wanted his assistant to spend the day relaxing. His mother assured him she would see to it.

Feeling as if he had taken care of the things in his world that needed tending, he left the palace with his father and brother.

Grace slowly surfaced to consciousness, a sensation of well-being pervading her. She'd had the most luscious dream about Amir. They had been married and deliriously in love. They were on one of their frequent trips to Zorha along with their four children. A little boy, so very serious and very much like his father at the age of ten. An eight-year-old girl who shared her grandmother's royal bearing and propensity to involve herself in the affairs of others. A sturdy little blond boy who at five years old reminded Grace of her second oldest brother and a sweet little baby girl that had surprised both her parents with her advent into the world. A very good surprise though.

The dream had been so real that Grace smiled as she stretched between the silky smooth Egyptian cotton sheets. Refusing to open her eyes, she wallowed in the joy left over from her dream. Four children? A soft laugh erupted from her throat. She could so see Amir as a doting father of a gaggle of children.

The unbidden thought that no matter how real the dream seemed *she* would *not* be their mother shattered the happiness burbling through her and Grace's eyes snapped open. The first thing she noticed was that her drapes were drawn. She didn't remember closing them last night. The second thing was that it was almost eleven o'clock. Her alarm had not gone off to wake her. She knew she had set it. She always set it. Always. The next thing she noted was that her computer was not sitting on the antique baroque desk she liked to work on when she was here in Zorha.

She sat up, the covers falling away from her as she tried to make sense of the inconsistencies. She rubbed the sleep from her eyes, but the scene did not change.

How had she slept so late? Even without the alarm, it was not normal for her. Okay, so maybe she *did* need to catch up on her sleep like Amir kept saying, not that she'd admit it to him. The man was already so sure he was always right. Of course, he would know the truth since she had just woken up and the morning was practically over.

But even if he *had* been right, that didn't explain the closed drapes, her alarm that had not gone off, or the missing computer. She had a feeling she wouldn't figure those things out until she tracked down her boss, which meant she had to get up.

Thirty minutes later, freshly showered and dressed comfortably, if not stylishly—she didn't *do* stylish—she made her way to the first floor of the palace. She was directed by one of the guards to the queen's personal study. A regal voice bade her enter when she knocked.

The queen dismissed her own assistant when Grace came into the beautiful, feminine room that nevertheless was obviously a working office. "Good day, Grace. I trust you slept well."

"Better than I should have," Grace replied ruefully. "I slept through my alarm."

"I believe my son turned it off when he went to see you this morning."

"He came to see me?" Again?

The queen nodded. "To tell you that he would be spending the day with his father and Zahir."

"But he came into my room? Turned off my alarm?" She was going to have to talk to Amir about just barging in. She didn't make it a habit of dressing or changing in the en suite and while it probably wouldn't bother him to catch her half-naked, it would certainly upset her. "Why didn't he wake me?"

"I believe he thought you needed additional rest." The queen smiled. "He said something about confiscating your computer for the day as well."

"I've still got my handheld computer," Grace said defiantly. She had notes from her projects on it and Internet access. It wasn't as easy to use as her laptop, but it could be done. She did not like having her activities dictated to her. Especially when it was already so hard to make herself work on her current, most pressing project.

"I had hoped you would do me the favor of giving me your company this afternoon."

Grace's heart sank. She knew without doubt that Amir was behind the queen's invitation, but that didn't make it any easier to turn it down. In fact, she couldn't think of a single way to do so without offending the monarch. "Of course, Your Majesty."

The slight elevation of the other woman's pencil-thin brow said she noticed Grace's use of her formal title despite the fact there was no one else in the room with them. But she did not call her on it.

"What did you have in mind?" Grace asked.

"I would like to do some shopping."

Grace couldn't help it. She laughed out loud.

The queen gave her a quizzical look. "What is so amusing?"

"Your son."

That seemed to startle the other woman. "My son?"

"Yes. He thought he had me all sewn up."

"Sewn up? Like a garment?"

"Sort of. He thinks he has me outmaneuvered."

"But you do not agree?"

"We are going shopping?"

"Yes."

"Then no, I do not agree."

"Do you mind explaining?"

"I assume my boss asked you to make sure I did not work today, right?"

"That is correct."

"Has he ever been shopping with you, Adara?"

The older woman was smiling herself, now. "No. He has not had the pleasure."

"I haven't for at least a year, either, but I'm looking forward to it. Let me get my purse."

"You have no need."

"Of course I do." Though she knew it would take quick action and forethought on her part to pay for any of her own purchases.

Grace smiled all the way to her room anyway. If it had been Amir's intention to make sure she relaxed today by stealing her computer, he had miscalculated badly. Shopping with his mother might be fun, but it was nowhere near restful.

CHAPTER SIX

LATER THAT EVENING, Grace relaxed in a hot bath fragrant with a special oil Adara had insisted on gifting her. Soft flower petals floated on the surface of the steaming water and brushed against Grace's skin erotically. She was sure that had not been her royal friend's intent when she had sent, via a servant, a basket filled with the floral offering for Grace's upcoming bath. The other woman had simply wanted Grace to enjoy being spoiled by the decadence. Adara was extremely kind and always had been, treating Grace with gentle courtesy not usually extended to a personal assistant by someone in the queen's position.

Grace wasn't sure, but she thought the queen might have recognized Grace's love for her son early on. She never said anything, but she had looked at the younger woman with feminine sympathy more than once. Grace had to admit that though shopping with the queen might not be restful, it *was* relaxing. She'd managed to forget her special project entirely for big chunks of time.

"Do you ever answer your d—" Amir's voice cut off

abruptly as he stood in the entrance to her private en suite bathroom.

At six foot four inches, he filled the doorway with his body. Her mind screamed that she should have had that talk with Amir over the cell phone if necessary as she gasped and sat straight up. Frantically looking for something to cover herself, she saw that the bath sheet was out of reach and the washcloth would hardly be adequate. With no other option open to her, Grace curled her knees up, hiding her nudity behind her folded legs. *"What are you doing in here?"*

"I came to speak to you." Amir's words came out disjointed and he made no move to turn away.

"Now is not a good time." She vacillated between wanting to hyperventilate and wishing the situation was something different than what it was. And no amount of inner castigation could make that desire disappear.

Amir cleared his throat. "I see that."

He definitely saw *something*. His eyes devoured her, or at least that's what it felt like. He wasn't really doing it…not to her. She wasn't his type. Not drop-dead gorgeous. Not sexually sophisticated. Not anything he usually found attractive.

The thought made her angry. "You could have knocked."

"I did knock. You did not answer."

"I didn't hear you."

"So, I came inside."

"You shouldn't have."

"You should have closed this door," he countered, again making no move to leave.

Clearly, he was so unfazed by her nudity, he planned to have whatever discussion he originally planned on. She was not so sanguine.

"I am in the private bath attached to my own bedroom, I did not think it was necessary," she said angrily.

"Apparently, you were wrong."

"Apparently, *you* forgot your manners, or is it only me you don't deem worthy of them?"

"What? Grace, you don't mean that." He looked upset, darn it.

How could he be so dense? "You need to leave, Amir."

"Leave?"

"Leave." She let out a tight breath. "I'm naked, in case you haven't noticed."

"I noticed." His voice sent shivers through her.

"Good."

"I'm not sure it is."

Frustration bubbled up inside her. "Amir, you cannot just walk into my room."

"There was no problem last night, or this morning."

So *he* said. "I want my computer back and there is definitely a problem now."

She couldn't believe they were having this discussion. Why hadn't he left the moment he realized she was in the bath? Was it because *her* nudity was so unremarkable, it didn't matter to him? She'd always know he didn't want her the way a man wants a woman, but to have him dismiss her femininity entirely was beyond demoralizing.

"I will leave."

She rolled her eyes. Finally! When had her brilliant boss ever sounded so simpleminded?

But he still didn't move.

"Amir," she said impatiently. It would be one thing if all she felt was embarrassment, but it wasn't. Being naked in his presence brought out feelings she could not act on, but if he didn't leave she just might try. And that would be bad. Really, very, beyond normally, survivable boundaries, bad. "You need to go. *Now.*"

He seemed to shake himself. "Of course. I apologize for invading your bath."

If only he would invade her bath, and not merely her privacy.

When she said nothing in reply, he sighed deeply and then he spun on his heel, bumping into the doorway with totally unfamiliar clumsiness, and then disappearing into the room beyond.

Grace stared at the open doorway for several seconds, waiting to hear the sound of her door closing in the outer room, but the sound never came.

"Amir?" she called out. If he'd left her door open, she was going to kill him.

"I'm here, Grace." His voice sounded strained.

"I'm taking a bath. Whatever you need to discuss is going to have to wait," she said in case he had the insane idea she was going to get out of her well-earned bath and prance out there with nothing but an oversized towel wrapped around her body, only to reenact another version of the mortifying scene.

"I am aware you are taking a bath." He said something else, but she could not hear him.

"Then why are you still in my room?"

Again he muttered something that she could not make out.

She stretched her legs out in front of her, settling back into the water and trying to come to terms with the weirdness of the situation. She forced her body to relax in a further attempt to let go of the hurt lingering from his unwitting rejection.

Amir stood in Grace's bedroom, willing himself not to go back into the tiled bathroom. However, the image of Grace's pink-and-white body floating in a pool of petal-strewn water in the big Roman-style bath was burned into his brain and wreaking havoc with his logical mind.

The sound of her moving in the water nearly undid him.

Was she washing herself? Rubbing skin that looked softer than the flower petals floating around her with soap that would leave her smelling more alluring than any personal assistant ever should? Especially one as efficient and controlled and damn it...*innocent*...as Grace.

"Please stop doing that," he said in a voice that almost cracked. How he managed to control it, he did not know.

"Doing what?" she asked, sounding genuinely per-plexed.

She had no idea. Innocent. Too innocent for his thoughts or libido.

"Moving, making the water splash around you."

A slow beat of silence met his words and then she asked, "Did you get too much sun today?"

He wished he had that excuse. "No," he groaned.

"I think maybe you did." He could hear her standing up in the bath. "I think maybe you need to see a doctor."

She was going to get out of the bath to check on him. If she walked out wearing nothing but a bath sheet, he was going to lose what remained of his control. His body ached for just such an eventuality, but his mind refused to be so weak.

The sound of quickly moving footsteps and a slamming door was the only answer Grace got to her suggestion about the doctor. She frowned. Deciding this situation required further action, she grabbed a towel and wrapped it around her to patter—dripping—into her bedroom. She picked up the phone and called the extension for the king and queen's suite.

The phone was picked up by the king himself. "Amir?"

"It's Grace, Your Majesty."

"King."

"*King.*" Sheesh, right now, how she addressed him was *not* at the top of her priority list.

"I thought Amir was coming up to speak to you."

"He was here, acting strangely. Did he get too much sun today, sir?"

"Not that I'm aware of. We only spent a couple of hours riding, the rest was spent conducting business indoors."

"Perhaps the sun was especially hot?"

"I did not notice it."

"Hmm…maybe he just needs a good night's sleep."

"In what way was he acting strangely?" the king asked, sounding amused.

"He wasn't his usual brilliant self." Which was as far

as she was willing to go with the explanations. No way did King Faruq need to know his son had caught her naked in the bath.

"I see." But he did not sound like he did and she wasn't about to enlighten him.

"Thank you for your time, King."

"You are welcome. You are always free to call if you have a need."

There seemed to be a message there that Grace did not get, but she simply thanked him and hung up.

She walked slowly back to the bath, her thoughts centered with concern on Amir. What had caused him to behave so out of character? And why had he come to see her in the first place? Before he had started to pull away, she would have thought he had simply wanted to tell her about his day. For the past five years, when they were apart unexpectedly, when they reconnected, they shared each of their individual experiences.

She'd heard more about his women than she wanted, but she had still enjoyed the intimacy of it.

Yet, that was no doubt *not* what he had wanted tonight. Perhaps a business issue had come up he had wanted her input on or simply to appraise her of. Regardless, as she had told him, it would have to wait.

She climbed back into the hot water and shrugged away the worries. She could not do anything about his odd behavior, much less understand it. She might as well finish enjoying the luxury of a hopefully now *un-interrupted* bath.

Amir brought the *gumia* down in a sweeping arc, part of a thousand-year-old pattern the men in his family had learned generation after generation. The perfectly balanced, curved sword fit his hand as if it had been made for it. Which, in fact, it had.

However, as satisfying as the sword practice was in a general sense, it was not doing what he most needed at the moment—helping him to forget his reaction to Grace's naked body. It made no sense. He could accept that he was attracted to his assistant, after all sexual desire did not follow rhyme or reason. But he found it intolerable that he had been so paralyzed by the sight of her lying in the bath that he had been unable to leave the room immediately.

He had made a complete prat of himself and she had asked him if he'd gotten too much sun. He almost missed a step as he shook his head in amazement. Absolutely clueless to her own appeal.

"Would you like a practice partner?" Zahir's voice interrupted Amir's troubled musings.

He turned to face his brother, who—like him—was dressed in a pair of loose-fitting pants and nothing else. Obviously, he wanted to work out as well.

"Definitely."

Without any further discussion, Zahir brought his own sword up into the beginning stance. They sparred for thirty minutes, both of them working up a sweat as they fought for dominance. But though his brother topped him by an inch and seven years of life, Amir refused to yield the field. With silent understanding, they both dropped their *gumias* at the same time and bowed their heads to one another in acknowledgment of the other's prowess.

"Did you work out your demons?" Zahir asked.

"Why do you think I was doing that?"

"I recognize the expression in your eyes because I've seen it in my own."

Amir's own worries went to the back of his mind immediately. "Anything you wish to talk about?"

Zahir shook his head, but because Amir was looking he saw the flicker of unhappiness quickly hidden.

"Is everything all right between you and our father?" Amir probed.

His brother shrugged. "As all right as it can be between two headstrong men bent on getting their own way."

"Does he pull the sovereign card on you often?"

"No, he respects me too much for that, but…" Zahir let his words trail off with another shrug.

"I do not envy you."

Zahir dried his face, chest and arms with a small towel. "I know. You and Khalil are too smart for that kind of stuff."

"We love you," Amir said, wiping away his own sweat.

Zahir almost smiled. "I love you both as well."

"Even when you have to travel half a world away to give a message of disappointment from our father?"

A look of understanding flashed across Zahir's features. "Maybe especially then. I felt badly for you and I cannot say I regret that Princess Lina refused to submit to the contract between our fathers."

"Thank you." Maybe Grace had been right. Given the correct set of circumstances, his brothers might actually support him if he chose a path divergent from their father's wishes. Then again relief was not the same thing as righteous indignation on his behalf. "A man wants to choose his own wife."

"Yes."

"What about you? Any plans to set up a royal nursery?"

"I would need a wife first."

"And?"

"There is no one." But something about how he said it made Amir know there was a story here even if his brother was clearly not ready to share it.

"I want Grace." Amir could not believe he had said the words aloud.

But his brother did not look shocked. "Naturally, you have done nothing about it."

"She is in my employ."

"Under your protection." Grace might not understand that concept but his brother did.

"Exactly."

"Not marriage material?"

The question shocked Amir into stillness. "She is hardly a princess."

"And you are not heir to the throne—that does come with some benefits. The expectations concerning your spouse are one of them."

"I don't think our father has made it that far into the twenty-first century."

"Before Khalil married Jade, I would have said the same."

"Khalil loves Jade. He would have married her with or without our father's approval."

"And yet he humbled himself to get it."

"Love." Amir was fully aware he made the single word sound like a curse—because to him, it was.

"Inshallah."

As God wills it. "I suppose, but I do not want a wife that makes me that vulnerable."

"That is understandable." More than anyone, Zahir had seen what losing Yasmine had done to his youngest brother. "But it does not answer the question of Grace."

"I want her. I cannot have her. Something must be done."

"Not marriage?"

"Absolutely not."

"So, what will you do?"

"I have a plan."

"I hope it is a good one." This time the smile was complete. "You have not given me such a good workout in memory."

He hoped so, too. Because his over-the-top reaction to the relatively tame circumstance of seeing Grace naked was not acceptable. He could not make love to her. Even if he didn't feel what she called his "ancestor instincts" to protect one of his own, there was the certainty that an affair between them would result in the loss of his perfect PA.

But there was another reason, one he was only now coming to admit to himself. It was the reason marriage to Grace was not an option. He already…cared for her. Even in his own thoughts, he was reluctant to admit that. If he married her, the friendship and lust he felt toward her might become something more. It might well become the one thing he did not want.

Of all the women in the world, Grace was the one who could never be his convenient wife.

Despite having no more concrete answers to his Grace problem, Amir felt better returning to his room ten minutes later. Whoever said it was lonely at the top, knew what he was talking about.

Look at Zahir. Clearly something was bothering the heir to the throne of Zorha, but who did he have to discuss it with? Amir would have to look for an opportunity to talk with his brother again, to see if there was anything he could do for him.

Amir was glad he had his brothers and part of him wished he could see them more frequently. Another more logical part recognized that to do so would test the boundaries of all their patience and perhaps even their love. They were too alike.

Grace spent the next few days attending meetings with Amir and his family or Zorhan business associates. In between working with him, she continued pulling together his list of potential wife candidates and developing a plan of attack for securing his choice.

It went slower than she would have liked because the queen also demanded some of Grace's time each day. She certainly didn't begrudge that time. She understood how the queen missed the company of her own daughters. And Grace enjoyed the older woman's company very much, but she needed to finish the personal project for Amir.

However, the closer she got to completion, the more certain she became of a painful fact. She could not continue to work for him. The emotional distress caused by her unrequited love grew by the day now. It had to be the result of his plan to marry. Compiling the list of names *hurt*. It hurt way more than she had been prepared for and she hadn't thought it was going to be easy. But it was mental torture of the worst kind. First, creating a profile of the ideal candidate—defining the type of woman she thought the man she loved would be most happy with had shredded an already battered heart. Every requirement she listed that was something she did not possess—such as physical beauty, the right breeding and/or sophistication—made her feel badly about herself. Even worse were the traits she did share with her picture of the ideal woman for Amir. As that list grew, she couldn't help wishing *she* could be the candidate. But she lacked what he wanted physically, and without it, no amount of personality and inner depth could compensate.

Especially for Amir, who had said the only compatibility he was concerned about was what they shared in bed.

Then, looking for women who actually met her requirement caused Grace no end of pain. She envied them and that made her feel evil. She could not be so petty, but she was. It destroyed her to realize each of these women had a chance at the life she craved—to be Amir's wife. Each moment spent creating dossiers on likely candidates brought home what it was going to feel like when Amir was married to another woman as well.

It was going to be hell. And Grace had come to realize that it was not a punishment she was willing to accept, or *even capable of* withstanding. She had no choice but to leave Amir's employ and that knowledge was decimating what bit of her sense of well-being remained.

He wasn't even engaged yet and she was beyond miserable.

The last question remaining was whether she left once she'd given him the list, or if she waited around until he actually got married. Her heart demanded she stay as long as possible, but her brain refused to ignore the way he'd pulled away from their personal relationship lately. Without his friendship, working for him would be untenable. The very heart that grieved at thoughts of her leaving would be demolished if she stayed. Watching him choose and then woo his intended would be the kind of torture she would not wish on her worst enemy—if she had one.

That thought, she had come to acknowledge, answered the question of *when* it would be best to leave. As soon as possible. Didn't they say that a clean cut hurt less than a slow, jagged incision? She certainly hoped that was true, because she didn't know how much more pain she could handle.

Amir noticed that Grace was looking more and more drawn each day, and when his mother brought it up to him, he knew he had to do something about it. He did not want Grace coming down sick.

He would take her to visit Khalil and his new wife, Jade. Grace had said before that she enjoyed their company. They had bought a new house outside the city Amir had not yet seen. And he would welcome the opportunity to ask Khalil if he knew what was going on with

Zahir. There would be the added benefit of being near Athens, too. The city boasted a nightlife that could easily distract Grace from her current obsessive focus on work.

She'd always been dedicated, but the only time she wasn't on the phone, her PDA or the computer, was during mealtimes they shared with his parents or when his mother managed to pry Grace away. He knew she was working late into the night as well, though he had not made the mistake of going to her room again. But on his frequent nocturnal walks, he had noticed light beneath her door. Even if he had not noticed that, he would know she'd been staying up too late, though. Because she looked tired and was drinking entirely too much coffee.

A weekend in Athens was exactly what she needed. And he would make sure she left her work behind at the palace.

CHAPTER SEVEN

GRACE LOOKED OUT the window as Amir's family jet circled for landing at a small airport outside of Athens. No doubt Khalil would have sent a car to meet them, or the diplomat would be there himself. She'd made token protests about this trip to Amir, but her heart had not been in them. She liked the couple very much and now that she had decided to give her notice along with her report on potential wife candidates to Amir, she knew this would be her last chance to see them. Once she no longer worked for her sheikh, the lives of the Zorhan Royal Family would be off-limits to her.

Amir did his usual check of her seat belt as they came in for landing. Though technically it was the steward's job to make sure she was buckled in, she couldn't remember a single flight Amir had not seen to the matter himself. It was one of the many things she was going to miss terribly about him, but she was a grown woman. She didn't need a sheikh whose mental processes reflected those of his ancestors taking care of her like that. She didn't.

"It will be good to see Khalil again," Amir said.

"Yes. He and Jade are good people."

"Of course, they are my family."

She smiled at Amir's arrogance. "I'm sure your brother says the same about you."

"That I am good?" he asked.

"That you are good because you are related to him."

"That is not what I meant."

She laughed at his look of chagrin. "I know."

A satisfied expression came over his features. "I knew this trip was a good idea."

"It was. Thank you."

"Wait until you see what I have planned for tonight."

"Spoiling your PA or your brother and his wife?"

"You, Gracey…you have been working too hard." She loved it when he called her that, but it was really infrequent and occurred only when he was feeling more than usually protective of her or charitable toward her.

"You're a good boss, Amir."

"Naturally."

She was still laughing when the plane's landing gear made contact with the tarmac.

Khalil and Jade were both waiting in the courtesy room of the small airport that catered to the wealthy and famous. Khalil looked a lot like his brothers and Jade was as gorgeous as a model. Grace smiled at them both as the brothers embraced and kissed cheeks in greeting. Of course, Amir's greeting with Jade was less physical. Though she did insist on a hug, which made her husband frown, though he tried to hide it.

Jade laughed at his expression before turning to

Grace and hugging her warmly. "He's an unrecon-structed man for sure, but I love him."

Grace grinned. "It shows. And he's a lucky man."

"You're so nice, Grace. How have you handled working so closely with my reprobate brother for so many years?" Khalil asked.

"He may be autocratic on occasion and more than a little demanding with a tendency toward workaholism, but he's definitely not a reprobate."

Everyone laughed as Amir mock-glared at her. "Damned by faint praise, I believe."

"Everyone knows Grace thinks you've hung the moon," Khalil said with a one-armed hug for his younger brother.

In that moment, Grace wondered if Amir's entire family were aware of her love for him. She'd always thought it was just his mother, but the way both Khalil and Jade looked at her for the briefest moment said maybe they did, too. A month ago she would have been horribly upset that her secret was so exposed, but now it hardly mattered.

She'd always worried that Amir would discover her love for him and fire her because of it, but now that she was leaving anyway, it did not matter. That did not mean she wouldn't be embarrassed for him to learn of it, but she didn't think Khalil or Jade were the type of people to tell tales out of school.

She hoped so anyway. That was the secret she'd like intact until she told Amir goodbye.

The trip to the couple's new house took only thirty minutes from the airport. "We like to be close to the city for both our jobs, but it is nice to live outside the congestion of Athens, especially for starting a family," Jade said as they pulled into a circular drive.

The couple shared a secretive look.

Amir grinned at his brother. "You have something to share, Khalil?"

"Not before we tell Father and Mother."

But the words were confirmation enough and Grace gave Jade an impulsive hug. "Congratulations! You're going to make a wonderful mother."

Jade beamed. "Thank you."

"She does not even suffer from morning sickness," Khalil said as if he was personally responsible for that blessing.

"My mother didn't with me, either," Jade said.

"That's fabulous." Though Grace thought that she wouldn't care if she had to suffer the pregnancy malady if it meant she could carry Amir's baby.

"It really is. I wouldn't have cared, of course, but it's nice to feel so good."

Grace nodded while Amir pounded his brother's back in congratulations.

Amir sat with Khalil on the lower terrace overlooking his brother's beautifully landscaped gardens and swimming pool. "This is a good place to raise children."

"That is what Jade thought. So we bought it."

"You are besotted, Khalil."

"Absolutely. I cannot imagine living without her." The naked vulnerability in his brother's eyes brought back painful memories of a time when Amir had been so weakened.

He would never go there again. He could only hope for his older brother's sake that Khalil never experienced the cost such feelings could bring with them.

Grace was surprised to learn that Amir's plans for the evening did not include the newlyweds.

"You need to relax completely and as much as I love my family, spending time with them will keep you feeling as if you have to maintain a certain level of focus. I have seen it before."

"You do not think I feel the same need around you?"

"Grace, we have spent the better part of five years living practically in one another's pockets. Any worry you had about putting the right foot forward with me had to have disappeared a long time ago or you would be crazy by now."

It was true, but she was surprised he knew her so well. On the other hand, why should she be? He was right. They had spent more time together over the years than either of them had spent with anyone else. Even Amir with his women if you added them all together.

Had she made the mistake of thinking that because she had hidden her love from him, that she had hidden the rest of herself as well? If she had, she now knew better.

"Thank you. I adore your family, but this *is* nice," she said, indicating the small Mercedes coup that Amir had led her to earlier.

"It drives like a dream," he said, tongue firmly in cheek.

She laughed. "You know that the car is not what I was talking about."

"Oh, you mean this time just to ourselves? I agree. It

is one of the things I miss about New York when we are over here visiting my family and conducting business."

If he missed it so much, why had he been so adept at avoiding any time alone with her in Zorha?

She asked herself if it mattered and realized it did not. Tonight was hers. He was hers…or sort of anyway. He was her companion for the night and if her hungry heart wanted to pretend it was more for a few hours, who would it hurt? Certainly, *she* could not hurt any more than she already did.

At least, for tonight, she could lose the pain in the fantasy.

"So, where are we going?" she asked.

"You will see when we get there."

"You are such a control freak sometimes."

"Not merely a man who wishes to surprise his friend with something special?"

"Well, put that way…I'll sit back and patiently wait to arrive."

"Good woman."

When they arrived, Grace couldn't stop looking around her. As many times as they had visited Zorha, she had never watched traditional dancers. Here they were in Greece, but Amir had managed to find a Middle Eastern restaurant that provided entertainment with the multi-course meal.

She steeled herself to deal with watching Amir watch other women who were not only beautiful, but sensual, too. They performed dances that showcased not only their bodies but also the amazing amount of control they had over them. She prepared herself to see lust in Amir's expression and to have his attention on the dancers—not her—during dinner. It would not matter, she told herself. She was determined to enjoy the show as well, if for entirely different reasons.

However, the lust-filled looks never came. While Amir showed evident pleasure in her fascination with the dancers and their finely honed talents, he, himself, barely watched them. Most of his attention and all of his charm was directed at his companion…namely, her.

It was a heady feeling and she reveled in it, loving the sensation of being the focus of his concentration. They laughed at the mess they made eating with their fingers and if sometimes when they touched, her entire body jolted with the pleasure of it, she wasn't telling. The dinner was several courses and lasted late into the night with a plethora of entertainment, including men who swallowed their swords, as well as fire.

After Grace's fifth gasp, Amir laughed.

She flicked her attention from the dancer juggling fire wands. "What?"

"You are like a child at the bazaar for the first time."

"I've never seen any of this in person. I always thought they faked it somehow, but they don't, do they?"

"No."

"Isn't it amazing to you, even if you have seen it all before?"

"You make it new for me, thank you."

She felt the blush climbing her cheeks and could do nothing about it. She smiled and then looked back at the show, not sure what to say, but feeling warm and tingly all through her body.

He muttered something, but when she looked at him as if to ask what, he shook his head and took a bite of food.

They returned to Khalil and Jade's home extremely late and Grace was careful to be quiet so she would not wake them. Amir was the same, so the end to her perfect evening was a quickly whispered good-night and thanks in the hall outside their bedroom doors.

The next day, they had a leisurely breakfast with Amir's family before Khalil had to leave for a meeting. Jade stayed home to work out of the home office her husband had installed for her volunteer position with a nonprofit children's agency.

"I'll cut my hours to less than a dozen a week after the baby is born, but until then, I'll be very busy training my replacement," she said with apology for leaving Amir and Grace to their own devices for a few hours.

"Do not worry about it, Jade. I plan to take Grace sightseeing today."

Grace smiled, remembering the other times Amir had either given in to her urging to explore a new locale or had come up with the idea himself when their travels took them someplace that held interest. "Where are we going?"

"What did I tell you last night?"

"That you are an acknowledged control freak?" she teased.

He shook his head, his expression of false exasperation not quite hiding his amusement.

Jade laughed as well and went off to her office shaking her head.

They spent the day visiting tourist spots he had always resisted going to before and she felt very spoiled for a mere personal assistant. She had told Amir he was her best friend, but she knew better than to think the moniker went both ways. However, he was treating her with special consideration that if he but knew was making her final days in his employ more special than she could have conceived of. She stored up the memory of her pleasure in his company along with the others she planned to pull out in the years ahead when the only piece of him she would be able to get was what she would be able to find in the media.

They had dinner with Khalil and Jade, and Grace could not help watching the way Amir's older brother treated the woman he loved. It was incredibly sweet. He was so obviously in love, but then that emotion was patently mutual. He watched over her so carefully and even when they argued, the underlying joy they had in one another's company was always there.

It was beautiful.

And if Grace needed any more evidence that Amir had no inkling of the same feeling for her, it was there. Khalil's attention was always on Jade. Even when he was speaking to someone else, part of him was tuned in to Jade and what she was experiencing. He often called her beautiful and complimented so many things about his wife.

They did not agree on everything, not even when it came to ordering their dinner, as, apparently, Jade preferred a spicier fare than Khalil considered good for her. They compromised on something Grace got the distinct impression had been Jade's first choice to begin with. She was sure of it when the other woman winked at her while her husband was engaged with the waiter.

They all chatted and laughed over dinner until the subject of Amir's almost wedding came up.

"I was surprised the princess eloped with another man, but I was not disappointed," Khalil said.

"Why is that?" Amir asked.

"A man wants to choose his own wife."

"A woman he can love," Jade added.

Amir shook his head. "Had Father not chosen her, I would have been most content to marry the princess. I am not looking for love."

"Why not?" Jade asked in shock. "This isn't the Middle Ages, you don't have to settle for a marriage of convenience simply because you are a royal sheikh."

"Love comes with a cost I have no desire to pay."

"Yasmine's death was an unfortunate accident, my brother, but you cannot believe that any woman you chose to give your heart to would suffer a similar fate."

"There is no chance of that happening because I will not give my heart away."

Jade cast a sidelong glance of sympathy at Grace. "That's no way to live, Amir…afraid of love."

"I fear nothing. I simply refuse to travel down a path I know is rife with pitfalls."

"Well, you have time enough to change your mind now that Father's plan was subverted by the princess's flit."

Amir said nothing, but Grace knew the truth. Her boss wasn't going to wait for his father to act again and it was up to her to protect him from himself. No matter how much it hurt. And she'd done it. The list was finished, along with the plan of action for the courtship.

Amir would be impressed. Heck, Grace was impressed with herself. She almost regretted that she would not be around to see the plan put into action. Almost. It was time for the torture of her heart to stop and she was the only one who could end it.

They spent one more night in Greece and then flew back to Zorha early Monday morning. Amir and Grace had a meeting with an investment group. He had decided to give their quarterly report in person since they were available to do so. His father planned to attend the meeting as well and Grace knew that pleased Amir. He was in a good mood and she had decided to wait until after the meeting to give him her own report…and the other typed message she had printed off that morning.

Perhaps that made her a coward, but why put him in a cranky frame of mind before he had to lead an important meeting? There was plenty of time to inform him of her decision. The time after she'd done so stretched out in an unending ribbon of loneliness in her mind.

Amir waited for Grace in the office he used when he was staying in his family's home. She had said she wanted to discuss something with him. He thought she might have finished the convenient marriage proposal. There was a familiar settled air about her that she got when she was done with a difficult or involved project.

He understood her desire to present it to him now,

rather than waiting until they returned to New York. What he did not understand was his own reticence to her doing so. He'd meant what he said to his brother and Jade in Greece. Amir had no interest in falling in love and becoming vulnerable to the pain he had barely survived when he was eighteen.

Admitting how close he had come to losing everything, even to himself, was unsettling. It was difficult enough to realize that he had a measure of vulnerability when it came to his family and even Grace, but never again would he be so wrapped up in another person that losing her made him feel as if his own life were over. Khalil didn't even bother to pretend he didn't feel that way, and while part of Amir admired his brother's courage, another part pitied him his naive belief that the joy now was worth the pain later.

Grace walked into the office with only a single light tap on the door to announce her presence.

He turned away from the e-mail that had not been holding his thoughts anyway.

She looked so serious, her hazel eyes behind her glasses reflecting a level of concentration that told him his earlier supposition had been correct. And suddenly he knew that regardless of logic he did not want to deal with this right now. When they returned to New York would be soon enough.

She went to lay a plain tan binder on his desk and he had to control the urge to tell her not to.

His gaze flicked down to the modest binder and then back up to her. "The project you took on before we left New York, I presume."

"Yes. I think you will be satisfied with the results."

"I'm sure I will. Your work is always exemplary."

"Thank you."

What was that tone in her voice? An emotion he could not quite identify.

"I will look it over. We can discuss it after returning to New York."

"You do not wish for me to present it to you now?"

"No." The single word came out more vehemently than he had intended.

Her eyes widened in surprise. "Okay."

"I want to have a chance to digest the information before we talk about it."

"No problem." But she didn't look any less single-minded.

"Was there something else you wished to discuss with me?"

"Yes."

When she made no move to hand him anything else and remained oddly silent, he prompted, "What?"

She opened her mouth and only a dry croak came out.

"Are you all right?"

She nodded, cleared her throat then said, "I wanted to give you this."

Were his eyes playing tricks on him, or was her hand trembling as she dropped the single sheet of paper on the desk in front of him? Wondering what could possibly cause such a reaction in her, he picked it up. As he read it, he went first hot then cold as fury unlike anything he had ever experienced with her welled up inside him.

He surged up from his chair and tossed the paper down on the desk. "What is the meaning of this?"

"It is my letter of resignation."

"I damn well know what it is…." He slipped into Arabic curses that would have made his father blush and his mother faint. "What I want to know is what the hell it means?" he finally managed to say in English, his accent thicker than it had ever been since his tutors had begun his language studies.

Not for a millisecond did he think the letter anything but genuine. Though he wished it was a practical joke. One in very bad taste, but he knew he was not so lucky. He knew from her reaction that she intended to leave him, what he wanted to know now was *why*. It had to be something he could fix. The alternative was completely unacceptable.

"It means that I will be leaving your employment a month from today." Her tone was neutral, but the way she held her body said the control over it had been hard fought.

"Why?" he asked in a voice as close to a growl as a human male could get.

CHAPTER EIGHT

SHE BIT HER LIP, her facade cracking slightly, but she said nothing.

His fury ratcheted up another notch. Miss Efficient, the PA that always had a reason for everything, had nothing to say about leaving his employ…about leaving him? He did not damn well think so. "Is it because you got a better offer? From who? Is it Jerry? Trust me, if that is the case, he will regret attempting to take what is mine."

"I don't belong to you, Amir. I'm a personal assistant, not a slave."

Like hell she did not belong to him. "You are not leaving me."

"I am."

"I'll ruin him."

From the flare of her eyes, he knew she understood he meant what he said. "I'm not taking a job with Jerry."

Amir gave her a disdainful look.

"I'm not," she insisted.

"Then why?" He gave her no chance to go on before demanding, "Tell me it is not about money. You know I will pay you more." He would pay her pretty much anything. "If you are feeling too hemmed in in that small apartment we will find you a larger one and the company will pay for it."

"It's not about money or apartments." Her expression was pained.

What did she have to be pained about? She was the one threatening to leave him. "Then. Tell. Me. Why."

"Personal reasons."

"Personal reasons?" he asked in disbelief. Not that she had them, but that she thought she could fob him off with something so vague. "What are these *personal reasons?*"

"By definition, they are personal. That makes them not your business." The words were defiant but her tone was ragged with hurt. What was going on?

"In the past, you did not make such distinctions."

"That was in the past. This is now."

"And what has changed?"

She opened and closed her mouth without speaking, then sighed and clenched her hands at her sides. "*Me.* I'm what has changed, Amir."

"You are not so faithless."

"This isn't about loyalty. I'm not going to a competitor. I doubt I will even stay in New York. I just have to move on with my life."

"Why? Your life as my personal assistant is not a bad one."

"No, but it does not allow me to have any other life, either."

"You have never complained before."

"I'm not complaining now."

"But you *are* leaving."

"Yes."

"So, we change your hours. You get more of what you consider a life."

"It won't work, as long as I work for you, it won't work." The words sounded like they carried heavier meaning, but for the life of him he could not figure out what it was.

He was still supremely angry, but hurt was crowding in, too. "You said I was your best friend."

"But I'm not yours."

"You are leaving because you do not think you are my best friend?" he asked with disbelief.

"Because I *know* I'm not."

"On what do you draw this conclusion?"

"On the fact that you do have a life outside your job. You have a family you see much more often than I see my own. Your siblings are your friends. You have your women and soon you will have a wife."

"And you only have me, is that what this pity party is all about?"

Anger flashed in Grace's eyes. "It's not a pity party. I'm simply trying to explain my decision to you."

"But you are leaving because I have more friends than you do," he said derisively.

"I'm leaving because I need to in order to move forward in *my* life. It's as simple as that."

"There is nothing simple about you abandoning me."

"It's not abandonment."

"You are my best friend," he admitted through gritted teeth. He hated this touchy-feely stuff, but for Grace he could make an exception.

"No, I am not."

"Damn it—"

"No, you listen. Since we came to Zorha, even before really, you've been pushing me away, pushing me into a box that is labeled *personal assistant* and nothing else. I understand it," she said, though clearly it bothered her. "You are getting married, it would not be comfortable for you to continue our friendship under those circumstances."

"That has nothing to do with it!"

"Please, you've never lied to me before, don't start now."

"How do you know I have never lied?" he demanded, his wrath at her wrong assumptions adding to the miasma of feelings inside him. "I lied every damn day when I pretended I wanted nothing more than a friendly business relationship with you, when what I wanted was to lay you across my desk and taste every centimeter of your pale skin. This is why I have pushed you away as you say. I could not risk being alone with you." And if she thought he found that easy to admit, she did not know him as well as he thought she did.

"What?" She shook her head, as if she could not translate what she had heard. "You don't mean that," she said faintly.

"I most assuredly do."

"You can't."

"And why do you believe this?"

"I'm not beautiful. I'm not sophisticated. I'm nothing like the women you usually go for."

"And yet you are the one I crave."

"No."

"Why do you attempt to deny it? You want me also."

"What? Why...I don't understand."

"What is there to understand? This desire." He stood up so she could not miss the physical evidence of his desire. "It is mutual."

She stared at him, her gaze not leaving his face. He shook his head.

"So damn innocent."

"What?"

"You."

"I'm innocent?"

"You wish to deny it?"

"Uh...no."

"It excites me, your innocence."

"But I thought you liked experienced women."

He was around his desk in a heartbeat and pulling her body into his a second heartbeat later. "I like you, Grace."

She stared up at him as if he were some alien come to earth to devour her, though she did not seem overly upset by the prospect. "You want me?" she asked with incredulity.

"I want you." Then he kissed her.

Despite his anger, regardless of the lust finally getting release, he could be nothing but gentle. It was, after all, their first kiss. And perhaps for his deceptively plain assistant, the first one she had ever had. She tasted sweet, like ripe berries, and her lips were so soft. Perfectly formed to give his mouth pleasure. She did not return the caress, but neither did she attempt to push him away.

He lifted his mouth from hers. "Kiss me back."

She looked at him with shock-glazed eyes. "I don't know how."

"Move your lips with mine, open them so I can taste you."

"Yes." The word came out sounding like a moan and he renewed the buss of his lips against hers with added passion.

She did as instructed and he was careful not to overwhelm, but to slowly lead her from innocent exploration to carnal bliss. His hands roamed up and down her back as he pressed his hardness against her, for the first time not worried that she could feel it. He wanted her to know how much she turned him on.

She made a sweet little mewling sound, her fingers kneading his chest.

His cousin Hakim sometimes called Catherine his kitten, and for the first time Amir understood such an endearment.

He tasted her mouth's interior, and the candied berries-and-cream flavor of her lips was even more luscious inside her mouth. It was a confection he could easily become addicted to.

The kiss grew in intensity and his virginal PA was learning quickly how to drive him wild. It took all of his self-control not to do what he had told her he wanted to—to strip her, lay her across his desk and use his mouth all over her.

One day, he vowed, he would do exactly that.

Suddenly, she shoved herself from his arms. "No, wait…why are you doing this?"

"What do you mean, why? I want you. I said it." Was

this one of those women things that men had no hope of understanding?

"Do you? Or are you trying to use sex to manipulate me?"

Shock coursed through him. "Do you really think such a thing of me?"

"You're ruthless when negotiating."

"I have no ulterior motives." Though that plan of attack had its merits.

If she was going to leave anyway, his biggest reason for not taking her to his bed was negated. A case *could* be made that protecting her included becoming her first lover. He would make sure her introduction to sex was a pleasant one. He also would not make false promises or use her and she *did* want him.

She was frowning at him. "I won't be your mistress while you marry another woman. You promised you would be faithful, remember?"

"I did not say I wished to conduct an affair after my marriage, but you are the one who says I cannot be seen with other women at this time. Yet, there can be no issue of me being seen with you."

"So, I'm *convenient?* Any female body will do?"

What did she want from him? Was this that latent streak of romanticism showing again? "Do not analyze this to death. You are not likely to get many offers like mine. Take what I offer and make us both happy."

She didn't bother to ask what he was offering. But saying a word he never thought would pass Grace's lips, she spun on her heel and she slammed out of his office with all the drama of a woman scorned, not an innocent, *über*efficient assistant who hadn't had a real date in five years.

Amir let a curse of his own out of his mouth, then spun and threw his fist against the wall. The pain did nothing to clear his head.

What had just happened? One second he was kissing Grace. *Finally.* And enjoying it very much. The next she was spouting accusations and then storming from the room. Okay, possibly that was at least partially his fault. He had not meant his words like they had come out. But damn it, she was threatening to leave him. So, some of his anger had come out in the things he had said. And she had left.

One thing he knew—he was not going to let Grace go, easily or otherwise.

Grace stormed into her room, the desire to smash something strong. But this was not really her room and she could not afford to replace any of the objects in it, except maybe the alarm clock on the table. Without another thought, she picked up the hapless piece of electronic equipment and threw it against the wall with all her might.

The plastic shattered satisfyingly.

She looked around for something more, but saw nothing. Frustrated, she did the only thing she could think of and threw *herself* across the bed. Then the tears came and they didn't slow down. Not for a long, long time. She cried over Amir's cruel words, but she also cried over five years of unrequited love. She cried for a future without the man that she was ready to punch, but still loved beyond reason.

And she cried for the pathetic creature she knew herself to be. Amir was her whole world and she was only a tiny part of his. Sure, replacing her would be difficult, but not impossible. She was nothing but a convenient body to him. Both in the office and out of it apparently.

Memories she would rather left her alone began to surface and she knew that assessment was unfair. Amir had treated her like someone special in his life, even if she was nothing more than his PA. The knowledge only made her cry harder.

How could he say that about her not getting a lot of offers? Okay, so it was true, but did he have to rub it in? Only he had not kissed her like a man who was only scratching an itch. She could feel the restraint he had exercised. He'd made her first kiss all that it should be, even teaching her patiently with his own actions how to respond.

Then he'd ruined it with those same lips mouthing horrible words. But he'd been angry. Much angrier than even she had envisioned. And maybe a little hurt.

How much of his words were lashing out and how much truly reflected what he thought? With anyone else, she would have taken his comments at face value, but this was Amir. And she knew him better than anyone else did. Even if she wasn't his best friend. *Only he'd said she was.*

What was the truth and what was the lie?

He said he wanted her—her, Grace Brown, average-looking, gangly and unsophisticated. The way he talked, he'd wanted her for a long time. And his withdrawal hadn't been about no longer wanting her friendship. It had been the result of how difficult he found it to resist her.

Could *that* be true? She'd said he had never lied to her—and he hadn't. Which meant she should believe what he'd said. One, he did want her. Two, he had for a long time. Three, he did not want her to leave.

That one she had no trouble believing.

Her gaze fell on the copy she'd kept of the project proposal—in some masochistic favor she could not understand even now. New questions started swirling in her mind. Hope that refused to die, probably because it was linked to a love that never would, sprang in her breast.

She had believed he didn't want her, but she had been wrong. What else had she been wrong about? She thought about the makeover shows she watched sometimes when she had a rare free hour. Women who looked positively homely came out the picture of sleek sophistication. Could she do that to herself?

Was there a chance she could create the perfect candidate for Amir's marriage of convenience? His only stipulation had been that they be compatible in bed. If that kiss was anything to go by, that wasn't going to be a problem. She could read up on the subject…this time without hiding the books away when they got to parts that made her uncomfortable. She could even watch videos…not porn, but instruction videos. Sex was a big industry, there had to be something like that out there.

Grace sat up, more resolute than she had ever felt before.

If there was any way of making her boss see her as

not only a potential candidate for his wife search, but also as *the best one,* then she was going to do it.

When it came to him, hadn't she always found a way to be what he needed? The only thing she had truly lacked was the knowledge that he wanted her as a woman. He might deserve a princess…her newfound confidence faltered—maybe he really did. But no other woman, no matter how royal or beautiful or *anything*, would ever love him like Grace. Of that she was absolutely certain.

It didn't even matter if he never loved her, as long as they belonged to each other, that would be enough. It would be so much more than she thought she could have. And she wasn't stopping him from finding love elsewhere because he didn't want it. He had as much chance of finding happiness with her as anyone else.

It was her very own pot of gold at the end of the rainbow. *She'd made the rain,* she thought, as she wiped away the wetness from her cheeks.

Now it was time to travel the rainbow.

CHAPTER NINE

"You are up early, little brother."

Amir looked up from his *gumia* practice. "I am often up early."

"But not down here, working up such a sweat."

Amir considered his damp, slick skin. "In New York, I go to the gym."

"And here, we have no punching bags?"

"Precisely."

"More demons?"

"The same ones, just bigger today than before."

"Do you want to talk about it, or work at exorcising them some more?" Zahir was not dressed for sparring, but Amir had no doubts that his older brother would change if he asked him to.

His hand clenched around the handle of his curved sword as he considered his brother's offer. He'd spent forty-five minutes down here already. He felt no closer to peace—much less resolution of his quandary—than he had when he first entered this room. It had been set aside years before his birth for royal family members who were training in the old fighting ways or, more recently, wanted to work out.

He'd often come here to work out his body while he cogitated on a problem. And left feeling better for it. This morning, it had not worked.

But then, never before had he faced such a predicament.

"Talk?" he asked.

Zahir's eyes widened as if the answer surprised him, but he nodded. "Then, let us talk."

"I am not interrupting your own workout?" Obviously, his brother had come down here for something.

But Zahir shook his head. "No."

"Perhaps we could go for a ride?" It was a compromise, but only if they did not spend the entire time talking. His brother would get no workout *walking* his horse.

"I will meet you in the stables in twenty minutes." Not only alpha, but firstborn as well and it showed.

Amir allowed himself a small smile at the other man's natural inclination to dictate terms. "Sounds good."

He was showered and in the stables fifteen minutes later.

"You are fast," his brother said as he finished inspecting the tack on the tall Arabian gelding that belonged to Amir.

His own black beast of a stallion was already saddled and waiting. They swung up onto their mounts at the same time, but Amir allowed Zahir to lead them out into the desert.

"So, what has you in such a quandary, little brother?" Zahir asked after some minutes of silent travel.

"She's leaving me."

"Grace?"

"Who else?"

"Well, you could have been talking about one of your women…Tisa perhaps."

"I told you I broke it off with her."

"You could have gotten back together. After Princess Lina eloped with her business tycoon."

"Not likely," Amir said with unconscious derision. Tisa might be gorgeous, fun to spend time with and quite intelligent—but she wasn't the woman he wanted.

"I see. So, it is Grace we are discussing?"

"Yes."

"And she is leaving you?" Zahir frowned. "I admit, that surprises me."

"I also."

"Why is she going?"

"She cited *personal reasons.*"

"And she refused to divulge what they were."

"Yes. It is very unlike her."

His brother made a sound that if Amir had not known it was out of the bounds of reality, could have been mistaken for laughter. "I see. Naturally, this upsets you."

"Yes. She is the best personal assistant I will ever have. She is perfect for me."

"And you still want her."

He averted his gaze to the surrounding desert. "Yes."

"Are you going to take her?" Zahir did not sound at all judgmental, but merely curious.

"She is a virgin."

"That is uncommon at her age, is it not?"

"Well, some commentators say that celibacy is

growing in popularity in the American culture, but Grace is not merely a virgin. She is completely innocent. She does not date."

"She has no admirers?"

Amir thought of Jerry and scowled. "She has some."

"But *you* do not want to marry her?"

"No, that has not changed."

"But your determination not to have her has?"

He sighed. "You know me well."

"We are brothers."

"Yes." And he was grateful for it. "She is a romantic. It is not something I knew about her, but now that I do, I am afraid that element to her nature will leave her lonely or getting hurt."

"You were unaware of Grace's romantic nature?" Zahir asked, his voice tinged with disbelief.

"You knew of it?" Amir asked, unaccountably jealous.

"I remember well her response to our mother assigning her to the harem-style room."

"And from that, you deduced she is a romantic?"

"Yes." And the look Zahir gave Amir said he wondered why his younger brother had not.

Amir frowned, but did not have a reply to that. So, he went back to his earlier point. "Be that as it may, I now wonder if her lack of dates is the result of some romantic ideal she has created in her mind that can never be met by a flesh-and-blood man."

"You think introducing her to her sensual nature will help her overcome her obsession with this fantasy?"

"She is vulnerable to me as she is not to other men. Perhaps I can help her realize that sex is not love, which would leave her more open to other connections and she would not be so alone." Something vicious moved in his heart at the thought of Grace with some future, faceless stranger, but he ignored it. "I will not lie to her, or make promises I have no intention of keeping."

"This is how you justify taking her innocence?"

"You think I am wrong?"

"I believe you need Grace more than you are willing to admit."

"I have already admitted I will be lost without her."

"Yes."

"But?"

"Did I say anything?"

"You are thinking something."

"You want her enough to overcome your natural and very good reasons for leaving her alone. Those reasons are strongly ingrained inside you. For you to set them aside, your feelings must be very deep."

"I have not denied I want her."

"You are so sure it is only physical?"

"She is my friend, too. *My best friend.*"

His brother looked at him for several seconds of silence, broken only by the sound of the horses. Finally, he gave one of his rare smiles. "You must do what you think best, of course, but I think your plan to make love to Grace will, in the end, do her no disservice."

Amir couldn't hide his shock. He had expected his brother to take him to task for being selfish and creating arguments that were nothing less than self-serving. "Are you serious?"

"Yes, but I expect to be the best man at your wedding.

After all, I am the oldest." With that, Zahir kicked his stallion into a gallop.

Amir's innate competitive streak took over and he kicked his own horse into a gallop, leaning over its neck to increase their speed. He did not know what his brother's desire to be his best man—once he'd found his convenient wife—had to do with Grace, but a certain relief lent strength to his movements as he encouraged his horse to run faster.

Zahir did not think Amir was wrong to seduce Grace. He understood Amir's arguments, which meant they were stronger than they seemed even to him.

Good. Because he did not think he could prevent himself from pursuing Grace intimately. Not after the kiss they shared. Not after she threatened to leave him.

Grace woke up feeling better than she had in two months. She had a plan and as Amir had said on more than one occasion, *Grace Brown with a plan is a fearsome thing.*

She rushed through her morning ablutions and then went straight to the queen's study. Grace was a strong proponent of going to a professional for advice. When it came to changing her image, she figured no one could give her better counsel than Queen Adara.

She was let in by the queen's assistant.

Adara looked up from a pile of papers spread before her. They looked like calendar sheets.

"Working on your schedule?"

The older woman rubbed her temple. "Yes. It is no small feat now that my daughters are married to their own sheikhs and have separate calendars I must take into account when creating my own schedule. The travel coordination alone is enough to challenge even the most adept tactician."

Grace smiled in sympathy. "Are you using the new scheduling program I recommended last year?"

"Yes, but even with it, the events must first be discovered—" she indicated the multiple calendars strewn across the table "—then entered into the system."

"Though it has made things much easier to track," her assistant added.

"Can I do anything to help with this?" Grace asked, indicating the papers.

"Amir does not need you to work with him today?" the queen asked in surprise.

"I've decided to take a day off."

Now the queen's eyebrows climbed to her hairline. She turned to her assistant. "Will you please fetch coffee from the kitchen? I believe we are going to need it."

The young woman left and then Adara turned her attention to Grace. "Tell me what is happening."

"What do you mean?"

"You have worked for my son for five years." The queen reached out and grasped Grace's wrist.

"Uh-huh."

"Have you ever, once, in all that time, taken a day off like this?"

Grace found herself being gently, but firmly, pulled until she was seated beside Adara. "Um, no."

"So, spill…"

Grace laughed. "You don't sound much like a queen right now."

Adara did not smile. "I do not suppose I do. What I should sound like is a concerned friend and mother, for that is what I am."

"I want to change my image," Grace blurted out.

Several expressions chased across the queen's features. First shock. Then speculation. Then satisfaction. "Finally."

"Excuse me?"

"I have been hoping for more than four years for you to come to me with such a request."

"You think I look that bad?" Grace asked, not sure whether to be hurt or annoyed.

"No, of course not, but you do not look like a future princess and that is what you would like to affect, I assume?"

"How did you know?" Grace whispered.

"I have known you loved my son since the first time I saw you two together."

"But *now,* how did you know I wanted to make him see me as potential marriage material?"

"It was inevitable."

"How so?"

"Did you ever wonder why I did not argue against my husband's contracting with King Fahd for the princess to marry Amir?"

"Actually, no. She's a princess, a much more suitable wife to Amir."

"Poppycock…that is what the English say, is it not?" Adara asked in her lilting voice. "We are not living in the Middle Ages, even if the men in my family behave in such a way from time to time."

"If you feel that way, why *didn't* you argue against the arranged marriage?" Grace asked, perplexed.

"Something had to be done to wake up my son."

"But what if he had ended up married to Princess Lina?" Grace almost wailed, remembering all the pain she'd experienced when she thought Amir was going to marry the other woman.

Adara dismissed the possibility with a wave of her hand. "I had a dossier compiled on her. Did you know she is an American citizen?"

"No," Grace breathed in shock.

"Neither did her family, but it was something I discovered. A woman who takes pains to protect her independence is not going to submit to a marriage of convenience."

"But she's a princess."

"She was not raised in her home country. Her father made the mistake of believing bloodlines could insure loyalty when love was what was needed."

"But what if you had been wrong?"

The queen's eyes flashed with arrogant certainty. "I was not." Then she smiled. "I was also right about something else."

"What?"

"You finally realized that with a little effort you could make my son see that you are what he needs."

"If you believe that, why didn't you say anything before? You knew of my feelings…I know you did."

"Of course. I am not blind, even if my children tend to be."

"So?"

"So…you had to find the strength in yourself to believe in the possibilities. I could not give that to you. Just as Khalil had to find the conviction to fight for his happiness with Jade."

"But…"

"Amir will not be easily caught. You are aware of this. You must not give up. You must have confidence you *can* be the one for him. No other, not even myself, could give you this confidence."

"Except Amir," Grace admitted.

"He has said something? I am surprised. I did not think he was yet open to his true feelings."

"I don't know about any emotions he might have, or not—" and she tended to think *not* "—but he wants me."

"And learning this was enough to give you the courage to embrace your inner beauty?"

"To go looking for it anyway."

The queen waved her hand. "However you choose to see it. I have been eager for this day and am almost as giddy as a girl, now that it is here." She stood up. "Come, we have a great deal to do and our time—as always—is limited."

Grace felt sorry for the young assistant who was told something urgent had come up as she was left to drink the pot of coffee and organize the multiple calendars on her own.

But she didn't have long to pity the other woman as she found herself being driven to the palace airstrip. "Where are we going?"

"Athens. Jade will join us. As will the image consultant I have brought in for just this purpose. She has been staying in the capital city and will meet us at the airport."

"But you couldn't know I was going to come to you."

"I had my plans." And something about the way the queen said it made Grace glad she'd come to Adara on her own.

The trip to Greece went quickly, with the image consultant asking Grace what felt like a thousand questions, but she was sure were probably only about nine hundred and ninety-nine. When they landed at the airport she and Amir had been at the day before, this time only one person was waiting for them in the courtesy lounge. Well, three if her bodyguards were counted.

Jade stepped forward and hugged both Adara and Grace warmly. "So, today is the big makeover?"

"Not a makeover so much as a makeup…we want to bring out Grace's natural beauty and style without losing the things about her that make her so special," the image consultant said.

Queen Adara nodded approvingly. "We are not looking to make a sex kitten out of her after all, even if my son might appreciate that more than anything else."

Jade laughed at this statement while Grace blushed a deep red.

The image consultant, an elegant French woman with skin the color of espresso and height that rivaled Grace's own five foot nine, merely smiled.

"Come, it is time to begin." The queen clapped her hands and, miraculously, bodyguards and women were all in motion, headed toward the most exclusive shopping district in Athens.

Sabrina, the image consultant, insisted Grace have her hair styled and makeup lessons first because the clothing they chose would be influenced by the outcome. Grace usually got her hair cut at shops that allowed walk-ins and she rarely wore the long, kinky red curls down around her face.

"We will start with a relaxer," the master stylist said. "The first time could take as long as three hours. However, when you go in to have your roots done every six months, it will be less time-consuming."

"Relaxer? Every six months?" Grace asked faintly.

The queen did not allow any time to be spent idle, however. She and Sabrina spent the first thirty minutes discussing Grace's color palette. Jade disappeared to have a late lunch with her husband and the queen had food brought in for everyone in the shop.

Exactly three hours later, Grace stared at her image in the mirror. Not only had her hair been "relaxed," but it had been cut as well. Not shorter…but given shape and definition. She was shown how to straighten it into silky waves with a flatiron.

"But you can wear it curly with a little product and still have a lovely style," the master stylist said. "It won't kink now, but fall in softer waves and frame your face nicely."

It had been left long enough she could still pull it up in a ponytail and, for some reason, she was absurdly grateful for that.

The makeup lesson was no less of a culture shock for Grace. The cosmetologist taught her how to apply different shades and combinations appropriate for casual and formal wear, both day and night.

"We'll have another lesson tomorrow, so don't worry if you don't take it all in on the first go," she said.

Grace looked to the queen. "Tomorrow?"

"You cannot expect a change like the one we are affecting to take a mere few hours."

"But Amir—"

"Will survive nicely with his father and eldest brother to keep him occupied."

"Are they in on this, too?" Grace asked, horrified at the thought.

"Of course not."

Her sigh of relief was the last real breath she drew for the next six hours. The group of women shopped more stores than Grace had ever been in if she counted all her previous shopping trips combined. She had never known trying on clothes could be so exhausting. Or liberating.

She'd discovered she liked a lot of the current styles and pretty much detested most of what she had in her wardrobe at home. So why had she worn the clothes? Because they let her hide, but her days of blending into the background were over.

But by the time they returned to Khalil and Jade's home that night, Grace was so tired, she could barely keep her eyes open.

"You've done very well today," the queen said.

"Yes," Sabrina agreed. "You are one of the easiest projects I have had in a long while."

"You call this easy?" Grace asked in a stunned croak.

Sabrina laughed. "It is tiring, yes, but you are naturally lovely and your image needed only to be let out, not created."

Grace wasn't sure she believed the other woman, but she was way too exhausted to argue about it.

Two days later, she stood in front of a mirror in Khalil and Jade's foyer while she waited for the driver to bring the car to return her to the airport. She did not recognize the woman staring back at her and yet she knew her intimately. That was what Sabrina had been talking about.

That woman *was* Grace Brown. The clothing she wore wasn't anything she ever would have bought herself without help, but it also wasn't anything she ever would have turned her nose up at.

The amber-colored, sleeveless button-up blouse had been left open enough to show a hint of her less-than-impressive cleavage, though the outfit highlighted the lines of her body in such a way she didn't look quite so lacking. The lighter shade doe-suede skirt hit her just above her knees, making her legs look really long. And the two-inch heels only enhanced that effect, which Sabrina insisted was a good thing.

Grace could remember the years of being teased as a beanpole, years she'd done everything she could to hide her skinny limbs and disguise her height. Sabrina said her body was trim—not skinny—and actually quite beautiful. Then, to back up her claim, she'd pulled out magazine after magazine that showed women with the same figure as Grace on their covers.

At first Grace's mind had shied away from the comparison, but even she could not deny the blatant resemblance in body shapes.

The outfit she had on was one they'd seen in one of

those magazines and Grace loved it. It was both comfortable and elegant. She felt good wearing it, but also
very natural. Not at all like she was trying to be someone
she wasn't.

She now had an entire wardrobe's worth of new
clothes that covered everything from casual to fancy. All
of them fit both her body and her personality…the one
that had emerged since she started working for Amir.

The one Sabrina told her she had been hiding with
her baggy, nondescript clothes and atrocious haircut.
Grace had laughed at the last bit. She'd never known her
hair could be so flexible, but she'd worn it in a different style each day, sometimes two—one for day wear
and one for evening—and the stylist had made sure she
knew how to recreate each one.

She felt confident of the woman staring back at her,
comfortable in her own skin and excited to find out
Amir's reaction to the change.

She'd realized sometime yesterday what his mom
had been talking about in her office though. Grace had
had to make this transformation for herself. Not on
someone else's urging, or even simply because she was
hoping to prove herself on par with Amir.

*But because it was time to stop hiding the real
Grace Brown.*

And that was, in the end, exactly what she had done.
Stopped hiding for her own sake. She hoped the new
Grace would catch Amir's matrimonial interest, but
even if she didn't, she wasn't going back to the woman
too uncomfortable with her own femininity to even wear
tinted lip gloss.

Heck, now she even knew how to use lip liner, lip color and a shine coat for evenings out.

She smiled and turned toward the door just as Queen Adara arrived in the hall.

She gave the older woman a fierce, impulsive hug. "Thank you."

"You did it for yourself."

"You made it possible."

The queen's eyes were suspiciously moist. "What can I say? I am a woman who likes to meddle in the affairs of others."

Grace laughed out loud.

CHAPTER TEN

SHE WASN'T LAUGHING when she arrived in Zorha,
however.

Amir was waiting for her at the landing strip, right
at the bottom of the exit step. Dressed in full traditional
desert garb, right down to the colored band and *guttrah*
that denoted his royalty, he looked as intimidating as she
had ever seen him. She'd always felt the desert robes
lent an aura of mystery to a man she knew almost as well
as she knew herself.

When he donned them, she could all too easily
imagine him a sheikh of a bygone era. The one some of
his more *interesting* ideas came from.

Regardless of the bright desert sunlight shining down
on them now, his countenance was so dark, she wanted
to shine a flashlight on him. He was obviously and completely, totally, one-hundred-percent *ticked off.* The look
he gave her cohort in crime, his own mother, could have
set fire to an ice flow.

The queen merely lifted her cheek for a kiss, which
he gave, despite the fact that his muscular, six-foot-
four-inch body vibrated with anger. Adara then stepped

around him and headed across the tarmac to a limousine, leaving Grace to what she had wrought.

Feeling just a wee bit craven, Grace went to follow the queen, but Amir stepped in front of the bottom stair so she could not hope to pass him. "Where the hell have you been?"

"I left a message for you telling you I would be busy with your mother."

"An e-mail message you knew I would not get immediately," he growled, making it obvious he had not appreciated her form of communication. "You gave no details. You did not answer your phone or respond to my messages. I had to ask my father where Mother had gone in order to discover *you* had returned to Greece."

And that had not sat well with him. He did not like having to go to a third party to learn Grace's whereabouts. She understood, but this time it had been necessary. Had she spoken to him, they would have argued again…she'd still been angry with him the whole time she was in Greece. Though that anger had not diminished her desire to follow through on her plan.

"It was a necessary trip."

"So you say. If it was so necessary, why did you not take me with you?"

"It wasn't related to work."

"So, we are back to the *personal thing,* are we? How is it that my mother is worthy of your confidences and I am not?" he asked, sounding every inch the outraged desert sheikh.

She stared at him, disconcerted that the reason was not obvious to him. "I didn't think you would be up for marathon shopping and makeover sessions. You don't even like shopping for your girlfriends. You make me do it."

And, seriously, how could she trust her own taste, considering the way she used to dress and the stores she frequented? Not such a good idea.

"Marathon shopping? You were shopping for three days?" he asked in a dangerously low voice. "While I wondered if you would be coming back to me, you were out buying, what…?"

"You really can't see?" she asked with disbelief.

His eyes scanned her body and then narrowed, giving her no clue what he thought of the changes. "Makeovers…clothing that is not inexpensive office wear… what is the meaning of this?"

"The meaning?" she asked faintly as the limo carrying his mother and her bodyguards pulled away, leaving her alone with a madman.

Well, sort of alone. The plane staff was still aboard, but not here…on the tarmac with the ultrafurious sheikh who was asking really odd questions.

"Is this for Jerry?" Amir indicated her new look with a wave of his hand. "Do you hope to entice him into being more than your employer?"

"For the last time, I am not going to work for Jerry," she yelled right in Amir's face.

He didn't even flinch. "Then why this?" he asked with another regal wave toward her.

"I did it for *myself.* Can you understand that?"

"I can. Of course I can, but why now, why when we have these unresolved issues between us?"

He considered her impossible-to-misconstrue letter of resignation an *unresolved issue?* "I needed a break. You needed a break."

"I needed no break. I needed *you.*" Then his jaw clamped shut like he wanted to bite the words back.

"I missed you, too," she said softly.

A lot of her anger at him had already resolved itself, but his admission that he needed *her*—not just anyone—helped dispel most of the rest.

"There was no need to do so. I could have gone with you."

"You had meetings."

"And you think they were a pleasure without you? I could not find anything."

She grinned. "You really are helpless without me."

"Do not sound so smug. It is unbecoming."

"My lips are sealed on the subject."

"Do not think I am done being angry with you."

"How long do you think it will last? Perhaps I should ask the pilot to take me back to Greece for a while."

"You will not leave me again." He was all too serious.

"I won't be returning to the palace, either, if you don't let me off these steps."

"I have need of staying very close to you—you might disappear again." Now, why did that sound so suggestive?

"Do what you think you need to." Oh, wow? Was that her flirting? She thought so. And nicely, too. Go her.

"Be assured, I will." The promise in his voice sent messages traveling along her nerve endings. He put his arm out toward her. "Come."

She put her hand on his forearm, feeling his body

heat through the sheikh's clothing. "Is this a bad time to mention your mother disappeared along with the limousine?"

"I have my own car."

She looked beyond him and saw the classic Jaguar. "I love riding in it. Thank you for bringing it."

"My motivation was not your pleasure, but I am glad it makes you happy."

"Are you sure? Not even a little?"

He sighed, looking at her with a mixture of perplexity and humor. "Very well, perhaps a bit."

"What was your bigger motivation in bringing the car?"

"I wanted a place to argue without interference."

She laughed. "And now?"

"You are here. I find my urge to beat my chest and make a lot of noise has diminished."

"You really do see me as somehow belonging to you." Couldn't he see how revealing that was of his subconscious thoughts toward her?

"I have said so."

"But Amir, I am your PA, not your girlfriend."

"Thank goodness for that. My girlfriends do not last very long in my life, but your place is much more permanent."

"Have you forgotten my letter of resignation?"

"I am doing my best to, yes."

She didn't know what to say. If this plan to show him she was the right candidate for his marriage plans did not work, she would still have to leave. But she didn't want her imminent departure hanging over their heads, making him angry and her jumpy. She supposed she could deal with it when the time came if she ended up having to leave.

In the end, it was the only viable choice. "We can table the motion for right now."

"It has been tabled." And she could tell that he meant it had been dismissed in his mind before she ever left for Greece.

"Arrogant."

"You are friends with my mother…you know my father…my brothers…you blame me?"

"Just because something is a family trait doesn't mean you have to wallow in it so completely."

"I do not think of myself as arrogant." He opened the passenger door to his car.

She looked up at him, cocking her head to one side as she stepped into the space beside the entrance to the car. "Really?"

"I prefer the term *confident*."

"I'm sure you do."

"You are getting saucy, Gracey."

"Is that a bad thing?"

"Only if you do not want me to do this."

"Wh—" But her word was cut off by his lips.

Hot. Soft. Yummy. Everything she remembered from the night before she'd left for Greece and so much more. She moaned, her body straining toward his as their mouths caressed one another. He felt and tasted *so* good.

His hands skimmed down her torso, leaving zinging nerve endings in their wake. "I like this," he said against her lips.

"Wh-what?"

"The new clothes. They feel good against my hands, but not as good as you are going to feel naked."

"They're comfortable," she mumbled as she renewed the kiss, before the full import of his words sunk in.

Then she went still.

He lifted his head just slightly, his mouth only a centimeter from hers. "Perhaps though, you should go back to your old clothing."

"Why is that?" she asked, but her mind was still grappling with the whole naked thing.

"Because other men will become a nuisance now that your sexy figure is highlighted by the things you wear."

"You mean like Jerry?" she dared to tease.

"Damn his eyes…he noticed you before the change."

"So did you."

"Remember that, Gracey."

She wasn't sure what he was trying to tell her, but warmth suffused both her body and her heart and she let herself melt against him as her body was so eager to do.

He went back to kissing her, reminding her of the things he had taught her that night in his office and then showing her more. The sound of the stairs being rolled away from the plane followed by a subdued voice infiltrated Grace's mind.

Amir broke his mouth away, his expression pained. "This is not the place."

Grace looked around dazedly. The tarmac was now empty, but the plane was closed and the stairs had been removed. The crew had to have seen them. Would news of the kiss get out?

The royal family were particularly intolerant of

gossip, but it could still happen. She couldn't believe Amir had taken such a risk. She stared up at him with a question in her eyes as he gently guided her into her seat because she couldn't seem to make herself move.

He went around the car and got in the driver's side. As the engine purred to life, so did the AC. Grace put her face in front of one of the vents.

Amir chuckled. "Need cooling off, do you?"

"Yes." She was beyond dissembling.

Unrequited love was hard enough to cope with, but fully requited lust was something else all together. Even with the air blowing into her face, she found it hard to breathe. She wanted him to pull the car to the side of the road and make love to her.

"I've never been parking."

"Parking?"

"Making out in a parked car."

"I see where your mind is at."

She looked over at him and his lap. "I see where your mind is at, too."

He laughed, the sexy sound filling the car. "So, finally you look, my little innocent."

She was back to letting the air-conditioning cool her cheeks and she didn't deign to answer. She didn't need her blush to get any hotter.

His fingers carded through her hair. "I like this."

"Less kinky you mean?"

"Oh, I'll like you kinky just fine, Grace, but I like your hair down. It's beautiful."

"You want me to be kinky?" she asked in shock. She *should* have read that chapter on bondage in the sex book.

"I want you to be who and what you are," he said with a smile in his voice.

"But you like my new hairstyle?" she asked. Now that the subject had finally arisen in a normal conversation, she wanted chapter and verse on his reaction.

"Yes. And the makeup. And the clothes," he said, giving it to her and proving once again he *knew* her and cared enough to give what she wanted and/or needed. "Though I liked you just fine before. If you could not tell."

"You never asked me to improve my image to reflect better on you," she said, just now coming to awareness of the truth of that statement.

"I have always found you pleasing, but this look—it seems like the you that has been hiding."

"That's how I felt. I think I spent a long time afraid to try to be anything special in case I failed."

"Because you saw yourself as always less than your siblings in talents and special abilities."

"Yes, but how did you know? I never told you that."

"We have spent a lot of time together in five years, Grace. I know more about you than probably anyone else."

"Ditto."

"Yes, though my brother comes a close second I think."

"Zahir or Khalil?"

"Zahir, he is very discerning."

"And here I thought he was too busy being the heir apparent to notice others so closely."

"It is part of the job, to be aware. He realized long ago you were a romantic."

"Are you serious?"

"Oh, yes. It embarrassed me to be so slow on the uptake regarding that hidden trait."

"Probably because it was hidden."

"Not to him." Amir sounded unhappy about that.

Grace reached out and touched his arm. "Sometimes, it takes distance to see things. We are very close."

"Yes…and you are very special. All together unique. Do not ever forget this."

"Thank you. I'm a good PA. I know that…it does take special skills to keep your life running smoothly."

"Yes, but you are more than your job, Grace."

"You would never know it by the hours I keep."

"Are you implying I am a difficult boss?"

"More like a straight-out, all-around, high-maintenance person."

"You believe I am high maintenance?" He sounded genuinely surprised.

She had to hide her smile. "I know you are. Don't forget, I know every aspect of your life."

"Except one and soon you will know it as well."

Wow, he was being blatant. "You mean sex."

"Lovemaking…yes."

He was awfully sure of her. "I need to know something."

"What?"

"Am I simply a convenient body?"

"There is nothing convenient about you, Grace. Just as you say I am high maintenance, you are a challenge…a significant challenge to me on many levels. Taking you to my bed will not be easy to keep from my family, nor will it be a simple matter once we are back in New York."

"But it is worth the work to you to make it possible?"

"While you were gone on your unexpected jaunt, I realized I have no choice. I want you, Grace, and I will have you."

It wasn't just confidence…it was desperation born of need. He had to have her and she knew exactly how that felt.

"I want you, too, Amir."

"That is good to know."

"You said you already did."

"That is true, but I find that hearing it is something I needed." His hand covered hers on his thigh.

The intimacy of the action warmed her clear through. "Okay."

"You understand…this thing…this…this…"

"Lust?"

"I am not sure I like that term. *Lust* is a word that can be easily misconstrued. What I feel for you is physical, yes, but you are also my best friend."

That was what she was counting on. "And?"

"And my desire for you…your desire for me…it cannot be labeled as mere lust."

"But it isn't love." She meant for him. She already knew she loved him, but no way did he return the feelings.

"Is that a problem for you?" he asked instead of answering.

"I…" Was it? She wasn't sure, but if she did not take a risk, she would never know if she could have the deepest desire of her heart. "No."

"You have a romantic nature, Grace….you want your first time to be with someone you love."

"I do love you." The words were out and she could not believe she'd said them—nor could she take them back.

"I know…as a friend…I am your best friend and perhaps that is enough for your romantic nature to be appeased," he said as if trying to work it out in his own mind.

She couldn't believe the save. She nodded, too incoherent with relief that he'd misunderstood her compulsive confession to speak.

"I am glad."

He said nothing else and it was only as the silence stretched between them that she realized he was not taking her back to the palace. It was just as she made this realization that he stopped in front of a nondescript building that seemed to be out in the middle of nowhere.

"What are we doing here?" she asked.

"Changing our mode of transportation."

He parked the Jaguar in a garage on the side of the building. Then he led her around to the back and she saw a sand-colored Hummer waiting for them. A man in full desert gear like Amir's, only without the signs of royalty, stowed her bags in the back along with two black leather duffels already there.

"If we were going to change cars, why didn't you bring the Hummer to the airport?"

"I was not sure we would make this trip today."

"Oh…because you were so angry with me."

"And I was not sure why you had left the palace and stayed away. After the things you accused me of, the cruel words I stupidly spoke, I was uncertain how angry you were with me."

It was the first sign of insecurity her sheikh had ever shown her and she was really touched by it.

"I was pretty upset, but I realize you said some of that stuff out of fury at the situation."

"This is most true."

"And I now realize you do want *me,* not just for convenience. That's very important to me."

"As it should be. Be certain, it is true."

"Good." She looked at the Hummer. "You probably didn't want your mom to latch on to the fact we were going into the desert, either. Bringing the Jag to the airport was smart. You can be sneaky that way."

"Only with the best possible motives."

Once they were again on the road, she asked, "Where are we going?"

"Always, it's the questions with you, Grace."

She laughed at his long-suffering attitude. "I'm not likely to change."

He gave her a sidelong glance that did some questioning of its own.

"You yourself said this wasn't a change so much as the real me coming out."

"It suits you, but it is a change. This willingness to be noticed, it is new. But it is good. I like it."

"I think I started taking my first steps away from blending into the walls when I took the job as your personal assistant. *You* don't blend at all."

"And since you are so closely connected to me, you cannot, either."

"No. Not even in my capacity as your PA. People notice me as a way to get to you."

"Or around me."

"Sometimes."

"But they quickly learn that only works when we both want it to."

They shared a smile. "Exactly."

"We make a good team, Gracey."

That's what she was hoping, but she knew that right now, the type of team they were each thinking about was quite different. She had to see if she could get him on the same page as herself.

CHAPTER ELEVEN

"SO, WHERE ARE WE GOING, *teammate?*"

He shook his head with a small chuckle. "You are also tenacious."

"It's one of my more endearing qualities. Now, answer the question."

"We are going into the desert. As you can see." At that moment, they turned off the main road and began traveling across the sandy, packed soil toward a set of cliffs in the distance.

"Where in the desert?"

"Someplace we can be alone without my family's interference."

"You're taking me to an assignation? Here in Zorha?"

"As far as my family is concerned, we are on a business trip. It works well that you are my assistant. No questions are asked."

"You lied to your father?" she asked in shock, and just a little awe.

"No, of course not. I merely let him draw his own conclusions."

"Which was that we were going on a business trip."

"Yes."

"But you didn't deny it?"

"He did not actually ask me. He told my brother the plan when he learned I had arranged to be away from the palace for three days upon your return."

"Three days?" *Three whole days of just them?*

"Yes."

"But, they'll figure it out."

"Perhaps."

"And that doesn't bother you?"

"If such a thing were to come to pass, would it upset you?" he asked, rather than answering.

"No. I don't think so, but I also think your father would be furious with you."

"Because you are innocent and under my family's protection?"

"As old-fashioned as I find that attitude, yes."

"Perhaps. It is worth the risk to me."

"But we could wait until we return to New York."

"I have no desire to wait."

Neither did she, but nor did she want him forced into marriage to her by his parents in a fit of outrage. "I'm not sure this is a good idea."

The Hummer stopped. Right there, in the middle of sand, scrub and the barren life of the desert. Amir climbed into the backseat through the open area between his and Grace's seats. "Come here."

She stared at him, feeling a bit like a rabbit facing a snake. "I…uh…"

He put his hand out toward her. "Come here, Gracey. Now."

Her body on autopilot despite the swirling thoughts in her brain, she unbuckled her seat belt and did as he commanded. He pulled her into him and then gently flipped her onto her back along the long bench seat. Then he came down on top of her.

She had to concentrate on not hyperventilating. "I've never had a man on top of me like this," she gasped out.

His big hands framed her face. "That is good to know. I want to be your first in every way, Gracey."

"You will be." She'd never even been kissed. "Wh-what are we doing here?"

"You said you have never been parking."

Parking? He wanted to go parking out in the middle of the desert? "But I thought we were talking."

"No, you were saying things I did not want to hear. Things that might lead to *wait*, or *let's not do this at all*. I am helping you to remember why those words should not pass these delectable lips," he said as he brushed his fingertip over her lips, making them tingle and part.

He slipped his finger inside, pressing it against her tongue. "No more talking, Grace, unless it is to say, *yes, right now* and *more.*"

She could do nothing but nod with his finger in her mouth.

He smiled, his white teeth flashing in triumph. "Good girl."

She didn't know what made her do it. Whether it was the condescending phrase he used, or simple curiosity about what it would feel like, but she started sucking on his finger.

Amir let out a groan and thrust his pelvis against her,

the long, rocklike hardness of his penis registering as an unmistakable presence. She sucked harder and he pressed her legs apart with his knee, causing her skirt to ride up. His lower body settled more firmly against hers and she felt a zing, like an electric current, go from the apex of her thighs through her body.

She bit down on his finger, then opened her mouth to offer a mortified apology, only to try to garble it around the still present appendage.

Amir hissed out a curse, but it didn't sound angry or even pain-filled. He thrust down against her again, harder this time, and her body responded without her telling it to do so. "More, Gracey…let me feel your teeth."

Oh…oh…he had liked it. She sealed her lips around his finger again, this time letting her teeth scrape along his knuckle.

He moaned and increased the speed and pressure of his movements. She was doing some moving of her own, trying to enhance the sensations of pleasure arcing through her most sensitive flesh. She was wearing thigh-high stockings and panties. The silky barrier between his steel-like erection and her pleasure spot might as well have not been there. His clothes, either, for that matter.

It felt so good, so utterly perfect.

His head was thrown back, the muscles in his neck chording in ecstatic tension. But then he tipped forward and pressed his lips to her neck, biting down with gentle teeth on a spot that made her entire body shake with sensation. It was her turn to moan and thrash as he kept moving in a steady rhythm against her. Then he yanked his hand away from her mouth and took possession of her lips with his own, his tongue immediately demanding and gaining entrance.

Pleasure and tension unlike anything she had ever felt before spiraled through her, increasing until she felt ready to explode.

Amir's hand came up to cup her small breast, kneading and rolling the beaded nipple between his thumb and forefinger. He kept doing it while moving his body against hers until she was going crazy with the new feelings coursing through her. She arched up toward him and he pinched her nipple…hard…and the cataclysm occurred, blasting through her body with wave after wave of pleasure.

She screamed into his mouth, the sensation much too big to keep inside and Amir went rigid above her. His mouth against hers, but no longer kissing, his own rough shout muffled by her lips.

Then he kissed her, passionately, possessively and thoroughly, before lifting his head and staring down at her with eyes that had gone almost pure black with desire. "Do we return to the palace, or continue on, Grace? The risks are worth it to me, are they to you as well?"

There was only one way she could answer that question. "Yes."

She only hoped he came to the conclusion she was the woman for him before his family discovered their affair and demanded redress. She didn't want Amir forced into marriage, no matter how much she craved being bound to him for a lifetime.

The trip out to the desert took an hour from their impromptu parking episode. They were almost to the cliffs when she saw the house. It was such a natural part of the landscape, she blinked her eyes to make sure it was really there. It was.

"What is it?" she asked as Amir pulled the Hummer to a stop in front of the building.

"One of my family's royal hunting lodges."

"Is anyone else here?"

"No."

"It's beautiful…like it's a part of the landscape."

"That was the intention. My great-grandfather designed it."

"How old is it?" she asked in surprise.

"It was built early in the last century."

"Wow. What is it like inside?"

"Come with me and find out." Amir grimaced as he stepped from the big vehicle.

"Is something wrong?" she asked.

He gave a low laugh. "It is nothing."

"What is nothing?" She'd definitely seen a grimace. "Are you hurt in some way, a twisted ankle I don't know about or something? If you are just being a tough, macho guy who should never have left the palace, I am going to be very angry with you."

He shook his head and started laughing for real.

"This is not funny, Amir."

"I assure you, it is."

"Explain what is so amusing about it."

"You, my dear innocent one."

"You think my concern for you is humorous?" she asked, hurt in her voice she made no effort to hide.

He came around the Hummer and took her in his

arms. She ducked her head against his chest. She wasn't laughing, but she had taken the time to note he was not limping.

"Gracey…" he said in a cajoling voice.

She refused to look at him. "What?"

"I grimaced because I am uncomfortable."

Her head came up quickly then. "I knew it. You are hurt."

"No, kitten. I am not hurt."

"Then what?"

"I have not found my pleasure while wearing clothing ever. As wonderful as it was, the aftermath is less than pleasant."

She stared at him, not understanding.

"You do know about ejaculation, do you not?"

"Of course I do. I'm a virgin, not an idiot." Then she understood and embarrassment washed over her. "Oh."

"Yes, oh. Definitely not hurt."

"And maybe just a little bit funny," she admitted.

"But sweet, too."

She unbent enough to smile. "I'm glad you think so."

He bent his head down until their foreheads touched. "There is so much about you that I find sweet, my Grace."

"Am I yours?"

"You know I believe so."

Yes, she did and if she needed it to be something entirely different than a sheikh taking possessive interest in his PA, now was not the time to think about that fact.

He kissed her temple. "You are precious, Grace. So very beautiful."

"It's the makeover."

"It's the woman who stands before me. I wanted you five years ago and I want you now."

Happiness rolled through her in waves and she let it show on her face when she raised her lips for a kiss. He looked at her and then groaned before taking her lips with gentle force.

They stood beside the Hummer, kissing for several minutes until Grace grew light-headed from both excitement and lack of air. Amir pulled his mouth from hers and she gasped in several deep breaths.

He chuckled softly. "Breathe through your nose, kitten."

"Why do you call me that?" she asked as she tried to ignore her blush at his instruction.

He looked pointedly down to where her fingers kneaded his chest.

"Oh."

"And you make soft mewling noises when you are enjoying my kisses."

"Mewling noises, like a cat?"

"Yes. It is very sexy."

"And so you call me *kitten?*"

"I have never called another woman that."

Oh, that admission made her smile. "Thank you."

"Thank you, Gracey. Your gift is beyond measure."

"My virginity?" She knew some people saw it that way, because she could only ever give it once, but her inexperienced condition felt more like a frustrating liability to her than a gift.

"That, too, but the gift of yourself is by far the greatest reward. I think it's time to go inside."

"Yes."

Then, he shocked her by swinging her into his arms and carrying her toward the door. His expression was so intent, she stifled any urge she had to protest or even ask a question. For whatever reason, this was a necessary action for him, and as far as she was concerned it was the perfect thing for him to do. She was not his wife…yet…but she felt like a bride and it was a good feeling.

He opened the door without putting her down and then carried her inside, stopping just beyond the threshold. "What do you think?"

She'd been so busy looking at him, she hadn't even glimpsed the inside of the house.

She forced herself to turn her attention to it now and gasped. "It's beautiful."

Inexplicable tears filled her eyes. The interior of the hunting lodge would have been impressive enough on its own, but obvious pains had been taken to make it romantic and inviting.

If the outside melted into the landscape, the interior would not have looked out of place in an *Arabian Nights* fantasy. The walls were draped with colorful silks, the furniture was of a bygone Middle Eastern era and the interior structure itself was marked with curves, shaped copper grillwork and recessed alcoves.

But the most impressive feature by far was the main living area. It was sunken two feet and in the center of it was a pile of silks and pillows. To one side was a low table with a selection of finger foods and a pitcher of something to drink. To the other side was another low table filled with candles of different

heights, all of them obviously new. Behind the
sitting/lying area was a huge fireplace, laid with wood
and ready to light.

She didn't know how he had managed to get all the
things here. She supposed there were benefits to being
royal, but right now all she cared about was that he had
cared enough to make the effort.

"Thank you," she said in a choked voice.

"I did not intend to make you cry, kitten."

"It's just so much."

"Too much?"

She shook her head vehemently. "Perfect."

He smiled then, just a small tilting of his lips, but she
knew he was pleased. "Your first time should be special."

"How can it be anything else with you?"

He said nothing, but the satisfaction burning in his
eyes spoke volumes. He carried her to a room beyond the
living area. It was obviously a bedroom. He set her down.

His cheeks were tinged with dusky color. "I need to
shower and thought you might want a moment to
collect yourself."

"I could do with a change of clothes."

He nodded. "You may find some things in that
wardrobe." He pointed to a huge antique armoire.

"If you could just get my cases."

"I'm sure you will find something."

She didn't want to press the point when he'd been so
nice, but if he thought she was dressing in some castoffs
left by him and his male family members after a hunting
trip, he was delusional. She would wait until he got in
the shower and then go to get her own suitcases.

He turned and went through an open doorway on the other side of the room that she assumed led to the bathroom. As soon as he was no longer in sight, she crossed to the wardrobe to open the doors. She would have a look so she could tell him she thought it was better to get her own things.

But when the doors swung back, revealing the contents of the armoire, she could not make sense of what she was seeing. Far from some man's hunting garb, even of the sheikh variety, there were several silky caftans in colors complementary to her skin tone. Something she knew now that the image consultant had taken the time to do Grace's color analysis.

Grace pulled out an emerald-green garment shot through with gold embroidery. It would bring out the green in her hazel eyes. She'd noticed the phenomenon when Adara had insisted she try a top on of the same color when they were shopping in Greece.

Grace held the caftan up to herself. It was exactly the right length for her. "How?"

"I had very little to do while you were gone on your jaunt with my mother." Amir stood just inside the bathroom door, his outer robes gone.

Right. The man had had several meetings scheduled and if she had not been so angry with him as well as determined to follow through on her plan, she would have felt guilty for leaving him without her assistance. "I don't understand."

"I went to the bazaar."

"Alone?"

"Zahir was with me."

"He knows you bought these for me?"

Amir shrugged.

Grace was stunned. He had no problem with his brother knowing about them. He'd taken a big risk that his parents might find out about this tryst in the desert. He was far too intelligent not to realize on some level what the ramifications of all this could be.

Once again she had to wonder if he had any clue at all what that said about his subconscious state of mind.

"They're beautiful," she said, indicating the silk garments.

"As are you."

"Because of my new look."

"Because of who you are, my Grace."

A lump of tears formed in her throat and she swallowed it down. "Thank you."

"As I said, the gratitude is mine."

"You aren't taking your shower," was all she could think to say.

"I came to ask if you wished to join me."

"I've never showered with anyone before."

"We could take a bath together." He took a deep breath and let it out. "I cannot forget the image of you in the bath with the petals of my favorite desert blooms floating around your luscious nude body."

"You think my body is luscious?" He'd thought it before the makeover?

"Yes."

"Wow." She thought of all the times she had felt inadequate as a woman next to those he had dated.

She had a choice now. She could continue to compare herself unfavorably or accept that she was the woman he was willing to risk his family's wrath for.

"Does this wow mean you will bathe with me?"

"What if you don't find me as exciting close-up?" she asked, trying to take a practical view of the situation.

But his laugh of incredulity said it all. Then he shook his head. "Not going to happen."

Nothing to misinterpret there.

"Um…I guess, if I get to wear the caftan later."

His eyes glowing with a predatory gleam, he stepped forward. "Count on it. I shall take great pleasure in removing it again."

She made an embarrassing *eep* as he once again swung her into his arms up against his hard chest.

He smiled, the look too primitive for words.

"There are times it is hard to believe you aren't one of your ancestors, rather than a twenty-first century man."

"There are times I feel like one of my ancestors." He carried her into the bathroom.

Her gaze skimmed the room. She'd never seen anything so decadent. Not even at the palace.

"This place does not seem like a bathing room for men all sweaty from a hunt."

"My great-grandfather liked his creature comforts. So did his wife."

"But…he took her hunting with him back then?"

"Theirs was an unusual marriage for the time. They were very much in love."

"He didn't have any mistresses?"

"The royal family of Zorha has always practiced monogamy, Grace."

"That's neat."

"I, too, like that particular aspect of our history."

"You never have cheated on your girlfriends."

A strange expression came over his features. "That is not exactly true."

"What?" she asked in disturbed amazement. He couldn't be telling her he was a cheater. She wouldn't believe it. She knew him.

"Every woman I have been with for the past few years has been a substitute for you, my Grace."

"What? You don't mean that…you can't."

"I do."

"But…" She didn't know what to say.

"I only got involved with Tisa because things had gotten so bad in regard to my desires for you that I had a perpetual hard-on in the office and often outside of it."

The earthy statement rocked her world. "You're kidding!"

"I assure you, I am not. It is not a comfortable condition."

"But you never said anything. You said you knew I wanted you…why didn't you ever try something?"

"You mean why did I not seduce you?"

"Um…yeah."

"I did not want to lose you."

Her brows drew together in a perplexed frown. "Why would you have lost me?"

"My liaisons did not last for very long and once we

were no longer lovers, I knew you would leave my employ as well."

He was right. She would have. "But why did it have to end?"

CHAPTER TWELVE

HE DIDN'T ANSWER, just shook his head.

"Amir?"

"This talking…it is not what I want to be doing right now."

"You want to take a bath with me."

"Yes."

"And I must be getting heavy."

"It is a weight I would gladly carry for much longer."

"You say the nicest things."

"I mean them."

"That's what makes them so nice."

"Is it nice to tell you I want you naked?"

"I don't know, but it makes me feel all tingly."

"Tingly is good."

"I think so."

He lowered her slowly to the marble floor, allowing her body to rub against his on the way down. "Let me remove your clothing."

"I've never been undressed by another person…at least that I can remember." In a family the size of hers, self-sufficiency was learned at a very young age.

"There are many things you have never done that we will do together this night, kitten."

She smiled, liking the endearment as much as when he called her Gracey, or this new "my Grace."

He put his fingers on the top button of her sleeveless top. "You permit me?"

"Yes."

He began to unbutton her top, one slow bit at a time. The backs of his hands brushed her skin and chills broke out along the surface of her skin.

"Amir," she gasped out softly.

"Yes, *aziz?*"

Had he called her beloved? But her thoughts skittered to the four winds as his hands spread apart the edges of her top and then cupped her modest breasts. It wasn't just the feel of his hands on a part of her body that had always been private, but the look in his eyes. He was impacted as profoundly by this touch as she was.

"Please, Amir."

"What do you want, kitten? Tell me."

"I don't know."

"I think I do." With that, he pushed her shirt all the way off, then he reached around her and undid her bra. He pulled her straps down her arms and the undergarment from her body.

The sensation of air against her nipples made them harden even more than they already were, her aureoles puckering around them.

"I…"

"What?"

"I don't know."

His laughter was soft and triumphant. "Just enjoy, my Grace."

"Yessss…."

His hands touched her breasts, skin to skin, and she shuddered.

"That's right, kitten. Enjoy my touch. Allow yourself to experience it completely."

"It's so good," she said on a moan.

"We have barely begun."

"I won't survive."

"I assure you…you will."

"I can't."

"You can."

"Prove it." What was she saying?

But he smiled. "Oh, I intend to."

Then, he kissed her. Not a long, drawn-out kiss, more like a promise.

Her lips curved into a smile as he pulled his head back. "You're very good at this."

"You expected anything less?"

"No, my sheikh, I did not."

"I like that."

"What?"

"When you call me your sheikh."

"For now, you are." And hopefully forever.

"Now is what matters, *aziz.*"

"Agreed."

His hands skimmed down her bare skin, leaving pleasure in their wake. "You are so perfectly formed."

She couldn't speak, so she didn't even try.

He undid her skirt, letting it fall to the floor, revealing her garter and panties.

He stepped back and just looked, an expression in his eyes unlike anything she'd ever seen. It wasn't just desire, but she didn't know what else it was, either. Something incredibly intense.

"Amir?" She covered her breasts with her arms.

He reached out and tugged her wrists so she was once again bare to his gaze. "Please…allow me to look. You are so beautiful to me."

"I'm average," she felt compelled to say. Honesty was not always a virtue, darn it.

But he only shook his head. "Believe me when I tell you that you are far from average. Perhaps, there was a time I, too, thought you were like many other women, but my body always knew your unique appeal and my brain caught up eventually."

"But Princess Lina is a pocket Venus."

"She is also married to another man and I could not be happier for it to be so. You are elegant, so very sexy, with the legs of a showgirl and a body that heats my blood to boiling." That look came back into his eyes. "You are everything I want, kitten."

If she didn't know better, she'd think he was trying to tell her he loved her. But even so, what he was saying was plenty special. "You really mean that," she whispered in awe.

"I would never lie to you, my Grace."

"No, I don't believe you ever would. You have always been honest with me…except when you hid that you wanted me."

"It was there for a woman with eyes. Only yours were luckily stuck on the body parts above my waist."

His meaning sunk in and she blushed, then shrugged. "I would have died of mortification if you saw me looking there."

"Take note, you are welcome to look now."

And she did. Oh, my... His loose-fitting trousers were tented in front of him with what had to be a very impressive erection. No wonder she'd been able to feel it through all the layers of cloth between them in the Hummer.

"You wish to see it?" he asked.

She was not up to teasing him. "Yes."

"Then, by all means...you shall see." He peeled off his shirt and then shoved his cotton trousers down his legs, revealing the most perfectly sculpted male body she could ever imagine.

"You like?" he asked, pride in his voice.

"Ver—" She had to clear her throat. "Very much."

"Now, we finish removing your clothes."

"Okay."

He knelt down and lifted one foot to his knee, then removed her shoe. She had to hold onto his shoulders so she wouldn't topple over. His skin was so hot, so silky beneath her touch.

He reached forward and kissed her tummy, right below her belly button. She made a noise she did not recognize.

He looked up at her and grinned. "That is right, my kitten."

Oh, man. Her sheikh was lethal.

He rolled the thigh-high down her leg, his warm hands caressing her as he did so. Her fingers dug into his shoulders as sensation upon sensation crashed over her. He gently placed that foot on the floor and then lifted the other and gave that leg the same attention.

She was a mass of quivering nerves by the time he reached up to tug her panties down her thighs. When he kissed her right on the silky curls covering her mound she let out a small cry.

He leaned forward and then his tongue was right there. On her most private place, delving between her nether lips to caress her pleasure button. She started making the "kitten" noises he mentioned in a continuous rotation, so the sounds filled the air around them.

His hands held her hips firmly, not allowing her to move away as the pleasure started to build from peak to peak until she thought she'd fall right off the edge.

She must have been talking out loud because he said. "Fall, *aziz*. I will be here to catch you."

Her untried body convulsed with such intense pleasure that her knees buckled. He caught her before she could crash to the ground and carried her to the bath.

As they stepped into the fizzing, steamy water, she realized the bath was actually an indoor mineral spring. A plethora of flower petals floated along the surface and even with her brain muzzy from satiation, she realized he had to have put them in…just for her. And he called her a romantic.

The bath was an experience in firsts for her. The first time someone had washed her adult body with cherishing care, the first time she had ever bathed another person, man or woman. The first time she had ever touched a penis. And she liked it. He was hard and soft at the same time. It fascinated her.

He used the time in the inlaid mosaic bathing pool to reawaken her desires and make her intimately aware of his own.

"I want to claim you as mine."

The words soaked into her and even if he didn't mean them the way she wanted most, they caused a primal reaction deep inside her. "Yes."

"You will let me join our bodies?"

"I will." It felt like a vow and she realized that for her, it was.

No matter what he felt toward her, she was giving him more than her body in this act. She was giving him her heart, the part of her soul a lover cherished and as much of her lifetime as he was willing to take. It couldn't be any other way. Not for her. She loved him too much. And she wouldn't want it any other way.

He carried her to the bed, laying her on the divan with careful gentleness.

He began making love to her body all over again and by the time he moved between her legs, she was pleading with him to make her his. But instead of entering her with his hardness, he put first one, then two fingers inside her. It felt so intimate, but so *right,* that she didn't even blush.

"Why?" she asked though, not understanding this part. It felt good, but wouldn't he feel better?

"I am preparing your flesh to take mine. I am not small and you are very tight."

"I didn't know you could do this."

"Be glad that I do."

"I thought you didn't date virgins," she gasped out as his scissoring fingers brushed a spot inside that made her whole body pulse with pleasure.

"I do not."

"Then how did you learn?"

"It is something the males in my family are taught, just as we are taught hand-to-hand combat and warfare with the *gumia.*"

"Thank goodness for your ancestors," she said as the blunt head of his manhood probed her entrance a few moments later.

It felt big…and just a little scary. But he went slow, oh, so slow. The pain was minimal, but when he hit the barrier of her virginity she knew to break through would *hurt.*

She didn't care. "Do it."

He kissed her while at the same time touching her pleasure spot with his thumb and just as she was ready to explode into a million bitty fragments of ecstasy, he surged forward. The pain was there, but so was the joy. Such incredible pleasure.

He joined their bodies with passionate force, his own shout of pleasure coming seconds after hers, his heavy body falling like a blanket over hers.

"Sorry," he mumbled into her neck.

"For?" she asked, having not a clue what it could be. He'd given her such intense ecstasy.

"I could not withhold my own pleasure any longer."

"You mean it can be better?" she asked, doubting very sincerely that could be the case.

"I guarantee it."

"This time I really won't survive."

But she did. Again and again over the next three days, as he made love to her out in front of the then lit fire, and then later in the bath, and again in the bed, and even once outside in the desert on a bed of silks and pillows like he had made in the living area of the lodge.

By the time their three-day idyll was over, she had learned infinite ways her body could experience pleasure and almost as many that she could use to give him joy. Neither had spoken of the future and while they were making love, talking and laughing…it did not matter. But now they were headed back across the desert and he had said nothing about what would happen when they reached the palace, much less New York.

She found herself worrying the problem in the back of her mind while he spent the hour-plus drive talking about the history of his family. He'd shared much about the history of his people with her over the years, but this was a lot more intimate a recollection of the past. Despite her concerns, she enjoyed every minute of it.

Until he got to the present day. Or close to it. "I met Yasmine when we were both small children. She was daughter to my father's closest advisor and friend. A princess in her own right, though her father's sheikhdom was defunct and he was part of my father's government."

"When did you realize you loved her?"

"I always knew. There was never a time I thought of marriage to anyone but Yasmine. We made it official when I was eighteen. No one in our families was surprised."

"And then she died."

Amir's face reflected an old pain. "Yes. Then she died."

"I'm sorry. You would be a father by now if she had lived. One day, you will be a good father."

"I have always believed so."

The last few minutes of their drive was finished in silence, both of them lost in their individual thoughts. She didn't know what he was thinking, but she was remembering the realistic dream she'd had when they first arrived in Zorha.

"We return to New York tomorrow," he said as he pulled behind the same building where they had made their car change three days before.

"I won't unpack when we get back to the palace then."

"Always my efficient Grace."

"It's part of my charm," she teased.

"No doubt. You are invaluable in my life."

"Am I?"

"Yes."

But did he mean what she needed him to mean? Did she have the courage to ask?

She hadn't managed it by the time he pulled the Jag into the palace drive. He came around to let her out of the car.

He reached for her hand and she gave it to him. He pulled her from the car. "We need to discuss the list of candidates for my future wife."

She was still reeling from that pronouncement when the king himself came outside. "Amir, you will attend to me now."

"I need a moment to speak to Grace."

"That will wait."

"No—"

"I am not asking merely as your father," the king said in a voice that brooked no argument.

Amir still looked ready to protest.

"Go with him," Grace said.

The last thing she wanted to talk about was that stupid list. How could he even bring it up right now, after the three days they had spent together?

Amir looked at her. "We need to talk, my Grace."

"Later. Go with your father now."

Amir nodded. "Later."

Then he set his shoulders and turned to join the king. They disappeared into the palace, but Grace did not follow them. She was paralyzed by the pivotal ramifications of the past thirty seconds.

It was the first time she'd ever lied to Amir.

A single word that would forever change their relationship. Because not only did she have no intention of talking about her final project for him at a later time, but she also had no plans to be there to discuss anything at all.

The decision was made in the same shattering moment her heart froze into painful lockdown. The moment when she realized the last three days had meant nothing to him. She should have known. He'd made no promises, but she had hoped.

They had been so close, more affectionate and intimate than ever before. And not merely physically. It had not just been about making love, but they had spent time talking and simply being together. He had shared his desert with her before on trips they had made to

Zorha, but this time, he'd shared how he felt about the land that his family ruled.

And yet he still wanted to talk about the list of candidates for a convenient wife.

What was the matter with her, that he didn't see that she would make the best choice? Was it because she wasn't from a noble family? America had its own class structure, but no recognized nobility and her family certainly would not have been included regardless.

No matter what his reasoning for not wanting Grace as his wife, she wasn't going to stick around bleeding from a lacerated heart while he picked someone else.

She forced leaden legs to carry her into the palace and up to her room, where she picked up the phone and ordered the plane readied for immediate departure. There were benefits to being Amir's assistant. No one questioned her orders, assuming they came from the prince.

All she had to do was pack her remaining possessions and order a car to take her to the airstrip. Then she would be out of Amir's life forever.

"I will not tolerate this behavior, my son."

"I have done nothing wrong."

"You took Miss Brown to the hunting lodge. She is your employee, under your protection." His father's expression was set in stone.

Amir found he was not intimidated. His realization that he loved Grace three days ago had freed him in ways he could never have expected. He felt strong enough to do anything, including stand up to both his father and his king. "She's a damn sight more than merely my employee."

"Ah, so you have figured it out," Zahir said from his position on the other side of their father.

He glared at his oldest brother. "You knew."

Zahir actually grinned. "I am only surprised you did not."

"I did not want to see, so I blinded myself to the truth for five years." And he both regretted and was thankful for that fact.

His fear was that if he had realized he loved Grace earlier, he would have pushed her out of his life to protect himself. But he could not help regret the years he had spent with other women when he should have been with her.

"You are no longer blind?" his father asked, sounding partially mollified.

"No. I see clearly now."

The king looked at his oldest son and then sighed with a frown. "You were right."

"You owe me a camel."

Amir burst out laughing. He should probably be offended, but he found their behavior too amusing. The competition between father and son was fierce. "You two bet a camel on whether I would figure out my feelings for Grace?"

"The bet was on whether or not you would figure it out *before* she left you," his brother said, still looking unnaturally—for him—amused as he answered his mobile phone.

"Grace is not going anywhere," Amir growled.

His brother clicked his phone shut. "I beg to differ with you. She's just ordered the plane to be readied."

Amir was headed out the door to the rare sound of his brother's laughter while his father demanded to know when the wedding was to be.

"As soon as Grace agrees to have me," he called back over his shoulder before taking the stairs to the next floor two at a time.

He burst into Grace's room without knocking. She was packing her computer, tears trickling in slow tracks down her cheeks.

"These unscheduled trips without me have to stop," he said.

Her head snapped up, her eyes filled with wounds he wanted to kick his own backside for. He should have said the words at the lodge, but every time he went to do so, they stuck in his throat. It was his final hurdle off the path set by Yasmine's death.

"You are done speaking with your father?" Grace asked in a low voice.

"We came to terms."

"What terms?" she asked, sounding suspicious.

"He wants a date for the wedding. I told him he had to wait until you agreed to be my wife."

"Then he'll be waiting a long, long time." She turned back to her packing.

Even though he deserved her words, they stung. "Gracey, we need to talk about the list you compiled for me."

"So you said."

"And you agreed to discuss it with me later."

"I lied."

"I must insist."

She spun to face him. "Fine, what do you want to know about it?"

"Why is it missing the only candidate that could possibly work?"

Her eyes widened. "It's a comprehensive list."

"And yet it is missing the only name of import."

"What name would that be?" she asked belligerently, swiping at the tears on her cheeks.

"Yours, kitten. Grace Brown."

"You didn't read the list," she accused, but looking both surprised and pleased at that fact.

"Guilty as charged, but how did you know?"

"My name *is* on it. I was going to pass it off as a joke, but it's there."

He smiled at her intelligence. "You are and have always been the perfect assistant."

"I can't marry you, Amir."

"Why not?" he asked, a tight fist squeezing his gut.

"You want a marriage of convenience and I cannot accept that from you."

He couldn't stand it any longer. He stepped forward and pulled her into his arms. "You might be the best personal assistant in the world, Grace, but you are anything but convenient."

"I mean it, Amir."

"Because you are a closet romantic?"

"Because I love you."

"That is a relief. I should not like to love you more than

my country, more than father's good will, more than my own life even and have the feelings not returned."

Her eyes widened with every declaration. "You can't love me."

"Kitten, you might know me better than anyone else, but even you cannot see inside my heart. I assure you, I *do* love you." How easy he found the words to say after all—when they stood as the final barrier between him and happiness. "More than I ever loved Yasmine, which is why I hid the truth so successfully from myself, I think. Losing her put my heart into stasis for years, but if I lost you, it would be destroyed."

"You're only saying these things because your father insists you marry me." But even she didn't sound like she believed herself.

He smiled and kissed the tip of her nose, then her delectable lips and then lifted his head so their eyes met. "I am saying these things because I realized while you were in Greece that I could not live without you. I still tried to convince myself that we could begin a physical relationship without leading to the loss of my heart, but I was being willfully, stupidly blind. I had already lost my heart so long ago, Gracey, I don't remember a time when you were not the center of my world."

"The other women."

"I will spend my life making up for them—they were cover both to you and to myself."

"When did you realize you loved me?"

"I am ashamed to tell you."

"Why?"

"Because it took me so long."

"Was it when we made love?"

He shook his head. "It was when you stood naked in front of me in the bathing room—that first time. You offered yourself so freely to me and I knew you deserved all I could give you. I also knew that the one thing I had tried to protect myself from had happened. I loved you and if I lost you, I would lose myself."

"No."

"Yes."

"But you didn't say anything…not in three days."

"It was hard," he admitted. "But I planned a special dinner for tonight. I was going to speak my feelings and propose."

"Really?"

"Really."

"I want it."

"The special night?"

"And the romantic proposal."

"Then you shall have it." As long as it was within his power, she would have all her heart's desires.

The romantic proposal was an easy one.

This time his mother had been *his* cohort in crime, co-ordinating participants while he and Grace cemented their unspoken love at the desert hunting lodge. With his instructions, his mother had organized the perfect evening for a proposal, including a decadent dinner he and Grace fed to one another along with kisses. It was almost impossible to keep his desire for her in check, but he managed it only with constant inner reminders of what was to come.

After dinner, he took her to the lower terrace, where his entire family and hers had been assembled.

Grace turned to him, her eyes shining with joyous tears. "What's going on, Amir?"

Instead of answering, he dropped to his knee in front of her and the entire assembly. "Grace."

"Yes?" she responded in a choked voice.

"I have a position to offer you."

"A position?"

"It is permanent, requires twenty-four-seven on-call status and offers no vacation or sick days. In fact, if you accept you will promise to stick with me through sickness and health. The pay is not that great, but the other forms of compensation make up for that…I hope."

She was laughing and crying at the same time. "Is this your idea of a romantic proposal?"

"I love you, kitten. Will you marry me, *my* Grace, and fill my life with a joy only you can bring?"

She nodded, her mouth open, but no sound coming out. Deciding that was good enough to count as a yes for him, he surged to his feet and took her into his arms, kissing her with all the love in his heart.

Everyone around them cheered.

EPILOGUE

THE WEDDING was a huge event, rivaled only by his brother's marriage to Jade. Their mother, in her element, arranged a wedding worthy of a princess, which was exactly what his Grace was to him.

The queen had made a point of inviting Princess Lina and her new husband, and they came. Amir thanked her for standing up to her family and setting them both free of a marriage that would have made them both miserable. She told him she hoped he and Grace would be as happy as she and Hawk were.

Though they looked like a positively besotted couple, Amir was positive he and his bride would be happier... after all, Grace Brown had been the ideal personal assistant, but she would make the perfect wife.